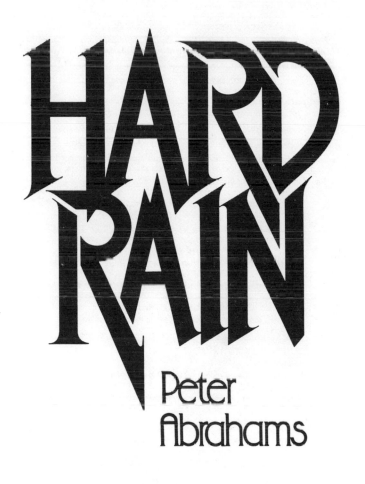

HARD RAIN

Peter Abrahams

E. P. DUTTON · NEW YORK

PUBLISHER'S NOTE: This novel is a work of fiction.
Names, characters, places, and incidents either are the product
of the author's imagination or are used fictitiously,
and any resemblance to actual persons, living or dead,
events, or locales is entirely coincidental.

Published in the United States by E. P. Dutton,
a division of NAL Penguin Inc.,
2 Park Avenue, New York, N.Y. 10016.

Published simultaneously in Canada
by Fitzhenry and Whiteside, Limited, Toronto.

Library of Congress Cataloging-in-Publication Data

Abrahams, Peter, 1919–
Hard rain / Peter Abrahams. — 1st ed.
p.   cm.
ISBN: 0-525-24581-2
I. Title.
PR9265.9.A2H3   1988
813—dc19   87-18947
CIP

COBE

Designed by Nancy Etheredge

1 3 5 7 9 10 8 6 4 2

First Edition

Grateful acknowledgment is made for permission to reprint lyrics from the following songs:

"Fourth Time Around" by Bob Dylan. Copyright © 1966 Dwarf Music. All rights reserved. International copyright secured. Reprinted by permission.

"I Am the Walrus" by John Lennon and Paul McCartney. Copyright © 1967 Northern Songs, Limited. All rights for the U.S., Canada, and Mexico controlled and administered by Blackwood Music Inc. Under license from ATV Music (Maclen). All rights reserved. International copyright secured. Used by permission.

"Changes," lyrics and music by Phil Ochs. Copyright © 1965 Barricade Music, Inc. (ASCAP). All rights administered by Almo Music Corp. (ASCAP). All rights reserved. International copyright secured.

"A Hard Rain's A-Gonna Fall" by Bob Dylan. Copyright © 1963 Warner Brothers Inc. All rights reserved. Used by permission.

For Nana

Everybody must give something back
for something they get.

—"Fourth Time Around,"
BOB DYLAN

Part One

Part One

1

The man they called Bao Dai lived in a three-colored world. Brown was the color of leeches. Orange was the color of Corporal Trinh's decayed boots. Green was the color of the jungle and of misfortune.

Bao Dai's own boots had rotted long ago. Now he wore sandals made from truck tires. His other possessions were a torn shirt, a loincloth and a tin bowl. The bowl was filled three times a day—rice with swamp grass at dawn, plain rice at noon, rice with watery gravy at night. It was a diet that had killed a lot of men. Bao Dai had watched them die. It hadn't killed him. He wasn't even hungry now, maybe because he believed that any extra food he got would only be consumed by the worms inside him.

Like his namesake, the playboy emperor, Bao Dai dreamed many dreams of escape. But that's not why they called him Bao Dai; everyone in the camp dreamed of escape. He was given the name because of his chubby knees, which reminded them of

3

pictures of the emperor in short pants, at his lycée in Paris. Corporal Trinh especially had enjoyed calling him Bao Dai, sometimes bowing to him before they got started in the torture room. But by now the joke had been lost—they called him Bao Dai because it was the only name they knew. And his knees hadn't been chubby for a long time. He was as tough and stringy as the hill people.

Nothing like hope remained in Bao Dai, but his dreams persisted, night after night. In the end, it was rain that made them come true: not flares, rockets, Hueys touching down from the sky—the fiction of his nightly adventures. Just rain, the hard rain of the late-summer monsoon. It struck with a force gravity alone could not explain, pounding stinging rhythms on all living things, drumming out all sound but its own, cascading in sheets off the trees, flooding the ground below.

Down in the mud, Bao Dai worked with the others. They were building a jetty by the river. A truck brought stones as far as the camp, where the road ended. They hammered the stones into pieces, packed them into big woven baskets and carried them on their backs to the river. Two hills stood between the camp and the river. The first was the easier—it had once been known as Hill 422 and wasn't completely refoliated yet. The second was overgrown and much steeper.

Bent almost double, Bao Dai toiled up the slippery path of the second hill, wrapped in a translucent curtain of rain. All he could see were the straining calves of Nhu, the wife-killer, a few feet in front of his face. On his own legs, he felt the panting breath of Huong, who had once owned two taxis and was now being reeducated. Huong's eyes never stopped crying—something had gone wrong with his tear ducts. Behind them all walked Corporal Trinh, unburdened by anything except his Marakov nine-millimeter pistol and his homemade whip.

They came to a little clearing, halfway up. Now the rain fell in powerful gusts, so hard it almost knocked Bao Dai to the ground. He fought to control the heavy basket on his back, fought to keep his shackled feet from tangling in the chain that linked them, kept going. The slight tug at the skin behind his knee meant a leech had fastened on. There was nothing he could do about it—he needed both hands pulling at the tumpline around his forehead to stop the basket from toppling him over.

4

Bao Dai went on. The mud sucked at his feet, belching rotten gases. He heard the taxi owner slip and fall, heard him struggling to his feet. He was too slow. Corporal Trinh's whip made its whistling sound. The taxi man cried out. Bao Dai tried to go faster. He rarely felt pain anymore, but he hated Corporal Trinh's whip. Corporal Trinh had tied a three-pronged fishhook to the end. Sometimes it stuck, sometimes it didn't. That's what made it sport for Corporal Trinh.

By the time Bao Dai started down the hill, he could no longer see Nhu in front of him or hear the taxi man and Corporal Trinh behind. He paused and leaned the weight of the basket against a tree, groping for the leech on the back of his leg. That's when Corporal Trinh went right past him, the Marakov in his hand. There was no sign of the taxi man.

Bao Dai straightened under his load and followed. They were supposed to stay together. Another rule. His back tingled in the spot it had last felt Corporal Trinh's whip. Bao Dai knew it would be worse if he tried to hide. Half-walking, half-sliding, he hurried down the hill.

Lightning flashed. Thunder boomed, a heartbeat later. Someone yelled. Bao Dai rounded a corner and saw Nhu, the murderer, lying under a fallen tree. The weight of the tree rested on his chest. His spine was doubled backward over the basket of stones. He was dead. Bao Dai sniffed and smelled burned air.

For a moment, he didn't see Corporal Trinh. That was because Corporal Trinh had been farther up the path when the tree caught him. Now he was trapped under its middle branches, partly covered with leaves. His head was bleeding.

Corporal Trinh strained under the tree with all his might, but he couldn't free himself. The Marakov lay in the mud nearby. Corporal Trinh saw Bao Dai and twisted his free arm around a branch, stretching it as far as he could. It wasn't far enough. Bao Dai went closer. Corporal Trinh's fingers clutched at the mud, inches short. Bao Dai squatted down and picked up the gun.

He looked at the gun, he looked at the tree, he looked into Corporal Trinh's eyes. Pounding in his head drowned out all sound, even the rain. Bao Dai heard the pounding for a long time. Then, slowly, he shook the basket of stones off his back and let it fall.

5

Corporal Trinh's eyes watched. There was no fear in them. Corporal Trinh had prepared himself to die before Bao Dai had fully realized that the man was in his power.

Bao Dai rose and stood over Corporal Trinh. The rain washed the leaking blood away from Corporal Trinh's head wound. It was a deep wound—Bao Dai could see gray corrugations inside. He reached down, took the keys off Corporal Trinh's belt, unlocked the shackles. Then he tore the leech off the back of his leg. It came with the sound of a bandage being ripped off a scab and rolled up in his hand, round as a half-dollar.

Bao Dai noticed that Corporal Trinh's eyes were fixed on the Marakov; noticed that it was pointed—that he was pointing it—at Corporal Trinh's head; noticed his own finger wrapped around the trigger. Bao Dai lowered the gun. He wanted badly to kill Corporal Trinh—killing Corporal Trinh was the stuff of his sweetest dreams. But not like this, not with a bullet, not quickly. And he had no time.

Bao Dai knelt in front of Corporal Trinh. He held the leech close to Corporal Trinh's eyes so he could see it. Then he shoved it as deep as he could into Corporal Trinh's wound. Corporal Trinh screamed. It was the most wonderful sound Bao Dai had ever heard—opening a world of possibilities, giving him hope.

Bao Dai turned and ran, slipping, stumbling, falling, down to the river. The river was muddy brown, not very broad, pocked with driving rain. The far side looked no different from his: dense jungle cowering under the monsoon. But it was another country.

2

Jerry Brenner was cele-
brating. All by himself, drinking cognac from a bottle with no
label, in a bar with a name he couldn't read, in a city he'd never
seen until the day before yesterday, he was as happy as he'd
ever been in his life. It was like the feeling he remembered from
the last day of spring semesters, back at USC, but blown up to
adult size: a feeling of accomplishment, followed by no immediate
responsibilities.

"Go Trojans!" he said aloud. The bartender, a young woman
in a tight silk dress slit high up both sides, glanced at him in
the mirror. He gave her image a big smile.

Son of a bitch. That afternoon he'd sold the Bank of Thailand
two million dollars' worth of data-base software. The contract
was signed and sealed, back in the hotel safe. It was going to
mean a bonus, at least twenty grand, and maybe a promotion.
And his flight didn't leave till late tomorrow afternoon. He had

7

time for an all-night celebration and a long sleep the next day. Son of a bitch.

A woman sat down on the next stool. The bartender gave her a drink without being asked. Jerry felt her hip pressing against his. He looked at her out of the corner of his eye. She was dressed like the bartender, looked like her too; they might have been sisters.

The woman smiled. "You like me?" she said. She had long fingernails, painted bright red.

Jerry laughed. "Sure," he said.

The woman reached over and laid her hand in his lap. Jerry looked down at the bright red fingernails. He was shocked; but not because he was a prude: he'd expected a longer preliminary, that's all. And in the end, he'd probably have refused: Jerry Brenner didn't pay for it, and in any case he tried to be faithful to his wife—he'd only had two little flings in the past ten years. But the woman's one touch was more exciting than the total of all Ginny's touches since their first date, and besides, what the hell, tonight was a special night. And he was far from home.

Jerry Brenner stood up. The room slipped its moorings and swung like a barge at the end of a long anchor line. Son of a bitch, Jer. Cognac wasn't his drink. Beer was his drink. But tonight was a special night. You don't drink beer on special nights. The woman laughed and took his hand. She led him up some wobbly stairs, down a long hall and into a little white room that was as neat and clean as a Buddhist shrine.

There, on a bed that smelled of Lysol, she pleasured him. There was no other way to put it. She made him cry out, again and again, like a woman in orgasm. It scared him.

On the way out, he had a few beers, just to put things in perspective. The bartender gave him the bill, which included everything—the cognac, the beer, the woman. It was very reasonable. Jerry put it on his MasterCard. His hand shook slightly as he signed his name, but the little piece of plastic, like a pilgrim's amulet containing a pinch of native soil, was reassuring; he began to get hold of himself. He even smiled a little as he stuck the card in his wallet. It was his business entertainment card: a tax-deductible fuck.

Jerry went outside. Night. Son of a bitch. Had it been night

8

when he'd entered the bar? He couldn't remember. Jerry started walking. It was cold   maybe that's why no one was about. He smelled water, rotting fish, sewage. Nausea bubbled up in his stomach—beer on top of cognac, a bad idea.

He stopped and looked around. Only one street lamp shone, a few blocks away: a smear of yellow, seen through a liquor-coated lens. Jerry walked toward it, all the while fighting a nagging feeling that the hotel was in the other direction. Maybe there'd be a cab parked under the light, he thought. He felt tired.

He kept walking. The distance was greater than it looked. Once Jerry thought he heard footsteps behind him, but when he turned no one was there.

And no one was parked under the light. The street ended a few yards beyond it, at a low wall. On the other side flowed a canal; he heard it slurping at the concrete. The smell of sewage and rotting fish was suddenly overpowering. The nausea bubble inflated and rose through his chest. Jerry stumbled into the shadow of a building and vomited.

He vomited the beer, the cognac, the satays he'd had for lunch, the shrimp in peanut sauce. He vomited on his brogues and on his Brooks Brothers tropical suit. But when he finished, he felt much better. "Son of a bitch, Jer," he said. "You're not as young as you used to be." He stood up, straightened his tie, and turned.

A man was standing in the shadows, watching. Jerry jumped. "Christ, buddy," he said. "You scared me."

The man didn't speak. He kept watching Jerry. He had strange eyes—blue for one thing, hard blue like glaze fired in an oven.

The man raised his fist. There was something in it, something that gleamed for a moment with reflected light from the street lamp: a gun. A burst of adrenaline swept through Jerry, sobering him at once. "Hey," said Jerry, "don't do anything foolish, I'll give you what you want." He reached for his wallet.

There was an explosion, not very loud. Then Jerry was lying on his back. The man was going through his pockets. "I'm hurt," Jerry tried to say, but no sound came. The man found his passport, opened it, looked inside. Then he stripped off all of Jerry's clothing—the brogues, the executive-length socks, the tan suit, the tie with the sailboat figures, the 100-percent-cotton shirt, the boxer shorts.

Jerry was very cold.

The man dragged him over rough concrete. He was humming a song. Jerry recognized it. "When the Music's Over." The tune rose high, higher, out of hearing.

"Oh God, help me," Jerry tried to say. But no sound came. He fell through air and splashed down in water. It felt cold on top, but much warmer below.

3

From the moment Bao Dai stepped on his native soil, he had problems with the glare. It bent the shape of everything he saw. He looked up at the sky, to see why home should be so bright, and saw that the sun wasn't even shining; it was a cloudy day. He rubbed his eyes, hard, as if dislodging distortion lenses that had been implanted without his knowledge, maybe in his sleep or when he'd been in fever land, but when he stopped rubbing the glare remained. It twisted the edges of things: the cars, the buildings, the hollow-faced mannequins in the clothing-store window.

Bao Dai went inside.

A tall black woman, hollow-faced as the mannequins, came through the glare and said, "May I help you, sir?" She didn't talk like a black person, not like any of the black people he'd known over there; she didn't talk like any white people he'd known over there either: too fancy. Her eyes gave him a quick

11

once-over, taking in the suit, the button-down shirt, the tie, the leather shoes with all the little round holes in the toe.

"Jeans," said Bao Dai.

"Pardon?"

He wondered if he'd pronounced it right. Had he said something like "jinns"? He repeated the word, taking care to stretch it out.

"You're looking for jeans, sir? That will be the Country Weekend Boutique." She led him toward the back of the store. "Do you have any designer preference? Calvin Klein? Jordache? Ralph Lauren?"

"Bell-bottoms," said Bao Dai.

"Pardon?"

He said it again, pronouncing it with special care.

The woman blinked, very rapidly, five or six times. In the glare, her long flickering eyelashes were like movements under a strobe light. "Do you mean bell-bottom jeans?" asked the woman.

Bao Dai grunted.

The woman gave him another quick once-over, this time taking in his face as well as his clothing. "There's a revival store near Coolidge Corner. You could try that."

Later he was on a bus, rolling along a highway, a paved highway, paved the whole way. A sign above the driver's head said: TOILET AT REAR. He went to it. He unzipped the suit pants and pissed in a metal toilet that made a sucking sound when he flushed. He thought of the black woman in the store. Then he looked up and forgot about her immediately. He saw a face in the mirror. It was his face, of course; he knew that. What he hadn't known was how much older it looked than the face of the black woman. He would have said they were about the same age. But it wasn't true. He returned to his seat, glancing at the other passengers as he moved along the aisle, trying to tell who was older, who was younger, who was the same age. He walked up and down the aisle several times until he noticed eyes peeking at him and the driver's eyes darting up in the rearview mirror. He went back to the toilet, locked the door, took off all his clothes and stared at the figure in the mirror until he realized the bus was no longer moving.

*   *   *

12

Bao Dai walked along a country road.

What was that song, he wondered as he walked. "Changes"? "Sit by my side, come as close as . . ." As what? He didn't remember. He remembered the chord progression though—C, D, G, E minor. His left hand made barring motions in the air.

It was a country road he knew well, glare or no glare. Rain was falling now, and he kept his head down, not because he felt the wet or the cold, but because he didn't like the hazy glare around every raindrop. He didn't need to see where he was going; he knew the road like the back of his hand. Bao Dai looked at the backs of his hands.

They were strange hands.

He didn't know them at all.

He kept walking, glancing down at his hands from time to time to see if they were beginning to look familiar. They never did, but at least he knew the road.

Bao Dai came to a mailbox: a normal rural mailbox, except it had been painted. He knew that; he remembered the smell of the wet paint, remembered how hard it had been to get the blue flowers just right and how he had copied the black symbol—a circle with an airplane shape inside—from somebody's button. It might have been yesterday. But it wasn't, because the paint had faded away, almost completely. He had to look very closely to make out the forms of one or two flowers, the outline of the symbol.

Bao Dai turned onto a dirt road. He saw the farm. He heard voices, laughter, guitars. His heart raced. He began to run, a clumsy, sliding run along the muddy road, in the tropical suit and the brogues, two sizes too big. He ran, but no one was there—no talkers, no laughers, no players.

There was only a middle-aged woman, scattering birdseed in the yard. She looked up. The glare was very bad. It took him a long time to recognize her, a very long time.

She didn't recognize him at all.

He had to tell her who he was.

And then what should have happened? What had he expected? What had he dreamed? He didn't know. All he knew was that his arms were lifting from his sides, all on their own. But she didn't step forward; she was still staring at his face. He didn't like the way she stared, didn't like the wrinkles on her skin.

He lowered his arms, stepped back.

At that moment, she opened her arms to him in a hesitant sort of way. He took another step back. She lowered her arms, bit her lip.

Their timing was off.

They went inside. She made him a meal. Fried chicken. Yellow wax beans. Banana bread.

It was sickening.

Night fell but the glare didn't go away. She made a fire in the fireplace, rolled a cigarette, lit it, sucked in smoke, held it out.

"No," he said.

"No?" She was surprised. "It's Colombian."

"No." The smoke scared him.

She turned on the radio. Music played. Rock music, he supposed, but he hated it. It was boring. Boring rock music **was** hateful. She was tapping her foot. He noticed that his hands were fists. He straightened them out.

A man rolled up in a wheelchair. "Company?" he said. The man in the wheelchair couldn't see.

"Business," said the woman. "No one you know."

The man rolled away. There was something familiar about him. Bao Dai was about to ask her when another question occurred to him, a far more important question.

She wouldn't answer. At first. He had to ask a few more times, and get up, and cross the room, and stand in front of her. It was then that they finally touched—when he took her hand and pulled her up and twisted her arm behind her back and twisted some more.

Then she told him.

Bao Dai left the next morning. He wore the tropical suit, the button-down shirt, the brogues, but he kept the tie in his pocket, together with the traveling money she'd given him—at least, she hadn't tried to stop him when he took it from her bag.

In the airport and on the plane, Bao Dai began to notice that people had things. All kinds of things. He didn't even know the names of some of them. He had a tropical suit, a tie with sailboats on it, a button-down shirt, boxer shorts, long socks

14

that needed washing, and shoes—with little holes in the toe—
two sizes too big. They gave him blisters. He'd seen the blisters
when he'd gone to bed the night before, but he couldn't feel
them.

"Cocktail, sir, before your meal?"

Bao Dai looked up, into the slanted eyes of a yellow woman.
"Cocktail?" she repeated.

He shrank in his seat.

"Or would you prefer a nonalcoholic beverage?"

Bao Dai grunted. She went away. He kept an eye on her
for the rest of the trip.

He got off the plane in a city where the air made his eyes
water. He found the house he wanted, near the beach. It was
a white Spanish house with a red tile roof. It made him think
of Zorro. He remembered how Zorro spun the 7-Up bottle with
the tip of his sword. *Zip zip zip*—the mark of Zorro. Every
Saturday afternoon. Four-thirty.

Bao Dai walked past the house three or four times before
he went up and knocked. No one answered. He went to the
garage and tried the door. It opened. He stepped inside, pulled
the door closed and stood by the window so he could watch the
street.

A car turned into the driveway and stopped. A nice blue
car. The windows were down so Bao Dai could hear music playing inside, just before the ignition was switched off. Music, full
and clear, as if the band had all its equipment right there in the
back seat.

A young-looking fair-haired man got out of the car, opened
the front door with a key and entered the house.

So fucking young-looking.

Bao Dai's hands were fists again. He straightened them,
reached for the handle of the garage door. At that moment,
another car drove up. A woman got out.

A beautiful woman.

She had healthy, glowing skin and a strong body—he could
see it was strong from the way it moved under her skirt. He
liked the way it moved. It gave him feelings he barely remembered feeling before, almost as though it were the first time.
Almost. Three female faces flipped through his mind—black
from the clothing store, yellow from the plane, and now white

15

a few yards away. And suddenly he wanted sex, not just sex, but rough sex. That must have been the yellow part. He hadn't thought of sex for a long time, hadn't had an erection for years. He didn't know if he could have one.

Bao Dai slipped his hand into the waistband of the suit pants and touched himself. Nothing happened. He kept his hand there anyway, while he watched the woman walking toward the house. There was a little girl with her. They had the same kind of hair. He wondered how hair like that would feel against his penis and felt a faint stirring. He glanced down. The feeling vanished. Maybe he had imagined it. He heard a low, angry growl. A few moments passed before he realized it was coming from his own throat. When he looked up again, the woman and the girl were disappearing into the house.

Bao Dai stayed in the garage. After a while, the woman came out alone. Now she had a frown line between her dark eyes. She drove away in her car.

The sky grew darker. The glare remained. When it was fully night, not black night, but a pink and orange, starless night, Bao Dai silently opened the garage door and silently moved toward the house.

4

Jessie Shapiro was in a bad mood. At a glance, anyone would have seen that from the way she was standing in her doorway, arms crossed. But no one saw. The street was deserted.

Jessie Shapiro's watch said 3:30. The colon dividing hours from minutes flashed every second to remind her that time marched on. Flash, flash, flash. She didn't need reminding.

3:31. Jessie looked down Idaho, anticipating the sight of a blue BMW going too fast, a fair-haired man behind the wheel and little girl beside him. But there was no BMW. No fair-haired man. No little girl.

No cars at all. Too cold for the beach, too early for going out. The massed boredom of fifteen million people was almost palpable. Soon they'd have to shop, but for now the traffic hum was no louder than beehives at a safe distance. The sky was the color of tin, and the sun hung at a strange low angle, small as a softball and drab white. Mid-November in L.A. Sunday afternoon.

3:33. That made Pat thirty-three minutes late. Kate was due at the birthday party at 4:00. Pat knew this. Jessie had told him when she dropped Kate off Friday afternoon. Twice. Coming and going. The second time he'd gotten that look in his eye, the bugged teenager look, and said: "How many times are you going to tell me?"

"Till I get some acknowledgment," she'd wanted to say. But there was no point fighting with him now. Fighting was for the married. Divorce was peace.

3:40. A mother went by, pushing a stroller. The mother was cracking her gum; her Walkman was turned up so loud Jessie could identify the song: "Sometimes When We Touch." The baby had a runny nose; he looked like Buddy Hackett. They were the only signs of life.

"Damn," Jessie said, going into the house and closing the door harder than she had to. The house shook. She was strong. It was weak: small, pretty and frail, like an aging belle with osteoporosis. Jessie had drawn up plans to rebuild it from the bottom up. All she was waiting for were money and time.

She went inside, under the only object of value she owned, a little Calder mobile that she'd taken as payment from a client, past a pile of tennis equipment, hers and Kate's, and into the kitchen. There was no point in calling Pat: he'd told her that they were going sailing for the weekend and that he'd bring Kate back directly from the marina. Jessie picked up the phone and dialed his number anyway. "Hi," said a woman's voice she didn't recognize and didn't like. "No one's here right now, but just leave a message and we'll buzz you back. Promise."

"Jesus," Jessie said, putting down the phone, too, a little harder than she had to. Doubts about letting Kate spend every second weekend with her father popped up in her brain. She forced them down with the usual arguments—Kate liked spending time with Pat, a girl needs a father, what possible harm could come of it? Besides, she'd agreed in writing to the visits when she'd signed the divorce agreement, a document as important to their lives as the Constitution, and just as difficult to amend.

She went back to the doorway, looked down Idaho. "Damn."

The party was in Beverly Hills. It would take at least half an hour to get there. She'd hoped to squeeze in a few hours of work. Instead she was standing in the doorway. In a bad mood.

3:50.

The phone rang. Jessie ran in and answered it.

"Hi, Jessie. It's Philip."

"Hi."

"Don't sound so excited."

"Sorry, Philip. I just thought it was someone else."

"Oh?"

"Pat, I mean," she said with impatience she hadn't meant for Philip. "He's late bringing Kate back." Now she was complaining to him; stop it, she told herself. "What's up?"

"It's finished."

"What?"

" 'Valley Nocturne.' "

Jessie heard a car parking in front of the house. "That's good. Listen, Philip, I—"

"When can you come and see it? We'll crack open a little something and—"

"Well, I'm not—"

"How about tonight? I'd really like—"

"I don't think tonight. Listen, I'll call you back, okay? I think there's someone at the door."

"But—"

Jessie hung up and went to the door. No one was there. The car belonged to the woman who lived across the street. Jessie caught a glimpse of her going into the house with her son, who carried a stuffed panda bigger than he was. Every week he returned with another trophy from the land of fathers. Jessie had a vision of children all over Southern California being shuttled back to their mothers: boosting gasoline sales, driving toy company stocks higher. There were probably studies that proved divorce was good for the economy.

"Shit." She thought of calling the marina, but she had no idea whose boat they'd gone out on. Pat knew a lot of people who'd grown nautical in the past few years. She dialed his number again. She had no need to look it up—the phone had once been in her name; the house in Venice had belonged to the two of them. "Hi," said the voice of the woman she didn't know and

19

didn't like. "No one's here right now, but just leave a message and we'll buzz you back. Promise." A word she disliked drifted into her mind. Bimbo. She banished it.

Was it possible Pat was at home, just not answering the phone for some reason? Jessie tried to think of a reason and couldn't, but went outside anyway. Passing the hall table, she saw the birthday present, a pen that wrote in twelve colors, chosen and wrapped by Kate before she left. Jessie took it with her.

She got into her car, a five-year-old American model that had been recalled three times, and drove south to Venice. The house was a white Spanish L with a red tile roof; the street, a dead end half a block from the beach. Every time she visited, the neighborhood seemed a little seedier. Today two men smoking joints were roller-skating toward the boardwalk. They eyed her without breaking stride and wheeled around the corner. A man with a bottle in a paper bag was coming the other way. Jessie stopped in front of the house. The BMW wasn't in the driveway. She got out of the car and looked in the garage. Empty. Jessie had a house key, but she didn't bother going in: two rolled-up newspapers lay on the stoop.

Jessie returned to her car. The knuckles of her hands, gripping the wheel as she sat there, turned white. She folded her hands in her lap. Perhaps, she thought, Pat had realized he was late and tried to make up for it by taking Kate right to the party. That didn't sound like Pat, but Jessie turned the car around and drove east. All her other ideas began with an accident at sea.

There were no joint-smoking roller skaters in the birthday girl's neighborhood. She lived on an estate behind a ten-foot wall. The only person in sight was the guard at the gate. He wore a well-tailored black uniform and looked like a movie SS man, minus insignia. Jessie rolled down her window. "I'm looking for my daughter—she was invited to Cameo's party, but there's been a mix-up and her father might have brought her."

The SS man didn't open the gate. Instead he consulted a clipboard. "What's your daughter's name?"

Jessie told him.

"She's on the list, all right, but she hasn't come yet. And the party's almost over."

"Maybe he's called. I'd like to go in and ask Cameo's parents."

"That won't be possible. They're cruising in the Solomons." He ran his eyes over Jessie's car. Maybe he was worried that Solomon Island references would be lost on the owner of a car like hers.

"Then—"

"I'll let you speak to Miss Simms. She's in charge of the party." He opened the gate.

Jessie followed a smooth, winding drive, lined on both sides with pink hibiscus. Ahead glittered a high-tech pleasure dome, built on a hill. The birthday party was taking place at the bottom of the hill, where a little state fair had been put up for the children. There was a midway with games and a fortune teller, clowns, jugglers and a ferris wheel. But none of the children were playing in the midway; the hired help had it to themselves.

Two girls sat in the bottom chair of the unmoving ferris wheel. They both had lank blond hair and high cheekbones. Jessie approached them.

"Cannes sucks," said one.

"Paris is worse," replied the other.

"Excuse me," Jessie said. "I'm looking for my daughter."

They looked up. Jessie could feel socioeconomic sensors scanning her surface. "What's her name?" asked one.

"Kate Shapiro."

The girls shook their heads.

"Or you might know her as Kate Rodney. Or Rodney-Shapiro," Jessie added with a smile.

The humor passed them by. "Is she the one with the frizzy hair? Like yours?"

"That's right. Just like mine."

Something in her tone made the girl's eyes shift down for a moment. "Haven't seen her."

Most of the children were gathered around a pool in the distance. When Jessie got there, two Mexican waiters were setting a pink cake on a long table. They could have used some help: the cake was eleven tiers high; eleven silver candles burned on the top. One of the clowns played "Happy Birthday" on an accordion, but no one sang except the waiters and a tall, thin woman with an English accent.

21

"Come now, Cameo," said the Englishwoman. "Make a wish and blow out the candles."

The birthday girl reclined in a chaise longue, a fruit punch at her elbow. She wore Vuarnet sunglasses and a cap that read Bora Bora Golf and Country Club. "I'm tired, Miss Simms," she said. "You do it."

The Englishwoman climbed on a chair, made a wish and blew out the candles in one breath. The clowns clapped with delight and stamped their floppy feet. Their eyes were very tired. Jessie thought she recognized one of them from a doughnut commercial on TV.

The Englishwoman began to cut the cake. A boy skimmed paper plates into the pool. "I've got the Mr. Mister video that's coming out next month," said Cameo. "Anyone want to see it?"

The children rose and straggled up the long hill toward the house. The Englishwoman stopped cutting the cake. "Hector," she said, "put the cake in the cold storage room."

The waiters picked up the cake and carried it away.

"Miss Simms?" Jessie said.

"Yes?" The Englishwoman, still standing on the chair, looked down. Her thoughts were far away.

"I'm Jessie Shapiro. I'm looking for my daughter Kate. Has she been here?"

"Kate?" said Miss Simms, brightening. She climbed down. "What a lovely child. So—" She began to say something, then censored whatever it was. "No," she said. "Kate hasn't been here." Miss Simms raised an eyebrow.

"Did her father call, by any chance? I think there's been a mix-up."

"Not to my knowledge." Miss Simms sat at the table, elbowed aside a stack of presents, all neatly wrapped in the paper of famous Rodeo Drive shops, and dialed a portable phone. "Mrs. Sanchez," she said. "Would you read me the log, please?"

While Miss Simms listened to Mrs. Sanchez, she opened a leather folder, took out some thick deckle-edged stationery and began to write. Jessie read the words upside down.

"Dear Missy, Thank you for the lovely gift. I hope you had a good time at my party. Thanks very much for coming. Your friend—" She left a space at the bottom for Cameo to sign.

Miss Simms hung up the phone. "Sorry," she said. "No call."

Jessie realized she was biting her lip, stopped herself. Miss Simms was watching her. Jessie let her breath out with a sigh. "Christ," she said.

"Yes," said Miss Simms, taking out another piece of paper. "Dear Hilary," she wrote.

Jessie got into her car and drove to the gate. The SS man opened it and ticked her off the clipboard. Jessie turned into the road, only then noticing that she still had the gift for Cameo.

She drove home. Traffic was suddenly very heavy, as though everyone were practicing for rush hour. Jessie switched on the radio. She heard a commercial for Levi's. It sounded just like a lot of commercials, except for the ringing guitar line. She recognized the style at once: Pat. He was very good: only by choice did he remain a studio musician. She switched him off.

It was night by the time Jessie got home. She hurried up the walk, then saw that the house was dark, and slowed down. But as she went inside she still called, "Kate? Kate?" There was no answer.

She called Pat's number. "Hi. No one's—" She called the marina. There had been no reports of overdue or missing boats.

Jessie went downstairs to her workroom. She turned on the powerful overhead light. On one side of the room lay a jumble of bicycles, skis, camping equipment. On the other was the big table. Orpheus and Eurydice lay on it, sick with craquelure. Jessie studied them for a moment; Mrs. Stieffler wasn't going to be happy.

She sat by the phone and started looking up Pat's friends in her address book. Almost all of them had been erased since the divorce. Now, after five years, only Norman Wine was left. He'd once been Pat's manager. Jessie supposed that she hadn't erased him because he'd been the only one of all Pat's friends she'd really liked. She dialed his number.

"Norman Wine Productions," a woman said. A trumpeter played scales in the background.

"Norman Wine please."

"Mr. Wine is not here right now."

"Oh."

The woman was silent for a moment. Then she said. "If it's important, I can transfer your call through the marine operator."

"The marine operator?"

"Yes."

"It's important."

"Your name?"

Jessie told her, then waited; something clicked and the trumpeter was gone. Jessie heard more clicks, a roar like a typhoon, and then Norman was saying, "Hey, this is a nice surprise." He could have been in the next room. "Over," he added. "You have to say over. Over."

"Are Pat and Kate with you?"

"You didn't say it."

"Are they?"

There was a pause. "No," Norman answered less boisterously. "Is something wrong?"

"Not that I know of," Jessie said. "Pat took Kate sailing this weekend and they're not back yet. I'm trying to find out who they went with."

"They were supposed to come with me," Norman said. "They never showed up."

"What do you mean?"

"We were scheduled to leave at nine on Saturday. Pat didn't appear. We waited till ten. It made us late getting into Catalina."

Jessie thought. She heard people laughing on Norman's boat. She wondered if Pat was on it, and Norman was lying. "I didn't know you were a sailor, Norman," she said.

"I'm not, I'm a puker. This is a tax scam." A woman laughed. "Over," Norman added. The woman laughed louder.

"Are they on the boat, Norman?"

"Who?"

"Kate and Pat."

"Hey. I just answered that."

There was a long silence. Then Jessie said, "Have you got any idea where he might be?"

"Search me." Maybe he heard the annoyance that lingered in his tone, because he smothered it and added, "What are you up to these days? Want to come for a sail sometime? My boat's called *Schlepper*." In the background, the woman shouted, "It cost two hundred g's."

"Did you try calling him?" Jessie said.

"Pat? He wasn't home. But hey. Stop worrying. He's not a child."

24

That was the point in question, all right, but Jessie just said, "Kate is."

Pause. She wasn't being fun. "They need me up top," Norman said. "Problem with a stuck cork."

The woman laughed uncontrollably. "Good-bye, Norman," Jessie said.

"I meant it about that sail."

Jessie put down the phone and went upstairs. She opened the front door and stood in the doorway. Street lamps made greenish pools in the night. She crossed her arms. 9:21. Flash, flash.

After a while, Jessie heard a squeaking sound. The gum-cracking mother went by again, pushing her little Buddy Hackett in his stroller. This time they brought tears to Jessie's eyes. "Shit," she said, angry at herself. The gum-cracking mother jerked around, startled. Jessie went inside and slammed the door.

She dialed Pat again. "Hi—"

From the cupboard over the refrigerator, Jessie took a bottle of brandy and poured herself a glass. She sipped it, leaning against the counter. It didn't calm her down. She drank some more.

Her gaze fell on a piece of notepaper, stuck on the refrigerator door:

> *My Mom*
> *My mom is like a turtle shell,*
> *so beautiful and strong,*
> *My mom has eyes like oceans,*
> *that know what's right and wrong.*

"Good use of simile," Miss Fotheringham had written at the bottom in red pencil, "but not developed enough. B − ." Jessie wondered what Cameo's poem was like.

She put down her drink. It was making her light-headed already. Perhaps she should eat. She made an omelette, set the table for one, sat down, didn't eat. Instead she thought about her marriage and what had happened to it. "That's simple," Barbara Appleman, her friend and attorney, had said. "His conscience is in his schlong. He refuses to grow up."

But that wasn't fair. Who was Barbara, or who was she, to say what growing up was? And, like drowning to a deep-sea diver, casual sex was an occupational hazard of Pat's career. But in the end, Jessie hadn't been able to accept it. He'd debased his sexual currency. She'd frozen to his touch. Their lovemaking had stopped.

Now she had Kate. She had her work. It wasn't enough.

Much later, Jessie realized she'd been staring at the omelette, staring until it looked like imitation food in the window of a Japanese restaurant. 3:00 A.M. Still flashing.

Her index finger jabbed out the digits of Pat's number. Cuteness waited at the end of the line. "Hi. No one's here right now, but just leave a message and we'll buzz you back. Promise."

"This is my message," Jessie said, her voice rising into realms that cuteness never knew. "You were expected here at three this afternoon. Where is Kate? Where the hell are—" She checked herself, swallowed the rest of what she had to say. It was a physical effort. "Just call me," she said, in as toneless a voice as she could manage, and hung up.

Jessie went upstairs, undressed, climbed into bed. She heard a small animal run across the roof. She heard a dog bark. She heard a plane fly overhead. But she didn't hear the phone.

5

Jessie slept: a short, tiring, anxious sleep. A dream flashed by. In it her womb turned to a block of ice, and Philip said, "No one coughs in the movies without dying in the last reel."

Jessie sat up, wide-eyed, shivering. 8:27. She got out of bed and went down the hall to Kate's room. The sunlight that slanted through the window every morning pooled as it always did on the quilted bed; but today it didn't gild a soft, sleepy face. The bed was empty.

Jessie picked up Kate's Miss Piggy phone and dialed Pat's number. "Hi. No one's here right now, but just leave a message and we'll buzz you back. Promise." The last wisps of sleep vanished from her consciousness. It was all real.

A little jolt went through her—a jolt of fear—but it triggered a hopeful image of Pat driving back from wherever they'd been and dropping Kate off at school. Jessie hurried into the bathroom. She jerked a brush through her hair. She splashed cold water on her face and rubbed it hard with a towel. She put on respectable clothes and went out.

A million dollars' worth of European cars were double- and triple-parked in front of the Santa Monica Children's School. Jessie squeezed into their midst and increased the total by $3,240, the current book value of her car. She had no objection to public schools, but Pat had insisted on private education for Kate, and he was willing to pay the cost.

Jessie didn't see Pat, Kate or the blue BMW. Children filed through the front door. Cars sped away. At 9:02 a black man in a security guard uniform came to close the door. Jessie got out of her car and entered the building.

Room 24 had a picture of the Great Wall of China on the door. Jessie opened it and went in. The children were settling at their desks. Kate's seat was at the back of the first row. It was empty.

At the next desk sat Cameo Brown, watching her with interest. Jessie tried to smile, but her face wouldn't cooperate. She turned to go. A bony little woman came in. Miss Fotheringham. "Bonjour, classe," she said, and then saw Jessie. "Miss Shapiro? May I help you?"

"I'm looking for Kate. I thought perhaps her father had brought her. There's been a mix-up."

Miss Fotheringham glanced at the empty desk, then at Jessie. She pursed her lips, then opened them and said, "Why don't you try the office?" Jessie felt her name going up on Miss Fotheringham's list of Bad Mothers.

In the office, the secretary riffled through the phone message slips. Jessie surveyed the bulletin board. It was covered with work by the children. A poem caught her eye.

> *My Mom by Cameo Brown*
> *Looks so good*
> *looks so nice*
> *always makes you*
> *pay the price*
> *lips so blue*
> *and eyes so green*
> *I only see her*

on Halloween
My Malibu mom.

"A," Miss Fotheringham had written at the bottom. Jessie had her first insight into Kate's and Cameo's friendship.

"Sorry," said the secretary, looking up. "No calls."

Jessie went home. She paced back and forth across the kitchen floor. Then she called Barbara Appleman.

"Yeah?" a sleepy man answered. For a moment Jessie thought she'd dialed the wrong number.

"Barbara Appleman, please?"

"She left for the office. Should be there in half an hour or so." He sounded very young. Jessie thanked him and hung up.

She called Gem Sound. She called the Hollywood Recording Studio. She called Pioneer Air. She called Electric Wing Recording. She called Bright Things A&R. Pat wasn't at any of them. No one expected him or knew where he was. There was no one else to call. She didn't know his friends, and he had no family: he was an only child, and his parents had died in a car crash back east; he'd dropped out of high school and gone to California soon after.

Jessie put the phone down. Then she picked it up again, toying with the buttons. Perhaps others had left messages on his machine, messages that might reveal where he'd gone. The machine had remote playback capability—Jessie had bought it herself, just after making her break from the Getty and going freelance. She searched her mind for the number code. It wasn't there. She tried Pat's number anyway, hoping her fingers would remember by themselves. She listened to the woman's voice, then punched 92–356. Nothing happened. She tried again, punching 92–365. The tape whirred.

A man said, "No one home? Shit. Call you later." Beep. Whir. A woman, the same woman who'd recorded the answering message, said, "Pat? Hi, listen honey, something's come up and I can't make it. See you when you get back. Don't get wet." She made a kissing sound. Beep. Whir. A man said, "Pat? Donnie. Did you get the sheets? Rehearsal's changed from two to two-thirty. At the Barn." Beep. Whir. Norman Wine said, "Patrick. Hey, let's go. We're all waiting." Beep. Whir. There was a long pause. Jessie thought she heard an intake of breath. Then an-

29

other woman spoke; her voice was tense, but faint, as though she were talking to herself. "Fuck, can't you answer your phone?" Another pause. Then, more loudly, she said, "Listen: you've got to split. I'm a—" Beep. The woman's time had run out. Whir. Jessie listened to the rest of the tape, wondering whether the woman had called back, but there was only one more voice, and it was her own: "This is my message. You were expected here at three this afternoon. Where is Kate? Where the hell are— Just call me."

Jessie stood up. All at once her legs were weak, her mouth parched. She got the key to Pat's house and started downstairs.

The doorbell rang. Jessie's heart fluttered. She raced down the stairs and threw open the front door, her arms already positioning themselves to wrap around Kate.

But it wasn't Kate. A plump young man and a middle-aged woman stood on the threshold. Jessie didn't know the man; it took her a moment to recognize the woman. She had a too taut face and wore a short ermine jacket against the morning chill: Mrs. Stieffler.

"Oh God," Jessie said, looking at her watch. 10:15. "I for—" A long explanation unreeled in her mind. She kept it there. "Come in," she said. "Please."

Mrs. Stieffler strode in. The man trailed after her. They eyed the living room. It hadn't been straightened up. It hadn't been cleaned, dusted or vacuumed either.

"This is Dr. de Vraag, from Berkeley," said Mrs. Stieffler. "Ph.D. He knows everything there is to know about Rubens."

"Well, I—" began Dr. de Vraag.

"Everything," said Mrs. Stieffler. "So let's see the baby."

Jessie didn't move.

"Are you sure this is convenient?" asked Dr. de Vraag. "Perhaps—"

"Mrs. Rodney set the time herself," Mrs. Stieffler said. "I wanted to make it earlier, but she had to take her son to school."

"Daughter," said Jessie and turned from the door.

She led them along the hall, under the Calder mobile, which Dr. de Vraag looked at closely and Mrs. Stieffler ignored, and down to the workroom. Her feet wanted to go the other way.

Orpheus and Eurydice lay on the worktable under the five-hundred-watt bulb. Mrs. Stieffler and Dr. de Vraag bent to examine the canvas. In the bright light Jessie could see the tiny scar under Mrs. Stieffler's hairline where the plastic surgeon had cut.

Mrs. Stieffler looked up. A smile spread across her face, the smile of a sugar lover who has just seen the dessert cart. "I love what you've done so far," said Mrs. Stieffler. "Love it."

"Thank you."

"The colors! Look at those tones! Look at that pink!" She pointed to Eurydice's pudgy arm. It was much like her own. "Doesn't that remind you of the Helena Fourment we saw in Antwerp last week, Dirk? I knew it. I just knew it all along. Instinct." She tapped her nose, a perfect object, untraceable to any ethnic group that ever walked the planet.

Dr. de Vraag looked uncomfortable. "Well, of course, we can't make judgments from palette tones alone. At this stage, the provenance must remain School of."

"Oh, don't be such an old fart." Mrs. Stieffler turned to Jessie, her breasts swelling under the ermine. "The moment I saw this painting, I felt it in my bones: the real McCoy."

"You don't mean you think it's a Rubens?" Jessie said.

"Of course. All it needed was a cleaning job. And voilà!" Mrs. Stieffler laughed with delight. Her pointed red tongue bobbed up and down. "Do you know what I paid for it?"

"Seventeen thousand, I think you said."

"Sixteen-five. And do you know what it'll be worth when we prove it's a Rubens?"

"A lot more."

"A million more. At least. Isn't that right, Dirk?"

"Well, prices fluctuate, and of course we're still a long way . . ." He stopped, having noticed something in the bottom corner of the painting, where Orpheus's muscular calf was frozen in mid-stride. "What's this?"

"The craquelure? I won't be able to get rid of it completely."

"I understand. It's . . . it's an odd shade of brown." He was watching her carefully.

"Yes," she said. There could be no postponing it now. "It's bituminous."

They exchanged a look. "Are you sure?"

Jessie shifted the heavy gilt frame, which she'd detached from the canvas, and picked up a folder lying under it. She

31

handed it to Dr. de Vraag. Inside was a lab report and a minute brown flake mounted on a slide. "I had it analyzed."

Dr. de Vraag glanced at Mrs. Stieffler out of the corner of his eye. "What's underneath it?"

"Nothing. That's the bottom layer. Maybe we can discuss this later. I've—"

"Hey, why the long faces?" said Mrs. Stieffler. "I don't give a shit about that craquelure." She waved it away. "It makes it look older, and that's in our favor."

There was a long pause while Jessie and Dr. de Vraag waited to see who would speak first. Finally, Dr. de Vraag said, "Mrs. Rodney has found a layer of bituminous oil paint under the varnish. It's the cause of the craquelure."

"Stop with the craquelure, will you? This is a coup, my friends."

Dr. de Vraag cleared his throat. "Bitumens weren't used in oil paints until seventeen-ninety, at the earliest."

"So?" Mrs. Stieffler said. The expression in her eyes began to change. Her neck thickened and her chin thrust forward. Dr. de Vraag couldn't meet her gaze. His lip twitched, but he said nothing. "So?" she repeated. "So, Mr. Five-hundred-a-day consultant?"

Jessie glanced at her watch. She had no more time to spar with Mrs. Stieffler. "Rubens died in sixteen-forty," she said. "It means he couldn't have done the painting. And . . ."

"And what?"

"It can't be from his school, either."

"Now," said Dr. de Vraag, "I'm not sure we can rule—"

"Hold it," said Mrs. Stieffler. Dr. de Vraag's jaws clamped shut. Mrs. Stieffler rounded on Jessie. "Are you telling me it's a fake?"

"In the sense that you paid for School of Rubens and that's not what it is, yes. But it's still a fine painting."

Mrs. Stieffler's face turned pink, then red. Her eyes bored into Jessie's. "I'm not paying you for lab reports," she said at last. "I'm not paying you to run your mouth. I'm paying you to do the cleaning."

"It's not a Rubens, Mrs. Stieffler." Jessie heard her voice sharpening. Mrs. Stieffler had made it sound like something done with Ajax and a mop. "And not School of."

"Bullshit."

"And there's nothing you can do to change that." The remark slipped out before Jessie could stop it.

"No? For starters, maybe I'll get my painting into the hands of someone who knows what they're doing." She picked up the frame and plunked it into Dr. de Vraag's arms. Then she put her hands on the painting itself.

"Wait," Jessie said, trying to soften her tone.

"Worried about your fee?" Mrs. Stieffler responded, slapping her checkbook on the table. She dashed off a check and flicked it toward Jessie. It glided to the floor. "There's your money. But you'll never work for me again. Or for any of my friends. You're through in Bel Air." She seized the painting and marched upstairs. Dr. de Vraag followed, struggling with the frame.

Jessie stood by the worktable, trembling. She'd never lost her temper with a client before, never handled her business so poorly. Suddenly she felt cold. The coldness brought her dream back to her. She went outside and drove to the house in Venice.

Everything looked the same as yesterday: no BMW in the driveway, all the curtains drawn, rolled-up newspapers on the stoop. The only difference was that now there were three of them. Saturday, Sunday, Monday. Jessie kicked them aside and went in.

The house was dark. Out of old habit, her hand flicked on the hall switch. This house still felt like home to her, much more than the little place on Idaho. But she hadn't had the money to buy Pat's share; instead he'd bought her out and stayed on.

Unopened mail was piled on the hall table. There was nothing unusual about that. The plants needed water, and the goldfish needed food. All normal. Jessie went into the dining room and stopped before a framed photograph she hadn't seen before.

Pat was standing at the wheel of a yacht, his fair hair blowing in the breeze. He wore it long, but not messy—like the Beatles' hair on the cover of the *Sgt. Pepper* album. That was the way he had worn it when Jessie met him, and he hadn't changed, as though he had found the truth, at least about hair, long ago.

Pat had one arm around a young, laughing woman: her even teeth gleamed in the sunlight; her string bikini showed she never indulged in any of the things Jessie liked to indulge in. An out-of-focus man hoisted a bottle of champagne in the background. Jessie could tell from Pat's eyes that he'd already had a glass too many; he was smiling, but his mind was somewhere else.

Cardboard boxes from King of Siam TakeOut lay on the dining room table. Their contents had congealed into a spicy goo dusted with the first hint of mold. Two chopsticks were stuck in something with shrimp and peanut sauce: the ivory chopsticks Kate had brought back from San Francisco last summer. Jessie took them into the kitchen, washed them and put them away.

She walked through the living room. It was clean and tidy: in the corners she could see the tracks of the vacuum cleaner. Pat had probably had the cleaning woman in Friday morning, just before Kate's arrival. Maybe because everything else was so neat, her eye fastened on the only untidiness in the room—the butts of two joints stamped out on the hearth. Jessie picked them up, sniffed to make sure. Pat had agreed never to do any kind of drugs when he had Kate. Jessie flung them across the room.

She went into Pat's studio. His sound equipment lined one wall; his instruments hung on the other: acoustic guitars, electric guitars, an electric bass, two banjos, a mandolin, a Dobro. One space was empty—in the corner, where Pat kept his Fender Stratocaster. That was odd, because he seldom used to play it and would never have taken it out of the house. The Stratocaster once belonged to Jimi Hendrix, who had played the "Star-Spangled Banner" on it at the Woodstock festival.

Jessie went upstairs to Pat's bedroom. He'd kept the king-size matrimonial bed. It was unmade, pillows, sheets and blankets twisted and tossed from one end to another, as if tag-team wrestlers had been working out on it. Jessie opened the drawer of the bedside table and found a mirror and a bag of white dust. In the drawer of the other bedside table, the one on the side of the bed that had been hers, she found a silk bag with *Clinique* written on it. Her fingers moved to the drawstring. She stopped them and put the bag away. For a few moments, she stood motionless beside the bedside table. The house was very quiet. Jessie reopened the drawer. She couldn't help herself.

Inside the silk bag were a diaphragm and a tube of spermicide. Jessie put them back, shut the drawer and went into the bathroom to wash her hands.

Kate's bedroom was at the end of the hall. It looked a lot like her bedroom at home, only bigger. There was a box of colored pencils on the desk, pictures of gorillas and orangutans on the walls, and a book lying open on the unmade bedding: *Jane Eyre*. Jessie picked it up. *Reader, I married him.*

Her foot brushed against something hidden by the overhanging comforter. Pulling it aside, she saw Kate's new Reeboks—the high-tops with blue stripes.

Jessie sat down on the edge of the bed, staring at Kate's shoes. Kate had worn them every day for the past two weeks. Jessie couldn't imagine her going anywhere without them, certainly not for a weekend on Catalina. She picked them up and examined the soles: perfect for sailing. She shook them, looked inside. There was nothing to see but the words "Made in W. Germany. Size 4." Sympathetic ape eyes watched from the walls.

Jessie rose and took the Reeboks downstairs. She was picking up the phone when she noticed the writing on the kitchen blackboard. The blackboard was used for jotting down memos and phone numbers. Jessie went closer. There were no phone numbers, and the memo, if it was one, had no meaning for her: "Toi giet la toi." The words were chalked in big block letters. A leather box, the velvet-lined one that contained the curving set Jessie had given Pat long ago—scrimshaw, but antique scrimshaw so there was no question of killing contemporary whales—lay on the ledge beside the chalk. The long-tined fork was there, and the sharpener, but not the knife.

Jessie dialed Barbara Appleman's office. "Barbara Appleman please."

"Who's calling?"

"Jessie Shapiro."

"One moment."

Jessie heard a click; then Barbara was saying, "—so what? So we'll sue his fuckin' ass. That's what. G'bye." And then, "Hi there, bubeleh. You on the line?"

"Yes," Jessie said.

"What's up?" Phones buzzed in the background.

Jessie opened her mouth to tell her, but the words wouldn't come. Instead a bubble of emotion started up her throat.

"Hey. You still there? Say something. Time is you-know-what around here."

Jessie forced the words out: "I don't know where Kate is."

There wasn't even a pause before Barbara said, "Was it the schlongman's weekend?"

"They were supposed to go to Catalina and be back yesterday afternoon. I don't think they went at all, but no one's been in the house since Friday." Jessie told her about Norman Wine, the newspapers, the cutoff message from the woman on the answering machine.

"I wouldn't worry. He probably changed his mind and took her to the mountains or something instead. Then he got stoned out of his skull and slept in."

"He wouldn't be that irresponsible."

"No? I did your divorce, remember? And if you'd done what I told you, you wouldn't be having these hassles now. Sole custody and no overnight visitations. The Appleman rule of thumb."

"Let's not go into that now."

There was a silence. Then Barbara said, "What do you want from me?"

"Advice. Should I call the police?"

Barbara snorted. "And tell them your kid's with her joint custodian and they're a few hours late getting back from a legal visit? This is L.A., baby, not 'The Andy Griffith Show.' You can't even report a child as missing for twenty-four hours, and then they don't go on the computer for thirty days."

Jessie clutched the Reeboks in her hand. "Then what do I do?"

Barbara sighed. "Look, I've got to be in court. I should be out by three. If you still haven't heard anything by then, pick me up at the courthouse and I'll have a look around schlongman's pad on the way back."

"But I've already had a look."

"Yeah. But I'd like to hear that tape." Barbara tried to make the remark sound casual; that only made it more worrying to Jessie.

"You can hear it from there," she said.

"Not now, Jess, not now. The D.A.'s going to be chomping at my ass in twenty minutes. G'bye." Click.

Jessie hung up the phone. She turned on the answering

machine, listened again to the message: "Fuck, can't you answer your phone? Listen: you've got to split. I'm a—" Beep.

Jessie called the school. No Kate. She wandered from room to room. She looked at the apes on the wall, the king-size bed, the take-out cartons, the woman in the string bikini. Then she tied the laces of the Reeboks together, swung them over her shoulder and went outside.

A man was coming quickly up the walk. He wore horn-rimmed glasses, a button-down shirt and a tie with ducks on it: he reminded her of a commentator on TV, but she couldn't think who. He saw Jessie and stopped. "Hello," he said. Drops of sweat clung to his forehead and upper lip. "I've been admiring your house." He held up a card—something-or-other Real Estate—and pocketed it. "Interested in selling?"

"I'm not the owner," Jessie said.

"Too bad," the man replied, wiping his forehead with the back of his sleeve. "It's a nice house. Is the owner in?"

"No."

"When is he expected?"

"I don't know."

"Too bad," he said again. He turned and walked away.

Jessie got into her car, put the Reeboks on the passenger seat and drove off. In the rearview mirror, she saw the real estate man at the house across the street, fist raised to knock on the door.

6

Barbara Appleman, in a dark pinstripe suit, came out of the courthouse and blinked in the brassy sun. The unkind light emphasized her pallor, sharpened her thin features, foreshadowed the lines of her face. Then she saw Jessie and smiled; and all of that somehow disappeared.

Barbara lugged her briefcase down the steps and got into Jessie's car. "You look like hell," she said, reading Jessie's thoughts about her and preempting them. That was Barbara.

"I told you—I'm worried."

"I was worried ten years ago, when you married him."

"You didn't tell me."

"You were too besotted to hear."

"I was in love. And he was too."

"So?"

"I was pregnant."

Barbara said nothing. They weren't going to get into all that. It always ended in deadlock: Jessie had liked Pat—she

38

probably still did, if she allowed herself to think about him—
and Barbara never had.

As Jessie pulled away from the curb, a big man came running down the steps. "Hold it," Barbara said, rolling down her
window.

The big man put his hands on the roof and leaned in; the
car sagged. Jessie could see the stubble of his beard, newly
shaved but ineradicable as crabgrass.

"No hard feelings?" he said.

"No hard feelings," Barbara replied.

"The heat of battle," he said.

"You bet."

He stuck out his huge hand. Barbara took it in her long thin
one and pumped. Up, down. Her ring, a little emerald that had
once belonged to Amelia Earhart, glowed in the sun. The man's
eyes took in Jessie. He saluted. They drove off.

"What was that?" Jessie asked.

"Lieutenant DeMarco. Homicide. He was pushing for a murder one indictment of a client of mine. We just bargained it down
to assault with a deadly weapon. The lieutenant got a little pissed
off and said a few things he's regretting."

"Homicide? You do family law."

"Sometimes the two intersect."

"At the corner of Love and Hate?"

Barbara laughed. "That's good, Jess. I should have it printed
on my card." Jessie felt Barbara's eyes on her, knew she would
reach for cigarettes a moment before she did. Camels, unfiltered.
Barbara had been smoking them since puberty, or maybe before.
The car filled with carcinogens. Barbara opened her briefcase
and took out a file. They drove the rest of the way in silence.

Jessie parked outside the red-roofed L. A bag lady in a
ragged polka-dot dress and wraparound sunglasses was going
by, pushing a shopping cart. Barbara, filling the margins of some
document with her spiky handwriting, didn't even see her.

No BMW. Three newspapers on the stoop, kicked to the
side. Jessie unlocked the door and led Barbara in. No mail on
the floor. The house smelled of Asia.

They walked through the hall, into the dining room. Barbara
glanced at the yachting blowup. "New filly?" she said.

"I guess."

39

Barbara lit another cigarette and looked at the photograph more closely, chin up, eyes squinting through rising smoke. "Nice bod," she said. "The schlongman looks tired, though."

"Shut up, Barbara." Green mold was spreading over the take-out food from King of Siam.

They went into the kitchen. Jessie bent over the answering machine and pressed the playback button. "This is what I want you to hear," she said.

"Hi. No one's here right now, but just leave a message and we'll buzz you back. Promise."

Barbara made a face. "Shh," Jessie said.

But there was no need for quiet. The rest of the tape was blank.

Jessie felt a cold prickle on the back of her neck. She hit fast forward, hit play, hit rewind, hit play. "Hi. No one's here right now, but just leave a message and we'll buzz you back. Promise." Jessie turned up the volume. The tape wound to the end, hissing softly.

"That's funny," she said, straightening; she'd been leaning over the machine, ear cocked. "There were lots—" She stopped. Her gaze had fallen on the kitchen blackboard. The foreign words were gone. There was nothing on the blackboard but wide swirls of chalk dust.

Jessie walked slowly to the blackboard and examined it.

"What's up?" Barbara said.

The words had been erased with some kind of cloth; the job had been done imperfectly. Jessie could make out a "T" and an "o" under the swirls.

"There were words here before," she said. "Foreign words."

"What foreign?"

"I'm not sure."

"What do you mean, you're not sure? You've got a B.A. in European history and literature. This is one of the few moments in your life it might be useful. Was it Spanish? French? Italian?"

"No."

"Chinese? Arabic?"

"No. It was our alphabet."

"German? Swedish?"

"I'm telling you I don't know."

"All right. Don't get excited."

40

"You bet." Jessie snapped the words across the room. Barbara opened her mouth to snap back, then closed it. She went to the answering machine instead, running her fingers over the buttons.

"What was on the tape?"

"A woman. She left a short message, cut off at the end. She ran out of time. I can't remember the exact words, but it sounded like a warning of some kind. 'Split,' she said. That was part of it."

"Local or long distance?"

She hadn't noticed. "I'm not sure." Barbara's eyes narrowed. "Long-distance, maybe."

"Maybe," said Barbara. "Did you recognize the voice?"

"No."

"But you think she called after he'd already gone?"

Jessie nodded. "The message before it was from Norman Wine. He—" Barbara's eyebrows rose. "You know him?"

"I acted for his wife." Barbara's eyes glittered at the memory.

Jessie ignored her. "Norman told me he'd called after nine Saturday morning. By that time Pat was already overdue at the marina."

"So he didn't hear the woman," Barbara said. She gazed down at the answering machine. Jessie gazed at Barbara.

"Well?" she said at last.

Barbara looked up. "I don't think you need to worry about what was on the tape. It could have been about a hundred things."

"But there was something in her tone. She sounded . . ."

Barbara waited for her to finish. Jessie wanted to add "afraid" or "scared," but she wasn't sure whether the fear had been in the woman's speaking or in her hearing. That's why she'd wanted Barbara to listen too.

"And," Barbara continued, when Jessie remained silent, "I wouldn't make much of the words on the blackboard either. Maybe it meant honey garlic satays in Thai. The point is someone's been in the house."

"Pat?"

"Who else? He came back, listened to his messages and took off. Maybe he's looking for you."

Jessie reached for the phone and called her own number, a

wavelet of hope already springing up in her veins. But Kate didn't answer. The machine took the call. Jessie checked it for messages. There were none. She called the school. It had closed for the day.

Jessie put down the phone. Hope stopped flowing inside her, leaving her inert. To look up at Barbara required conscious effort, especially since she knew there was a helpless expression in her eyes, and Barbara loathed helpless women.

Barbara looked back. Over the years she had perfected the ability to shield her eyes from penetration; now Jessie saw even she could be barred.

"I've got to get back to the office," Barbara said.

"Take the car. I'll see you later."

"What are you going to do?"

"Look around here."

"Is that a good idea?"

"Tell me a better one."

Barbara went outside. Jessie followed her. She tried once more. "Kate left *Jane Eyre* behind. She reads it in bed every night."

"So?"

"And she left her Reeboks. They're practically brand-new."

"So?"

"That obtuseness may work in court; it doesn't work on me. Those Reeboks mean as much to her as that ratty Peruvian poncho meant to you at Stanford."

Barbara laughed. "Shit. I'd forgotten all about that."

"Not me."

"No, not you." For a moment Barbara's eyes were unshielded, far away, back in the days of the Peruvian poncho, burning incense, all-nighters at the Fillmore. But she fought off memory, Jessie saw, and said, "You can't make a case of the Reeboks. And she probably got sick of *Jane Eyre*. It's pretty sickening stuff."

"I don't think so. And she was halfway through the last chapter."

"You're giving me a headache, Jess." Barbara sighed. She took a last, deep drag from her cigarette. "Look, even if you could make a case out of a pair of shoes and fucking *Jane Eyre*, what case would you make?"

Jessie had no answer. Barbara squashed her cigarette butt under her heel and got in the car.

The bag lady was sitting on the sidewalk, writing hurriedly on a scrap of paper with a pencil stub. "I wish you'd heard the tape," Jessie said through the car window. Barbara turned the key. Jessie took a deep breath. "Come on, Barbara, you know about these things. What do you really think? Has he gotten in trouble with dope dealers or something like that?"

"It happens," Barbara said. She revved the engine. "Parental kidnapping happens too."

"No," Jessie said, holding onto the car. "It couldn't be that. He's never even asked for more time with Kate. Why would he kidnap her?"

"Junkies do the damnedest things."

"He's not a junkie. Junkies are heroin addicts. Pat smokes grass and does some cocaine, but it doesn't interfere with his life."

Barbara's voice rose. "Don't be an asshole. You've been divorced for five years, and you're still defending him. He's a loser, Jessie. When you get Kate back . . ."

"What?"

Barbara softened her tone. "You'd better make some changes, that's all."

Barbara drove off. Jessie watched the car until it turned the corner. Her hands were shaking. She put them in her pockets.

The bag lady finished writing and stuck the pencil behind her ear. "Beam me the fuck out of here," she whispered urgently. Jessie reentered the house.

She went from room to room. Was Pat a loser? She looked at the flat stomach of the laughing woman on the wall and the fast-food containers on the table; she looked at the bag of cocaine in the bedside table; she looked at the Clinique bag too, but didn't open it. She looked at *Jane Eyre*. She looked at the empty space where Jimi Hendrix's Stratocaster had hung. If Pat was a loser, what was she? They'd lost their marriage together. Maybe she should have handled things differently; maybe she should have . . . Jessie stopped herself. It was over. All it had left behind was a residue of regret; and from time to time she missed him, a lot.

Jessie looked at the hall table. Hadn't there been unopened mail on top of it? She went through the drawers. She found advertising circulars, receipts from clothing stores, a few unpaid bills in small amounts, a handful of pesos, guitar picks, but no unopened mail. At the back of the bottom drawer, she found a crumpled piece of carbon paper. She smoothed it out. It was the copy of a money order, signed by Pat. On March 18, he'd paid ten thousand dollars to Eggman Cookies.

The name meant nothing to Jessie. She called information for Eggman Cookies and found no listing in L.A., Santa Monica, Hollywood, the beaches, the Valley. She tucked the carbon in her pocket. Ten thousand dollars was a lot to pay for cookies.

"I am the Eggman," John Lennon sang in her mind. "Goo goo ga joob." Could Eggman Cookies be the name of a band? Jessie went into the music room. Pat had hundreds of records, tapes and compact discs. He had Merle Travis, Carl Perkins, Muddy Waters, Doc Watson, Eric Clapton and everything Blind Lemon Jefferson had recorded. He had Charlie Christian, Django Reinhart, Wes Montgomery, Joe Pass, Bucky Pizzarrelli. He had Andrés Segovia, Narciso Yepes, Julian Bream, John Williams. He had a rock collection that went from Abba to Z.Z. Topp and included Blue Cheer, the Blues Magoos, the Moody Blues, David Blue and Two Jews' Blues. But he didn't have Eggman Cookies.

Turning to go, Jessie noticed a tape inserted in one of the cassette players. Just to hear what it was, she flicked it on. Joni Mitchell. She was singing about Woodstock and the future she hoped she had seen there. Not Pat's kind of music, Jessie thought as she turned it off. Perhaps the woman with the flat stomach liked it.

"Shit," Jessie said. She went into the kitchen and splashed cold water on her face. As she dried herself with a paper towel, her eye was drawn again to the blackboard. She turned on the overhead light and examined it closely. She could make out the "T" and the "o." Now she saw that the third letter was "i." "Toi." It was French for "you," wasn't it? And hadn't the last word been "toi" as well?

After searching unsuccessfully for a magnifying glass, Jessie unhooked the blackboard from the wall and carefully wrapped it in dry cleaners' plastic. In her workroom at home, she had

44

the big light, a powerful magnifier and fine brushes for uncovering chalk dust, layer by layer. She called a taxi. When it arrived twenty minutes later, she picked up her package and went out.

It was late afternoon. A cool, damp wind was blowing in off the ocean. The blue oblong at the end of the street stretched to the horizon, turning gray under a graying sky. Rain was in the air.

The taxi driver looked her up and down, then got out of the car to open the trunk for her. He had to step around the bag lady, who was leaning against her shopping cart, watching the sky; reflected clouds drifted over the lenses of her sunglasses.

The taxi driver held out his hands to take the blackboard, but Jessie wanted to put it in the trunk herself. As she leaned forward, a metal wheel squeaked. Then the bag lady backed into her, knocking the package from her arms. The blackboard shattered on the pavement.

"Christ almighty," Jessie said, turning on her.

The bag lady hunched down as though in the teeth of a storm, her gray head tucked into her thick shoulders. Then she spun around and hurried away toward the beach. The shopping cart ran over the blackboard, crunching fragments under its wheels.

"Beam me, beam me," the bag lady whispered.

Jessie bent down and looked at the pieces. They were all there in the plastic, dozens of them.

"Mierda," said the taxi driver.

A cold raindrop landed on Jessie's face.

7

It was just like a jigsaw puzzle, except the pieces were all jagged and black. Find the four corners, find the four sides, fill it in. Under the five-hundred-watt bulb, Jessie's fingers dipped into the plastic wrapper, found the piece they wanted, stuck it in place, working quickly and surely, like a well-trained team that didn't need coaching anymore. The puzzle began to take shape on a big sheet of brown paper she'd laid on the worktable—"Night Sky with Milky Way," or a rectangular blackboard with swirls of chalk dust. And under the chalk, Jessie could distinguish block capital letters: "T," "o," "i," and now a "g" and "e" as well.

When she had fit most of the pieces together, Jessie glued them, one by one, to the brown paper. Then she swiveled her magnifier into place, adjusted the focus, took her number eight flat brush and got to work. She knew that wiping with a dry cloth dislodges loosely packed chalk particles, spreading them over the blackboard, but underneath, unless the wiping has been very thorough, the tightly packed core remains. Particle by particle, Jessie brushed a narrow border around the "T," the "o," the "i," the "g"; then she found the top of the next letter, found its side, brushed away the covering layer of chalk dust: another "i." By the time the doorbell rang she'd exposed it all: "Toi giet la toi." It still meant nothing to her. She copied the words on a sheet of paper and went upstairs.

Jessie opened the door and let Barbara in. Rain danced on the roof of her car, parked in the driveway. "Peace," said Barbara, handing her a stack of Lean Cuisine packages.

Jessie took them and went into the kitchen. "What'll it be?" Jessie asked, going through the packages—Chicken à l'Orange, Turkey Dijon, Linguine with Clam Sauce. "Two hundred and twenty-two calories? Two sixty-seven? Or do you feel like pigging out on two ninety-six?"

"I don't care," Barbara said. "What's to drink?"

Jessie shoved the frozen food into the oven and looked in the booze cupboard. "Wine?"

"Check."

"Red or white?"

"Red. Let's live a little."

Jessie filled two glasses with Beaujolais and took Barbara down to the workroom. "Toi giet la toi?" Barbara said. "Isn't 'toi' French?"

"Yeah. But 'giet'?"

Jessie looked it up in her French-English dictionary. "Giet" wasn't there.

"Maybe you need a better dictionary," Barbara said.

"This is the Robert."

"I beg your pardon."

They went upstairs. "Have you got anything I can put on?" Barbara asked. "I'd like to get out of this man suit."

"Why? It's you."

"Fuck off," Barbara said. "Blake's picking me up a little later. Businesswear intimidates him." Barbara reached for her Camels, shook one out and stuck it in her mouth.

Jessie remembered the sleepy voice on the phone. "Who's Blake?"

Barbara's eyes darted toward her, then away. She lit her cigarette, frowning over the match flame. "You'll meet him."

Jessie lent Barbara a pair of jeans and a sweater. They were both tall, but Jessie had a bigger frame and more flesh on it. Barbara came out of the bedroom looking softer, as though she'd put on a boyfriend's sweater.

They sat down at the kitchen table. Jessie pried the tops off the Lean Cuisines and poured more wine. But neither of them ate. Barbara smoked and drank her wine. Jessie just drank.

"I was at a meeting the other day where someone proposed we lobby the U.N. to declare the twenty-first century the International Century of Women," Barbara said.

"Why don't we shoot for the whole fucking millennium?"

They looked at each other. Barbara began to laugh. She threw her head back until the cords in her neck stood out, laughing and laughing. Smoke curled up between her parted lips. All at once, Jessie was laughing too. She too laughed and laughed. Her body shook with it; her stomach muscles ached. She laughed until only ugly honking sounds came out. She couldn't stop. Tears rolled out of her eyes and down her face. The next moment she was holding onto Barbara.

"Help me, Barbara. Help me get her back."

Barbara held her close. "Don't worry, Jessie. We'll get her back." Barbara was crying too.

They went into the bathroom, washed their faces, patted their hair. "God, he's a shithead," Barbara said. "This time we're going to nail him to the wall, baby; I mean it."

"He's really not that bad. His parents died when he was a kid, don't forget, and he never finished high school. It was very destabilizing."

"My heart bleeds. Explain to me why he has to shove his dick into every woman that comes by."

But that's what Jessie couldn't explain. "He's just a boy who can't say no, I guess."

" 'Boy' is the operative word, Jess. Boys are all that's out there. I'm in a position to know. Boys in three-piece suits, boys with seven-figure salaries, boys with silvery hair like lions' manes—like your friend Norman Wine. I heard a rumor of a man being sighted the other day, but it turned out to be false."

They stared at each other in the mirror: two heads of frizzy hair, two dark faces, one very thin and modern, the other a little

48

fuller and classical. "How much did you get for Norman's wife?" Jessie asked.

"Ten grand a month."

Jessie whistled.

"The schmuck can afford it. He's making a killing in real estate."

"Norman's a record producer."

"That's his job. But he gets rich from real estate. Wake up, Jess. The music's over."

Jessie woke up. The amount of Norman's wife's settlement reminded her of the Eggman Cookies money order. She showed it to Barbara.

"Beats me," Barbara said. "I'll pass it on to DeMarco when he calls."

"DeMarco's calling?"

The thin face in the mirror smiled. "I figured DeMarco owes me one. So I told him he could pay me back by bending the rules a little and running a check for Kate."

Jessie put her arm around Barbara. Barbara went on: "They're not actively looking for her, you understand. But if there are any reports having to do with Kate, Pat or . . . the car, he'll find out. He should call sometime tonight."

"Thank you, Barbara."

"You can thank me by letting me nail him to the wall when this is over. Agreed?"

Jessie didn't reply.

"Agreed?"

"Okay. Agreed."

Barbara held out her hand. They shook on it. Their images shook hands in the mirror. "I wish I had your nose," Barbara said.

"You can afford it."

"Prices have gone up. What was yours—a sweet sixteen present?"

"Keep guessing," Jessie said.

"Bitch."

"Hey," called a voice. "Anybody home?"

It was Philip. He came in carrying an artist's portfolio and a small bag. He wore baggy white flannel trousers, a black T-

49

shirt, a satin Lakers jacket and a little diamond in his left ear. "You should lock your door," he said. "This is L.A."

"It's Santa Monica," Barbara corrected him. Jessie introduced them.

"I've got something to show you," he said, opening the portfolio with his quick, agile hands. " 'Valley Nocturne.' This is just a study. The real thing's twenty by thirty."

"Yards?" asked Barbara.

Philip smiled uncertainly. "Feet," he said, unwrapping the protective plastic. "The slides are coming tomorrow."

They all looked at "Valley Nocturne." It was smooth and sleek, the colors mainly purple and silver, although the subject matter seemed to be an orange grove on a foggy evening. A naked girl was folded into it like a truffle in cream sauce.

"Well?" said Philip.

"Nice bod," said Barbara.

Faint pink patches appeared on Philip's cheeks. He looked at Jessie. It was hard to hide from Philip. His soft gold-brown eyes saw everything. She tried to think of something to say. Philip's paintings were already attracting attention. He was very talented. He could do with his brush, she suddenly thought, the kind of thing Pat could do with his guitar. She knew at a glance that "Valley Nocturne" had the commercial goods and would one day hang on a big wall in Palm Springs or Malibu. On the other hand, she didn't like it.

Before she could say anything, Barbara spoke. "Did you know that Kate was missing?"

"Kate?" said Philip. He looked inquiringly at Jessie. "Did you mention that yesterday?"

"I said Pat hadn't brought her home yet. He still hasn't."

Philip came closer and patted her shoulder. "I'm sure it'll be all right," he said. She felt his soft eyes on her. He patted her again, this time putting more into it. "Is there anything I can do?"

"Maybe there is," Jessie said, taking out the sheet of paper on which she'd copied the foreign words. "What do you make of this?"

Philip examined it. "French, isn't it. 'Toi' is 'you,' and 'la' is 'the.' 'You something the you.' We just have to find out what 'giet' means."

50

Jessie explained that they hadn't found it in the Robert. "No problem," said Philip. "I've got a friend at Berlitz. I'll call her tomorrow." He folded the sheet of paper and slipped it into his portfolio; then he fished around in the bag he'd brought and drew out a bottle. "Do you like champagne, Barbara? I know Jessie does."

"She's a real fun lover." The patches on Philip's cheeks went a little pinker.

"Knock it off, Barbara," Jessie said.

Barbara saluted. "Champagne's my fave," she said to Philip. "Crack her open."

They drank the champagne. Philip talked about a series of paintings about California he had in mind, "Valley Nocturne" being the first. Jessie said it was a good idea. Barbara said nothing. They finished the red wine and started on the white. The doorbell rang. Jessie answered it. A young man stood on the doorstep, a very young man, twenty-one or -two. He had two giant pizza boxes in his hands. He also had clear green eyes, clear golden skin, shining golden hair, the body Michelangelo's David might have developed if he'd spent time in the weight room and a shy smile. He was beautiful. "Hi," he said. "I'm Blake. Is Barb here?"

"Barb? Oh, yes. Come in."

Blake came in. "I brought some pizza, " he said. "I hope you like everything on it." He gave Barbara a kiss. He towered over her. Her lips lingered on his. Jessie saw that her eyes actually closed. "Any beer?" Blake said. "I forgot beer."

"I'll get some," Jessie told him. "I could use a walk."

"It's raining," Blake said. "I'll drive."

"That's all right. I don't mind the rain. What kind of beer do you like?"

"Wet," Barbara answered for him.

Philip laughed nervously. Blake smiled his shy smile. Jessie threw on her big yellow slicker and went out.

The rain was falling heavily now. Thunder rolled in the west. Jessie put up her hood and walked quickly, across Idaho, around the corner and south three blocks to the liquor store. She bought a case of beer. "Nasty night," said the old man behind the counter.

Jessie walked back. She didn't mind the rain, never had. It was probably part of the same complex that made her a sucker for *Jane Eyre,* guitar players, painters and all the rest. *Don't think about that. Think about what needs thinking about. Maybe Lieutenant DeMarco's called.* Jessie quickened her pace. As she turned onto Idaho, a car pulled away from the curb and shone its high beams in her eyes, blinding her for a moment as it flashed by. She crossed the street and went into the house.

Barbara was hanging up the phone. "That was DeMarco. He checked every jurisdiction from Santa Barbara to San Diego. Nothing."

All at once the case of beer was unbearably heavy. Jessie put it down.

"That's good news," Barbara went on. "It means nothing bad's happened." Jessie nodded, but it didn't feel like good news to her. "DeMarco says not to worry. It's only been one day. He said that if they went chasing after every kid who's disappeared for a day, they'd be doing nothing else."

Jessie waited for that to make her feel better. When it didn't, she said. "There's the beer."

They sat around the coffee table. Philip showed Blake 'Valley Nocturne.' "It's great," Blake said. They all drank the beer. Philip ate one slice of pizza. Blake ate the rest.

"How about some music?" Blake said.

"What do you like?" Jessie asked.

"Sixties stuff."

"God, no," said Philip.

"Pick something out," Jessie said.

Blake picked out Jimi Hendrix. He sang along to "Purple Haze." Barbara rested her hand on his thigh. "Did you know Jessie's ex-husband has Jimi Hendrix's guitar?"

"You're kidding. How did he get that?"

Jessie tried to remember what Pat had told her. "I think he bought it at an auction after Hendrix died."

Blake thought about that. Then he said, "Gee, so many of those sixties people OD'd, didn't they, choking on their own vomit and everything. I wonder why."

"Because the sixties were bullshit, that's why," Barbara said.

"Really?" said Jessie. "What about the night we hitchhiked to Reno?"

Barbara burst out laughing, spraying beer on Blake's neck. He didn't seem to mind.

"What happened in Reno?" Philip asked.

"We never actually got to Reno," Barbara replied. "Did we, Jess?" She began laughing again.

"What happened?" Blake said.

Barbara took out a cigarette, lit it, frowned over the match. "Some other time," she said. Jimi Hendrix ran off several dozen notes, but nothing happened that you could dance to.

Blake turned to Jessie. "It must have been exciting in those days. Wasn't your husband a musician?"

"He still is. But he's not my husband anymore."

"He lived on a commune, didn't he?"

Jessie glanced at Barbara, wondering what else she'd told Blake about her and Pat. Barbara was squinting into her smoke. "That was before I met him," Jessie said. "Spacious Skies, they called it. Somewhere in Vermont. Pat wrote a song about it."

"Did it get recorded?"

"A few times."

"By anybody famous?"

"Dave van Ronk."

"Who's he?"

"A folkie, I think," Philip said. "Right?"

"Right," Jessie said. Barbara took a deep drag of her Camel.

Jimi Hendrix's guitar roared itself out in an ocean of over-dubbed feedback. Blake rose and stretched. "Well," he said, "Tomorrow's a working day."

"Where do you work?" Jessie asked.

"Nautilus on Pico. I'm an instructor."

Barbara led him up the stairs to the guest room. Philip helped Jessie put things away and went up a few minutes later. Jessie stayed behind to dial Pat's number. "Hi," she heard. "No one's here right now, but just leave a message and we'll buzz you back. Promise."

"Fuck you," Jessie said, slamming down the phone.

She went upstairs, down the hall to her bedroom. As she passed the closed door to the guest room, she heard Barbara cry out.

Philip was waiting in the bed. Jessie took off her clothes.

"You look great," he said. She got into bed. He kissed her and rolled her nipple between his finger and thumb, not too gently, not too rough. Philip was good with his hands. Jessie felt an enormous orgasm building inside her.

But Philip entered her a little too soon. And he came a little too soon. Or maybe it was just the image of Kate, getting in the way. Jessie's orgasm stayed inside. She heard Barbara cry out again down the hall.

They lay on opposite sides of the bed, not touching. "Didn't you come?" Philip said.

"No."

"God, I'm sorry. That's never happened before, has it?"

No, Jessie thought, it's a first in the history of the human race. But she just said, "No."

There was a silence. Then Philip said, "Do you want me to . . . do something about it?"

"Go to sleep, Philip. It's no big deal."

He patted her thigh. His hand had gone cold. He cleared his throat. "Do you like it?"

"Do I like what?"

" 'Valley Nocturne.' "

"It's good. You don't need me to tell you that."

"I do."

A little later, Philip said, "You know Mrs. Stieffler, don't you?"

"Yes."

"I wouldn't mind meeting her. And some of her friends."

Jessie explained why she couldn't help him. He said nothing.

Rain drummed on the roof. Jessie tried to sleep, but couldn't. She allowed herself to take some comfort from Lieutenant DeMarco's nonnews. She took some more from the fact that Barbara was helping her. Rain drummed on the roof.

"What's that?" Philip said, much later. He was a light sleeper.

Jessie listened. She heard someone moving in the hall. Jessie smiled in the darkness. "Barbara," she whispered. "Looking for cigarettes."

They heard feet going downstairs, heard a briefcase opening, heard an irritated mutter. "Barbara's a . . . hard person, isn't she?" Philip said.

"She's the best of the best," Jessie said.

Philip rolled over the other way. Jessie thought about Barbara's boy theory.

She heard the front door open and shut. The liquor store was closed by now, but they had cigarettes next door to it at the all-night grocery. Jessie closed her eyes. She listened to the rain.

An awful shriek of rubber snapped her up into a sitting position. The next moment came the sickening thump of something hard striking something soft. Then rubber shrieked again.

"Oh, God," Jessie said, and she was out of bed, running down the hall, down the stairs, out into the rain. Barbara lay in the middle of the road.

"Oh, God."

Jessie fell to her knees and took Barbara in her arms. Barbara's eyes were open. "I was wrong about the sixties, Jess," she said, so faintly that Jessie could barely hear. "There was you."

She said no more. A moment later there was no life in her at all. "Oh God, oh God, oh God." Jessie held Barbara tight, rocking her back and forth, back and forth. She didn't stop until the police came and pulled her away.

Only then did Jessie notice that Barbara had borrowed the big yellow slicker to protect her from the rain.

8

SENATOR FRAME: Mr. President, I ask unanimous consent that the text of the prospective legislation be printed in the RECORD at this time.

There being no objection, the material was ordered to be printed in the RECORD as follows:

S. 4076

Be it enacted by the Senate and House of Representatives of the United States of America in Congress assembled,

Section 1. SHORT TITLE AND TABLE OF CONTENTS

a) SHORT TITLE—This Act may be cited as the Federal Polygraph Law.

—from the Congressional Record

□

"This won't hurt a bit," said the young man, slipping a blood pressure cuff around the woman's arm. He pumped in air until it felt uncomfortable; you couldn't call it hurting. Then he strapped two sweat detectors to her fingers, fit a narrow rubber belt around her chest and a wider one around her waist, and flicked a switch on a metal box that lay on a desk between them. Four styluses quivered in anticipation.

"Follow the Redskins?" the young man asked.

"Is that the first question?"

"Ha, ha," he said. "Nope. Just making conversation." But he didn't make any more of it. Instead he adjusted a dial on the metal box, pumped a little more air into the blood pressure cuff and took out a notebook. He wore an identification tag on his lapel: John A. Brent, Jr.

"Must it be so tight, Mr. Brent?"

"Excuse me?"

"The blood pressure thing."

He looked at a dial on the metal box. "We're well within the standard range," he said. "It won't be long."

"How long? My husband didn't tell me."

"Not long." The young man opened his notebook; his eyes scanned the writing inside.

"My husband gave me to understand that this would be . . ."

He looked up. John A. Brent, Jr.'s eyes were instruments for seeing; the revelation capacity had been shut down. "Yes?"

"Pro forma."

"Pro forma?" he said. His eyes returned to the notebook. The woman didn't know whether he was ignorant of the expression or was merely avoiding answering it. To find out she'd have to be on the other side of the metal box; he'd have to be the one connected to it.

The thought made her angry. She could feel her heart beating faster, her breathing becoming more labored, her pores starting to open: all grist for the black box, and they hadn't even begun. This insight reminded her of a dinner party where someone had said that beating the machine was easy. All you had to do was artificially raise the tension level during the control questions—"Bite the insides of your cheeks; squeeze your feet into the floor; simply remember the worst pain you've ever felt."

"What about thinking of sex?" someone had asked.

"Only if it's adulterous." A rather witty conversation for Washington, these days, she thought. It must have taken place at the Canadian embassy. What a pass things had come to.

"Now, I'm going to ask you a series of questions," Brent said. "Please keep your answers simple." He licked his thumb and turned a page. "What is your name?"

Something about his gesture made the woman lose perspective, made her see things not as they were—a publicity exercise that would soon be over, to be followed by lunch at Le Pavillon and some shopping—but as they would appear to an uninformed observer or a camera: state functionary, human peeling machine, citizen. What had it been—simply the sight of his thick pink tongue wetting the ball of his thumb? A glimpse of something animal lurking under all the high tech?

Glancing first at Mr. Brent, who was watching the styluses, the woman bit the inside of her cheek. She discovered that her dinner party informant had never put his ideas into practice: cheek-biting precluded normal speech. Instead she dug a fingernail into her palm and answered, "Alice Frame."

The graph paper in the metal box began rolling. The styluses dove down and started scratching. The young man glanced without expression at the four lines appearing on the paper and went on.

"Where do you reside?"

"We have a farm near Sweet Briar, Virginia."

Styluses scratched. Paper rolled. Brent watched the spidery lines grow. Silence continued until Alice felt compelled to add, "We also have a house in Palm Beach and a ski chalet in New England."

"Where in New England?"

"Does it matter? Near Morgantown, Massachusetts."

58

Brent licked his lips. Then he asked, "Are you married?"

"That's the whole point of the exercise, isn't it?" The styluses did something that made Mr. Brent frown.

"Please make your answers direct. Are you married?"

"Yes."

"What is your husband's name?"

"Edmund."

"What does he do?"

"What he likes."

Brent frowned. "What is his job?"

"As you know, he's a member of the United States Senate."

Brent watched the styluses. The frown lines receded on his forehead, but didn't quite disappear.

"Do you have children?"

Alice drove her fingernail into her palm, but not to fool the machine. It just happened. "No."

"Could you speak up a little, please. Children?"

"No."

Brent's eyes tracked the black lines moving across the paper in the metal box. He frowned again. Then he licked his thumb and turned another page in his notebook.

"Have you ever had an unauthorized meeting with a representative of a foreign power?"

"No."

"Have you ever been the subject of a blackmail attempt?"

"Object," said Alice.

"Excuse me?"

Alice sighed. "No. No one has tried to blackmail me."

She stopped digging her nail into her palm. She answered the rest of Mr. Brent's questions as quickly as she could. All she wanted was for it to be over.

Brent unhooked her. He didn't thank her or say good-bye. Protocol for these situations hadn't been developed. The world awaited the coming of a new and steely Emily Post.

Alice went out the door, into an elevator, out into a lobby. Photographers clicked cameras in her face. Microphones were stuck in front of her mouth. Then Edmund was beside her, his hand around her waist. He flashed his white smile, proud as a papa whose kid had won the race.

*   *   *

"Shit," said Dahlin.

"Fuck," said Keith.

They were watching a twenty-five-inch Mitsubishi video monitor. Dahlin jabbed at the remote-controlled pause button. A woman's face froze on the screen. She was middle-aged, but obviously possessed the kind of bones and money that would keep her beautiful for another ten or twenty years. That was no comfort to the two men confronting her image.

Keith rose and walked across the room. He stared abstractedly at a framed blowup on the wall: a grainy photograph shot from overhead. It showed a bald man with a big strawberry mark on his forehead. He appeared to be urinating against a hedge. Keith turned to Dahlin, sitting behind his desk.

"Don't blame me," he said.

"Who mentioned blame?" replied Dahlin.

"I wouldn't blame you."

"If I mentioned blame?"

"I wouldn't. Maybe you think I put him up to it."

"That's too strong."

"But I encouraged him."

"That's about right."

"He would have gone ahead anyway."

"Probably."

Their heads turned toward the screen.

"Shit," said Dahlin.

"Fuck," said Keith.

"He doesn't have to worry about crap like this."

"Who?"

"Him." Dahlin pointed his chin at the urinating man on the wall.

"Hell no. That's what makes America great."

"That's a good one," Dahlin said. But he didn't laugh.

"What are we going to do?" Keith asked.

"How about nothing?"

Keith took off his horn-rimmed glasses and polished them on a monogrammed handkerchief. "Nothing?" he said.

Dahlin frowned. "You missed a smudge."

"Where?"

"The right lens."

"This one?"

"The other one."

"That's my left."

"It's my right."

Keith nodded. He polished both lenses. "I'm not sure it can be nothing," he said.

"From where you sit."

"That's part of it."

"Then," said Dahlin, "it'll have to be something."

Keith gazed out the window. In the distance flowed the river, dark gray under a light gray sky. Beyond it rose the city with its monuments to this and that. "Maybe I should handle it myself," he said.

"You? What kind of talk is that? How can it be you? He knows you. She knows you. Why do I have to do all the thinking myself?"

"Sorry."

"Objectivity," Dahlin said, "appearance of. Commandment one." He opened his desk drawer, took out a pipe and reamed it violently. "We'll just have to treat this like a normal . . ." He searched for a word. After a while, he gave up.

They looked at the woman, quivering very slightly in the freeze-frame. It was a close-up —none of the fluttering equipment showed. Dahlin lit his pipe. Time passed. Smoke rode convection currents through the air. The phone on Dahlin's desk buzzed. He didn't pick it up. The river flowed. On the far side, little figures chased an invisible football across a football field. They darted around, lay down in piles, jumped up, darted around.

"I've had a thought," Dahlin said at last.

"Shoot."

"How about Zyz?"

"Zyz?"

"Why not? At least it would get him out of the office."

"Surely that's not our first—"

Dahlin interrupted: "And what possible harm could he do?"

"He's not exactly toothless."

"Maybe not. But what harm could he do? What possible harm?" Dahlin repeated. When he found a point to make he

61

made it over and over. It was the foundation of his career, maybe the foundation of all successful careers in Washington.

Keith had no answer.

Dahlin puffed his pipe. The room began to smell like a waste disposal plant. His lips moved around the pipe stem. "Zyz," he said. "Just the ticket."

9

Number 22, gleaming in white and gold like some knight of yore, was game enough, but he just didn't have the speed. Two thick-necked boys in purple hit him before he could turn the corner. The impact made noise— an artificial one of plastic on plastic, a natural, deeper one of flesh on flesh. Number 22 went down hard; pain knocked the grown-up mask off his face, exposing to all the boy his mother knew. But no one saw, except the man jogging on the track around the field.

Squirting from number 22's grasp, the ball bounced over the chalk sideline onto the track. The jogger, a big man in a plain gray sweatsuit and all-purpose ten-dollar sneakers from J. C. Penney, kicked it back without breaking stride. He didn't appear to aim it anywhere, didn't appear to kick it very hard, but the ball flew straight to the referee, standing at midfield. The referee eyed the jogger for a second or two. Then he signaled fourth down and blew his whistle.

Three laps to go. Ivan Zyzmchuk's feet thudded softly on the red cinder track, very softly for a man of his build. He wasn't much over six feet tall, but he weighed two hundred and twenty pounds and none of them moved independently as he jogged.

"Jogging" was not a word he himself would use. "Roadwork" was his name for it. He'd started putting in roadwork a long time ago, before the discovery of Lycra, waffle soles or runner's high. Training. Three miles a day. Back then he'd been fighting for a place on the school boxing team. Later he'd been schoolboy light-heavyweight champion of his country. Then had come an interruption: a long interruption that still hadn't ended. But he'd kept up his training.

"Hut one, hut two, hut, hut." Zyzmchuk, who had been gazing with unfocused eyes at the red cinder track, looked up. A coach with a square jaw and a round belly sent number 22 back in the game and ran him off-tackle. Perhaps the coach was testing the Get-Right-Back-on-the-Horse Theory. The test yielded immediate results: the boy fumbled the ball away and returned to the bench with his head down. He became invisible to the coach, his teammates, the few dozen spectators clustered along the sidelines—to everyone except Zyzmchuk, circling the field. It wasn't that Zyzmchuk was a ghoul, or was attracted to others' humiliation, or was particularly interested in the boy—it was just that he had an eye for seeing things as they were. It was a talent mentioned on all his fitness reports, in one way or another.

As he ran, Ivan Zyzmchuk's mind wandered from the game being played beside him to memories of the other kind of football, the kind he had played. Not many of these memories remained: the image of a faded blue singlet, patched many times by his mother; bloody fragments from a match played in pouring rain against a team of German cadets; the bony face of a wonderfully quick goalie named Miro, who'd once shared a bag of stolen chocolates with him.

Zyzmchuk kept going. He felt damp patches spreading under his sweatshirt. The chill snapped his reverie. Just as well. The blue singlet had finally fallen apart; they'd lost the match to the German boys; Miro had been shot against a wall in 1944. Two laps to go.

Zyzmchuk heard footsteps coming up behind him and moved

to the inside. A young woman in orange jogging tights glided by. He glimpsed her effortless body, her determined eyes, her bare ankles, lovely and slim—the Achilles tendons contracted like perfectly machined springs with every stride. She reminded him of the mountain girls from his boyhood summers, but the mountain girls had never had that determined look. His body sped up, all by itself. He slowed it down. This wasn't a footrace, he wasn't built for footraces, and even if he caught up to the woman in the orange tights, what then? The object of her determination was unlikely to be him. It was more likely to be making the payments on a Saab, or making the right connection, or making partner. Zyzmchuk couldn't help her. He soon lost sight of her perfect ankles.

One lap to go. He was straining just a little now. Running wasn't his sport. Football, soccer, whatever they wanted to call it hadn't really been his sport either. His sport he'd had to give up when they fled Prague after the war. No time for boxing in America. They'd had too much catching up to do, too much, in the end, for his father or his mother. But Zyzmchuk had caught up.

He finished the last lap and walked down to the river. A cold breeze blew across the water from Virginia. It knocked dried leaves out of the trees and carried them on spiraling descents. Zyzmchuk lay under an oak. His eyes closed. Miro's face drifted across his eyelids. He opened them.

Mat work. Twenty push-ups. Twenty sit-ups. Twenty leg raises. Thirty push-ups. Thirty sit-ups. Thirty leg raises. Forty push-ups. Forty sit-ups. Forty leg raises. Enough, Zyzmchuk thought: enough for a twenty-year-old, and I'm going to be fifty-seven in two months. The thought made him do a few more. But not fifty, fifty, fifty. Those days were gone.

When he sat up, he saw the woman in the orange tights, stretching nearby. She was watching him. Surprise. She looked away when she saw he noticed, finished her stretching and walked to the parking lot on the other side of the field. Zyzmchuk rose and followed.

The football game was over, the field deserted. The woman got into her car—a Peugeot, not a Saab—and drove away. Zyzmchuk had time to memorize her license number.

He went to his own car, a Blazer with one hundred and

twenty-two thousand miles on the odometer and an engine he'd rebuilt himself, and paused, his hand reaching for the keys. He looked around and saw no one. Then he got down, lay flat on his back and looked under the chassis, like a used-car buyer checking for rust. He found plenty of it, plus a loose bolt on one side of the muffler and a perforated catalytic converter that wouldn't last the winter. He unlocked the door, got in, stuck the key in the ignition and turned it, all without disappearing in a ball of fire.

Zyzmchuk switched off the engine. He opened the glove compartment, took out a Thermos and unscrewed the top. The smell of coffee filled the car. He poured a cup, not hot, but still warm at least. A blessing, coffee. One of the great blessings of his life. Count your blessings: one. He took a sandwich from a paper bag. Smoked salmon on fresh pumpernickel. Two and three. The smells blended with the coffee smell, harmonious as a Beethoven trio. Ivan Zyzmchuk ate his lunch.

1:30. Time to get back to the office. Zyzmchuk caught himself thinking of going to the gym for a steam instead. He was amazed. Maybe he was changing. Change was coming, whether he liked it or not. "It's nothing personal, Zyz. A question of dollars and cents, that's all." Oh well then.

He picked up the phone and dialed a number. "Grace," he said, "I'd like you to check a license plate for me. Maryland, SEO 833."

He sat in the car, waiting for her to call back. A pair of ducks, male and female, glided down from the sky in a graceful curve and landed beneath one of the goalposts. Their heads bobbed back and forth. Then the male mounted the female. She tried to get away. He pinned her head down with his bill. Another male flew down, pushed the first away and took his place, bill planted on the back of her head. The first male bit the second's neck. The three ducks wove under the goalposts in a bad-tempered scrum. "Nature," he remembered Leni saying, "is what we're put on earth to rise above." He felt a warmth, cozy and domestic, spreading through him. It always did when he thought of Leni, but he knew from experience not to encourage it. Zyzmchuk pushed her out of his mind. In the backseat he had some brochures. He put on his glasses and reached for them.

66

Arizona Sunset. Condo Country. The Time-Sharing Experience. Zyzmchuk studied the glossy pictures of sunburned old people playing tennis and eating ice cream cones. Being old was a gas. Zyzmchuk could hardly wait. He rolled down the window and tossed the brochures into a trash barrel.

They'd started appearing in his mailbox a few days after he'd been asked to take early retirement. Condo Country had its own intelligence capability. "It has nothing to do with the way you do the job, Zyz. Nothing like that." Oh no. "It's a budgetary matter. You've seen the figures, you know what I'm talking about. It's time to get some younger men in. We've got to think of the future. You know how long people last in this business. You're our Satchel Paige already."

"Zyz didn't play baseball."

"Our Pele then. Our Archie Moore."

"I know who Satchel Paige was."

"Of course, of course."

And more palaver like that. But they all knew the real reason. Ivan Zyzmchuk wasn't cut out to work in an office, and there was nothing else for him to do. That was departmental policy—no one in the field after fifty. Zyzmchuk had hung on for an extra six years thanks to a series of special six-month contracts, but now it was over. Assets: a pension of $2,272.65 a month (but it didn't start until he was sixty), a savings account with a little over three thousand dollars in it. Liabilities: an apartment that cost eight hundred a month, car insurance, medical insurance, food and drink for one. Conclusion: he had to find a job. Credentials: a bachelor's degree in economics from the University of Chicago, 1951, and a twenty-five-page résumé. Its contents were top secret.

The phone buzzed. Grace had been quick. "Yes?" he said.

But it wasn't Grace. "Caught you, Zyz," said Keith.

"Caught me?"

"In the middle of an old-fashioned three-martini lunch. Am I right?" He paused, waiting for Zyzmchuk's reply. Zyzmchuk said nothing. He didn't like being called Zyz. "Well," Keith said, "you've earned it, if anyone has." There was a longer pause. When Keith spoke again, his voice had lost its bonhomie. "Stop by the office this afternoon. We've got something to show you."

"What?"

"Show, not tell. I think you'll be interested."

The line went dead. Zyzmchuk looked across the river; he could make out a square gray building halfway up a hillside. From a distance, it looked like any other government building designed by middle-echelon architects for middle-echelon workers. Perhaps it had a little more rooftop equipment than most. Zyzmchuk started the car and drove toward the bridge.

He was on the Virginia side when the phone buzzed again. "Mr. Zyzmchuk? It's Grace. Maryland SEO 833 is registered to a Ms. Lisa Turley. She lives alone at 483 Hawthorn Street, Bethesda, and is employed as an analyst at the Bureau of Economic Indicators. She's divorced, twenty-nine years old and graduated from Wellesley College. No federal or state arrests or convictions, no known travel to any Soviet bloc countries. She had an abortion in nineteen eighty-three and owes fifty-five dollars in overdue D.C. parking tickets. Do you want more?"

"What more could there be?"

"I could do some digging on her ex-husband for starters."

Zyzmchuk laughed. "Only for your own fun," he said.

"What a suggestion, Mr. Zyzmchuk!"

"Isn't it?"

Zyzmchuk drove to the gray building on the hillside and pulled into the small parking lot at the back. The lot was marked with numbered spaces. Zyzmchuk parked in number 9, although it wasn't his; 31 was his space, but 9 was closer to the door and its owner in the hospital for tests.

The gray building had no nameplate, just a carved stone over the door—an eagle that looked more like a vulture holding a banner that read 1952. Inside there was no security check, no guard, no office directory. The sole decoration was a big mirror on the rear wall of the lobby; a woman was pursing her lips in it. The RAG, as it was called by those working there who enjoyed sufficient clearance to know the name of their employer—the Research Analysis Group—was a mediocre, unpretentious office building that made no statements, unless you knew about its hidden cameras, metal detectors and plastics sensors, and the two men watching on the other side of the mirror, one with a logbook, the other behind a fifty-caliber machine gun.

Zyzmchuk took the elevator to the top floor and entered his

office. Grace was sitting at her desk, eyes on her VDT, hand fishing in a can of Almond Roca.

"Caught me red-handed, Mr. Zyzmchuk," said Grace.

"It's one of those days," Zyzmchuk said, although he caught Grace red-handed every time he went in or out. She weighed more than he did. The soft pounds sagged in folds from her chin to her ankles. Grace also had glossy chestnut hair and a flawless complexion. She popped another Roca in her mouth. Zyzmchuk went into the inner office, pulled off his sweatsuit and put on gray flannels and a tweed jacket.

"That's a nice tie, Mr. Zyzmchuk," Grace said when he emerged. "Are those ducks?"

"On the wing, at least," he said.

Grace raised an eyebrow. She had alert, dark eyes that didn't miss much. "As opposed to what, Mr. Zyzmchuk? Flat on their backs?"

"That kind of thing."

Zyzmchuk went out and walked down the hall. He heard Dahlin and Keith laughing before he was halfway to the corner office. They liked a good joke. You could tell that from their satellite picture of Gorbachev pissing outside his dacha.

Dahlin, sitting on the arm of a deep-red leather couch that might have come from the bankruptcy sale of a second-rate men's club, had a magazine open in his hands when Zyzmchuk walked in; Keith was looking at it over his shoulder.

"What a character!" said Dahlin, shaking his head.

"The worst and the dullest," said Keith.

They laughed again. Dahlin closed the magazine: *Harvard*. They'd been browsing through the class notes section at the back. They looked up at Zyzmchuk. Both wore pinstripe suits, wing-tip shoes, horn-rimmed glasses: the Tweedledum and Tweedledee of prepdom. It was easy to underestimate men like them. Zyzmchuk had watched a lot of Europeans make that mistake.

"Ivan," said Dahlin, "nice to see you." They'd last seen each other, Zyzmchuk recalled, the day before. Dahlin rose and held out his hand. Zyzmchuk crossed the room and shook it. Dahlin had a firm, dry grip, not that it mattered. Anyone in his position had long ago mastered the handshake, just as he knew which fork to use for the kiwi fruit and how to say no. The only interesting part of it was that they'd never shaken hands before.

"What's up?"

"Sit down, Ivan, sit down," Dahlin said, crossing his legs. Zyzmchuk sat.

Keith got up and looked out the window. He reminded Zyzmchuk of George Will, somewhat rounder and a little younger. Zyzmchuk noticed that he had ducks on his tie, too. They looked like a better class of duck.

"Nice to see you," Dahlin repeated. He took out his pipe and began reaming it. "You're going to be missed."

Zyzmchuk nodded. He wasn't about to say that he'd miss Dahlin, too. Dahlin was the fifth director he'd worked for. He'd lost track of the number of deputies that had come and gone in that time; usually, like Keith, they were political appointees. They came, learned secrets, spent money, departed. Perhaps Keith had more pretentions than most. In his first month on the job, he'd written a monograph called "The Role of Disguise in the Modern Intelligence Matrix," had it classified, then widely distributed in the intelligence community. Zyzmchuk had an inscribed copy: "To an old pro."

"I was talking to someone the other day who spoke very highly of you," Dahlin said. "He referred particularly to Budapest in 'fifty-six."

"Who was it?"

Dahlin named a name that was in the papers almost every day.

"He wasn't there," Zyzmchuk said.

"I know that," Dahlin said, a little sharply. "He'd been going over some of the reports from the time."

"Why?"

"Now Ivan," said Dahlin, "how would I know a thing like that? Don't you ever stop working?"

"Sure. Five o'clock every day. And all day Saturday and Sunday, since Gramm-Rudman."

Dahlin's mouth opened. It made laughing motions, but no sound came out. He stuck his pipe in it. Keith turned from the window, glancing at his gold watch. I might be funny, Zyzmchuk thought, but not screamingly, like Gorbachev or the Harvard class notes.

70

Dahlin's mouth stopped doing whatever it was doing. "We've got something that looks like your kind of thing," he said. "It'll get you out of the office, at least, for these last few . . ." Dahlin abandoned that approach, without substituting a replacement.

He needn't have been so careful: getting out of the office sounded fine to Zyzmchuk. "What kind of something?" he asked.

Dahlin nodded to Keith. Keith picked up a remote tuner and touched a button. Light glowed from the big screen on the wall. It took the shape of a face, the face, Zyzmchuk saw, of a woman about his own age, poised, well-cared-for, but slightly uneasy: the kind of face you might see in the waiting room of the best dentist in town.

A man on the screen leaned over and blocked the view. He had a fat neck, recently shaved clean by a barber's razor. He did something to the woman, saying, "This won't hurt a bit." He did a few more things. Zyzmchuk glimpsed one of the woman's eyes as the man bent forward. It had widened very slightly: a little hole through which poise could start leaking away.

"Follow the Redskins?" said the man, with his back to the camera.

"Is that the first question?" the woman asked, sounding very puzzled.

The man on the screen laughed, the kind of laugh children provoke when they ask if God put the baby in Mummy's tummy. "Nope," he said, "just making conversation." He took out a notebook and moved offscreen.

The woman ran her finger across her upper lip, as though wiping sweat away, but there was no sweat to see. "Must it be so tight, Mr. Brent?"

"Excuse me?" said the man, turning. The camera caught his face in profile. Zyzmchuk could see that he had heard the woman perfectly well.

"He can't stop being tricky," Dahlin said. "They're mass-producing boobs like that at Langley."

"But boobs who enjoy their work," Zyzmchuk said.

"That's what makes them boobs," Keith said and laughed, drowning out the video. He had his hands folded comfortably across his belly, like a customer with a good seat at a Neil Simon hit.

The man from Langley had moved offscreen. "Pro forma?"

71

he was saying, as though he couldn't believe what he'd heard. The woman's face tensed. The man announced that he was about to ask a series of questions, then put the first one: "What is your name?"

There was a long pause. The woman cast a quick look in the direction of the man; then she balled her right hand into a fist and said, "Alice Frame."

"For Christ's sake," Zyzmchuk said. "Is that the senator's wife?"

"You're quick to see the problem, Ivan," Dahlin said.

"I don't see anything," Zyzmchuk replied. "What's she doing in the flutter room?"

"You must have heard of the senator's polygraph bill."

"I've heard of it. He wants to flutter every firstborn son and daughter in the land."

Dahlin's mouth made its laughing motions, revealing teeth full of metal and a tobacco-stained tongue. "It's not that bad, Ivan. No more than a few hundred thousand people will be involved in all, mostly more State and Defense people, some independent contractors, a few agencies like NASA, that kind of thing."

"And their families."

"In some cases. The senator's trying to help."

"By testing his own wife?"

"He's just trying to show that he's not asking anyone to do anything he wouldn't do himself. All the networks picked it up last night."

"Surely you're not going to defend fluttering," Zyzmchuk said.

"Not within these four walls," said Dahlin, through a cloud of smoke.

"Except in terms of discouraging potential leakers," Keith added.

"You mean intimidating the little guys."

"Why not?"

"Because the machine can't detect when someone's lying. It can just write lines on paper. Its name describes it perfectly, no more, no less." Zyzmchuk paused. He could see from their faces he'd gone too fast—it often happened when a man who spoke nine languages posed arguments based on word derivations to those with only one. "The point is that soon everyone's going to know. And then it won't even be scary anymore." Out of the corner of his eye, Zyzmchuk saw Alice Frame, unaware of the camera in a light fixture or behind a ventilator, digging her nail into her palm and saying, "No, never." "You can't make a joke your first line of defense," Zyzmchuk said. "The professionals are laughing already."

"I'm not going to argue with you, Ivan. The point is the senator has sat on the intelligence committee for twenty years; he's one of our biggest supporters; and he's very enthusiastic about this bill. That's fact one. Fact two: his wife took the test. Call it a publicity stunt if you want, but if we had results like this from anybody else, we'd investigate. I'm not talking about the polygraph report—don't waste your time reading it—but just look at her. Fact three: anything we do has to be discreet. We can't have the senator finding out we're investigating his wife."

"Investigating her for what?"

"That's the problem."

"Not mine," Zyzmchuk said, looking at Keith. "If there is a problem, it's his."

Keith flushed very slightly, but his voice was calm when he said, "It wasn't my idea."

"I know that. But you could have discouraged him."

"You overestimate my powers. The senator only calls on me for technical advice, never on policy."

"That's crazy. You've written every word he's ever uttered about intelligence."

Keith flushed a little more. It made him look very young. "Not since I left his office. He's got two staffers now working on nothing but intelligence. I haven't even seen him for a year."

Zyzmchuk opened his mouth to say something, but Dahlin interrupted. "Ivan, please. We need your help."

"To do what?"

Dahlin looked surprised. "A follow-up. In case, you see, there really was anything . . . we couldn't have it said we'd done . . ."

"Nothing," Keith finished for him.

"So?" Zyzmchuk said.

"She'll have to be watched," Keith replied.

73

"Oh, come on. She's not a spy. She's probably worried they're going to find out about some junket her husband took her on at the taxpayers' expense. Why don't we just drop it?"

"She's in a position to know a lot of things."

"Then give it to the FBI. It's not our problem."

"Not legally, perhaps, although I could make a case," Dahlin said. "But as a practical matter, we have a close working relationship with the senator and we don't want it jeopardized by some oaf from the Bureau."

"But suppose we do find something," Zyzmchuk said. "What happens to your close working relationship then?"

"We'll tackle that when we have to."

"Why don't we cross that bridge when we come to it instead?"

The room went still. Alice Frame's voice filled it. "Soviet nationals? Well, I met the ambassador at a reception once. And a few of his aides. I—I'm sorry, I can't remember any of their names." They all looked at the screen. Alice Frame was biting her lower lip; she might have been on the verge of tears. "But I never—"

"Wait for the question, please," said Mr. Brent.

"Turn that fucking thing off," Zyzmchuk said. Keith touched a button. Zyzmchuk rose and walked across the room. He was giving physical expression to a mad vision of taking Keith and Dahlin by their necks and cracking their well-barbered skulls. For a moment he studied the Gorbachev photo. The resolution wasn't sharp enough to actually see urine, but there was enough supporting evidence to infer its presence.

"Why me?" Zyzmchuk asked at last.

"I think I can answer that," Keith said. "Because it has to be flawless."

Zyzmchuk smiled. "That's nice," he said. He kept smiling. "I wonder," he added, "since the senator is such a good friend, why our budget is getting so tight?"

There was a silence. Keith stood by the window, leaning his shoulder against the wall. Dahlin sat on the men's club couch with his legs crossed and his executive-length socks showing. They didn't look at each other, but signals passed between them. They were intercepted by Zyzmchuk, but not decoded.

74

"Specifically," asked Dahlin, "do you mean why our budget is getting so tight that we've had to let you go?"

Zyzmchuk nodded.

Keith looked hurt. "But that's not why we're letting him go, Zyz. We've been through this. You're way over the age limit for a field man. You were a great field man. The kiosk operation was a classic—the trainees study it every year. But—"

Turning to Dahlin, Zyzmchuk interrupted. "That's what I mean, all right. Specifically."

Dahlin folded his hands together. Zyzmchuk saw him consider and reject cracking the knuckles. "Perhaps," Dahlin said, "something might be arranged, if you made a nice discreet job of this Alice Frame business."

"I'm not talking about office work," Zyzmchuk said. "It would have to be in the field."

"Ivan, you know that's impossible."

Zyzmchuk rose. "Then I'm sorry, I can't help you."

Dahlin cracked his knuckles. "Oh, Christ," he said. "Why can't you just go quietly?"

"Do you want to just go quietly?" Zyzmchuk asked. He was already at the door.

"When the time comes, yes."

"Me too. But the time hasn't come yet."

Dahlin sighed. "I may be able to work something with Langley. If you don't mind being seconded temporarily to them."

"Tell them I want Prague. Second choice Budapest."

Keith cleared his throat. "We could simply order you to do it." He turned to Dahlin. "Couldn't we?"

Dahlin said nothing. Zyzmchuk answered for him. "I'd refuse. And then what would you do? I'm already fired." Zyzmchuk expected some laughter at the irony of it all, but none came. Dahlin and Keith were no longer in a laughing mood. He opened the door and went out.

But he hadn't reached the end of the corridor before Keith caught up. He straightened his tie with the high-class ducks on it, cleared his throat again and said, "I hope we weren't too obscure."

"Not at all."

"I mean, I hope you didn't get the idea he wants you to

75

move heaven and earth. It's not that kind of thing at all." From
behind his glasses, Keith was watching Zyzmchuk for some sign
that he was following along. Zyzmchuk gave none. Keith sighed.
"What he really wants, what the department really wants, is
something more . . ."

"Pro forma?"

Keith smiled. "Exactly, Zyz. Exactly."

10

Everything was fine.

Zorro did the driving. Zorro, the fox, so something and free; Zorro, who makes the sign of a P.

Zorro's little girl sat at one end of the backseat. Bao Dai sat at the other.

"Call me Uncle Bao," he told her. But she didn't. She didn't call him anything. She'd been put off by the episode with the whalebone knife. A brief episode, nothing really, just waving it around. Bao Dai regretted it—he just wanted to go for a nice long drive—but Zorro had needed persuading—not to go on a nice drive, but to go on a nice long one. Now the knife was tucked away and everything was fine.

The dark countryside, the Doors—Bao Dai still couldn't believe the sound in the car—the black sky: all fine. Even the glare wasn't so bad.

Bao Dai rested his head against the rear speaker. There were six speakers in the rear. Fat bass notes pulsed in his ear.

The singer sang about the scream of the butterfly. Bao Dai heard the scream. Dark night rolled by outside. He could almost forget everything. Then the music ended. Bao Dai sat up. He glanced at the girl. She was asleep.

"Where are we?" he asked.

The car slowed down. "Missouri," Zorro said.

The car pulled over to the side of the road and stopped. "Why are we stopping?" Bao Dai said.

"I'm tired." Zorro turned around to face him. He looked so fucking young.

"Tired?" Bao Dai had forgotten the feeling.

"I think we should head back."

"Back?"

"Home."

"Home?"

Zorro took a deep breath. "Please don't take this the wrong way."

"Take what the wrong way?"

"I think maybe you need some . . . professional help."

"What's that?"

"Someone to talk to."

"I'm talking to you."

"I'm not a professional."

"Sure you are," said Bao Dai. "You're a professional, all right. When it comes to me. A real pro."

"I don't know what you mean."

"No?"

There was a long silence. A car whizzed by, then another. Zorro's face paled and darkened as the headlights swept past.

"You've been through a lot," he said at last.

"Why do you want to talk about me all of a sudden?" Bao Dai said. No answer. "I don't want to talk about me," he said. "Let's talk about you."

"Me?"

"You have a nice life. You know that?"

"It's not so—"

"A nice car. A nice house. Nice sounds. Nice axes. Nice little girl. Where's your nice wife?"

"I told you. We're div—"

"You told me a lot of things. What does she look like?"

"Who?"

"Your wife."

"I told you, we're not—"

"What does she look like?"

"Well, not bad-looking, I guess."

"Nice tits?"

No answer.

"I said, 'Nice tits?' "

"I suppose. It's been five or six years now."

But Bao Dai knew she had nice tits. He'd seen from the garage. "How'd you ever give up tits like that?"

Zorro laughed, man to man. "Shit, they're not that good. And anyway, there're lots of girls around, you know. Women, I mean." Zorro turned his head, and tried a man-to-man smile.

"I don't know," Bao Dai said.

Silence.

"Your little girl have tits yet?" Bao Dai asked. He looked at her. Fast asleep.

"I wish you wouldn't talk about her like that. She's just a little girl."

"That's what I said. A little girl. She's the same age . . ."

"Same age as who?"

"As my little girl."

"But you don't have a little girl." Pause. "Do you?"

"As my little girl would have been, asshole. If I'd had a little girl. And a wife with nice tits. You know what I mean?"

"I'm not sure."

"You have a nice life—that's what I mean," Bao Dai said. "Let's go."

"Back?"

"Don't look back," said Bao Dai. "Not you. Not while I'm around."

"I meant where do you want to go?"

"You know."

"It's far."

"Far?" That was very funny. Bao Dai almost laughed. "You don't know what far is," he said. "Drive."

Zorro drove. The little girl slept. Bao Dai watched night turn to day.

"You're passing all the cars," he said after a while.

79

"I am?"

"Slow down."

"Sure."

"You're still passing them."

"I am?"

But it was too late. Red lights flashed in the mirrors. "You shit," Bao Dai said.

"He wants us to pull over."

Bao Dai took out the whalebone knife. He held it in his hand, covered with the tan suit jacket. "Then do it," he said. "But if anything happens, it happens to her first. Understand?"

"Yes."

They pulled over. A cop approached, bent over, looked in the open window. "Clocked you goin' seventy-five."

"Sorry, officer."

The cop peered inside the car, saw Bao Dai and the sleeping girl. "Nice car," he said. "We don't get many of these hereabouts."

The cop looked a lot like a platoon sergeant Bao Dai had known long ago. Maybe that's why he said, "You should hear the sound he's got." The words just popped out.

The cop gave Bao Dai another glance. "Yeah?"

"Show him," Bao Dai said.

Zorro switched on the music. It filled the car.

"The Doors, huh?" said the cop, cocking an ear. "Not bad. What'd it set you back?"

"The sound system?" said Zorro. "It came with the car."

"And how much was that?" asked Bao Dai.

"Well, fairly expensive I guess."

"Like what?" pressed Bao Dai. "Don't go all bashful."

The cop and Bao Dai exchanged a quick smile.

"A little over thirty," said Zorro.

The cop whistled. Zorro was looking at the cop. Bao Dai could see his eyes were full of pleading. The cop took mercy on him, but misread the plea. He tapped the roof of the car. "Okay, buddy. I'll let you off with a warning. But take it easy next time." He walked to the patrol car and drove away.

When he was out of sight, Bao Dai said, "I don't like this car anymore. It's too . . . open."

Zorro, holding his head in his hands, wasn't listening. "What do you want from me?" he said. "We can't undo the past."

"We can give it the old college try," Bao Dai replied. "Drive."

They drove. The tape ended. The radio came on. A commercial for jeans.

"That's Daddy," said the little girl. Bao Dai looked at her. She was wide awake. "Playing on the radio," she added. She looked at him in a funny way and said, "Didn't you know he was a professional musician?"

Bao Dao couldn't say a word. It had never occurred to him that Zorro was anything, except rich. He listened to the guitar, and his whole body stiffened as the notes went by. He could have played them, every one, and just that way. And no other way—that was how he played. Exactly. That was his style.

"It's nothing really," came the voice from the front seat. "Just a job."

"You're too modest, Daddy," the little girl said.

Bao Dai said nothing. Under the suit jacket he squeezed the handle of the knife, very hard, and kept squeezing it long after the commercial was over.

11

Kate was crying. The sound came from below. Jessie ran down the stairs. The basement was flooded. Kate's cries were louder, but still came from somewhere below. Jessie stepped off the last step onto the wet floor. There was no floor. She plunged into water over her head.

Jessie dove down through the blackness. Kate's cries grew louder and louder. Jessie kept swimming, down, down. Her lungs were bursting. She fought to hold her breath, groped with her hands, reaching for the bottom, reaching for Kate. The cries were all around her now, but her hands felt nothing. Then, when she could hold her breath no longer, her fingers brushed something. She grabbed it and kicked toward the surface. The crying stopped. She broke through into air, gulped it in. In her arms she held the cracked painting of Orpheus and Eurydice.

Jessie sat up. She was soaked, but with her own sweat instead of water. Daylight filled her bedroom, not the fresh light of dawn, but light already a little used. "Shit." She was late.

Jessie hurried into the bathroom and fixed herself up, trying not to see the hollow-eyed image in the mirror. Then she went to the closet and pulled on the blackest thing she owned.

Outside, nature wasn't imitating the moods of man, at least not hers. It was a beautiful day, bright, sunny, almost hot. The smug man on the car radio told her it was cold and rainy right across the country, everywhere except the Southland, amigos. He seeemed just as proud to report that freeway traffic was heavy, the way Chicagoans secretly enjoy corruption scandals and New Yorkers get a kick out of muggings in Central Park.

Jessie didn't need the radio man to tell her about the traffic; she was stuck in it. She changed the station. The Levi's commercial came on. Pat played his ringing line. Jessie could see him turning his hips into the guitar body as he ran up the scale. Sure. Levi's. Hips. They knew what they were doing. She switched him off.

Jessie ran out of gas just before the Seal Beach exit. For a minute or two, sitting in the breakdown lane, she didn't even know what had gone wrong. Then she saw the gauge. "Shit, shit, shit." She pounded the steering wheel, once, twice, but didn't cry. She was all cried out.

By the time she reached the cemetery, they were sliding the coffin out of the hearse. Everyone wore sunglasses. Everyone but her. She ran up and took one of the brass handles. No one objected.

Jessie helped carry the coffin to a hole in the ground. It didn't feel very heavy. Maybe that was because Blake manned the brass handle in front of hers; his broad back blocked her forward view. To the side were three pallbearers she didn't know and one she did: Noah Appleman, Barbara's son. He was three years older than Kate and lived in San Diego with his father, Sid. The sight of his thin arm straining under a blue blazer brought home to Jessie what was in the coffin. She squeezed the brass handle with all her might to keep her hand from shaking.

A Reform rabbi in a paisley tie spoke some nonsectarian words. Jessie stood around the edge of the hole with the others, feeling the heat. Her blackest thing was wool, bought long ago for a party at the Getty; she sweated into it, feeling inappropriately physical. The rabbi quoted Bertrand Russell, Hannah Arendt, Bruno Bettelheim. He was a modern man. That meant he had no comfort to give. Jessie tuned him out. She watched Noah, standing on the far side of the hole, holding his father's hand. Sid wore a yarmulke, but it didn't hide his baldness. He'd had a full head of hair the last time Jessie saw him, six or seven years before; in that time, he'd become middle-aged, faded and stooped. Or maybe the whole change had hit him at once, in the past two days.

The rabbi finished speaking. It was very quiet, except for airplane noise trailing down from the sky. The rabbi nodded to a man in a soiled coverall.

"En bajo," said the man. A machine lowered the coffin to the bottom. The man in the coverall tossed a spadeful of earth in after it. End of ceremony. A bulldozer waited nearby to do the rest.

"Jesus," Sid said, glancing at Jessie as he passed her on the way to the parking lot. From that angle she could see one of his eyes, naked and helpless behind the green lens of his sunglasses. Noah climbed into the back seat of a big American car. Wife number two was waiting in the front, redoing her face in the vanity mirror. She bared her teeth to get the lip gloss just right.

"Jessie Shapiro?" said someone behind her. Jessie turned and saw a black-suited man taking off his sunglasses; the circles under his eyes matched the suit. "I'm—"

"Dick Carr. Barbara's partner."

"We've met?" He put his sunglasses back on.

"Once. At her Christmas party a few years ago."

He smiled. "No wonder I don't remember." He held out his hand. She shook it. It was very wet. So was hers. "Got your daughter back yet?"

"No."

"I'm sorry to hear that. Barbara was very upset about it. She talked about nothing else that afternoon, what was it, Monday?"

"Monday."

"God." He looked out across the cemetery. Jessie followed his gaze. The bulldozer moved back and forth, back and forth, shoving earth into the hole. Dick Carr sighed. "I'd like it if you'd drop by the office some time. About Barbara's will."

"Barbara had a will?"

"Of course. Don't you?"

84

"I've never seen the—" She stopped: the legs had been chopped off that argument.

Carr turned to her. "Barbara left the bulk of her estate—meaning the proceeds of the sale of her house and car, mainly, which should come to a nice little sum—to Noah. But there are small bequests of a more personal nature to two or three other people."

"And I'm one of them?"

"Yup."

"Can you tell me what it is?"

"What what is?"

"What she left me."

"I'd prefer you came to the office."

"All right."

Carr drove off. So did everyone else. The rabbi was on his cellular phone before he was out of the lot. In the cemetery, workers rolled strips of grass over the earth and maneuvered a square gray stone into place. When they had finished and gone, Jessie walked back along the crushed rock path and stood in front of the stone. "Barbara Ann Appleman." The dates of her birth and death were carved below the name. She hadn't quite reached thirty-five. Jessie had a wild vision of overturning the stone, clawing down through the earth, ripping open the coffin, pulling Barbara out. That brought back the dream of Kate. The two visions closed on her like a vise, paralyzing her in front of the marble marker, as though she'd been turned to stone herself.

When, how much later she didn't know, Jessie finally found the strength to move, she backed away and bumped into someone standing behind her. Spinning around she saw a big, dark man with a heavy beard.

"Don't," she said, raising her arms.

"Don't?" said the man; and then she recognized him: Lieutenant DeMarco.

Jessie lowered her arms. "I'm sorry."

"You're a little jumpy."

"I said I'm sorry."

He nodded, then looked at the gravestone. "She was something," he said.

The thought that Barbara might have slept with DeMarco popped up in Jessie's mind. It was an unpleasant thought; perhaps that sharpened her tone a little when she asked, "Have you found her murderer yet?"

"Murderer? Isn't that a bit strong? The most we ever shoot for in hit-and-runs is vehicular homicide. And that's in flagrant cases. With witnesses. Here we've got no witnesses. No leads."

"You do have leads. I explained to the officer that someone flashed headlights at me earlier that night. Later, when Barbara went out, she was wearing the same yellow—"

DeMarco held up his hand; it was big enough to smother her whole face. "I've read your statement."

"Then you're involved in the investigation?"

"I'm keeping an eye on it."

"Does that mean it's being treated as murder?"

"I answered that already. I'm keeping an eye on it because Barbara and—because I knew her personally."

"And?"

"And what?"

"What did you think about my statement?"

His eyes shifted. Jessie could see he'd expected something else, maybe a question about Barbara. "You mean the part about you being the intended victim and it all having something to do with your daughter?"

"Yes."

"I didn't give it much credence."

"Why not? My daughter disappears with my ex-husband. Then my best friend gets killed wearing my raincoat. Doesn't that make you suspicious?"

"Look, this is hardly the time or place for an argument."

"No? You think she'd mind?" The words were out before Jessie realized she'd pitched her voice a little higher—like Barbara's—and jabbed her thumb at the gravestone, the same way Barbara jabbed hers.

DeMarco's mouth opened involuntarily. He was a homicide detective who must have seen everything L.A. had to offer, but she'd shocked him with an unconventional remark. That hadn't been her intention—she had no idea why she'd imitated Barbara. Was her subconscious trying to keep Barbara alive? Jessie didn't know. All she knew was that she had finally gotten through to DeMarco.

"Well," she said, "do you?"

DeMarco let out his breath. "I guess not," he said. "She'd love it."

"Yeah?" he said. His lips curled up, just a little.

"Yeah. You'd know that if you knew her at all." She looked right into his eyes to see just how well he had known her.

Well enough, she saw, to make his lips curl a little more. "Yeah," he said. "Come on to the car. We'll talk."

They walked along the crushed stone path to the parking lot. They had to step aside to make way for another group carrying a coffin. This one was fancier, with gold-plated handles and lots of scrollwork. That'll impress the worms, Jessie thought. There was no point in saying it out loud. The only person she knew who appreciated that kind of humor was gone. She overcame the urge for one last look back.

A rabbi came hurrying up the path. It was the same rabbi, but Jessie didn't recognize him at first. He'd had the sense to change his tie.

She sat in DeMarco's car. On the scratchy radio a bored woman dispatched patrols to scenes of mayhem. DeMarco turned on the air-conditioning. "Ever been to an Italian funeral?"

"This is my first one, ethnic or non."

"Yeah? Shit. People don't die in your circle?"

"Evidently they do."

DeMarco looked at her, "Got me," he said.

"Two-two-six-eight-oh La Cienega, robbery in progress," said the bored woman. "Make that two-two-*eight-six*-oh. That's the Seven-Eleven on the corner."

"Thirsty?" asked Demarco.

"Not really."

"Mind if I?" He had a cooler in the backseat. He took out a can of beer and snapped the tab. "Ah," he said, tipping it to his mouth. He looked at her. "You need some release at a time like this."

"Release?"

"Make that Sepulveda," said the bored woman.

"Instead of Pico?" crackled a voice.

"Instead of La Cienega," snapped the woman.

DeMarco drank his beer. The man in the coverall came up the path, smoking a cigarette. A woman in a clanking heap drove up. She had four kids in the back, drinking Coke. The man got in and spun his cigarette out the window as they drove away. Sparks flew.

"Doing anything tonight?" DeMarco asked.

"Looking for my daughter."

He didn't miss the sharpness in her tone. "Sorry," he said. "Maybe I'm going too fast, but you're a very attractive woman."

"It's not just the speed. You're going in the wrong direction."

He laughed, turning toward her; at the same time he threw his arm over the back of the seat. "That's what Barbara said, too. At first."

Jessie reached for the door handle.

"Don't," DeMarco said. "I shouldn't have said that."

Jessie kept her hand where it was, resting on the handle.

"It was misleading, for one thing," DeMarco said. He reached around and opened another beer. Jessie realized her first funeral was over; now came her first wake. "She dumped me," DeMarco continued. "I was ready to leave my wife for her, you know."

"I didn't know. Are you happily married, Mr. DeMarco?"

"No." DeMarco allowed a little sadness into his tone. It sounded sentimental to Jessie.

"Then it wouldn't have been much of a sacrifice, would it?"

"I've got kids too," he said, "not just a wife." His voice rose, more in pleading than anger.

"I don't want to hear about it, Mr. DeMarco. I want to hear about who killed Barbara and what you're doing to find my daughter."

DeMarco turned to her, but whether he was trying to stare her down or blinking in astonishment, she didn't know, because of his sunglasses. "Shit," DeMarco said. "Okay. But get it straight—this is a hit-and-run, not a murder. I already told you that." He put the beer can between his thick legs and took a notebook from his shirt pocket. "No witnesses," he said, summarizing what he saw there. "Both sides of the street have been canvased. A few people heard it. No one saw diddley. No reports of any speeders apprehended in the area. Automobile paint flakes were taken from Ba—from the victim's hair. We'll have the lab report tomorrow. Then we can start calling the body shops. Okay? That's number one." He turned the page. "Number two: your daughter. Three days overdue on a legal custodial visit with her father. Whereabouts of father also unknown. Status: they're both on the computer."

"Does that mean you're looking for them?"

"It means if they're picked up for anything—speeding, running a red light—we'll hold them."

"That's not good enough."

"It's better than anyone else gets, at this stage. Missing children come in three categories. The biggest, by far, are runaways. Then come custodial scuffles like this one. The last, and by far the smallest, are genuine abductions."

"But this isn't custodial. My—my ex-husband doesn't want sole custody."

"Then he's probably off on some toot. Barbara told me something about him."

"He wouldn't do that."

"No? Is he a drug user?"

"I wouldn't put it that way."

"How would you put it?"

Jessie searched for the words. They were blocked by the times she'd grown up in; by DeMarco's job; by residues of loyalty to Pat; and by loyalty to something else she couldn't name precisely: a generation, perhaps, or a culture. She added it all up; it didn't add up to much compared to Kate. "He's a drug user," she said.

DeMarco nodded. "Then just hang on. He'll be back. I had a case identical to this once. Busted my ass from one end of the county to the other."

"And what happened?"

"He came back. All on his own. They always do."

"I meant what happened to the child."

DeMarco looked surprised. "He brought the kid back. That's what I'm saying. Too much responsibility. A druggie looks out for number one. Period."

"But it's not just that Kate's missing. It's Barbara too."

DeMarco raised his big hand.

Jessie kept talking. "Supposing it wasn't just an ordinary hit-and-run. Supposing someone was trying to kill me."

"Who?"

"I don't know."

"Why?"

"I don't know that, either."

"Do you have any enemies?"

"Not that I know of."

"Barbara had plenty."

"She did?"

DeMarco lowered his hand. "She mauled a lot of men in court. That makes her a more likely candidate than you, doesn't it?"

"I don't know."

"Did she do your divorce?"

"Yes. But we didn't go to court, and no one got mauled."

"Yeah. What color's your ex's car, by the way?"

"Blue. A blue BMW."

DeMarco shook his head. "The flakes were green." He closed his notebook, took off his sunglasses and picked up the beer can. Jessie smelled beer. It made her want to puke. "Hot today," said DeMarco. "Change your mind about a beer?"

"No."

"You don't drink?"

"Sometimes."

"Sometimes you do or sometimes you don't?"

"Right."

DeMarco smiled. He had a nice smile; his eyes joined in, if that meant anything. "What about tonight?" he asked.

"No."

The smile faded. He put the sunglasses back on. "Make that an Amoco station," said the radio woman, "not a Seven-Eleven." DeMarco tipped the beer to his lips. "Anything else?" he said.

"No." Jessie got out of the car. Before closing the door, she said, "What if you're wrong?"

"I'll take you to Disneyland, all expenses paid."

Barbara spoke to her from the grave. Jessie passed on the message. "You won't be able to afford it. I'll sue you for every penny you've got." She slammed the door, got into her car and sped out of the lot. For a few moments, she had the strong feeling, despite her disbelief in the supernatural, that Barbara was watching her, that Barbara was smiling. Then, all at once, the feeling was gone. It never came back.

On the way home, Jessie stopped at the printer's. The posters were ready. She'd ordered two hundred. Now she didn't know why. Why not a thousand, or a million? At the time two hundred had seemed like a measured response. Jessie opened the package on the counter and inspected them. "Have You Seen This Girl?" they said in big black letters. That was followed by pictures and descriptions of Kate and Pat, a description of the car, and her phone number.

"Okay?" said the clerk.

"Okay?" she repeated. What was he talking about?

"The way you wanted it."

"Oh. Yes, it's okay."

"Thirty-three eighty-eight. Plus tax."

Jessie paid. The clerk rang it up.

Jessie had her staple gun in the car. She drove around Santa Monica looking for places to tack up the posters. Almost every street had suitable trees or telephone poles. She passed a notice-free telephone pole at the corner of Ocean and Olympic; an empty hoarding beside a busy gas station on Pico; a notice board outside a laundromat near the beach. She didn't get out of the car; she didn't even stop. It wasn't that she was embarrassed, or even that a public display would shred her last illusions that nothing was really wrong; those illusions had vanished. She didn't want Kate splashed all over the place, that was all.

Jessie drove home. She went into the silent house, checked for messages, called Pat's machine. She put the phone down and listened to the silence. Then she looked in the cabinet where the booze was. It was still there. She looked at the bottles for a while. Red or white? Red. *Let's live a little.*

She called Philip to tell him about the posters. The posters had to go up. Maybe he'd come over and help.

"Jessie! How are you?"

"I've just come from Barbara's funeral."

"Oh. It's terrible."

She mentioned the posters.

"Gee, I can't come over right now. The most exciting thing has happened—someone's coming from the Museum of Modern Art tomorrow to see 'Valley Nocturne.' "

"That's great."

"Isn't it? I couldn't sleep a wink last night."

Jessie said nothing. There was a long pause. Philip said, "Hey, don't worry about the posters. Just tack them up wherever you want. Everybody does. The worst they can do is tear them down."

"That's not—"

"Oh shit, there's someone at the door. Listen, could I—"

"What about the translation, Philip?"

"Translation?" Jessie heard someone talking to Philip in the background: it sounded like Mrs. Stieffler.

"You said you'd find out what those words on Pat's blackboard meant."

"Damnation. I forgot all about it. Shit, I'm sorry. I'll try—"

Jesse hung up. She didn't slam the phone down. She just hung it up.

Then, still in her black dress, she went out, got in the car and drove to Malibu. She started tacking up the posters, moving north to south. She ended in Venice, stapling the last one to a palm tree outside Pat's darkened house.

Jessie went home. She checked for messages, called Pat's machine. She hung up and listened to the silence. She looked inside the booze cupboard.

Much later, Jessie went upstairs and lay on the bed. Kate was crying, far below. Jessie ran down the stairs, into the flooded basement. No floor. She plunged in over her head.

12

A bell was ringing, far above. Jessie swam up, up, and opened her eyes. She was lying on her bed; the black dress clung to her damp body. She picked up the phone.

"Hello." She cleared her throat and said it again.

"DeMarco."

Jessie looked at her watch. 4:32 A.M. Flash, flash. "Yes?" she said.

"I just called to say you win."

Jessie gripped the phone with both hands. "You mean you've found her?"

"Found who?"

"Kate, of course."

"Oh, no. Nothing like that. But I can promise you that our search is going to be more active from now on. We got a warrant to search Pat Rodney's house. I'm there right now."

"You didn't have to do that. I'd have let you in."

"It's better this way. I don't want any screwups when we get to court."

"Maybe I'm being stupid, Mr. DeMarco; you woke me up. But what are you talking about?"

"I'm talking about the three ounces of coke we found in your ex-hubbie's drawer. Plus a few bags of weed and sundry pills we're sending to the lab. We'll have a warrant out for his arrest on trafficking charges by ten this morning."

"God damn you," Jessie said. "I told you he used drugs, yes, but he's not a trafficker."

"Don't get all hot and bothered. It's just standard procedure. He can always plea bargain it down to simple possession. In return for the name of his supplier."

"Christ."

"What do you care? Unless you've still got a thing for him, that is."

"Shut up." DeMarco was silent. "You're not fooling me," Jessie said. "I know why you did this."

"Do you?"

"You're a bastard."

"You're hurting my feelings," DeMarco said. "I expected gratitude."

"What for? I know the way you people make drug arrests—with your finger on the trigger. If anything happens to Kate because of you—"

"You're getting hysterical."

Jessie fought to control her voice. Accusations of hysteria worked like cattle prods: they hurt and they made the cows behave. "Stay right there, Mr. DeMarco. I want to talk to you."

"Talk."

"In person."

Jessie pressed the button cutting the connection. Then she got Dick Carr's home number from information and dialed it. She wanted him with her when she saw DeMarco. DeMarco didn't have his arrest warrant yet. There was time to stop him. But no one answered at Dick Carr's house.

Jessie drove to Venice by herself. It was still night when she pulled into Pat's driveway. A fat moon the color of a sodium lamp shone on the oblong of black ocean at the end of the street.

Jessie didn't see any police cars. The house was dark, the door locked. She opened it and went in.

"DeMarco?" she called.

No one replied. Jessie switched on the lights and searched the house. She found some changes; the plants were turning yellow and the goldfish floated upside down in the tank in the front hall; someone had left a cheap cigar smell in the house and an El Producto butt in the kitchen sink; someone had closed the copy of *Jane Eyre* in Kate's room; the bag of white dust and the little mirror were no longer in the drawer of the night table on Pat's side of the bed. The silk Clinique bag was gone too. DeMarco had made a tidy job of it, but Jessie still thought of male dogs pissing on their territorial borders.

She went into the front hall, scooped the goldfish from the tank. "Christ." Why hadn't she fed them? She threw the goldish in the garbage and tossed the cigar butt in after them. She was watering the plants in the front hall when her glance fell on the table: no mail. Hadn't there been a pile of unopened mail there before? And no letters lay on the floor under the mail slot. That meant Pat had received no mail in the past two days or DeMarco had taken it.

Jessie climbed the stairs to Kate's room. She opened the window and waved the cigar smell out of the room. The sodium moon had sunk from sight; the ocean was turning blue. A boy in a wetsuit walked quietly toward it, a surfboard under his arm. Jessie drew the curtains. She sat on Kate's bed. She put her feet up. She lay down with her head on Kate's pillow. She pulled Kate's quilt on top of her, the one with the puffy clouds. Outside a squeaky wheel came closer, stopped, moved on. Jessie gazed at the gorillas and orangutans on the wall. Their liquid eyes gazed back. She closed her eyes. She was sure she smelled the sweet smell of Kate's hair after a shampoo.

Jessie slipped toward sleep. Far away, someone was crying, very faintly. The smell of Kate's hair drifted away, replaced by the smell of water. It grew stronger and stronger.

"Shit." Jessie sat up. She didn't want to be in dreamland. She got off Kate's bed and went downstairs. She dialed a number on the hall phone.

"Appleman and Carr," answered a voice.

That threw her.

"Hello?" said the voice.

"Is Dick Carr there?" Jessie asked.

"No. Who's calling please?"

"Do you know where I can reach him? I tried his house and there's no answer."

"Mr. Carr is in Sacramento till Saturday. He'll be calling in. Is there a message?"

"No."

Jessie hung up. She stood motionless in the front hall, her hand on the phone, her eyes on the empty fish tank. She almost didn't notice the mail coming through the slot.

Letters fell softly on the floor. Jessie hurried to the door, opened it. The mailman was walking away.

"Excuse me," Jessie said.

The mailman stopped and turned. He had a toothpick in his mouth and water in his eyes. "Yeah?"

"I notice you brought some mail today."

He blinked. "Yeah?"

"It's funny there hasn't been much this week."

"Huh?"

"Mail."

The mailman's eyes narrowed a little, as though she were accusing him of something. He shifted the toothpick in his mouth. "Depends what you mean by much, don't it? Some gets more than others."

"I suppose, but we didn't get any this week."

The mailman blinked again. Then he looked at her carefully, chewing his toothpick. "Listen, lady, I don't know what you're saying, exactly, but I delivered mail to this house every day this week. If you didn't get it, don't blame me. I handed it to the maid, in person."

"The maid?"

"Yeah. Who sweeps up the steps."

Jessie moved closer to him; he backed away, keeping a constant distance between them. "Something funny's going on," she said. "But it has nothing to do with you." The mailman stopped backing away. "Do you remember what this maid looked like?"

96

"Sure. Kinda big. Heavy. Grayish hair, kinda."

"What else?"

"Hard to say, exactly. She was always wearing sunglasses."

"Sunglasses?"

"You know. Wraparounds."

Jessie glanced down the street. There was no one to see but the surfer, walking back with his board. She turned back to the mailman. "I see," she said. "Thanks." She went into the house and picked up the mail.

There was a menu from a Chinese takeout on Montana and three letters: a bill from American Express, something from a Dodge dealership and a letter addressed to Pat in purple ink. Jessie opened it.

Dear Pat,

Just a little note to say how much I enjoyed the other night and I mean that. I was sort of hoping you'd call and such but I've been out a lot (working double shifts at the club I'm going to be rich!) and maybe you've been trying to reach me (you can always call at the club you know—they don't mind a bit the number's 962-7011).

Pat, I just loved the way you played those old Beatle songs. You made me understand for the first time how amazing those times must have been. You're so lucky to have been there really been there at the time. With Hendrix at Woodstock!

And about afterwards please try to understand. I mean I got a bit shy it's not like me at all I haven't got hangups about that kind of thing. I think it was the c——. It really hit me in a funny way. It wont be at all like that next time if you dont mind me saying next time. So dont forget the winding road that leads to my door.

Yours very, very truly,
Tania

Jessie folded the letter and replaced it in the envelope. She felt a sliding in her stomach, as though she'd just flown into an air pocket. Swift justice: her punishment for reading other

97

people's mail. She went into the kitchen and drank a glass of water.

Then she sinned again, opening first the American Express bill—Pat owed $927.85 for eating at restaurants, mostly in Hollywood, and buying a shirt at Giorgio's in Westwood—and then the letter from the Dodge dealership.

Dear Mr. Rodney,
Thank you once again for purchasing your new Dodge Ram-Van at Buddy Boucher's Dodge and Dodge Trucks. We appreciate your business and promise the utmost in service and satisfaction. Enclosed please find your entry ticket for this year's Buddy Boucher Win-a-Week-in-Bermuda Sweepstakes. The draw will be held next June 1. Good luck!

All the best,
Buddy Boucher

Jessie read the letter again. And again. The paper began to shake, very slightly, in her hands. That was due to two facts. Buddy Boucher's letter was dated and postmarked on Monday, three days before. Solid fact one. Solid fact two: Buddy Boucher's Dodge and Dodge Trucks dealership was located in Bennington, Vermont.

Jessie picked up the phone.

"Information for what city please?"

"Bennington, Vermont."

"Go ahead."

"Buddy Boucher's Dodge and Dodge Trucks."

A machine took over the other end of the conversation: "732-8911," it said.

Jessie dialed the number.

"Buddy Boucher's," said a man.

"Is Buddy Boucher there?"

"This is Buddy. What can I do you for?"

Jessie struggled to frame her question. Static buzzed on the line.

"Hello there?" said Buddy Boucher.

98

"Yes. I—I just got a sweepstakes ticket in the mail and—"

"The draw's not till June, sweetheart."

"I know. It's just that my husband seems to have bought a car from you recently, and I thought maybe you'd know where I could reach him."

"Where you calling from?"

"Los Angeles."

"You Mrs. Rodney?"

"Yes." Silence. "Do you know where he is, Mr. Boucher?"

"No. I haven't seen him since he came in and bought the van on Monday."

"Monday?"

"Check. Right after lunch. Boom. Couldn't have been here for more than twenty minutes."

"Was he alone, Mr. Boucher?"

"Nope. He had a friend with him. And his niece."

"His niece?"

"Little girl."

"Can you describe her, Mr. Boucher?"

There was a pause. "Why are you asking all this stuff?"

"It's very important, Mr. Boucher. It's—it's about an investment opportunity that's just come up."

"Oh." Pause. At the end of some long wire, a woman laughed, almost beyond Jessie's hearing. "Then why," Buddy Boucher continued, "did you want to know about the niece?"

"Just curious. Pat's got a few nieces back there."

"Yeah?" Buddy Boucher blew out his breath; it sounded like a faint explosion. "Well, this one's about ten or eleven, I guess. Cute little girl. Kind of shy, maybe. Didn't say boo. Ring a bell?"

"I think so. What color was her hair?"

"Dark brown. Frizzy."

Jessie felt the blood pounding in her fingers, wrapped around the phone, and in her lips, millimeters from the receiver. "Do you think he's staying with his friend?" she asked.

"Maybe. I didn't actually meet his friend. Wasn't feeling well. Stayed in the car the whole time."

"What car?"

99

"Why, your husband's BMW. It's still on the lot. He said he'd be back for it later this week, but he hasn't been in yet."

"He didn't trade it in?"

"On a Dodge? Never happens, Mrs. Rodney."

"How did he pay, then?"

Buddy Boucher cleared his throat. "Are you separated or something like that?"

"Nothing like that." The lie came without hesitation. Some instinct told her she couldn't put Buddy Boucher in the position of feeling like a traitor to his sex.

"Then I guess it's all right. He paid in cold cash. A bit unusual, but not as unusual as it used to be. Hope it wasn't the grocery money." He laughed.

When his laughter trailed off, Jessie said, "Would you do me a favor, Mr. Boucher?"

"Depends what."

"When he comes in tell him to call me. That's all."

"Easy enough," said Buddy Boucher.

Jessie gave him her number and hung up. Then she couldn't stay still. Her body moved her: out the door, onto the sidewalk, down to the boardwalk, back and forth. But no expenditure of energy could stop the trembling.

Jessie went back into Pat's house. She considered calling DeMarco. But why? DeMarco had been right. Pat was on a toot, tripping down memory lane with some old pal from Vermont, right back to the sixties, singing Beatles songs, throwing money around and snorting his fucking c——.

Calling DeMarco would lead to telexes crisscrossing the country and lots of waiting and maybe Vermont state troopers descending on some dope fest with drawn guns. Vermont was five hours away, eight with the time change. Eight hours was nothing, measured against days of waiting.

Jessie found Bennington on a map. Then she booked a flight to Boston. The next available plane was the red-eye, leaving at midnight. She'd be in Boston Friday morning, in Bennington by noon. If she got there before Pat returned to Buddy Boucher's for the BMW, it would be easy; if not, it might take a little longer, that was all. Jessie's mind drew a picture of Kate and

100

her on the Friday-night flight back to L.A. She didn't rub it out.

Jessie ran upstairs and got *Jane Eyre*, in case Kate wanted to read on the plane. Then she bounded down the steps of Pat's house and hurried home to pack *Jane Eyre*, the Reeboks with the blue stripes and the few things she herself would need for a day or two in Vermont.

13

Jessie stripped off her black dress and left it on the bathroom floor: a funerary heap like the remains of the Wicked Witch of the West. Then she scrubbed herself under a hot shower, shaved her legs, washed her hair with shampoo that had enough protein in it to keep an Ethiopian family going for a week. Hair, body, and now, in front of the mirror, face: a black line or two around her eyes, a touch of gloss on the lips. Jessie seldom wore makeup, but how could it hurt, especially on a traveling day?

She packed: *Jane Eyre*, the Reeboks, a red sweater for Kate, a blue one for herself; jeans, underwear, socks, a suede jacket in case it was cold; comfortable old loafers; Buddy Boucher's letter. She checked her wallet. Fifty-two dollars. Wouldn't do. In the bank she had just enough to cover the next mortgage payment. And the return airplane tickets would put her over her credit card limit. She thought of Mrs. Stieffler's check.

Mrs. Steiffler's check was a problem. She should have torn it up and scattered the pieces in Mrs. Stieffler's wake, but she hadn't, and the check was still lying on the big table in the basement. Five hundred dollars. Hold your nose and cash it, Jessie told herself; wasn't that the American way? This light-headedness surprised her. Tone it down, Jess. Barbara hasn't even been in the ground for a day.

Jessie took the check to her bank. Thursday afternoon. Long lines. They didn't bother Jessie. The world reopened before her eyes. She listened to normal conversations: the couple in front of her worrying about 10 percent take-backs, the women behind her talking about soft weights. When her turn came, she endorsed the check and handed it to the teller. "Twenties will be fine," she said.

That was wishful thinking. Mrs. Steiffler had stopped payment.

The women behind Jessie forgot about going for the burn; the bank fell silent in speculation. Jessie restored normality by withdrawing two hundred dollars—she'd worry about the mortgage later—and going home.

The phone was ringing. Jessie answered.

"Ms. Shapiro?" a man said.

"Yes?"

"Jessie Shapiro?"

"That's right."

"Are you the one who put up the poster? 'Have You Seen This Girl?' "

"Yes, what is it?"

"I may have some information for you."

"Are you calling from Vermont?"

"Vermont?"

"I—where are you calling from?"

"Los Angeles. Why did you think I was calling from Vermont?"

"I don't know why I said that. What sort of information do you have? Is it about my daughter?"

"I'd prefer not to discuss it over the phone."

"But—have you seen her?"

"Perhaps we could meet somewhere tonight."

Did she hear a slight accent in his voice? Jessie wasn't sure. "Tonight's not—can't you just tell me if you've seen her?"

"Is tomorrow evening better?"

"No. I—why can't you discuss it over the phone?"

"How about the Santa Monica Pier? At eight."

Jessie had a thought. "Has Pat asked you to call? Are you a friend of his?"

"I'll explain everything tonight."

"What's your name?"

"Mickey."

"Is that your first name?"

"My first name?"

"Or last?"

"Oh," said the man. "Mr. Mickey. Call me Mr. Mickey."

It was a name Pat had never mentioned. That left other possibilities. "Is it money you want?" Jessie said slowly. No reply. "Is that it?"

"We can discuss that tonight."

An icy current raced through Jessie's veins. "Have you got Kate? Is this some kind of ransom demand?"

The man laughed, or rather, Jessie sensed, made patronizing sounds in the guise of laughter. "Of course not," he said. "I have information I think you shall want, that's all. But for reasons that will become perfectly clear, I should make it known to you in person. Okay?"

Jessie didn't know the answer. What sort of information could he have? Kate was in Vermont, but he hadn't appeared to know that. "I don't really know," she said. "Is Kate safe? Is Pat still with her? Was he in an accident?"

The man sighed. "Let me put it this way, Ms. Shapiro. I'm a private detective, working on another matter. I happened to stumble on something I think you'll want to know."

"Are you selling it or giving it?"

"I already suggested we discuss that at the proper time, Ms. Shapiro. See you at eight." Click.

Jessie slowly replaced the phone. Stapling notices around town was an invitation to crank callers. The man hadn't offered one fact that couldn't have been taken from the notice itself; he hadn't offered any facts at all. On the other hand, he could have been much more insistent about the meeting, and he hadn't sounded like a crank. He'd sounded like a Swedish art historian she'd met at Philip's.

Jessie looked under detective agencies in the L.A. yellow pages. There was no listing between Michaelson and Mitchum. She tried Santa Monica, West L.A. and Valley listings. No Mr. Mickey. That didn't mean he wasn't who he said he was. DeMarco might know. Jessie looked up his number, and dialed it. Someone picked up the phone at the other end. Children were crying. A woman screamed, "You've ruined my life." A man yelled back, raw and uncontrolled, but it was DeMarco. The woman said, "Hello?"

Jessie hung up.

At 7:45 Jessie picked up her suitcase. On her way out of the house, she passed the "My Mom" poem on the fridge door. She took it off, folded it carefully and slipped it in the pocket of her jeans Then she put the suitcase in the trunk of the car and drove down to the pier, parking on a side street. The sun had set; the sodium moon had risen, but fog was rolling in, dulling its glow and spreading an orange sfumato through the night, reminding her of "Valley Nocturne." A strange light, and not much of it, but enough to see Mr. Mickey. What could be lost by having a look at him, hearing what he had to say, before she drove to the airport? It might make her better equipped to deal with Pat.

Jessie walked down the pier. On a summer evening, and maybe even a few hours earlier, it would have been crowded with tourists, high school kids, beachers, dope smokers, beer drinkers. Now all the concessions were closed—the hot dog stand, the T-shirt place, the bumper cars, the merry-go-round—and everyone gone. Only smells remained: grease, onion, motor oil, urine, and, from below, the sea.

Jessie came to the end of the pier. She almost missed the man sitting there, his feet dangling in the air, his back to a trash can. He wore a straw hat with a frayed brim and held a fishing rod loosely in his hands. "Mr. Mickey?" Jessie said.

"No hablo inglés." The man didn't look up.

She walked back. The thickening fog closed around her,

damp and cold. A foghorn sounded, somewhere at sea. Up the coast, another answered. Jessie began to worry about whether planes would be flying. She quickened her stride.

As she passed the merry-go-round, a shadow separated itself from the other shadows. "Ms. Shapiro?" a man said.

"Oh. You scared me. Mr. Mickey?"

"I'm forever doing so." Up close the man still spoke with the very faint accent she couldn't place.

Mr. Mickey came a little closer. Jessie saw he was taller than he had seemed; his perfect proportions disguised his height. He was huge. She fought an urge to back away.

"What do you know about my daughter?"

"I am not at liberty to discuss this matter myself."

Jessie backed away. "What does that mean?"

"I have a . . . supervisor. He will answer your questions."

Jessie looked around and saw nothing but the carousel, shrouded in fog.

"I'm here to take you to him," Mr. Mickey said. "But first there are a few preliminaries."

"Preliminaries?"

"Formalities." The man held out his hand. "Your ID, please."

"What for?"

"Procedure."

"You already know who I am. You called me by name."

"We need proof."

"Who else would I be, for Christ's sake."

He withdrew his hand. "Very well, then. I'm afraid there's no more to say."

Jessie stood where she was. The man's face, in the dim orange light, remained indistinct; she had an impression of high cheekbones, fair skin, fair hair, but no impression at all of what was on his mind. "How do I know you have anything to tell me about Kate? Everything I do know makes it seem unlikely."

"How is that?"

"What do you mean?"

"I mean what is it you know that makes our knowing unlikely?"

Without understanding exactly why—maybe it was his size, or the smell of the sea from below, or just the fog—Jessie avoided his question. Perhaps it was its very precision that scared her off. "You're supposed to be the one with the information," she said.

Orange light glinted off the man's teeth. Was he smiling? "I find your attitude very strange," he said. "We are trying to help you."

"Why?"

"Isn't that what you expected people would do when you put up the posters?"

"I don't know."

"Perhaps that's true. Nevertheless, it's happened. We have information concerning the whereabouts of your daughter. You, on the other hand, may have information, unsuspected I'm sure, about a case we're working on. We propose a simple exchange."

"Then you know where Kate is."

"That is for my supervisor to say."

"Why this secrecy?"

"It has nothing to do with you. The other matter is rather delicate."

"But I don't know what it could be. What kind of information do you want?"

The man held out his hand again. "First, please," he said, "your ID."

"Is it a drug case? Is Pat in some kind of trouble?"

Mr. Mickey sighed. "Do you want your daughter back, Ms. Shapiro?"

Jessie took out her wallet and handed him her driver's license.

Mr. Mickey shone a pencil flashlight on it. Jessie got a good look at him. He had high cheekbones, all right; they threw shadows almost into his eyes, but not quite. The eyes were clear blue, pale as the farthest sky in a Venetian painting; the hair platinum blond, lit with orange from the fog. He combined all the colors of "Valley Nocturne" and added the extra something that would have made the painting disquieting.

"Thank you." He gave back her license and switched off the light. His features slipped back into the fog.

"I looked you up in the yellow pages," Jessie said. "You're not there."

"The agency is not in my name."

"What name is it in?"

"My supervisor prefers to make his own introductions." Mr. Mickey took out a notebook.

"Are you from Scandinavia?"

"No," he said; annoyance edged into his tone. "Hermosa Beach." He flipped through the pages. "I must clarify a few details before we proceed. First: did you see anything unusual when you were in Pat Rodney's house, subsequent to the disappearance?"

"What makes you think I've been in the house?" The image of the real estate man standing outside Pat's house flashed through her mind. "This isn't all part of some real estate deal, is it?"

Mr. Mickey laughed. "That's very funny. But please, Ms. Shapiro, don't play at detective. That's our job. Just answer the question."

"But I have a right—"

"Ms. Shapiro." Mr. Mickey's voice rose a little; his accent thickened. "You act as if there were lots of time for talk. Let me inform you that in disappearance cases, time is the crucial factor. Try to understand that a crime has been committed, a crime, not directed at you or your daughter, but which has affected you all the same. I believe that my supervisor is prepared to put you in possession of the facts, if only you will cooperate in this simple interview."

"Was this crime directed at Pat? Or by him?"

"Neither. We're not interested in him. We're interested in recovering a sum of money. That's all. There. You have it. Now you know all."

Jessie let out her breath. "Okay," she said. "There was strange writing on the blackboard in Pat's kitchen. Is that what you're after?"

"Strange?"

"Foreign. It had been erased, but I was able to restore it, enough to read, anyway."

"What did it say?"

"I haven't been able to translate it. The words were 'Toi giet la toi.' We thought it was French, at first, but it's not."

"We?"

"Me and some friends."

"Who were they?"

"Does it matter?"

Mr. Mickey was silent. The sea made sucking sounds round the pilings below. "I suppose not," Mr. Mickey said at last, "given the nature of the message."

"Why? Do you know what it means?"

"Yes. It's a saying. Freely translated, it means something like 'Make hay while the sun shines.' "

"In what language?"

"Arabic. It's a common saying in the Arab world."

"But it wasn't written in Arabic."

"It's the phonetic equivalent," Mr. Mickey said impatiently. "Does Pat Rodney have any Arab friends?"

"Not that I know of. Why do you know Arabic?"

"What an American question," Mr. Mickey replied. "I've worked in the oil business. There's an American answer." He turned a page in his notebook. Jessie wondered why Mr. Mickey had needed a light to read her license but wasn't using it now and why anyone would write "Make hay while the sun shines" on Pat's blackboard. Mr. Mickey looked up. "Did you see anything else unusual in the house?"

"Not exactly. But I heard a portion of a message on his answering machine. Later, when I went to listen again, the tape had been wiped."

"Do you remember what it said?"

"It was a woman. She seemed to be warning Pat of some danger, telling him to get away."

"Away where?"

"She didn't say."

"Would you recognize her voice if you heard it again?"

"I don't know."

Mr. Mickey closed the notebook and put it in his pocket. "I think we're ready for my supervisor."

"Where is he?"

"This way." Mr. Mickey led her off the pier, but instead of heading toward the street, he turned down the staircase that led to the beach.

109

"Where are we going?" Jessie asked.

"To see him."

But Jessie saw no one on the beach. That didn't mean there was nothing to see: a dark shape bobbed on the water, a few yards offshore. Mr. Mickey blinked his flash at it. Jessie heard an engine, muffled by the fog; the dark shape edged closer to the beach. "Is he on the boat?" Jessie asked.

"No, But we'll get to him faster this way." He didn't repeat that time was the crucial factor in disappearance cases. He'd made the point.

The sand slid under a ruffle of foam. Cold seawater lapped at Jessie's feet. From where she stood, she could see that the boat was a large cabin cruiser; a dark figure stood high above on the tuna tower, hands on the controls.

"I haven't got much time," Jessie said.

"No? We're ten minutes away." Mr. Mickey waded in. It was worth ten minutes. Jessie followed.

Mr. Mickey turned to her. "Here," he said.

"No."

But he picked her up anyway, as easily as a sack of laundry, and lifted her onto the deck. Maybe he thought he was being gallant; maybe he was just demonstating their relative strength. Jessie hated it.

Mr. Mickey climbed in after her. He glanced up at the figure on the tuna tower, a man, Jessie now saw, wearing a straw hat with a torn brim. Had the boat been tied under the end of the pier? She was still scanning her memory when Mr. Mickey said, "Andale." The word stiffened on his tongue.

The bow swung slowly around. Then the boat surged forward with a roar of power. Jessie was knocked down. She lost her breath. Lying on the deck she felt the strength of the engines. It scared her.

Mr. Mickey helped her up, half-dragged her to a fishing seat in the stern. He yelled something in her face. It might have been an apology. She couldn't hear over the engine noise. Mr. Mickey yelled again.

"What? I can't hear you."

He made drinking motions.

"No," Jessie shouted at him. "Nothing."

Mr. Mickey smiled and made more drinking motions. He turned and went into the cabin. A column of yellow light poked out of the doorway for a moment. Jessie glimpsed a wall full of electronic equipment, lit with a swinging Tiffany lamp, before the door closed. A television had been on. John Wayne was manhandling a saloonful of greasy customers. Even with all of MGM's help, he didn't look quite as powerful as Mr. Mickey.

Jessie's eyes readjusted to the darkness. The boat flew through the fog on a boiling white V. She'd never been on such a fast boat. L.A. had already vanished in an orange cocoon.

A hand touched her shoulder. Mr. Mickey. He set down two crystal snifters and a bottle on the table between the two fishing chairs. Armagnac. Le Comte de Quelque-Chose. Mr. Mickey poured, held out a glass to Jessie. The smell of the Armagnac rose up, a good smell. She drank. Mr. Mickey smiled and, leaving the bottle where it was, took his own drink inside.

The Armagnac began to drive the chill out of Jessie's body. She took another sip and another. Stop it, she told herself. She had a long night ahead. Mr. Mickey's supervisor. The plane to Boston. She looked at her watch. Only 8:45. Plenty of time: must be almost there. What direction were they headed? She'd be able to tell better from the bow.

Jessie rose. Her legs felt weak. She took a few steps toward the bow. The orange cocoon lay on the right side: they were heading north. Above she saw the man in the torn straw hat, his bare feet planted on the platform.

She turned and went back to her chair. On the way she noticed a life ring hanging from the gunwale. Something was written on it in block letters. She went closer—it took a long time—and read the word: *Ratty.*

Was that the name of the boat? Jessie made the long journey to the stern. Holding tight to the rail, she leaned over, her head directly above the point of the boiling V, throbbing with the noise of the engines. There was nothing written on the stern. She touched the point where a name should have been. It felt sticky.

Jessie stood up. She felt dizzy. Seasick? No, just dizzy. She moved toward the fishing chair, but so slowly. Dizzy. And sleepy, too. A sudden, irresistible sleepiness was metastasizing through her body, up to her brain. "Oh, God," she said.

Jessie didn't quite reach the chair. The boat dipped over a swell, making her lose her balance and fall over the table, knocking the bottle of Armagnac and the crystal snifter to the deck. Jessie went down too. She lay in a puddle of Armagnac, feeling the sharpness of the broken glass against her skin and the power of the big engines, down below.

14

Thursday night was Bela's night. That meant slivovitz in thimble glasses, the "Opera Box" on the radio and Bela saying things like, "This is a pansy country, Ivan. It always was; I just didn't see it at first." Then he'd lean forward in his armchair, the way he was doing now, a little man who'd once been built like a pit bull, with stubby legs and a barrel chest; now all that remained was the fighting instinct.

"Do you mean sexually?" Zyzmchuk asked. "Homosexuality exists in the old country, too, Bela."

Bela knocked that argument aside with the flat of his hand. "I don't mean that," he told Zyzmchuk, who knew it already; he'd just been hoping to sidetrack the old man. "Not just that, anyway. I'm talking about the whole mentality. Macho!" he snorted. "Bankers with manicures! Politicians with dyed hair! Pleaders, beggars, whiners. They call that macho. I'll tell you what macho is, Ivan. Macho is pansy. It has to be, right? It's

113

Latin. Latins can't fight. Everybody knows that. You know who can fight, Ivan?"

"Who?"

"And I'm not talking about the Koreans, the Japs, the fucking Russians. You know who can really fight?"

"Who, Bela?"

"The Brits. I don't mean the little Lord Pansies. I mean the lower-class Brits."

"The ones who riot at soccer games?"

Bela's eyes hardened; his jaws snapped shut. Björling was on the radio. *Dein ist mein ganzes Herz*. Not Zyzmchuk's kind of thing, but definitely the old man's. His eyes misted over, all anger gone. His hand reached for slivovitz, poured it into his mouth. The sweet voice filled the room. Bela had excellent sound: a CD from Nakamichi, Acoustic Research speakers that could handle two hundred watts, an amplifier that could provide them. Was that pansy too?

Zyzmchuk kept that thought to himself. Björling came to the last big note and blew it effortlessly away. Björling had always been a big favorite in Bela's family. Zyzmchuk remembered the chipped Blaupunkt, stolen from the Germans, that had sat on a kitchen table, long ago. The radio was gone, the house was gone, the family was gone, the country, in a sense, was gone too; but Björling was as good as ever, maybe better, on Bela's sound system.

Bela drained his glass but didn't let it go, cradling it in his hard hands. When he spoke again, his voice was much softer. "You know why the Brits, the lower-class Brits, are such great fighters?"

"No."

"They're not afraid to die. Get them mad and they don't give two fucks about dying. That's the secret. Everyone else these days is afraid of dying. They're so scared of dying they're dying like flies. Like flies, Ivan." Bela began to laugh. His face reddened, his laughter turned to choking, Zyzmchuk crossed the little room and banged him on the back.

"Like flies, like flies," he gasped as soon as he recovered his breath. "It's the funniest thing I've seen in my whole God-damned life."

At that moment, Zyzmchuk found himself looking at the

photograph of Leni on the mantel. He glanced down at the old man and saw that his eyes were on it too. "Any beer, Bela?" he asked. He didn't want one of those evenings: slivovitz and Leni.

"In the fridge."

Zyzmchuk snapped open a can and returned to the living room. The old man was still gazing at the photo. "Good pansy beer," Zyzmchuk said. "Want one?"

"I can't drink that piss," Bela said, filling his glass with slivovitz. "Americans don't know how to make beer. They don't know how to do anything."

Zyzmchuk knew that Bela meant the Americans hadn't known how to do one specific thing: keep the Russians out of Budapest. An unforgivable sin. But he didn't say it. "What about me, Bela? I'm American."

"Ja, but it didn't take."

"Come on. I've been a citizen all my adult life."

"Don't make me laugh. You're a big Czech—too smart to be smart, like most of your countrymen—but you're not an American."

Bela's eyes shifted back to the photo; so did Zyzmchuk's. Leni sat in a cafe, smiling at someone out of the frame; not a very good photograph, but it had Leni's smile going for it. "You know what I'm thinking?" Bela asked.

"Don't say it."

Björling polished off a few more beauties. Bela swallowed more slivovitz. He was going to say it. "I'm thinking what kind of boy a big dumb Czech like you and my Leni would have had."

"It wasn't necessarily going to be a boy," Zyzmchuk said.

"You don't know what you're talking about. It was lying up high in her belly. That means a boy."

"That's an old wives' tale," Zyzmchuk said, but not with the conviction he'd meant: his mind had suddenly jumped a groove and tossed up the image of number 22 in white and gold, distracting him.

Bela pounded the padded arm of his chair. A puff of dust rose in the air. "There would have been a boy eventually. You know what I'm saying." He leaned forward, ready to fight again.

"I know what you're saying," Zyzmchuk said.

Bela sat down and lowered his voice. "Maybe two."

Zyzmchuk got up. The room was small and overheated, full

of gemütlich bric-a-brac from a Central Europe that no longer existed. "How about a beer instead of that shit," he said. "Nobody drinks it in Hungary anymore."

"Nobody does a lot of things in Hungary anymore."

Zyzmchuk went into the kitchen and got another beer. A calendar hung beside the fridge. All the days were blank, except Thursdays. On Thursdays it said: "Z. + Opera Box." Zyzmchuk stayed in the kitchen, drinking his beer. He didn't want to go over it all again—the mix-up at the kiosk, the broken carburetor, the crumby little village near the border, Colonel Grushin. A classic operation, according to Langley. But the patient died.

"Hey," Bela called, "did you get lost?"

Zyzmchuk went into the living room. Bela's glass was empty again. His eyes were blazing. "That son of a whore at the kiosk." The conversation had gone ahead without them.

Zyzmchuk sighed. "You had your revenge."

"It wasn't enough. I should have done it with my bare hands." He lifted them, grasping, in the air. His thimble glass fell to the floor and smashed. Zyzmchuk went into the kitchen for the broom. The phone rang. He picked it up.

"Mr. Zyzmchuk?"

"Hello, Grace."

"One moment for Mr. Keith."

There was a click. Then the line went fuzzy as Keith was patched through. He sounded far away. "Greetings," he said. "Little Miss Muffet is on the move."

"You're not tapping their house?"

"I thought about it. No. Actually it's public knowledge. It was listed on the daily schedule put out by his office. She's on her way to some ceremony. Grace has the details."

"Okay."

"And Zyz?"

"Yeah?"

"Don't say tapping. This is an open line."

"You just did."

Keith laughed; he'd been very jolly since they'd reached their agreement. "What fools we mortals, huh, Zyz?" Zyzmchuk said nothing. He listened to the bad connection: surf rolling on a sandy beach.

"Where are you?"

"Red Square," Keith said. "Any more questions?"

"No."

"Okay, then. On your horse."

"Sure."

"Bye bye."

The line cleared. Grace came on and gave the details. Zyzmchuk hung up the phone. He knew Bela was watching from the kitchen doorway before he turned to see him.

"Back to the office?" Bela said.

"Nothing pansy like that. They're letting me out."

"To do what?"

"The usual. Dangerous top-secret capers."

Bela made the chopping motion with the side of his hand. That got rid of the sarcasm and left the naked words. Bela always tried to get to the basics. He'd never learn. "Does that mean the Russians?" he asked, eyes narrowing.

"Worse than the Russians."

"Worse than the Russians?"

"Much. A stadium full of English soccer fans."

Bela didn't laugh. He didn't smile. He thrust out his pit bull chin and said, "You know something? I was wrong."

"About what?"

"You. You are an American. You don't understand anything and you don't know you don't know. That's the part that makes you American. Even a Bohunk like me knows when I don't know."

"Time for one more drink," Zyzmchuk said, putting his arm around Bela's shoulders and leading him back to the living room. Björling was singing the Ingemisco. "That's more like it," Zyzmchuk said. He swept up the broken glass, tossed the fragments into the grate, poured slivovitz for two. "Here's to Verdi," he said.

"And to killing Russians," Bela added.

"Shit, Bela."

They drank. Zyzmchuk rose. "Ivan?" said Bela.

"Yes?"

"Can I go with you?"

"Where?"

"Wherever you're going."

"You know the answer to that."

"Is it because of the danger? I can still fight, damn it." Bela balled his right hand into a fist as proof.

"There's no danger. It's stupid and boring. To get me out of the office, that's all."

"I won't be bored."

"Sorry, Bela. See you next week."

Zyzmchuk let himself out. Bela was turning up the volume as he left. Björling, now in the role of Dick Johnson, followed him outside and all the way to the car.

Zyzmchuk sat behind the wheel, watching the lights in Bela's apartment. They went out; but he thought he could still hear "The Girl of the Golden West," drifting down.

Grace had booked him on the last flight to Logan and reserved a hotel room; that would give him plenty of time to be ready for the arrival of Little Miss Muffet's flight in the morning. But Zyzmchuk didn't like hotel rooms, and he preferred driving to flying. Why not? He had a change of clothes in the back of the Blazer; he had his sweats and his J. C. Penney sneakers; he had his toothbrush and his toolbox. The only thing he didn't have was his gun, and you didn't need guns for following people like Alice Frame.

Zyzmchuk turned the key and began the long night's drive to Boston, the taste of slivovitz in his mouth and Leni on his mind.

15

A voice. Familiar. "Horse," it said. "Bye bye."

No more voice. Just the sea, very near. Jessie opened her eyes.

A Picasso hung on a white wall: Rose Period. The subject was an angular woman on a pale beach, a woman who looked something like Barbara. She gazed out to sea with mismatched eyes.

Jessie was lying on a rattan bed. She sat up. The movement made her head pound. She stayed still for a few moments, waiting for the pounding to stop. When it didn't, she got off the bed and crossed the room. It was a long trip: the carpet was deep pile; her body weighed a ton; her legs were flab.

Jessie stood before the painting. It had the familiar signature in the bottom corner, a work of art in itself, and it wasn't a print: a real Rose Period Picasso on a white wall, in a room with a rattan bed, a deep-pile carpet and the ocean very near.

119

The room had two other white walls, but no more Picassos, no more paintings of any kind. The fourth wall was sliding glass. Jessie slid it open and stepped out onto a balcony. Foggy orange night. With an automatic movement, she pulled back her sleeve and glanced down to check the time. Her watch was gone.

One level below hung another balcony, somewhat bigger, extending eight or ten feet beyond the railing of hers. Far below that lay the ocean. A cabin cruiser swung gently off a mooring, bow pointing to the horizon, stern facing her. No name.

Her heart fluttered. Fresh blood washed some of the lethargy from her legs, but made her head hurt more. She reentered the white room, crossed it and tried the door. It was unlocked. She opened it very softly. A staircase, carpeted in more deep pile, led down. Jessie followed it.

She came to an arched doorway. Beyond it spread a big room with a marble floor that matched the Picasso. A fire burned in a pink granite hearth. In front of the fire was a glass table; on it lay the taped-together pieces of Pat's blackboard with the restored message in white chalk. "Toi giet la toi." A gray-haired woman knelt by the table, studying the blackboard, her back to Jessie.

Jessie took a quiet step, off the carpet and onto the marble. The gray head snapped around. Sunglasses. Wraparounds.

"You're up early, dearie." It was the bag lady. She had a funny voice, high but full of male sounds. The combination made Jessie's stomach slide. "We're not quite ready for you."

Jessie's body got ready to bolt. She fought against it. "Where is Kate?" she said; her voice sounded cracked and thin.

"You do like to ask questions," said the bag lady. "But you'll have to wait your turn. First we've got some questions for you."

"What questions?"

The bag lady pointed her heavy chin at the blackboard. "Like what you make of this, for example."

"I don't know what to make of it. Why is it important?"

"There you go with another question." The bag lady smiled a patronizing smile. She had good teeth. "What did other people make of it?"

"What other people?"

"Your friend the police lieutenant, for starters."

Jessie stared into the wraparound sunglasses. All she saw

was her tiny, distorted self. "Did you kill Barbara Appleman?"

"What a thing to say!" The bag lady rose; she was tall and heavy. "And yet another question. You're an unruly young woman, aren't you?" The bag lady took one step toward her. Blue shadow showed on her upper lip. "What have you heard about Wood stock?"

"Woodstock? I don't know what you're talking about." Her tiny distorted self gestured feebly in the wraparounds. The sight made her angry. "Why have you brought me here?" she said, her voice rising. "Who are you?"

The bag lady moved closer, reaching into the pocket of her dress. "You really are difficult," she said.

Jessie lost the struggle with her body. In an instant, she jumped back, spun around and ran up the stairs to the bedroom. She closed the door, but couldn't lock it: no key. The bag lady's steps clicked on the marble. Jessie ran out onto the balcony and looked over the railing. She'd never dived from higher than the ten-foot board; this was more like fifty, if she could clear the lower balcony.

Jessie turned and started back into the room. Too late. The bag lady came in. She had a gun in her hairy hand. "Let's not be hasty, dearie."

Jessie glanced around. There was nothing to throw but the Picasso, hanging on the wall beside her. She flung it at the bag lady, ran across the balcony and climbed onto the railing. She didn't think; her body had taken over. Behind her the bag lady called, "Mickey!" The high notes had disappeared from her voice.

Mr. Mickey appeared on the lower balcony, looked up, saw Jessie. Jessie's body coiled; she sprang off the railing with all her strength. Mr. Mickey rose up at her, reaching; his fingers raked the front of her body, scratching, ripping; but her momentum bent him backward, over the wrought-iron railing, and carried him with her.

Mr. Mickey's hands found Jessie's arms, clamped onto them. They fell: a long fall, locked together like lovers. She saw murder in his pale eyes.

Mr. Mickey was underneath when they hit the water. The impact knocked his breath out in one grunt; she felt it on her face. Then the clamps released her, and she plunged down in the cold sea.

121

The water slowed her. Plunging turned to sinking. She sank, stunned and limp, and kept sinking until something slimy touched her face. Then, instinctively, she kicked up and away from it, legs scissoring, frantic. Her head broke the surface. Blackness closed around her, darker than the night; the world shrank away. She fought for air, sucked it in through wide-open lips, filled her lungs with it. The world came back.

A cone of yellow light cut through the fog; it ended in a yellow circle. The yellow circle zigzagged across the water. It swept over Jessie's face, paused, returned. She squinted up into the cone. From above came a cracking sound. Something slapped the water, a few feet away.

Jessie ducked down. *Slap*, just above her head. *Slap, slap*. Her legs panicked; air bubbled out of her throat. She clenched her jaws and tried to make her legs kick in strong, smooth strokes. *Kick, kick, hold on. Kick, kick, hold on.* Another bubble of air escaped, then another. Her legs panicked. She couldn't hold on any more. She shot to the surface; her feet touched bottom—she was standing in water up to her chest.

Jessie gulped in air and started running—out of the water, across a beach, into a palm grove. She ran, not toward anything, simply away from the sea. The night was full of shadows; she dodged them and kept going. For a while she heard nothing but her own panting. Then a dog began to bark. It quickly barked its way from suspicion to rage. The barking came closer. Jessie veered away from the sound, trying to run harder. The shadows parted. She'd come to a road: a broken white line divided the night. But as she ran onto it, something cut her across the shins, and she went down.

A voice in the trees said, "You are trespassing on private property. Do not move." The voice said it again in Spanish, a treble voice, blurred with static. Jessie stayed where she was. The barking came closer. The voice said, "You are trespassing on private property. Do not move." The voice was halfway through the Spanish for the second time when Jessie realized it was recorded. She scrambled up and started running.

Too late. Jessie hadn't taken two steps before a light shone in her eyes, blinding her. Another voice spoke, "Move and you're dead." No treble. No static.

She froze. A growling form hurtled out of the trees, hitting her from behind and knocking her down. Paws scratched the tarmac for traction; the light swung across the road, found the animal—a Doberman, big and black. It turned and charged Jessie. "Heel, Sonny," shouted the voice. The dog halted, saliva dripping from its bared lips, msucles taut. "Heel." The dog's muscles quivered for a moment. Then it trotted past Jessie, not even looking at her, toward the source of the light. "You are trespassing on private property," said the bilingual voice in the trees. "Do not move." Sonny growled.

Footsteps appproached. "Get up." Jessie got up. The light ran over her body—down, up, down. It was only then that she realized she was naked. Two eyes gleamed behind the light. They liked what they saw. With the light off her face, Jessie made out the contours of a heavy, balding man, wearing some kind of uniform, and beside him the dog, leaning on a taut leash.

"Hands up," said the man. "Not like that—on top of your head. Yeah. That's nice."

The man knelt by the side of the road. A trip wire glinted in the beam of his flashlight. He followed it to a post a few feet away, stuck a key into a hole in the post, turned it. The voice in the woods stopped talking. He rose. "Okay, start walking."

"Where are you taking me? I've been kidnapped and assaul—"

"Shut up."

Jessie turned and started walking. She felt the light on her back. Sonny growled, low in his throat.

Jessie walked along the broken line: a woman's shadow in a wobbly yellow oval, followed by a dog's and a gun's. The sound of the sea grew fainter. "You—"

"Shut up."

The road met another, slightly broader road. A gatehouse sat in the intersection, light glowing within. "Hold it right there." She stopped. "Sit, Sonny." Sonny sat, but he kept growling.

The man went by her and pushed open the door to the gatehouse. "Inside." Jessie hesitated. The man put the flashlight in the small of her back and pushed her in.

"Don't touch me."

"Well, la de dah," said the man, but he didn't touch her again.

The man sat behind a metal desk. There wasn't another chair. Jessie stood. A magazine lay on the desk. *Big-Titted Mamas*. The man saw her eyes on it and swept it into a drawer.

He folded his stubby hands on the desk and gave her a level stare, but only for a moment—he had trouble keeping his gaze from sliding down. "You're in big trouble, baby," he said.

"What are you talking about?"

"Trespassing."

"I haven't been trespassing. I was kidnapped in Santa Monica tonight. I don't even know where I am."

"You can do better than that."

Jessie looked at him carefully for the first time: a middle-aged man with a paunch above his belt and a smaller, naked one under his chin. He wore a green uniform with a name tag on his chest: Hubble. He also had a security-guard patch on one arm: Mille Flores Estates—somewhere in Malibu, she thought, surprised she was so close to home.

"Or what?" she said. Looking carefully made all the difference. Or maybe it was just that whatever had been added to the Armagnac was wearing off.

"Or I'll call the cops."

"Call them."

Hubble squinted at her. The conversation had taken a turn he didn't like. "That won't be so good for you."

"What's my choice?"

"Well, now, maybe we can come to some kind of arrangement. You and me."

"Call the cops. In fact, why don't you call Lieutenant DeMarco in Santa Monica?"

"DeMarco?"

"Yes," Jessie said. "Homicide."

Hubble's hand moved slowly toward the phone, hovered in mid-air; he really preferred some kind of arrangement.

"My name's Jessie Shapiro. He'll want to know that."

Hubble picked up the phone, dialed, and took it outside. When he came back in, he opened a locker, removed a blanket and tossed it to her. "Here," he said.

She wrapped it around her and sat on the floor. Hubble opened his mouth to say something, closed it. They waited. It wasn't long before headlights arced through the gatehouse windows. Sonny started barking. "Shut up, Sonny." Sonny stopped barking. A car door closed. DeMarco came in, wearing a stained fisherman's sweater and a two-day growth of beard, but he looked like Fred Astaire next to Hubble.

"Let's have it," he said.

"Well, Lieutenant," Hubble began, "I apprehended this—"

"Not you," DeMarco said. "Her."

Jessie rose, pulling the blanket around her. "I was—what time is it?"

"Quarter to one."

"Friday?"

"What else?"

"It seems later, that's all. I was kidnapped tonight. Around nine. I think they gave me some kind of sleeping drug."

"Who?"

"A man named Mr. Mickey. Or maybe just Mickey. And a woman, or maybe a man, who might have been his boss. They took me to a house, somewhere near here. Are we in the Colony?"

"Near it," DeMarco said. "What did these people look like?" Jessie described them. "Anyone around here like that?" DeMarco asked Hubble.

"Huh—a woman or maybe a man who might have been the boss of someone named Mr. Mickey or maybe just Mickey? She stoned or what?"

"I'll do the thinking," DeMarco said.

"She was the one who mentioned drugs," Hubble said. "Just trying to help."

DeMarco ignored him. "Describe the house," he said to Jessie.

She described it—the balconies, the pink marble floor, the long drop to the sea. "Recognize it?" DeMarco asked Hubble.

"Sounds a little like the Blugerman house," he said. "But it's been empty for a year. He sold it."

"Who to?"

"I don't remember I ever heard," Hubble said. "But I got a list of property owners." He opened a drawer, shifted *Big-Titted Mamas* aside and consulted a directory. "D. C. Investments, Limited."

"What's that?"

"Dunno."

"Do they own any other property here?"

Hubble ran his eyes down the list. "Nope."

"Is there an address?"

"Just says Panama."

"Okay," DeMarco said. "Let's go."

"Where?"

"To look at the house."

They got into DeMarco's car, Jessie in front with DeMarco, Hubble in back with Sonny. "Can't you get him to stop growling?" DeMarco said.

"That's just purring. He likes riding in the car."

Hubble directed them up a hill to a bluff overlooking the sea. They parked beside a high wall. Through a wrought-iron gate, they could see a long drive leading toward a house. There were no cars in the drive; the house was dark.

"Told you," said Hubble.

"Is that it?" DeMarco asked Jessie.

She pulled the blanket closer around her; the fog was lifting and the night growing cold. "I don't know. I didn't really see it from outside."

DeMarco turned to Hubble. "Got the key?"

"Well, now," Hubble said, "I really got no author—"

DeMarco turned from the gate and looked at Hubble. "Don't give me that."

Hubble's lips moved, but he didn't speak. Sonny growled. "Shut up," DeMarco said. Sonny stopped growling. "Okay, pal," DeMarco said: "How much?"

"I'm not—"

"How much?"

"Fifty."

"Twenty."

"I can't—"

"Open up." DeMarco stuffed a bill into Hubble's shirt pocket.

Hubble unhooked a key chain from his belt and opened the gate. "Leave the dog," DeMarco said. Hubble shut Sonny in the car. They walked up the drive to the house, stopping in front of the door. The house was silent; the sea made noise on the other side.

DeMarco pressed the button by the door. A three-toned bell

sounded inside. He knocked. He rang the bell again. "Got a light?" he said.

Hubble handed him the flash. DeMarco shone it through a window. Pink marble glowed in the beam. "That's it," Jessie said.

DeMarco put his fingers on the bell and kept it there. The three-toned bell rang and rang. DeMarco turned to Hubble. "Okay, pal."

"Oh, no, that could mean my—"

DeMarco jabbed his finger at Hubble's shirt pocket. "Too late now—you've already lost your cherry. Don't make me broadcast it."

"Broadcast?"

"Yeah. To your boss."

"You bastid."

"Everyone says so. Open up."

"It's worth more."

"But you called me names. Open."

Hubble unlocked the door. Then he went toward the car. Jessie followed DeMarco into the house. He turned on the lights. Their footsteps echoed on pink marble. The house was empty. Mr. Mickey was gone, the bag lady was gone, Pat's blackboard was gone, the Picasso was gone, even the fire—not just out, but gone: not an ash remained. Jessie felt the granite hearth: slightly warm. "Feel," she said.

DeMarco felt. "So?"

They went out to the balcony. He shone the light on the water. No boat. No mooring. "It was right there," Jessie said.

"Yeah. What kind of boat?"

"A cabin cruiser. At least forty feet."

"Did you get the name?"

"That was the funny thing."

"What?"

"There was no name."

"That's a funny thing, all right."

"You don't believe me."

"Oh, I believe that you were in the house, that there might have been a fire in the fireplace, that you probably went in the water, that drugs were involved. It's the rest of it that seems a little shaky."

Jessie rounded on him. "What is wrong with you? Why would I make this up?" Hot tears flooded her eyes; she couldn't stop them. "Don't you see there's something terrible happening?"

"What?"

"Some terrible . . ." She searched for a word. "Conspiracy."

It was a bad choice. "Sure," DeMarco said. "Everything's a conspiracy. And Paul's dead, if you play the song backward."

"God—" Jessie stopped. She'd seen something floating on the water. "What's that?"

DeMarco steadied the light. "A leg."

Jessie ran out of the house, around the side, down narrow stairs cut in the bluff. DeMarco followed her. She dropped the blanket and waded in. Something floated on the water: one leg, two. She reached out and pulled in her own jeans.

"Do you see?" she said to DeMarco.

"See what? I said I believed you'd been in the water. It's the rest of it."

Jessie felt in the pockets, took out the sheet of soggy paper. The sea had washed the ink away. "My Mom" was gone. She pulled on the jeans and wrapped the blanket tightly around her.

They returned to the car. Hubble and Sonny were gone. DeMarco drove Jessie to Santa Monica. She was trying to decide whether to tell him about Buddy Boucher when he said, "You're not handling this very well. Maybe you should see a shrink."

"What for?"

"Because. You're going a little crazy. Barbara used to get that way a bit too, under pressure. You need some trancs."

"Barbara never took trancs."

"You're not Barbara."

"That keeps me from making some of her mistakes."

"Are you referring to me?"

Jessie didn't answer. The rest of the drive was silent.

DeMarco dropped her on the side street near the pier, beside her car. Her keys were still in the pocket of her jeans. So was her wallet.

"You owe me twenty," DeMarco said.

"Are you joking?"

"No."

She gave him a wet twenty-dollar bill. For some reason she felt better the moment it left her hands. He drove off.

Jessie went home. She took her suitcase out of the trunk and went inside. Everything looked normal: door locked, drawers all neatly closed, furniture in place; nothing missing but Pat's blackboard. And Kate.

All normal, but her teeth were chattering. She had to think. Jessie went into the kitchen, brewed tea, swallowed it strong and steaming. That stopped the chattering, but did nothing for the thinking. She could make no sense of what had happened that night. Was DeMarco right? Had she imagined some of it? But what? She tried to reconstruct the events, detail by detail. That only started her teeth chattering again.

Do something, said an inner voice, her own voice, and angry. Nothing that had or had not happened in the past few hours changed the fact of Buddy Boucher. Wasn't that true? Jessie tried to find a counterargument and couldn't. Perhaps someone else could come up with a counterargument, or even another idea. But there was no one else.

Jessie rose and went to the phone. All at once, her movements were slow and heavy, as though the earth had suddenly swollen and doubled its gravity. Her voice was slow, too, and thick. She called the airline.

"I was booked on the midnight flight to Boston, but I missed it. Is my ticket good for the next one?"

"Speak up—I can hardly hear you."

Jessie raised her voice. The effort was huge. Her body was demanding to fold up and stay that way.

"Your flight has not departed yet. We've been closed by the fog."

"Can I still make it?"

"You've got forty-five minutes."

Jessie made it.

16

Bao Dai was an expert at binding people so they couldn't move. He'd learned the hard way, from Corporal Trinh. Thin nylon rope was good; copper wire was the best. Bao Dai got both at the hardware.

Bao Dai bound the guests. He didn't want to think of them as prisoners. Corporal Trinh had prisoners. Bao Dai had guests—the little girl, at least, was a guest. He wanted to get to know them, all about them. Then he'd know what to do with them. And if something happened to the fox, so cunning and free, then maybe he'd have to bring up the girl himself. After all, he could have had a little girl just like that if . . . if he'd said no instead of yes on the last day of Peace and Love.

Not too late. Plenty of time, as long as he didn't make any mistakes. Bao Dai sat in the bus station, wondering if he'd already made any. He thought of one.

That night he took a bus. It wasn't a long ride. There were

only a few people on the bus. One was a man with long hair—the first longhair Bao Dai had seen. He smiled at the man. The man sat down beside him.

"Smoke?" said the man.

"I don't smoke."

The man laughed. "I meant you looking to cop some."

"Cop some?"

"Yeah," said the long-haired man, pulling out a pack of cards and opening it. Inside were hand-rolled cigarettes packed tight with dark green leaf.

"Joints?" asked Bao Dai.

"You got it. Two bucks a stick."

Bao Dai bought five.

"You're the first head I've seen," he said. *Was that another mistake?* Bao Dai felt across the front of his wrinkled tan jacket, where he had the whalebone knife tucked away.

"Head?" said the man.

"Hippie," explained Bao Dai, looking at the man again and wondering whether he might be a younger man, possibly more than a few years younger. "You know."

The man laughed. "No hippies anymore, amigo. Not here or anywhere else. I'm a salesman, pure and simple."

Bao Dai relaxed. "What do you sell?"

The man laughed again. "I just sold you some. I got pills too." He pulled out a vial, filled with blue tablets and red capsules. "The reds are ludes; the blues are acid."

"Acid?"

"Yeah. Five bucks each."

Bao Dai bought five blues and five reds. The long-haired man took out the pack of joints and lit one. He inhaled, passed it to Bao Dai.

Bao Dai shook his head. He was afraid. He would wait until he wasn't afraid.

The man looked puzzled for a moment, then took another drag and said, "You work around here?"

Bao Dai didn't answer.

"Or just passing through?"

"Yeah."

The man finished the joint. "I used to be in wood stoves.

131

For the condos, right? Then they put in the new pollution laws and priced them out of the market. Can't even burn fucking wood anymore." He stamped out the roach and got off at the next town.

Bao Dai got off at the town after that. It was quiet. Everyone had gone to bed. Bao Dai found the mistake, just where they'd left it. He unlocked the door, drove away.

The sound was thrilling. He turned it up as loud as it would go: ". . . to hear the scream of the butterfly." And Bao Dai heard it, as never before.

He forgot his fear of the smoke. Just one little puff, he thought. He lit a joint, had one puff, then another. All at once he found himself up at the top of the right-hand speaker, where the cymbals splashed and the high notes squealed. Squealed like a pig.

Then he was remembering the Year of the Pig: pus in his eyes, worms wriggling in the rice bowl, shitting liquid green, a face with no skin, the things Corporal Trinh made him do. Corporal Trinh, his black gun, his homemade lash, his little yellow cock: all in the Year of the Pig.

Pa had had a lash too. Also homemade—a knotted rope, hanging near the crucifix in the kitchen. It was a painted crucifix. Bai Dao could see it in his mind: the blood where the nails stuck in, the strange look on the face of Jesus, not the look of a man in pain, not like Corporal Trinh's face, when Bao Dai did what he did. But crucifixion must have hurt, must have hurt a lot.

Bao Dai turned off the sound, but the image of the crucifix didn't go away. He couldn't push it out of his mind. He stopped the car. He took deep breaths. Then he had a funny feeling, almost like he was going to cry. But he didn't cry. The image of the crucifix went away. He forgot Pa's lash and the Year of the Pig.

After that, it was easy. He didn't have to think. That was because he knew the country like the back of his hands. Bao Dai looked at the back of his hands. They had scars, marks, lines all over them, could have been the hands of some old geezer. He remembered that he didn't know his fucking hand backs at all. Someone had to pay for that.

He didn't know his hand backs, but he knew the country.

132

It was easy: past the old wall, down the lumber track, through the trees to the big rock.

Bao Dai got out of the car. He got everything lined up, then gave a little push. The splash was tremendous, like a thousand cymbals warring in a thousand right-hand speakers.

Then silence. He was safe.

Part Two

17

One by one, the conveyor belt dumped the bags onto the spinning carousel. A good animator could have given them funny faces and made a singing-dancing movie about the class system. Louis Vuitton, fake Louis Vuitton, imitation Louis Vuitton, Samsonite, backpacks, duffel bags, cardboard boxes, battered luggage tied with string—all came bumping down to the carousel. Hands reached for them; people took their places in society. All except Jessie. Her bag—worn leather with solid brass fittings, picked up at a garage sale in Menlo Park in 1970: how would the animator classify her?—didn't appear.

After a while, the carousel was empty, her fellow fliers gone. Letters and numbers flickered on the sign above her head, changing from L.A. UA 418 to WASH EA 102. The conveyor belt stopped. New, fresher-looking people appeared in the concourse, moved toward the carousel. Jessie was about to go looking for the lost luggage office when the conveyor belt shuddered and spat out her suitcase. She reached for it and pulled, only then realizing how tired she was—the suitcase banged the rubber guardrail, slipping from her grip. It would have fallen, had not a man standing nearby caught the handle and lowered it gently to the floor.

"Thanks," Jessie said. He nodded; a broad man in a plain gray sweatsuit.

She carried the suitcase to a corner and looked inside. Everything accounted for: the Reeboks, *Jane Eyre*, Buddy Boucher's letters. Jessie closed the suitcase and went to the car rental counter.

Not long after, furnished with a subcompact car and a map, Jessie drove away from the airport. As soon as she got on the turnpike, she felt the north wind: it buffeted the little car, trying to blow it into the next lane; overhead it slapped the trees around, tearing off their few remaining leaves. Jessie rolled the window all the way up and turned on the heat. She still felt cold. A cup of coffee might have warmed her, but she didn't want to stop. She turned the radio on instead; no warmth there: the Levi's commercial was almost the first thing she heard. It was one nation, all right, conceived in liberty and dedicated to making a sale. Jessie drove on in silence, through a stripped-down, naked world that seemed to be waiting for the covering of the first snowfall. It reminded her of another long, brown drive, all the way to the tip of Baja, with Kate sleeping in her lap. For a moment, she almost felt the weight of Kate's head; but her lap was empty, cold and empty, and she was empty inside, too.

Bare hills rose on Jessie's right. She took the next exit and followed a narrower highway up into them. The wind blew harder; the sky grew grayer. Now, off the turnpike, Jessie had her first close look at New England countryside: rocky meadows, a piebald herd of holstein cows in the lee of a spruce grove, a big Rockwell-red barn with a roof that read: ANTIQUES BOUGHT AND SOLD. FLEA MARKET EVERY SATURDAY. MAJOR CARDS."

She entered Bennington a few minutes after three and almost went right by Buddy Boucher's dealership, just inside the town limit. Buddy Boucher had red, white and blue plastic pennants, a big sign with a smiling lumberjack, and a small lot with about a dozen shiny cars on it. She parked in front of the office, swept her eyes over the cars. She didn't see the blue BMW, but there were more cars parked around the building, where the sign said, SERVICE. Jessie went in.

A chocolate-colored sedan with white tires and wire wheels took up most of the showroom. Along the back wall were three-sided offices, the size of cobblers' stalls in an Oriental market. All but one, slightly bigger than the others, were empty. In the occupied cubicle a man talked on the phone. He had swept-back silver hair that needed washing and a face as busy as a B-movie actor's.

"Hey," he was saying, "we'll work something out. That's what we're here for." He nodded a few times, smiled, winked, raised an eyebrow. "Darn tootin'," he said. "Darn tootin'." He hung up. His face relaxed. Then he saw Jessie and got back to work, a little distractedly at first; he reminded her of a singer given an unexpected curtain call. "Hi there," he said, coming to her. "Nice little automobile, huh?" He patted the chocolate-colored roof. He glanced past her, toward the lot. "What're you driving?"

"I'm looking for Buddy Boucher," Jessie said.

"You found him." Buddy Boucher puffed on the spot he'd been patting, buffed it with a handkerchief and said, "What can I do you for?"

"I spoke to you yesterday," Jessie began. She told him who she was. His eyes shifted when he heard the name Rodney. "Has my husband come for his car yet?"

Buddy Boucher cleared his throat. "Well, Mrs. Rodney, I'm not sure what to tell you."

"I don't understand."

"See, the fact is, the car was on the lot when I locked up last night. Right over there beside the green Charger. But when I came in this morning it was gone."

"Do you mean it was stolen?"

"That's what I don't know. It might have been stolen. On the other hand, your husband had the keys. So he could have come after we closed and just taken it. I wisht he'd left a note, is all."

Jessie gazed for a few moments at the empty space on the lot. Red, white and blue pennants snapped in the wind. "What were the exact arrangements?"

"He said he'd be back at the end of the week. He didn't make it more exact than that."

"Have you called the police?"

"Not yet. I was kind of waiting to see if he came in over the weekend."

Jessie nodded. "How was he when you saw him?" A clumsy question: she regretted it the moment it passed her lips.

"How was he?"

She stumbled again. "I've been a little worried about his health, lately."

"Well, I don't know. As I said, he was only in here for half an hour, tops." Buddy Boucher screwed up his eyes. "Seemed okay, I guess. Tired, maybe. Kept a close eye on the little girl. Never let go of her hand. Well-dressed—had on a suit and tie."

"Tie?"

"Yeah. Tan suit and a tie with sailboats on it."

"How do you remember that?"

"I've got an eye for clothing, Mrs. Rodney. Got to, in this business." He couldn't stop his eyes from giving her outfit a quick once-over.

"What was the little girl wearing?"

"Didn't notice. Kids don't write the checks." He started to laugh, stopped when he saw she wasn't. "Just joshin'. I love kids." He thought. "In fact, she had on a Coca-Cola T-shirt."

It was a T-shirt Jessie knew well. "Did she . . . seem all right?"

Buddy Boucher took a deep breath, let it out slowly. "Are you sure there's nothing, uh, wrong between you and Mr. Rodney?"

"I told you—an investment opportunity's come up. It's urgent that we talk." He was watching her closely. "We've had an offer on the house," she added.

He nodded. Had she finally spoken his language? "The girl. She was okay, I guess. Didn't say boo, like I told you." His gaze rested on Jessie's face. "She's your girl, all right. Doesn't take after her old man much."

"It's just the coloring, really. Take away his blond hair and they resemble each other a lot."

Buddy Boucher blinked his little eyes. "Blond hair?"

"Pat's," she explained. "Mr. Rodney's."

Buddy Boucher stepped back. Exit Animation Face. Jessie awaited the entrance of Flaccid Face. It didn't appear. Instead a shrewd small-town face, economical in its movements and not very friendly, put in its appearance. "Would you mind explaining what's going on here?" Buddy Boucher said.

"What do you mean?"

"I mean your husband doesn't have blond hair, lady. At least he didn't when he came in here."

"What color was his hair?"

"You tell me."

"What are you getting at?"

Buddy Boucher's thin lips parted, pressed together, parted again, very narrowly. "I'm not getting at anything."

"Maybe we're having a misunderstanding, Mr. Boucher. Pat's hair isn't light blond. It's a dirty blond: maybe you could call it brown."

The thin lips parted again. "I'm not arguing about the color. This guy was bald."

"How—" Jessie heard the word jump out of her throat, an octave higher than nomal, and began again. "How do you know he was Pat Rodney?"

"He had ID." Impatience roughened his tone. "I saw his driver's license, his social security. I get that from everyone who buys here."

"Even a cash sale?"

"Even a cash sale."

"Did you write it all down?"

"I did."

"I'd like to see it."

Buddy Boucher took her into his cubicle. He had Dale Carnegie diplomas on the walls and pictures of a round wife and three round children on the desk. He showed Jessie what he'd copied. The address and birth date on the driver's license were right; Pat's social security number she didn't know, so couldn't verify.

"Was he bald in the photograph on the license?"

Buddy Boucher thought. "I don't remember." The admission pulled a plug somewhere inside him; his impatience drained away. "I'm not sure I really looked. I was just taking down the numbers."

"What kind of baldness was it?" Jessie asked. "The natural kind with a fringe or the shaved kind?"

Buddy Boucher stared at the pictures of his round family: on skis, under beach umbrellas, behind birthday cakes. "The shaved kind, I think. I couldn't swear."

Jessie wished she had brought a photograph of Pat. She did have one of Kate. She took it out of her wallet: Kate at the beach, making a silly face and standing like a stork.

"That's her," said Buddy Boucher.

The phone rang. Buddy Boucher's animated face reasserted itself. "Hello. Hey, where you been?" Jessie leaned forward. The small-town face peeked out for a moment, as Buddy shook his head at her. "You'd best get your butt down here. I've only got one left on the lot, and a fellow from Putney's coming to see it Monday. . . . Air, AM-FM cassette, power everything. . . . Can't tell you over the phone. Right. Bye." He hung up, looked at Jessie, changed faces.

"Can I ask you a question?" he said.

"Yes."

"Is he wanted?"

"Wanted?"

"By the cops."

"Why do you ask that?"

He held up his fingers and folded them back one by one: "Paid cash. Shaved his head. And you looking for him with a story about an investment and all kinds of questions like you don't know him too good."

"You think I'm with the police?"

"It's hard to tell these days."

"God. Look, Mr. Boucher. He's my ex-husband. He has my daughter illegally. I want her back. That's all. The police have nothing to do with it."

"Why don't you call them?"

"It's hard to get them interested in something like this. And I'd prefer to resolve this peacefully, if I can."

Buddy Boucher looked her in the eye. He might have been making up his mind about something. Or he might have been plotting to sell her the chocolate-colored sedan. Jessie waited. "Tell you what," Buddy Boucher said at last. "You going to be around?"

"For as long as it takes," Jessie replied. She realized the truth of her words as she spoke. "For as long as it takes."

"Give me a number. If he comes in, I'll call you while he's here. Then you can sort it out, the both of you."

"That's very kind."

"I've got kids of my own," he said, glancing at the photographs. "And I love kids—I told you that."

"Thank you," Jessie said, wondering if that love was something unimpeachable for Buddy to cling to in a tricky world, like a cathedral to the burghers of a grubby town.

"But no rough stuff on the premises."

"There won't be. It's not that kind of thing."

Jessie held out her hand. Buddy Boucher shook it. "If," he said.

"If?"

"There's no guarantee he'll call."

Jessie had a thought. "Do you know the license number of the car you sold him?"

"Better than that. I've got a Polaroid of the van itself. It's got a temporory license because he's from out of state."

He gave it to her: a black van with opaque side and rear windows and red flames, more discreet than some she'd seen, painted on the side. But still, red flames. "What about his friend?"

"Like I told you on the phone, I didn't really get a good look at him. He stayed outside in the BMW. A little rocky, your husband said."

"A little rocky?"

"Stomach flu."

"The little girl wasn't sick, was she?"

"Not that I saw."

Jessie turned to leave. "Did Pat say why he wanted another car?"

"Nope. And I didn't ask. My Pop brought me up smarter than that."

Jessie went out into the cold. She didn't go to her car right away. Instead she walked to the space beside the green Charger. It was just a rectangle of asphalt, swept clean except for a broken piece of plastic comb. Jessie picked it up: part of a barrette, the color of a turtle shell. A few frizzy dark hairs clung to the teeth:

143

just the right darkness, the right tightness of frizz. Jessie held it close to her nose and sniffed: no smell. She put it in her pocket. *My Mom is like a turtle shell.*

A few minutes later she checked into a motel, called Buddy Boucher and gave him the number. Then she sat on the bed. The mattress sagged and she sagged with it. She stood up. She hadn't come all that way for a nap.

Jessie went into the coffee shop, had coffee and a tuna sandwich. The coffee didn't make her more alert; it just made her stomach nervous. The tuna rolled up in a hard ball and got stuck in it. She put on her blue sweater and walked to the car. The thick wool, worn at home only on the coldest nights, didn't warm her at all. She got into the car, turned on the heat and started driving. She didn't go fast, her eyes were too busy looking for a black van with discreet red flames on the sides.

But she didn't see it. She saw few cars of any kind. There wasn't much to buy in Bennington; few people were shopping for what there was. Hardly anyone was driving through the countryside, either. Maybe they were all at home, chopping firewood, putting up jam, ordering from L. L. Bean. After a while, Jessie parked in front of a diner on the main street, had another cup of coffee and called Buddy Boucher.

"No cigar," he said. "And I'm getting ready to close. I'll be in at ten tomorow."

"I'll call you."

"Sure thing."

Jessie stepped outside; still afternoon, but the air already had a nighttime bite. Hands deep in her pockets, Jessie walked along the street, glancing at the parked cars. She saw bumper stickers for and against abortion, nuclear war and secession from the Union. She didn't see a black van with flames.

As she turned to go back to her car, Jessie noticed a sign around the corner on a side street: FOOD OF LOVE, it said, RECORDS AND TAPES. Jessie moved toward it, thinking of Spacious Skies and the man who had stayed in the BMW: a friend of Pat's, an old friend perhaps, possibly old enough to have known him on the commune. Then she had another thought: what if Pat hadn't shaved his head, as Buddy Boucher had suggested? What if the friend was bald, and it was he who had gone into the showroom, taking Kate and Pat's ID? Jessie couldn't think of any reason for that; but neither could she explain why Pat would shave his head.

The record store occupied the bottom floor of a narrow two-story building made of unsandblasted bricks. Yellowed shades were drawn behind the small windows of the second story. The store's windows, not much bigger, were thick with dust. They displayed a psychedelic mural of lovers reclining on a giant mushroom and, in front of that, dusty album covers: *Surrealistic Pillow, Strange Days, Disraeli Gears*, the White Album. Jessie didn't know much about Pat's life in those days, not even where in Vermont the commune had been, but she thought some town had been named in the lyric of his song. She opened the door and walked in.

Music played inside: "Oh where have you been, my blue-eyed son?" Rows of record bins extended into gloom at the rear of the store. Posters hung on a wall: an embracing couple at a rock concert, John and Yoko in a bag, Jim Morrison without a shirt, Jerry Garcia with a fat joint stuck between the tuning pegs of his guitar, the Freak Brothers salivating over a girl in a miniskirt, men in berets—Che Guevara, Huey Newton, Eric Anderson. Jessie smelled incense. She saw no customers, no staff, heard not a sound but those made by Bob Dylan. She might have been in a museum after hours, a museum dedicated to 1968.

Jessie moved along the record bins until she came to V. There he was: van Ronk—a thick section. She was still flicking through the albums when she heard a door open at the back of the store. She turned.

A man walked out of the gloom, but he didn't break the mood. How could he? He was perfect in his embroidered jeans, plaid lumber jacket, granny glasses and long ponytail. Jessie hadn't seen a ponytail on a man in some time; once they'd been common, even in Santa Monica.

"Hello," the man said, waving to her, or had he actually flashed the peace sign? It was too dark to tell. The man had a long, loose stride; he came closer, into the light. Then Jessie saw the lines on his forehead, the gray in his hair. "Can I help you?" He had a soft voice and soft, bloodshot eyes behind his granny glasses. He brought smells with him—wood smoke and stale sweat.

145

"I'm looking for a song Dave van Ronk recorded," Jessie said.

He looked her up and down, but very quickly and furtively. "You like brother Dave?"

"Yes, as a matter of fact."

"Far out."

"But it's a particular song I want."

The man made a loose-jointed gesture at the bin. "I've got everything he ever cut. Maybe not in mint condition, but it's all there. I mean he's seminal, right? What's the name of the song?"

" 'Spacious Skies.' "

"*Travelin' Light.* Vanguard R143. Side two. Cut three." He moved past her, pulled an album out of the bin and handed it to her. Jessie flipped it over. Side two, cut three: "Spacious Skies (Artie Lee)." Artie Lee was Pat's nom de plume—something to do with a tax scheme Norman Wine had set up, he'd told her.

"Can I hear it?"

He tugged at a loose strand of hair. "That's a sealed record. Like I'd hate—"

"I'm buying it anyway."

"Okay. Eight ninety-five." Jessie paid. He tucked the money in his jeans. "I've got a turntable in back."

He led her into the gloom and through a doorway. On the other side lay an all-purpose room: desk piled with business papers in the center, boxes of records along the wall, wood stove in one corner, unmade bed in the other. The turntable rested on an empty crate within arm's reach of the bed. A record was spinning: "I saw a highway of diamonds with nobody on it."

The man took off the Dylan, opened the van Ronk and placed the disk on the turntable, handling the records as though they were made of glass. Lowering the tone arm, he paused and said, "Like some tea?"

Jessie didn't want tea. She wanted to listen to the lyrics and get out of there. The man watched her with his soft red look, the needle hovering over the vinyl.

"I'm having a cup," he said, swinging the arm back onto its cradle.

"Okay," Jessie said, feeling suddenly like a foreigner negotiating for something in an Oriental bazaar. "Thanks."

146

He took a kettle off the wood stove and filled two lopsided ceramic mugs. Then he opened a desk drawer and removed a plastic bag. "Herbal," he said, sprinkling green leaves into the mugs. He handed her one. She smelled dandelions. "Sit," he said. The only place for sitting was the bed.

"I'm fine," Jessie replied; she leaned against the desk. The man sat on the bed and lowered the tone arm. Dave van Ronk played a little intro and started singing:

> *I dreamed*
> *I dreamed a dream of dreams*
> *And woke as Sergeant Pepper.*
> *All wrapped in light*
> *And feeling right*
> *And high, high, high.*
> *Higher than mountains*
> *And higher than air*
> *It was all so fine*
> *Under Spacious Skies.*
>
> *I dreamed*
> *I dreamed a dream of dreams*
> *And woke as just plain me,*
> *With a mouth like dust*
> *And a tongue like rust*
> *And down, down, down.*
> *Lower than earth*
> *Deeper than graves*
> *I must have been back*
> *Down in Morgantown.*
>
> *I dreamed*
> *I dreamed a dream of dreams*
> *And woke as Sergeant Pepper.*
> *All wrapped in light*
> *And feeling right*
> *And high, high, high.*
> *Higher than mountains*
> *Higher than air*
> *It was all so right*
> *In Spacious Skies.*

147

"That's what you wanted?"

Jessie was silent for a moment. She'd forgotten the power of Dave van Ronk's singing, especially when he used his whispery voice. But that was only part of it. "Yes," she said. "That's what I wanted. Is Morgan near here?"

"Morgan?"

"The town in the song."

Dave van Ronk started singing "Cocaine." The man lifted the needle, put Bob Dylan back on. The song resumed at the exact point of interruption. "I saw a black branch with blood that kept dripping."

"Why do you ask?" he said.

"I thought the song was about a commune in Vermont. I'm looking for it."

Wind rattled the windows. The man reached into the pocket of his lumber jacket and took out a joint. He lit it, took a deep drag, held it out to her. Jessie shook her head.

"You're not rejecting my hospitality?" he said, smoke curling out of his mouth. The question sounded funny, but there was nothing humorous about his tone. "Everyone's in such a hurry these days." Slowly he got off the bed, replaced the van Ronk record in its cover and gave it to her. "I won't keep you."

Jessie didn't move. "Is it about a commune in Vermont?"

"Maybe," said the man, raising the joint to his lips; the smells of marijuana, sweat and wood smoke acted on the tuna balled in Jessie's stomach, nauseating her. "I mean, could be." He held out the joint again.

The soft red eyes were on her. They knew something about Spacious Skies. But first she had to take communion. The wafer was in his hand. Jessie took it.

She hadn't smoked marijuana in years. She brought it to her mouth, inhaled hot smoke and passed it back to him. He waved it away.

"Take another hit. Live a little."

The phrase—Barbara's words coming from his mouth—paralyzed her for a moment.

"Something wrong?"

"No." Jessie inhaled a little more and held out the joint; this time he accepted it.

148

"Good shit, huh? Homegrown."

Jessie didn't feel a thing. "Was there or is there a commune called Spacious Skies?"

The man took another drag, sat back down on the bed. "There was. How come you're interested?"

"How come?" she repeated. Then someone pounded a bass drum; an organ came in like a far-off wail; guitars, electric and acoustic, made the air vibrate in metallic and woody ways; and a raw scared scary voice, not Bob Dylan from *People* magazine and MTV but Bob Dylan back then, started to sing: "Visions of Johanna." It took her away on musical roads that divided and subdivided in her mind.

"Good shit, huh?"

Jessie looked up, into soft red eyes. "Yes. It is." All at once her voice sounded very young, like a teenager's.

"Come have a seat."

"I'm fine here." Where? Leaning against the desk; blackened roaches in a beer bottle; stacks of bills and letters: "Dear Mr. Flenser," she read, "Your account is now five months overdue and we can no longer . . ."

"You know, I dig your taste in music. Your musical likes and dislikes, I mean. 'Visions of Johanna.' A world in itself, right?" He sang along in a very light, high voice, but in tune and surprisingly sweet.

"Look, Mr. Flenser—"

"Call me Gato."

"I'd like to find Spacious Skies."

"How come?"

"How come? Because . . ." But the music grabbed her again, much harder than before: she lost her feeling for the desk, the floor; she lost her sense of smell, for the sweat, wood smoke, marijuana; her vision shrank to a soft red smear; all was hearing—she bounced along the bass notes, felt the thump of the drums in every fiber, lingered in the meaningful bent silences that marked the guitarist's long runs, came face to face with the raw scared scary voice.

This was tedious.

It was just an old record. Straighten up. She pushed herself away from the desk. Wobble, wobble.

149

"Homegrown. But I've been breeding selected plants for fifteen years. This is the best shit you've ever had. Right or wrong? Be objective."

"You're asking me to be objective and stoned at the same time?"

Gato began to laugh. He kept laughing until his body shook with it. Jessie felt like laughing too, but she didn't let herself. Once started, she'd never stop, and it would be the furthest thing from laughter. She took a deep breath to clear her head, but got caught up in the process of breathing: how the air felt cool in her nostrils, warmed as it dipped down into her throat; how she filled like a balloon, ribs stretching, bra straps tightening.

After some time, Jessie realized she was holding her breath. She let it out. Deflating. The man on the bed wasn't laughing anymore. He was watching her.

The man on the bed took the elastic out of his hair and shook it loose. "It is good shit," he said. "But more than that, we're sharing it." The record finished playing. "What do you want? More Dylan? Or how about Leon Russell? You make me think of him—that zippy way he plays the piano."

"I'm not zippy."

"No?" Gato's fingers wound themselves into his long hair. "I didn't mean anything by it."

"That's okay. But if you know anything about Spacious Skies, please tell me."

"See—that's zippy."

"For God's sake."

Gato glanced at her. He looked hurt. "Why?"

"Why what?"

"Why are you so interested in Spacious Skies?"

"I want to go there."

"Why?"

She toyed with telling him the truth; given her state of mind at the moment and the way he was, it might take days. So she said, "I'm writing a story on communes."

"Yeah? Who for?"

"*Rolling Stone.*"

Gato perked up. "You work for them?"

"Free-lance."

150

He bit his lip. "Do they pay your expenses?"

"It depends."

"Maybe the information is worth something."

"Maybe."

"How much?"

"Twenty," Jessie said. It seemed to be the going rate.

"Make it thirty."

"Split the difference."

"Okay."

"Where's Spacious Skies?"

"Where's the money?"

"After you tell me.'"

"How do I know you've got it?"

"Because you looked in my wallet when I paid the eight ninety-five."

He sank into thought, biting his lips again. "You're a sharp chick. You know that? Zippy, but on you it's good."

"Spacious Skies," she reminded him.

"Amber waves of grain." He laughed. "Shit," he said. "Funny how quick the mind is." He shook his head at the wonder of it. Long twists of hair fell over his face. "Two human beings in a room with a record player and some grass. What else do you need?"

"The information."

Gato laughed. For a moment Jessie feared another laughing binge, but he came out of it quickly. "Okay, okay. The song. 'Spacious Skies.' Words and music by Artie Lee. A somewhat mysterious figure in the music business—seems to be his only song. They say he lived on the commune for a while, but that was before my time."

"Before your time?"

"Here. I spent three years in Marrakesh." He lingered on the word.

"Who says he lived on the commune?"

"Dudes. On the other hand," he said, holding up a finger like a logician splitting a crucial hair, "the woman says she never heard of him."

"What woman?"

"Blue."

"Who's Blue?"

"Woman from the commune. Only it's not a commune any-more. At least it wasn't the last time I talked to her."

"When was that?"

He bit his lip. "I guess it was around the time *Exile on Main Street* came out."

"That was a long time ago."

"Yeah? Well, that's the last time I saw her. She came in the store. The old store. I had the old store, then."

"Where was that?"

"Bennington." He made it sound dreamy, like Marrakesh. "They dug music in Bennington."

"This *is* Bennington, isn't it?"

"Not the old Bennington. Now it's all . . ." He searched for a word, but soon gave up, falling silent.

"Is the commune near Bennington?" Jessie asked.

"It's not a commune anymore."

"What happened to it?"

Gato was looking down at the floor. "What happened to everything?"

"Is the woman still there?"

"What woman?"

"Blue, you said."

"As far as I know."

"Have you been to her place?"

"Not when it was just hers. Back when it was a commune, I was there once. *Sticky Fingers.*" He used album releases to keep track of time, the way Cro-Magnon man watched the stars.

"Was Artie Lee there then?"

"No. I told you. He'd been and gone. If the song's about it at all. You can't always tell." He perked up again. "Manson thought the White Album was about race war, right? Which is bullshit: it's about death. So that chick—what's her name—got forked for nothing. Can you dig that?"

What the hell are you talking about? Jessie wanted to say. But she asked, "Do you remember where the place was?"

"Right off Route Eight. Third left after the stop sign."

"What stop sign?"

"At Nine."

"The stop sign at Eight and Nine?"

"Right."

"Is that far from here?"

"Why are you asking me all these questions?"

"I told you," Jessie said. "I'm doing a story on communes."

"But it's not a commune anymore."

"That's the point of the story."

He laughed. He laughed and laughed. Jessie watched. He looked like a windup troll toy, run amok. "The point of the story. The point of it. Point. Point. Oh, wow. You're really something."

Abruptly, the laughing stopped.

Gato Flenser lit another joint. He gave her the soft red look, holding out the joint. Jessie pushed away from the desk, crossed the room, took out her wallet and gave him twenty-five dollars. He let it drop.

"Do you have to go right away?"

"Deadline," Jessie said.

He nodded. "I don't want your money."

"Keep it."

Jessie picked up the van Ronk album. She walked out of the back room, out of the gloom, into the cold wind. Before the door closed, a needle scratched vinyl; music followed her down the street. The volume on Gato's record player was turned up high. Leon Russell did have a zippy way of playing the piano.

18

Route 9 unreeled like a long movie about white lines. No plot, no dialogue, no characters, but it absorbed Jessie like *Citizen Kane* or *The Seven Samurai*. Only when a car honked or flashed by would she remember what she was doing and glance down at the speedometer, to find the needle dipping down to forty, thirty, twenty-five miles an hour.

The pressure behind her eyes slowly eased. By the time she reached the stoplight at Route 8, the fog had lifted from her mind, leaving her somewhat like a country after a long drought: dry-mouthed, inert and wanting a shower. In her case the weather had been internal, and any famine mental.

A mailbox marked the third turning on the left. No name appeared on it, nothing but faded homemade decorations: blue flowers curling around what might have been a peace symbol; the paint was too weathered to tell.

After a few hundred feet, the road narrowed abruptly and the pavement ended. Jessie steered around the ruts and bumps, up a long hill lined on both sides with bare trees and banks of fallen leaves. At the top of the hill, she stopped the car. A broad meadow lay on the other side, stretching to a wooded rise in the distance. Tucked into a clearing at the base of the rise was a farm: white house, red barn, unpainted sheds. Spacious Skies. Jessie looked up: the sky was a single low dark cloud, like a cast-iron lid over a simmering pot, and darkening with the approach of night. She drove down the hill.

The house looked better from a distance; big and rambling, it might have been something long ago. But now the white paint was peeling; water stains darkened the dormers; and the porch sagged. Jessie parked beside a rusted engine block and a heap of bald tires, climbed the steps and knocked on the door. Nothing happened.

She knocked again, harder. No one opened the door. No sound came from inside. "Hello?" she called. "Hello?" Silence.

The door, heavy and scarred, had a crescent-shaped window at eye level. The glass was cracked and held together with masking tape. Jessie peered through it.

She saw into the front hall: a high-ceilinged room with faded wallpaper and a bare wooden floor. A down jacket hung on a wall hook; stairs led up into darkness.

"Hello?"

Silence.

Jessie walked around the house, thinking a car might be parked on the other side. There was no car, just a dirt yard with a fat brown turkey pecking in it. Jessie crossed the yard to the barn.

This wasn't the kind of barn Norman Rockwell would have liked: most of the red stain had faded away, lingering only in patches like a skin disease; the boards were warped, cracked, rotting. There were no windows to peek through, and the big sliding door was closed. Jessie knocked, but got no answer. She didn't hear shifting hooves or the flapping of clipped wings. Had the farm been abandoned? Only the presence of the single turkey said no, and the down jacket in the front hall.

Jessie reached for the handle of the barn door. Entering someone's house without permission was wrong, but what was the rule on barns? City people couldn't be expected to know. Jessie slid the door open.

The barn was almost empty: no horses, no cows, no birds, no hay, no machinery. Just cobwebs and a big hump under a tarpaulin at the back. Then she looked up. And saw—

What?

A second-rate reproduction?

An oversized joke?

Or the Sistine ceiling of a hippie chapel?

The ceiling of the barn was covered with an enormous painting of the album cover of *Sgt. Pepper's Lonely Hearts Club Band*. John, Paul, George and Ringo, and all those other faces, heads and in-jokes, blown up bigger than life-size. They gazed down in silent splendor, frozen in 1967. The signatures of the artists were strewn among the red flowers that spelled "The Beatles": Digger, Hank, Jojo, Jim and Ruthie, Blue, Oddjob, Hart, Rama, She, François et Marlene, Disco, Stork, Sunny, Lara, Susie, Cityboy, Pat, and others she couldn't read—the paint, applied directly to the wooden boards, was fading.

Jessie stared up at *Sgt. Pepper's Lonely Hearts Club Band* for a long time. Then she walked through the shadows to the back of the barn. She wanted to see under the tarpaulin. It was coated with dust and mold. She raised one corner.

There was a car underneath. A blue car, the same shade of blue as the BMW. Jessie tore off the tarpaulin in one jerk; but it wasn't the BMW.

The car was a Corvette, shiny and unmarked. Jessie was about to replace the tarpaulin when she realized there was something odd about the car. It was immaculate, but not new. The design reminded her of the model Buzz and Todd drove in "Route 66." The blue Corvette must have been as old as *Sgt. Pepper*.

Jessie opened the door and checked the odometer: eighty-seven miles. It was what it seemed—an old car that had hardly been driven, with a Vermont vanity license plate: PAT 69. Jessie covered it with the tarpaulin and went outside.

The turkey was still pecking at the dirt. All at once it straightened, twisted its head around, paused. Jessie heard a car approaching. She walked quickly around to the front of the house.

A scraped and dented pickup was bouncing up the road. It stopped beside Jessie's car. A woman got out of the cab. Clothes: flannel shirt, down vest, peasant skirt, hiking boots. Face: broad, with even features. Hair: salt and pepper, parted in the middle, hanging down to the small of her back. Makeup: none. Jewelry: a big gold hoop in one ear.

The woman faced Jessie: "Looking for something?"

"A woman named Blue," Jessie said. "I was told I could find her here."

But Jessie already knew she'd found her: the woman had eyes of Wedgwood blue, clear and hard as porcelain.

"By who?" the woman asked.

"A man who owns a record store in Bennington."

"Not Gato?"

"Yes."

"Shit. Is he still around?" Jessie nodded. The woman gave her another look. "If you're in real estate, you're wasting your time. I'm not selling. I thought all the agents knew that."

Jessie shook her head. "My name's Jessie Shapiro. I'm not a real estate agent. I'm looking for someone and thought you might be able to help me."

"Who?"

"Pat Rodney."

"Pat Rodney?" Jessie felt the clear blue eyes probing hers. She herself could read nothing in them, although there was something familiar about Blue. She couldn't identify it. Perhaps she was simply a familiar type—earth mother—grown older and harder.

"That's right," Jessie said. "He used to live here, didn't he?"

"Did Gato tell you that?"

"No."

"Who, then?"

Jessie's mind quickly sketched in a lie involving *Rolling Stone* and communes recollected, but she abandoned it. Hadn't the truth swayed Buddy Boucher? Yes, but he had children. Jessie had seen no sign of children at Spacious Skies, few signs of life of any kind. She went with the truth anyway.

"Pat told me himself," she said. "He's my ex-husband."

Blue's mouth opened, wide enough for Jessie to see she was missing a molar. "He is?"

"Yes. He's disappeared with my daughter, Kate. Our daughter. I know he's in Vermont, and I thought he might have come here."

157

Blue quickly turned and looked down the road. It was empty. She took a deep breath. "I haven't seen him," she said. "Not in years. What do you mean he's disappeared?"

"He didn't bring Kate back from a weekend visit. And he hasn't been seen since last Friday."

The blue eyes seemed to focus on something far away. "Where is this?"

"Pat lives in Venice, California."

Blue nodded, almost imperceptibly, as though that made sense. "You came all the way from California?"

"Yes."

"What makes you think he's been here?"

Jessie told her about Buddy Boucher. Blue's eyes stopped gazing far away; they looked quickly at Jessie, then glanced off. She muttered something Jessie didn't catch.

"What?"

"Nothing." Blue looked down at her; she was slightly taller and much broader than Jessie. "He really has a kid?"

"Yes." Jessie showed her the picture; Blue barely glanced at it. Jessie saw no sign of recognition on her face.

"And you were married to him?"

"Yes. You make it sound strange."

"I do? You just don't seem his type, that's all. If you don't mind my saying so. Maybe he's changed."

"Why don't I seem his type?"

"I didn't mean anything by it. You're too . . . straight-looking, I guess."

Jessie swallowed her annoyance. Nothing would be gained by quarreling with Blue. "You're probably right. We're divorced, after all."

"A real divorce?"

"What does that mean?"

"You were really married? Officially? Or just living together?"

"Really married. It happens."

"I heard. But it doesn't sound like the man."

"Pat?"

"That's right. Pat. He wasn't the marrying kind, at least not when I knew him."

"When was that?"

A cold gust of wind blew across the meadow, whipping Blue's long hair across her face. Overhead the sky was the color of charcoal, and even darker in the east. "You might as well come in," Blue said. "If you don't mind watching me work."

Blue unlocked the door and led Jessie into the house. It wasn't much warmer inside. They walked through dusty, unlit rooms—furnished with dilapidated chairs, stained futons, shelves of bricks and boards, rickety card tables—into the kitchen at the back of the house.

Blue turned on the light over the sink, revealing a country kitchen that would never be featured in *Town and Country:* unsanded, unpolyurethaned floor; yellow walls that hadn't been painted in a generation; dirty windows overlooking the barnyard. Only the stove and refrigerator didn't fit: they were big and new.

Blue took a stainless steel bowl full of dough out of the refrigerator, mixed in a package of chocolate chips and started scooping cookie-sized blobs onto baking sheets. Her hands moved quickly, without wasted motion. Not once did she dip a finger into the dough for a taste. Jessie had never in her life baked cookies without sampling the dough.

Blue turned on the oven. "Did he . . . did Pat ever mention me?"

"No. He didn't talk much about the time he spent here."

Blue slid the baking tins onto the oven racks. "It's been a while," she said. She closed the oven door. Suddenly the implication of Blue's question hit Jessie, and she felt the full force of her fatigue. She'd spent a lot of time coping with the women in Pat's life during their marriage; she'd never thought about those who came before. She sat down at the kitchen table.

"Yeah, sit," Blue said. "Like some tea?"

"Please."

Blue boiled water, sprinkled tea leaves in mugs a little less lopsided than Gato's. Her tea, too, smelled of dandelions. Jessie didn't need dandelions. She needed caffeine, and lots of it. Still, she was grateful for its warmth; a cold draft came through the walls and found its way down her back. Blue didn't seem to notice; but she wasn't wearing a thin wool sweater from Bullocks; she had on her flannel shirt and down vest and a turtleneck underneath.

Blue opened the window by the table and flung out a handful of birdseed. The turkey squawked and ran stiff-leggedly across the yard, an intense look in its tiny eyes. Blue sat down. "Six more days of birdseed," she said.

"Six more days?"

"Till Thanksgiving. What kind of car did he buy?"

"A black van with red flames on the sides."

"Red flames?"

"Have you seen it?"

Blue shook her head. "Red flames don't sound like him."

Jessie was getting impatient with Blue's expertise on Pat's character. "Will you keep an eye out for it at least?"

Blue's mug hovered, halfway to her lips. "Sure," she said. "But why would he come here? I haven't seen him since nineteen sixty-nine."

"Because I think he's come back to look up some old friends. There was one with him when he bought the car."

"Oh? Who?"

"I was hoping you'd have some ideas."

"Sorry. Everyone's gone from those days."

"Not everyone, apparently. The car dealer saw Pat, Kate and another man."

"Another man?"

"Yes."

"What did he look like?"

"I don't have a description. The friend didn't go inside." Then she remembered that he might have.

Blue sipped her tea. She was staring at the liquid over the rim of the mug. Jessie said, "Do you have any children?"

"No."

Blue rose and took the cookies from the oven. Jessie smelled buttered almonds and chocolate, but she wasn't hungry: the tuna sandwich was stuck inside her. Blue didn't offer one, anyway, didn't try one herself. She began putting them in brown paper bags, six to a bag.

"How long did Pat live here?

"Not too long. Less than a year, I'd say."

"That's all?"

"Yeah. But he'd hung around before that."

"Where was he living?"

160

"I don't know. Here and there."

"So he must have had some friends."

"Sure. But they're gone now. The only person still around from those days is me."

"Where did they all go?"

"To flowers, everyone." Blue piled the paper bags into a wicker basket. She returned to the table, picked up her mug, but didn't sit down. "I've got to get going," she said. "Sorry I couldn't help you."

Jessie gave Blue the number at the motel in Bennington. "If he shows up, get in touch with me."

"A van with red flames."

Jessie nodded. "And he may have shaved his head. Either that or his friend has."

Tea slopped over the rim of Blue's mug. She put it down. "Why would he do that?"

"I don't know. None of this is like Pat. He's always been a bit . . . irresponsible, and he has had some trouble with drugs, but he'd never do anything disruptive to Kate. He seems to have gone off on—"

Jessie stopped talking. Someone was banging on the floor above them. "What's that?" Jessie said. She was on her feet.

"God damn him," Blue said. She smacked the wicker basket down on the table and started out of the room. Jessie went after her. Blue turned, holding up a hand to stop her. "You'll have to show yourself out," she said.

"Where are you going? Who's up there?"

"Disco."

"Disco?"

"My boarder. He's bedridden."

"There's no one else?"

"Like who?"

Jessie didn't say. Blue left the room.

Jessie stayed where she was, listening as hard as she could. She heard nothing. After a while, Blue returned. "You still here?" She picked up the wicker basket, switched off the light. "Let's go.

Jessie followed her through the cold dark house and out the door. Night. She looked up at the second story. It was dark too. "What's wrong with your boarder?"

"He got hurt in a fall."

"Is he from around here?"

"Yeah. Why?"

"Did he know Pat?"

"No. Look, I'm running late."

"Get in touch if you see him."

No answer. Just the unreadable blue look.

"Please."

"Yeah. So long."

Blue got into the pickup and waited for Jessie to back her car and turn down the road. Blue's lights followed her down the bumpy road to Route 8, left onto 9 and into Bennington. Then they swept away onto a side street. Jessie parked, sat in the car for a few minutes, then made a U-turn and headed back to the farm.

It was a dark night—no moon, no stars and no lights shining from the house. Jessie stopped beside the rusted engine block and the heap of tires and switched off the headlights. After a few moments, her eyes had adjusted to the darkness; she got out of the car and walked around to the barnyard. The cold cut through her clothing; she hugged herself as she went.

She found the kitchen. Above it was the room where the banging had come from. Its windows were dark. Jessie found the kitchen window Blue had raised to throw out the birdseed, wriggled her fingernails under the frame and pushed. The window slid open with a squeak. She stood still, listening. She heard nothing but the wind moving in the bare branches of the trees. Jessie climbed inside.

In the kitchen, darkness was complete. No amount of waiting would help: her pupils must have been fully dilated already. She should have brought a flashlight; but that would have meant a premeditated break-in, and it wasn't like that—she'd just come up to Blue's house for another look, that's all.

Jessie remained motionless, one hand on the windowsill. Without light, she would never find her way to the stairs, up them, to the back room. Time passed. Jessie felt a strange, paralyzing calm. She stood on the border—one step forward led to a country she didn't know; a land of law-breaking and looking for trouble. One step back led—where? One step back. And

162

Kate wasn't there. Jessie's hand slipped off the windowsill. She stepped into the room.

The movement destroyed the paralyzing calm. In a moment, her pulse was racing, her pores opened, the hairs on the back of her neck began to rise. Of course she'd been fooling herself about the lights: she knew the stairs were in the front hall, and she'd already been through the house twice; no need for lights. Slowly, she felt her way around the table, crossed the kitchen floor and went through the doorway.

With her weight on the balls of her feet, Jessie moved through the house. She passed one room full of shadows after another, until she saw the dim glow of night through the cracked crescent window and knew she'd reached the front hall. She put her hand on the bannister and started up the stairs. They creaked with every step.

At the top was blackness. Jessie reached out and touched a wall on either side. She was in a narrow hall. Using the walls for guidance, she followed it to the end.

Long before she got there, she smelled marijuana. The smoke was coming through the open door of the back room: a gray rectangle in the blackness. Jessie stopped at the edge and looked in. She saw night outside the windows, shadows within, and the red point of a burning cigarette in one corner.

"Pat?" she said quietly.

No answer. The red point continued to burn.

"It's me. Jessie." She spoke a little louder, but still no answer came. She knocked on the door. Silence.

Perhaps no one was in the room. Jessie tried to imagine a nonhuman agency for the marijuana smell and the red light and couldn't. She reached into the room, felt along the wall, found a light switch, pushed it up.

A naked ceiling bulb flashed on. Jessie blinked away her momentary blindness, quickly took in the room: a bed, a chest of drawers, a man in a wheelchair. Not Pat. The man was listening to a Walkman; that's why he couldn't hear her. The reason he couldn't see her was that he had no eyes: just empty sockets with eyelids sunk into the concavities. He didn't even know the light was on.

Disco. Hurt himself in a fall, Blue had said.

Jessie stood in the doorway. Disco had legs, but they were shrunken to skin and bone, and marked with long scars. She could see them very clearly because all he wore was a sweater.

Disco's head was bald on top, but a stringy fringe grew all the way to his shoulders. His nose was flattened like a boxer's; he had scars on both brows and a rough white patch of skin on one side of his face. He also had long eyelashes—soft, curled, beautiful.

Disco's fingers were stained yellow with smoke. They held a joint. He raised it to his mouth, sucked till his cheeks were hollow. His other hand tapped once or twice on his scrawny knee, then rested. Jessie's heart was beating wildly; she wanted to fly down the stairs, jump in the car, drive far away. She started to back out of the doorway, then stopped herself. Backing out wasn't the way to find Kate. She took a deep breath and pounded on the door.

Disco jerked in his wheelchair. He fumbled with the headset; the joint fell to the floor. "Blue?" he said, turning his head in the general direction of the door.

"No," Jessie replied, making her tone as gentle as she could. "I'm a friend."

Disco backed the wheelchair against the wall. "I don't know your voice." The skin on his legs was raised in goose bumps.

"I'm a friend of Blue's."

"What's your name?"

"Jessie."

"I never heard her mention you." He twisted the headset in his hands.

"We met recently."

"Where?"

"It doesn't matter. I'm looking for Pat Rodney."

"Pat Rodney?"

"Do you know him?"

"I knew him." He kept twisting the headset. "A long time ago. Before . . ."

"Before what?"

"Before I dropped acid and flew off the mountain."

There was a long silence. Tinny music came out of the earphones in Disco's lap. He switched it off.

"When was that?" Jessie said at last.

164

"When I flew? Firecracker night. The fourth of July. Nineteen seventy-two. Or maybe three."

"I meant when did you know Pat Rodney? When was the last time you saw him?"

"Before that. Everything was before that." His lip curled. It might have been a sneer, or just an involuntary twitch caused by brain damage.

"How long before?"

His face slowly straightened itself, assuming a peaceful expression. Jessie was wondering if that was due to the soothing tones she was trying to project, when he said, "I got a good buzz coming."

"That's nice," Jessie said.

Disco frowned. "I'd share, but my stash is getting low and the bitch won't . . ." His fingers twisted in his lap.

"That's all right," Jessie said. "I have a feeling Pat Rodney's been here recently. This week." Disco said nothing; he clasped his hands together to keep the fingers from twisting. "Hasn't he?" Jessie said, putting more force in her voice.

"Pat Rodney?" Disco began to rock back and forth in his wheelchair. "He's been gone for years. Didn't I say that?"

"When did you last see him?"

"When I could see." His hands felt along the arms of the wheelchair. "Where's my J?"

Jessie picked it up. "Here."

As he took it, his hand brushed his naked thigh. "God fuck," he said. "She didn't even get me dressed."

Jessie took a blanket from the bed and draped it over him. His face turned up in her direction, as though he were giving her a careful look. "Are you a cop?"

"Why would I be a cop?"

"You know. Looking for Pat Rodney."

"Why would a cop be looking for him? What's he done?"

Disco didn't answer. His fingers began twisting the headset. "You don't sound like a cop."

"I'm not a cop. I was married to Pat. Out in California. He's disappeared with our daughter. I know he's in Vermont and thought he might have come here."

Disco contemplated that; at least, he sat motionless, the joint burning in his fingers. "You were married to Pat Rodney?"

"I was."

"When was this?"

"Until five years ago."

Long silence. "What did Blue say?" Disco finally asked.

"She said he hasn't been here; but I thought she might not be telling me the truth."

"Oh yeah?" Jessie thought she heard amusement in his voice. "Why not?" he said.

"Because I got the impression she might be protecting him. They were . . . lovers once, weren't they?"

Disco said nothing for a moment. Then he laughed, a harsh, grating laugh, but she'd been wrong about the amusement—there was no humor in the sounds he made.

"What's funny?"

"Nothing. Blue's done some things in her life, but nothing as sick as that."

"What do you mean? What would be sick about that?"

Disco laughed his harsh laugh, but didn't reply. He put the joint to his lips for one last smoke, then stubbed the butt out on the wall and let it drop. "I'm thirsty," he said. There'd been fear in his voice before; now it was gone.

"Do you want me to get you something?"

"What's your name?"

"Jessie."

"You sound nice, Jessie."

"What can I get you?"

"I had a girlfriend. She went away."

"That's too bad."

"Everyone went away. Except me and Blue."

"Where did they go?"

"Who knows?"

"Where did Pat Rodney go?"

"Don't ask me."

"When was the last time you saw him?"

"When I could see."

"That joke wasn't funny the first time," Jessie said before she could stop herself.

"You think it's a fucking joke?" Disco's voice cracked. He made ragged crying sounds in his throat, but no tears came. Jessie saw a bottle of Coke by the bed. She opened it and put

it in his hand. Abruptly, he stopped crying—it was more like a
trailer for crying than a feature-length presentation—and drank.
His teeth were brown and rotting. "I hate when she leaves me
alone," he said.

"Did Pat come here when you were alone?"

"No. Why do you keep saying that? I told you I haven't
seen him. I haven't seen him. I haven't seen him. Now do you
get it? I haven't seen him." He lowered his voice. "It's the truth.
Not since Woodstock."

"Woodstock?"

"Yeah."

What have you heard about Woodstock?

"Do you mean the festival?" Jessie said.

"What else?" Disco drank more Coke, then pulled the blanket closer around him. "The fucking festival."

"Why do you say that?"

"It was the end. My friend."

"The end of what?"

"Everything. The commune, for starters."

"Why?"

Disco shrugged. The movement pained him. He winced.

"How was it the end of the commune?"

"Everyone went away."

"Pat Rodney?"

"Him and all the musicians."

"What musicians?"

"They had a band. They were fucking good. Hendrix jammed
with them in the woods."

"Jimi Hendrix?"

"The one and only."

"Who was in the band?"

"Lots of dudes. It kept changing. But it was mainly him
and Hartley Frame. The two-guitar sound. Like the Stones, you
know?"

"Hartley Frame?" said Jessie.

"Pat's buddy from up at the college."

"What college are you talking about?"

"Morgan. It's the only college around here. Just across the
state line."

Jessie had heard of it: a small liberal arts school with a

167

stuffy tradition and a two-hundred-year-old endowment. "Is it in a town called Morgan?"

"Morgantown. Mass. Not far."

"Is Hartley Frame still around?"

Disco didn't answer right away. When he finally spoke, his voice was much quieter. "No one's still around."

"Where did he go?"

"Everybody split. Or aren't you listening?"

"Why?"

"Why, why, why. Fuck." His hand closed tightly around the Coke bottle. "You're way off base. And you're starting to bug me. How did you get into the house, anyway?"

"The door was open. I thought Blue was inside."

"How do you know her, again?"

"She's helping me find Pat."

Disco's head tilted to one side, as though he were trying to see things from a different angle. "What are you paying her?"

"Why should I pay her?"

"Huh? Are you stupid or what?"

"What do you mean?" Disco didn't answer. Jessie went close to him, touched his hand. It was hard and cold. "Disco?"

He drew away. "How do you know my name?"

"Blue told me."

"She's got a big mouth, all of a sudden. Did she tell you about my flight?"

"Your flight?"

"Nonstop to oblivion."

"She said you hurt yourself in a fall, nothing more."

"Nothing more. Yeah."

She touched him again. "I think you know something you're not telling me. You have nothing to be afraid of. If you tell me Pat's been here, I promise you I won't tell Blue. I just want my daughter back, that's all." A horrid thought struck her: What if Blue wanted children, but couldn't have them for some reason? She pictured her family reforming without her.

Again Disco drew his hand away. "What are you talking about? How could he be here?"

"I told you—he's in Vermont. He was in Bennington on Monday."

"And I told you—you're way off base."

168

"How?"

Disco began to laugh his grating laugh. It went on and on, pitching itself higher and higher and finally out of hearing. "Are you loaded?"

"Loaded?"

"Do you have lots of bread?"

"No. Why?"

"Then you're as fucked as the rest of them."

"Who do you mean?"

He laughed again, rocking back and forth as the sound rose; a tic quivered in one of his eyelids. Then it was quiet. Disco said, "I've got a nice buzz on now. And you're bugging me." His hands found the Walkman, put on the headset. He turned up the volume until Jessie could hear it: heavy metal music played by a thimble-sized band.

Jessie rose.

"And turn out the lights," Disco said.

Jessie turned out the lights, walked down the stairs, through the front door. She drove across the state line, booked a room at the first motel she saw and flopped on the bed. Her eyes closed immediately. Some time later, she awoke and hurried to the bathroom, where she vomited the remains of the tuna sandwich.

After that Jessie couldn't get back to sleep. Every time she tried, her mind filled with images of eyelids plastered to eyeless sockets; eyelids with long, soft lashes, curled and beautiful. She knew that if she slept she would dream, and if she dreamed, those eyeless eyes would turn into Kate's.

19

The dark-haired woman knelt on the baggage room floor and started rummaging through her suitcase. Ivan Zyzmchuk watched from a distance. There wasn't much in the suitcase—a pair of shoes, some clothing, a book, an envelope. The woman closed the suitcase and hurried away. Ivan Zyzmchuk watched until she was out of sight.

He was very good at guessing people's occupations from their appearance: for example, the two women in business dress, moving toward the carousel, were housewives—too much jewelry and too relaxed to be in the working world; and the man in the windbreaker by the exit was a cop—a cop who didn't know how to watch without appearing watchful or how to buy a big enough windbreaker to conceal the gun in his armpit. But despite all the data Zyzmchuk had on the dark-haired woman—her LAX luggage tag, the old, expensive suitcase, what he'd seen inside it—he had no idea what she did in life. All he knew was that she was very worried, beyond the stage of being able to hide it in public. He wondered for a moment if she was sane. Then Alice Frame came down the escalator in a long mink coat, and Zyzmchuk stopped thinking about the dark-haired woman.

Alice Frame looked worried herself, but to a much lesser degree. Glancing at the other Washington passengers, Zyzmchuk saw they were all worried. Air travel induced it. More than that, it was structured on worries, the way a Shakespearean play had five acts: delays, overbooking, security checks, stacking up, crashing; now, in the finale, the passengers worried whether their bags would appear.

Alice Frame didn't have to worry alone. She hadn't quite reached the carousel when a limousine pulled up outside the door. A man in a gray suit and matching cap got out and hurried inside. Alice saw him and raised her gloved hand in the kind of gesture that gets a waiter's attention. Together they turned to the carousel, now spinning the bags around. Alice's job was to point. The man's job was to grab her tapestry suitcases and place them in a neat row. When he'd collected all four of them, Alice started for the exit. Picking up the suitcases, the man followed.

The plainclothesman's eyes followed her too. Zyzmchuk didn't blame him. She was a handsome woman and rich enough to afford mink, limousines, chauffeurs and a face ten years younger than she was.

Zyzmchuk went outside. Alice was already in the backseat; the chauffeur was getting into the front. The Blazer was parked a few places behind, lowering the tone. A uniformed cop was there to uphold standards; he was frowning at Zyzmchuk's license plate and taking out his ticket book. Zyzmchuk went past him and got in. The cop put his hand on the roof. "Can't you read, pal?" he said, nodding at the NO PARKING sign.

"Braille only," Zyzmchuk replied. He started the car. The cop moved his lips, but still hadn't formulated a reply when Zyzmchuk drove off. Zyzmchuk sympathized with cops, but it wasn't the moment for a long discussion.

He stayed close to the limousine through the tunnel, onto the expressway, south to the turnpike exit. On the turnpike he slipped four or five cars back, and sometimes, between exits, six or more. It didn't matter. Even the rawest amateur was incapable of losing a car like that. Zyzmchuk settled back for the ride.

For a while he watched the scenery go by: brown, bare, in the yawning stage of dormancy. Then he switched on the radio and heard easy listening and hard listening, but no good listening. He tried some coffee from his Thermos. Finally he let himself look down at the odometer. He'd only gone twenty miles.

Zyzmchuk picked up his phone. A lot of people left the office early on Friday, but not Grace. She didn't have a family, and she liked her job. He called her number. He had a question for her computer. He also felt like talking to someone.

Grace answered on the first ring. "Mr. Z.?"

"How did you guess?"

"You're the only one with an engine that needs a tune-up. Mr. K.'s engine purrs, and Mr. D. never uses his car phone."

"Why not?"

"He likes to keep both hands on the wheel."

"Natch."

" 'Natch,' Mr. Z.?"

"Before your time." The limousine topped the crest of a hill and dipped out of sight. Zyzmchuk pressed the accelerator. "Can you find the owner of Mass. plate JTA 395?"

"Momentito," Grace said. Something crunched; it might have been Almond Roca. Keys tapped. "That number's registered to Morgan College, Morgantown, Mass."

"Any human names?"

"Signed for by, you mean?"

"That kind of thing."

Tap, tap. "Dr. Jameson T. Phinney. That's pee aitch. College president."

"Thanks."

"Welcs."

Zyzmchuk put down his phone. For a few miles, he tried to imagine what it would be like to live with Grace. He decided theirs resembled a lot of office relationships: the opposite of an iceberg, it was nine-tenths above the surface. That's why they usually led nowhere. Then he began to think about relationships that led somewhere; that took him, like a car hitting an ice patch, to Leni; and Grace faded away.

As the road rose into the Berkshires, the towns grow less industrial and more picture-perfect. Above an unmarked frontier, they had no visible means of support at all; except for the dark gray sky, he might have been driving in a postcard.

Morgantown had the same prosperous appearance, but differed by revealing the reason for it: dormitories, libraries, office and classroom buildings, a museum, an observatory—all made from the best brick and stone, all with the good taste to seem smaller than they were—playing fields, gym, ice arena. Morgantown, Zyzmchuk saw, was in the college business. That meant *Spellbound* and *Vertigo* playing at the cinema on Main Street, with *Animal House* and *Animal Farm* to follow. It meant a weekend keg special at the package store and clothing store mannequins dressed like Mr. K. and Mr. D. at a cocktail party. It meant young men and young women crossing airy quadrangles, dressed like Mr. K. and Mr. D. on a country weekend. They had determined faces and good haircuts and were on their way to places that were already charted. The college business, upscale division.

The limousine turned onto a quiet street and stopped in front of a big white house set well back from the road. Mercedes, Jaguars and Volvos lined the long lane. Zyzmchuk drove past and parked at the corner under a big, leafless maple that offered the illusion of cover. In the rearview mirror, he saw the chauffeur help Alice Frame out of the car, remove the tapestry suitcases from the trunk and accompany her to the front door. The door opened when they were halfway up the walk. A man stepped out. He was tall and thin, with a full head of dark hair, graying at the sides in soap opera baron style. He took Alice Frame's hand in both of his and shook it warmly. Then he led her into the house. The chauffeur followed. Before the door closed, Zyzmchuk glimpsed a long-haired woman with a violin and a man carrying a tray of champagne glasses.

Zyzmchuk sat. The north wind blew a low ceiling across the sky, gray clouds sagging with moisture. Zyzmchuk poured more coffee; it had grown cold and bitter. He drank it anyway. This was what he liked to do, wasn't it? Hadn't he fought with Keith and Dahlin to let him keep doing it? This was supposed to be fun. But sitting in this spruced-up Arcadia waiting for charm-school innocents to finish their champagne wasn't fun: it was a parody of what he liked to do, and he didn't want to be a figure in a parody.

He screwed the top on the Thermos and drove to Main Street. In the Morgantown Book Store he bought the *Morgan College Guidebook* and went into COL. MORGAN'S BAR AND GRILLE, BASS ALE ON TAP to read it.

The guide opened with a friendly forward from the president, Jameson Tucker Phinney. Pee aitch. All his names were surnames, Zyzmchuk noticed. In two hundred years, Americans still hadn't learned to feel comfortable without a titled class. That failure was responsible for their nervous energy, Neil Armstrong's walk on the moon, the behavior of headwaiters in Manhattan.

And names like Jameson Tucker Phinney. A photograph of Mr. Phinney's smiling face appeared beside his signature: a handsome face that wouldn't have looked out of place in *Gentleman's Quarterly* or a summer-stock production of *My Fair Lady*. It was also the face of the man who had taken Alice Frame's hand in both of his and greeted her so warmly.

Zyzmchuk drank a bottle of beer and a glass of whiskey and returned to the big white house, parking under the maple at the corner. He read the guide from cover to cover, learning that tuition, room and board came to $16,600 a year; three-quarters of the senior class went on to graduate school; and the football team had gone two and nine the year before. He was memorizing a map of the town when the door opened and pink-faced people began coming out, head bobbing, mouths thanking, arms waving. They got into their Mercedes, Jaguars and Volvos and politely yielding the way to each other while laughing at the absurdity of it all—maneuvering automobiles, drinking champagne all afternoon, having their cake and eating it too—soon emptied the lane. A few minutes later, the chauffeur came out. He tossed his cap onto the seat of the limousine and accelerated away.

Time passed. Evening slid across the sky like a dark filter. Then the garage door opened and an ordinary little car backed out, square, dark, Everyman's, if Everyman was Japanese. It turned onto the street and drove past the spot where Zyzmchuk was parked. Jameson T. Phinney was driving; Alice Frame sat beside him. Zyzmchuk followed. They didn't look back.

The little car drove for only a few hundred yards before

stopping in front of a massive stone building with a spotlighted cornice. Zyzmchuk made a U-turn and waited on the other side of the street.

The cornice was the kind where names were carved to set an example for others: in this case, Bach, Handel, Haydn, Mozart and a few more on the far end, which Zyzmchuk would have needed his glasses to read. Phinney and Alice got out of the car and walked onto the lawn in front of the building.

A large shape stood on the lawn, twice as high as a man and draped with a heavy tarpaulin. Phinney raised one side, holding it over his head so Alice could step under and look. Zyzmchuk tried to look too, but could see nothing in the dying light.

Alice stepped back. Phinney lowered the tarpaulin. They spoke for a few moments, but Zyzmchuk was too far away to distinguish the words. Then they got in the car and drove away.

They didn't return to the big white house. Instead they headed south, out of town. They passed a prosperous-looking motel, the 1826 House, that advertised a buffet dinner and rooms with fireplaces. Zyzmchuk almost stopped, and might have, had Phinney not turned onto a side road. Zyzmchuk drove after him.

The road was narrow and soon began to climb—the road to Mount Blackstone, Zyzmchuk remembered: unbidden, the map drew itself in his mind. The lights of the little car flashed on. Zyzmchuk kept his off.

The road twisted up the mountain. The air grew colder, the wind stronger. Phinney, a law-abider, signaled a right turn to nobody that he knew of and entered a gravel lane. Zyzmchuk stopped. The little car disappeared in the woods. Zyzmchuk switched off his engine and rolled down the window. After a minute or two, he heard a car door close. Without turning on the engine, Zyzmchuk shifted into neutral and backed down the hill until he came to a clearing by the road. He steered onto it and parked the car.

Late evening: the sky would soon be fully dark; no moonlight or starlight could penetrate the thick black-purple cloud Zyzmchuk saw as he got out of the car. The arrival of darkness did something that coffee, beer and whiskey had failed to do—it woke him up. He felt his senses sharpening; listening to the quiet— no birdsong, no rustle of animals, nothing but the wind in the bare trees—he realized it was not merely an absence of sound, but an invitation to it, opening up infinite possibility, like a keyboard to a pianist. That's what made quiet exciting, especially at night. Zyzmchuk just wished he had something more promising to do.

Without making a sound, he opened the back of the Blazer. He put a heavy wool sweater on over his sweatshirt and a black waterproof jacket over that. Then, taking his toolbox, he walked up the lane, keeping to the grass verge that bordered the gravel. The only sound was the wind in the trees.

Zyzmchuk smelled wood smoke. Then he rounded a corner and saw a light glowing in the distance. He stopped behind a tree and gazed in its direction. He saw the dark, square shadow of a cabin, yellow light in its windows, sparks sailing from a chimney into the night. Everything else was indistinct. His vision wasn't what it had been; there were no push-ups he could do for that. Once he'd been able to tell the color of a man's eyes at fifty feet.

Staying in the trees, Zyzmchuk made his way toward the cabin. Open lawns sloped up to it from the front and sides, but at the back, against the mountain, it almost touched the forest. Zyzmchuk circled the cabin. He stopped every minute or two to listen and didn't hurry. Finally, he reached a squat cedar directly behind the house. Ten feet of open ground lay between him and the nearest window. Leaving his toolbox by the tree, he got down on the ground and crawled.

The grass felt cold, the earth hard. Music leaked into the night: Sarah Vaughan. Now he had the divine Sarah to go with the wind in the trees. Two forces of nature. Smiling, Zyzmchuk placed his hands on the windowsill and slowly raised his head.

Alice Frame and Jameson T. Phinney sat on a thick red Persian rug before a roaring fire. She was dressed for après-ski at Gstaad or Megève. He wore cashmere and tweed. They were eating pâté and drinking Burgundy: Zyzmchuk could tell from the shape of the bottle. A wicker hamper lay between them. Alice's manicured hand reached in and pulled out a bunch of grapes. She plucked one and held it up. Phinney opened his mouth. He had little white teeth and a little red tongue. Alice tossed the grape in the air. Phinney caught it like a good little seal. They laughed—a third sound, to go with Sarah Vaughan and the wind. Zyzmchuk was reminded of D. H. Lawrence, Scott Fitzgerald, or one of that crowd. He wasn't reminded of Mata Hari or one of hers.

A cold raindrop landed on the back of his neck. Then another. Zyzmchuk crept back to the cedar tree and sat under its branches. The sky made a whispering sound, a whisper of the insistent kind. Rain fell. The wind drove it at an angle, lashing the ground all around him. He tucked his knees under his chin to keep his whole body in the shelter of the cedar tree. But at last the rain penetrated it, too, dripping off the branches and onto him. First wet, then cold; he thought about whiskey in pint bottles. He thought about it with such concentration that some time passed before he realized that Sarah Vaughan had stopped singing.

Zyzmchuk slid out from under the tree and stood up. Lights no longer glowed from the house; he was about to move around to the front to check on Phinney's car, when he heard a faint sound from above.

There was a big window on the second floor of the cabin. Zyzmchuk could see nothing through it. He opened his toolbox and took out an extendable steel pole, painted black. He screwed a little round receiver-transmitter onto its end and approached the house. Sticking the base of the pole into the ground, he pulled out the extension until the bug reached the height of the window. Slowly he tilted the pole forward until the bug touched the glass. Then he sat down under the tree, pressed the record button on his tape machine, donned earphones and listened.

First he heard rain striking glass. It sounded like a percussion instrument, halfway between a snare drum and cymbals. Then a woman moaned. "Oh, God," she said. "Jamie. Oh God."

A man moaned too, deeper and throatier. "Jesus. Jesus Christ. It's so . . ."

Perhaps, being cultured people, they recognized the lack of original things to say. In any case, they stopped talking. Instead, they made moans together, intensified them, climaxed them. Then there was just the percussion of the rain on the window.

A sigh.

"When is Maggie coming back?" asked Alice Frame. She sounded wide awake.

"Tomorrow night," Phinney answered, sounding sleepy.

177

Rain on the window. Rain dripping through the cedar tree, under the neck of Zyzmchuk's waterproof jacket, soaking through his sweater, his sweatsuit and down to his skin: God's punishment, he thought, for a professional voyeur, or auditeur, this time.

Alice blew out a long, slow breath. "God, he's a shit," she said.

Zyzmchuk turned up the volume. That made the percussion louder.

"It must have been awful," Phinney said.

"You don't know the half of it."

Phinney cleared his throat, perhaps in an effort to expel his sleepiness, or just to speak words he didn't want to. "Tell me."

"I don't want to talk about it." Pause. "But I've never felt so humiliated in my whole life." Her voice broke on the word "humiliated."

"Don't cry."

"Sorry."

"Don't be sorry. Cry if you want. Don't be sad, that's all I meant."

Alice stopped crying. "He's such a shit. He's not even coming for the unveiling. His staff couldn't get the *Times* or the *Post* interested enough to send photographers."

Phinney said nothing. Rain played its music on the window. "Is there any wine left?" Alice asked.

"Here."

Zyzmchuk heard her sip. He had good equipment in his toolbox.

"When is Maggie coming back?"

"I already told you."

"Sorry."

"Tomorrow night."

Sip. Time passed. Sip.

"Come closer," Alice said.

Bedding rustled. "I can try," Phinney said.

"That's all I ask. I . . . need you, Jamie. But I'm not supposed to say that, am I?"

There was no reply.

They moaned together, low and passionate. Zyzmchuk took off his earphones. He didn't want to hear their lovemaking, not without a good reason. And the reason was gone, the investigation finished. He knew the cause of Alice Frame's behavior at the lie-detector test, and it had nothing to do with the spy game. It had to do with the adultery game. So he continued to record the sounds in the cabin on Mount Blackstone—Keith could listen to the whole tape if he wanted—but he didn't listen himself. Instead he tried to think of some way to force them to keep their promise. The investigation had been so easy, the results so trite, he couldn't imagine them not trying to wriggle out of the agreement. He thought of all the ways they might try. He thought of all the ways he might counter. He ended up thinking about the job market.

At first light, Zyzmchuk rose, stretched his damp body, packed his toolbox and walked to his car. He drove down Mount Blackstone, out of the rain and into drizzle. He'd planned to drive home, but passing the 1826 House, he saw again the sign advertising rooms with fireplaces. And showers too, he thought. Comfort and rest. Why not? It was Saturday morning.

Zyzmchuk drove up to the office, thinking about warm showers and glasses of whiskey in front of a fire. The office door opened. A woman came out. Zyzmchuk, with one foot already on the pavement, drew it back into the car and closed the door.

The dark-haired woman.

He pulled out of the parking lot before she could see him. Then he drove a few hundred yards down the road and stopped at the Morgan Inn. The Morgan Inn advertised rooms with fireplaces too, but that wasn't why he booked one. The room was booked—chintz and maple, too-soft mattress, no fireplace, they were all taken—because Ivan Zyzmchuk was paid not to believe in coincidences, and he liked to earn his money.

20

A man, or maybe a boy, said, "It's supposed to be fun."

A woman, or maybe a girl, said, "Not when you treat me like this."

"Like what?" he said.

"Like last night," she said.

"Like what last night?"

"Precisely."

"God, it's true what they say."

"What who says?"

"Your roommates—that you're a bore."

No reply. A door closed. Jessie opened her eyes. Gray light leaked in through a gap in floral curtains. She took in the outlines of her room: desk, television, fireplace, the double bed she lay in. She got out of it and looked through the curtains.

A young man was walking away, across the parking lot. He

had his head tucked down into the turned-up collar of a jacket that said MORGAN on the back, tucked down against the drizzle or because he craved anonymity. The next moment a young woman went quickly by Jessie's window. She was the kind of woman who might one day realize how beautiful she was, but hadn't yet. And it wouldn't be today: her eyes were puffy from crying and she needed sleep. The woman got in a car with a Vassar decal and sped away. Jessie remembered carefree college weekends just like that, but at Stanford they'd had the sunshine to make it all less depressing.

She went to her suitcase, put on the last of the fresh clothing. She'd packed for a day or two. Saturday. Day two. All she had to show for her trip was a broken barrette with a few strands of frizzy hair caught in it. She picked up the phone and called Dick Carr's home number.

"Jesus," he said. "It's the middle of the night."

"Sorry, I forgot."

"You forgot?"

"I'm in Vermont. Or Massachusetts, I guess."

"You guess? I've been trying to get in touch with you for two days."

Jessie held the phone in both hands. "Have they found Kate?"

"No, no, nothing like that," he said, almost impatient. "And nothing new on the hit-and-run. It's about Barbara's will. You were supposed to stop by the office. I'm trying to wrap it up in the next few days."

"I don't know when I'll be back," Jessie said, hearing the edge in her tone and doing nothing about it. "Kate's somewhere around here. Or she was on Monday. They both were."

He paused, and when he spoke again his voice was gentler. "How do you know?"

"They were seen."

"Does that mean DeMarco was right? He's off on a toot?"

"I think so," Jessie said. "What did you want to see me about?"

"Signing some papers."

"Why?"

"Barbara left you her ring."

181

"The Amelia Earhart one?"

"Yes."

"Sell it. And send me the money."

"I don't like to do that."

"Me either. But I need the money."

Silence. Then Dick Carr sighed. "I'll advance you some from the firm. We can formalize arrangements when you get back."

"Okay."

"Five hundred all right?"

"Thanks," Jessie said.

"Where are you?"

Jessie opened the desk drawer and found the stationery. "1826 House." She read him the address and hung up. She didn't want to wear Amelia Earhart's ring—Barbara's maybe, but not Amelia Earhart's.

Jessie dressed—the jeans, blue sweater, suede jacket—and went into the office. She got a map of the town and paid for two nights. That left seventy-eight dollars in her wallet. She was worrying about that as she went outside. A big rusty jeep shot out of the parking lot. Jessie got into her own car and drove to the campus.

The Morgan campus was the kind that came to mind when someone said "college." It had broad lawns, green even in November; ancient spreading trees; and impressive buildings—Georgian, Greek Revival, Federal, Colonial. Harold Lloyd could have walked out of any door.

Jessie hadn't expected to find the Alumni Affairs Building open; she only wanted to find it so she could be there first thing Monday morning. But the Alumni Affairs Building—a trim white house with skylights and flowering plants in the windows—had smoke rising from its chimney. Jessie knocked on the door.

"It's open," called a man inside.

Jessie went in, through a front hall with lacrosse sticks hanging on the wall, and into an office. A man sat behind a monitor, one hand hovering over a keyboard, telephone receiver wedged between shoulder and chin. He pointed Jessie to a chair. "There is no suggested figure, Tad," he was saying. "This isn't Harvard. It has to come from the heart." Tad said something; Jessie could hear his tiny voice but couldn't make out the words.

Whatever it was made the man behind the monitor laugh. He screwed up his face and twinkled his eyes as though Tad could see him. At the same time, his fingers tapped at the keyboard. Words appeared on the screen: "Addison T. Wheeler, Jr.—$1,000." "Really nice talking to you, Tad. Don't be a stranger." The man pressed a button on the phone, opening another line; he didn't waste time by putting the receiver down.

He swiveled around to Jessie. "Can I help you?"

"I hope so," Jessie said. "I'm trying to find the present address of one of your alumni."

"You've come to the right place," the man said. "What's your connection to the college?"

"None, really. It's my . . . husband. I think he's visiting the alumnus I'm looking for. I'd like to find the address."

The last twinkle of merriment left over from his conversation with Tad faded from the man's eyes. "Is your husband an alumnus too?"

"No."

"I see."

"But it's important."

"I don't doubt that. But we can't just give out alumni information to anyone who asks for it. School policy. I'm afraid you'll have to apply in writing."

"Apply to whom?"

"To this office." He held out a card: Curt Beringer, Alumni Affairs.

Jessie got off her chair and approached him. "Please listen to me, Mr. Beringer." She said it again, leaving out the please. "I've come all the way from Los Angeles. I've got a ten-year-old daughter. She's a week overdue from a visit with her father. I know they're in the area, and I'm pretty sure they're with a friend of his from this school. I need your help."

Curt Beringer listened. His eyes didn't leave her face. But the expression in them didn't soften as she spoke; it became quizzical instead and a little put-off, as though she'd raised the curtain on something distasteful.

"You're divorced?" he said.

"What does that have to do with it?" Her voice rose despite her efforts to keep it even.

"This sounds more like a police matter to me," Curt Beringer said. "Of course, if you've got authorization from them, it's a different story."

"I don't. But—"

"Then I'm very sorry." Beringer turned to the monitor. He touched the ENTER key. "Name?" asked the screen. Beringer checked a list. "Wallis," he typed. "Newton E." The disk drive spun. Beringer dialed the phone as information on Newton E. Wallis lit the screen. "Newt?" said Beringer. "Hey, how are you. Curt Beringer up at Morgan. Fine, fine. Still whalin' that killer forehand? Ha ha. Say, I'm calling on behalf of the Field House Fund. . . . You haven't heard of the Field House Fund? Oh boy. Listen, Newt—"

Curt Beringer glanced up and frowned at Jessie. That look made her want to hit him; instead she felt tears welling in her eyes. Before Curt Beringer noticed, she hurried out of the Alumni Affairs Building and started to cry. Then the image of the young woman from Vassar sprang into her mind; that stopped her. She didn't have time for tears. This wasn't a bad date.

Jessie began walking, with no destination in mind. Morgan College had a human scale. Even under a gray, drizzling sky it calmed her. Think, she told herself. She was letting anxiety grow wildly insider her for no good reason. Look at the facts. She was close to finding Kate, much closer than she'd been in California. And if Buddy Boucher could be believed, nothing like kidnapping had happened. Kate was with her father, and they were in the company of an old friend, possibly Hartley Frame. That meant she still needed Hartley Frame's address. Curt Beringer mentioned police authorization. Fine. Instead of losing her self-control, she should have played by his rules: simply picked up the phone and called Lieutenant DeMarco. Jessie started back toward the Alumni Affairs Building. She was running by the time she got there.

Jessie knocked on the door. No answer. She turned the knob. The door opened. Jessie went through the front hall and into the office, expecting to find Curt Beringer at his desk. But he wasn't there. "Hello?" she called. "Hello?" No answer. Jessie poked her head around a corner and saw a corridor leading to a door at the back of the house. "Mr. Beringer?" she called down it. Silence.

She'd have to come back later; turning, Jessie was about to leave the room when she saw Beringer had left his monitor on. "Kinsley," it said. "Forrest J. Class of '56." Jessie went closer. Her hand moved toward the keyboard, a normal keyboard, with an ENTER key on the right side. She glanced once around the room. Then she lowered her index finger onto the ENTER key and pressed.

"Kinsley, Forrest J." vanished from the screen. "Name?" it asked.

"Frame," Jessie typed. "Hartley." ENTER.

Words scrolled down the screen. "Frame, Hartley E. Class of '69. Father: Edmund S. Frame. Class of '43. U.S. Senator, Virginia. Mother: Alice (Sangster). Faculty advisor: Prof. M. R. McTaggart, Dept. of Music. Academic Record: SAT: Verbal-670. Math-640. Achievement Tests—"

A foot crunched on the walk outside. Jessie's hand jerked away from the keyboard. She heard the front door open. Now was the moment to assert her self-control. It was embarrassing, that's all—she hadn't committed a sin. Just tell Mr. Beringer exactly what happened; he'll understand.

Then the door closed and a board creaked in the front hall, as if under a heavy weight. The sound made Jessie bolt across the room, down the corridor and out the back. She didn't stop running until she came to a small quadrangle with a statue of a judgmental-looking man in the center. Colonel Morgan, said big letters carved on the base. Jessie turned. A woman with an armful of books was walking the other way. An Irish setter was chasing a bouncing ball. No one followed her.

Jessie returned to the 1826 House. Step one: completed— not smoothly, or even with dignity, but done just the same.

Step two: Jessie picked up the phone and called information in Washington. Information gave her Senator Edmund Frame's office number. Jessie wrote it down. She looked at the number for a while. She'd never called a U.S. senator before. But it was the next step. Jessie dialed the number.

A man answered immediately. "Yes?" he said. Saturday, but he still sounded pressed for time.

Jessie felt the pressure. It made her condense what she had to say and bend the facts a little. "Hello. I'm an old friend of Senator Frame's son Hartley. I wonder if you could tell me how to get in touch with him."

"The senator?"

"No. Hartley."

There was a pause. Then the man said, "If that's supposed to be a joke, it's not a very funny one."

Click.

21

"Boucher's Dodge and Dodge Trucks. Buddy here."

"It's Jessie Shapiro, Mr. Boucher."

"Who?"

"Jessie Rodney."

"Oh yes, Mrs. Rodney."

"I wondered—"

"Sorry. Nothing new."

"He hasn't been back yet?"

"Nope. And nothing on the BMW, neither."

Jessie gave him her number at the 1826 House and hung up. Then she lay on the bed, pulled the spread over her body and closed her eyes. She wanted sleep, not because she was tired, which she was, but because she had to get away. After only a few moments, she knew that sleep wouldn't come. The powerful inertia that had seized her body had no control over her mind. Broken images reeled in it: Reeboks with blue stripes, wraparound sunglasses, curling eyelashes, graying ponytails. She opened her eyes. *Help me*, she thought. She almost said it aloud.

But there was no one to help. Barbara was dead. Philip wouldn't help, even if he could, which she doubted. Philip was the wrong type. DeMarco was the right type—tough, a man of action—but he lacked the imagination to share her fears; he had just enough to doubt her.

Jessie gave in to temptation. She opened her wallet and took out the picture of Kate making a silly face at the beach. It had been taken at the class picnic. They'd played Botticelli— Kate had stumped everyone with Yosemite Sam. Jessie looked at the photograph until it stopped making sense. Then she looked at it some more.

Jessie got off the bed. She opened the phone book and found a listing for McTaggart, M. R. She stared at the name until the letters lost their symbolic meaning and reverted to the mysterious shapes illiterates see. *Go on*, she had to tell herself. *As long as there's another step to take, take it*. She dialed the number.

"Yes?" answered a man on the other end. He sounded impatient. A piano played in the background.

"Professor McTaggart?"

"What?" The piano playing stopped. "Keep playing, keep playing," McTaggart shouted, his voice partly muffled. The piano playing resumed. "No, no, from the third bar." It sounded like Bach, maybe not played very well. McTaggart might have been thinking on parallel lines. He groaned, then said, "Yes, what is it?"

"I'm sorry to interrupt," Jessie said, "but it's important. I'm looking for information about someone who was a Morgan student in the sixties. You were his faculty advisor, and I thought you might be able to help."

"Oh for God's sake," McTaggart said. "Who?"

"Hartley Frame." McTaggart said nothing, so Jessie added, "He was in the class of 'sixty-nine."

Jessie heard nothing but the piano, tinny as a child's toy instrument. Finally McTaggart spoke: "You've got the wrong number."

"But—"

"You want my ex-wife. Good-bye." He broke the connection.

"God damn it," Jessie said. The next moment she hurled the phone across the room. It hit the wall with a ringing sound and fell to the floor. Jessie lay on the bed and buried her face in the pillow. She'd never done anything like that in her life, and people who did disgusted her.

But nothing she tried brought results. Each logical step led to something grotesque. Putting up posters led to Mr. Mickey and the bag lady. Tracing Pat's friend led to unpleasant, incomprehensible phone calls. None of it brought her any closer to Kate.

Kate had been in Bennington on Monday. Fact. Pat had told Buddy Boucher he would return for the BMW. Fact. But Buddy Boucher hadn't seen Pat, and the BMW was gone. Facts three and four. What was logical now? To return to Bennington and wait? To go home? To keep trying to find Pat's friend?

None of the choices seemed especially logical. But only the third meant doing something. She couldn't just sit and wait: that she'd known from the start.

Jessie reopened the phone book and again found McTaggart, M. R. The next listing, and the only other McTaggart, was Erica, 15 Mariposa. Jessie didn't dial the number. Phone calls about Hartley Frame didn't work; perhaps a personal visit would. She went into the motel office, got directions, and drove.

Mariposa Street was a little cul-de-sac that ended at a marsh. The clapboard houses were small and rundown; they might have been cottages at one time. Number 15 was the last one. It had a narrow lawn at the front and along one side, covered with a thick mass of soggy leaves. The other side—a tangle of undergrowth and stiff yellow bullrushes—marked the edge of the marsh. The drizzle had almost stopped; it hung in the air now, wetting Jessie's face as she walked to the door and knocked.

Footsteps approached on the other side. The door opened. A dark, wiry woman stood in the doorway. She wore paint-stained jeans, a torn black T-shirt and a silver and turquoise Navajo pendant; she carried a palette on which glistened a single blob of oily red. "Yes?" said the woman; her voice sounded thick and scratchy, as though she hadn't spoken for some time.

"Mrs. McTaggart?" Jessie said.

The woman nodded. She hadn't let go of the door.

"I'm looking for a former student of the college. I was told you might be able to help me."

"By whom?"

"Mr. McTaggart."

"Doctor, please. Don't let's forget Ross's precious Ph.D. That's where the oh-so-generous alimony comes from, as he'd be the first to tell you."

The bitterness spilled out so quickly and unexpectedly that Jessie could think of nothing to say. Mrs. McTaggart watched her; she had alert eyes, surrounded by smears of black makeup that might have been left over from the day before, and topped by eyebrows that had been almost tweezed away. "When did you see the lovely man?"

"I didn't actually see him. We spoke on the phone."

"Oh," she said, her tone less sharp; perhaps Jessie, having only spoken to McTaggart on the phone, was free of contamination. What's the name of the student? I haven't been connected with the college for five years, by the way. Didn't he mention that?"

"This student was here before that," Jessie said. "He was a member of the class of 'sixty-nine." Mrs. McTaggart's eyes began to narrow. "His name is Hartley Frame."

Mrs. McTaggart's eyes narrowed a little more. Red patches rose to the surface of her pale cheeks. "Whose joke is this? Yours or his?"

Jessie's voice rose, abruptly and angrily. "Why does everyone keep saying that? Every time I mention I'm looking for Hartley Frame I'm told I must be joking. Why?"

Mrs. McTaggart's voice rose too. "Because Hartley Frame is dead."

Suddenly Jessie felt very weak and very tall, far too high above the ground. "Dead?" she repeated. Her voice sounded disembodied.

"Yes," said Mrs. McTaggart. "He died in Viet Nam."

Jessie took a deep breath. "I—I'm sorry," she said, backing away. She stumbled, regained her balance. "I didn't mean to trouble you."

"If you really didn't know it's no trouble. Didn't the professor tell you?"

"No."

"The prick." Mrs. McTaggart said. Then she gave Jessie a sharp look. "Are you all right? You don't look well."

"I'm fine," Jessie said. But she was too tall, and her voice was coming from somewhere else.

Mrs. McTaggart made a clicking sound of disapproval. "You'd better come in and sit down," she said.

"That's not ne—"

Mrs. McTaggart took Jessie's hand and led her into the house. Fleetingly Jessie glimpsed a cramped front hall, a small living room, an easel, a worn velvet couch. She sat down on it, hard. Mrs. McTaggart brought her a glass of water. Jessie sipped. The wave of dizziness passed over her.

"That's better," Mrs. McTaggart said. "You were white as a sheet."

Jessie drained the glass. The woman took it from her. "Thank you, Mrs. McTaggart."

"Call me Erica. I don't much like the McTaggart label. For personal reasons." She went to put the glass down on a side table. Her route took her past the easel. It drew her like a magnet. She dipped a brush in the red pool on her palette, hesitated, dabbed paint on the canvas. From her place on the couch, Jessie could see the almost finished painting: two misshapen naked men standing by a gas pump. They might have been arguing. It wasn't a bad idea, but Erica McTaggart didn't have the skill to make it work. Philip could have fixed it in ten minutes.

Erica saw Jessie looking at the painting and said, "I'm thinking of calling it 'Pumped Up.' It's Exhibit One-A in my 'A Man's Gotta Be What a Man's Gotta Be' series—men at boxing matches, men in bars, men at urinals. Therapeutic, if nothing else." She stepped back, laid down the palette and the brush. "I know what you're thinking—to send a message call Western Union. Right?"

"Not at all."

But Erica detected her lack of enthusiasm, if not its cause. She snorted. "Thanks for the vote of confidence, uh . . ."

"Jessie. Jessie Shapiro."

Erica's ruined eyebrows rose. "Jewish?"

"That's right." Jessie's father was Jewish, her mother Protestant, but she didn't go into that rigmarole. Instead she repeated, "That's right," and added, "Jewish."

"Hey," said Erica McTaggart, "no offense." She sat on the floor, crossing her legs in a modified lotus. Jessie watched her, but she was thinking about her parents. It had been the second marriage for both of them. Now her mother was in Costa Rica, working on her fourth. Her father, retired in Florida, had also retired from the marriage game. Now he just had girlfriends. Like a lot of people Jessie knew, they were their own children, still occupied with their own development, their own growing up. That put their real children in an awkward position. Jessie had resolved never to let that happen to Kate.

"You're not offended, are you?" said Erica McTaggart.

"No."

"Christ, my so-called maiden name was Rabinowitz. I don't like that label, either. For aesthetic reasons." She smiled. She had sharp little teeth. "But if you want to know the truth, I'm most comfortable in the company of Jewish women. Don't you find that?"

"No."

Erica's smile hardened. The room was quiet. A fly buzzed between the double windows. "So," Erica said, "you were looking for Hartley Frame. Can I ask why?"

"I thought my husband . . . my ex-husband," Jessie began. The words trailed away. Thinking about her parents had knocked her off the rails. "When did he die?"

"Hartley?"

"Yes."

"I don't remember the exact year. 'Seventy-one, or 'seventy-two. Around there. You still haven't explained why you're looking for him. Does it have something to do with the memorial?"

"I don't know about any memorial. I'm—I was looking for him because he was a friend of my ex-husband." In a few sentences, Jessie described the disappearance and Buddy Boucher's letter.

"What's your ex-husband's name?"

"Pat Rodney."

Erica McTaggart tilted her head back, as though trying to see Jessie from a new angle. "You were married to Pat Rodney?"

"Yes."

"You had a child by him?"

"Yes. What's so odd about that?"

Erica looked away. "Nothing. People change, I guess, although I've never found that to be the case—you just gradually learn what they're really like." She turned back to Jessie. "You don't look his type, that's all."

"So I'm told. Why not?"

"You're too . . . classy."

Jessie shook her head. "I'm middle class. So's Pat."

"I didn't mean it quite so literally. Pat Rodney is—or at least he was—a bit . . . crude."

"How do you mean?" Jessie said, at the same time hearing the edge in her tone and wondering why she was defending him.

"Well, he used to—touch me when I didn't want to be touched. Things like that."

"Did you go out with him?"

"Good God, no. I went out, if that's the right expression, with Hartley."

"I thought—"

Erica smiled a malicious smile. "You thought right. I was married to Ross at the time. He wasn't pleased when he found out—took it like a man, you might say. Put *fin* to our *mariage*, in fact. Such as it was. The funny thing was that by the time Ross found out, Hart was already . . . Hart and I were starting to grow apart."

"When was this?"

"The fall of 'sixty-eight. Hart and I were really all finished by the winter. That's when he dropped out."

"He dropped out?"

"Yes. Before he flunked out. He was failing all his courses, except for music. He always got straight A's in music. Hartley was a real artist. I think that's what Ross couldn't stand. Ross was the first one to spot his talent—he even tried to persuade his parents to send him to Juilliard, but they had other ideas."

"His father's a senator, isn't he?"

"Is and was. But they didn't get along. Hartley had a complete rupture with his family sophomore year."

"What about?"

"His life-style in general, I guess. Drugs. They didn't approve. Ross came around to that way of thinking too, after he found out about our little fling. Then he started taking the line that Hart wasn't really talented, just facile."

"What instrument did he play?"

"Anything. He could play anything. He had a band. Sergeant Pepper."

"That was the name of the band?"

"Yes. Sergeant Pepper. Hart loved that record, so that's what he called the band. I sang in it sometimes. 'Descartes Kills.' "

"What?"

"It was one of our songs." Erica's eyes brightened. "Do you want to hear it? I've got a tape."

"Sure."

Erica opened a drawer and rummaged through piles of cassettes. She muttered their names as she tossed them aside: *"Tapestry, Best of Buffalo Springfield, After Bathing at Baxter's.* Here it is." She snapped a cassette into a player by the wall. The room filled with tape hiss. Then a woman's voice shouted, "Descartes Kills," and a band began pounding behind her. The lyric that followed was unintelligible, the playing chaotic. Only one sound came clearly to Jessie, a ringing guitar that faded in and out of the background. When the song finished, Erica popped the cassette out. "A bit rough, maybe, but you don't hear that kind of passion anymore." Her face was flushed. "Sometimes I think rock music is like opera—all its great moments have already happened." Erica stuck out her sharp, little chin, ready for an argument.

But Jessie let the invitation pass by. "Pat played on that song, didn't he? Did he write it too?"

"Hart wrote all the songs," Erica replied with annoyance. "It was Hart's band. Different people played in it at different times, including Pat. Pat was a primitive—couldn't read a note." A veil slipped over her dark eyes. Her voice softened. "We used to drop acid and jam in the tunnels. The sound was incredible."

"Tunnels?"

"There are miles of maintenance tunnels under the campus. It's black as black down there. Sometimes we'd just drop acid and explore. But other times we'd take the instruments and jam

194

all night. And . . . once in a while, just Hart and I would go down—we had a little room way at the end of one of the crawl tunnels. With a little mattress." She lapsed into silence, her dark, veiled eyes on the past. "It was like *La Bohème*," she said at last. Then she turned to Jessie, as though snapping out of a reverie. She saw the expression on Jessie's face and misinterpreted it. "You know, the opera."

"I thought all the great moments in opera were in the past," Jessie said.

Erica didn't like that. Her brow wrinkled as she searched for a cutting reply; for a second, Jessie saw how she would look as an old woman. "Pat wasn't very good, to tell you the truth," Erica said. "I think Hartley kept him in the band just because he felt sorry for him. The poor townie routine."

Energy fluttered through Jessie's body, as though an engine had started. "Townie? Does that mean Pat came from here?"

Erica looked surprised. "Not Morgantown specifically, I don't think, but from somewhere around here, yes. Didn't you know that?"

"Pat never spoke much about his past."

"That's probably because he didn't have much of one, at least when I knew him. What did he end up doing?"

"He's a studio musician in L.A."

"You're joking."

"No."

"But he couldn't read a note."

"So you said."

Erica McTaggart's dark eyes flickered around the room. "Maybe people do change, after all."

Jessie leaned forward on the couch, but not with excitement at Erica's psychological speculations. "If Pat came from here, he must still know people in the area."

"I wouldn't be surprised," Erica said.

"Do you know of any?"

Erica yawned. Jessie noticed for the first time how tired she looked. Maybe she'd been painting all night. "You could try across the Vermont line," she said. "They had a commune—Pat, his sister, some others. Hart stayed there after he dropped out. I went up once. Not much of a place. That was the last time I saw Hart."

Erica was sliding back into nostalgia again, but Jessie had no time for that; she was on her feet. "Pat has a sister?"

"You didn't know that? How long were you married to him?"

Jessie ignored the question. "What's her name?"

Erica thought. "Doreen, if memory serves. But in those days, she had a hippie nom de guerre."

"Which was?"

"Blue," Erica replied. "Preferable to Moonbeam, I suppose, or Sunflower. She was the one Hart left me for, in fact. One of the ones." She rose, quite gracefully, from her lotus position. "But you know something? I don't regret any of it. Not one minute. It was wonderful." She paused; the light faded from her eyes. "Do you think that's just because we were so young?"

Jessie didn't know the answer. She thanked Erica Mc-Taggart and hurried away.

22

Lacrosse sticks hung in the front hall. The house was silent. Quietly, Zyzmchuk shut the door and turned toward the inner room. A floorboard squeaked beneath him. He paused. From the inner room came the sound of quick footsteps. He got there in time to see the dark-haired woman run down a corridor and out the back door.

Zyzmchuk started to follow, then stopped himself. The monitor. He turned back. More haste less speed, slow and steady wins the race, and other comforting adages took the place of thinking.

Zyzmchuk looked at the screen. "Frame," it said, "Hartley E. Class of '69. Father: Edmund S. Frame. Class of '43. U.S. Senator, Virginia. Mother: Alice (Sangster). Faculty advisor: Prof. M. R. McTaggart, Dept. of Music. Academic Record: SAT: Verbal-670. Math-640. Achievement Tests: French-610. Grades: 1965: Fall Semester: Music 101-A . . ."

Zyzmchuk scrolled through the academic record of Frame, Hartley E. Except in music, his grades started high and dropped steadily; the music marks remained high. By the spring of 1968, he was on academic probation. No grades were listed for the fall term of 1968. Instead there was a notation: "Withdrew Dec. 3, 1968." Then came a few blank lines, followed by: "Alumni contributions: $0. Present Address: Deceased. (See file WR/DD)." There was nothing else in the file on Frame, Hartley E.

Zyzmchuk looked down at the instructional template fastened to the flat border of the keyboard. To close a file: Control KD. Simple enough. He closed the Frame file. The screen displayed an opening menu. To open a file: E. Zyzmchuk pressed E. "Name of file?" asked the screen. WR/DD, typed Zyzmchuk. Nothing happened. "Enter?" asked the screen. "Okay, okay," Zyzmchuk muttered. He pressed ENTER. That made the disk drive hum. Then green words appeared on the screen: File WR/DD—Alumni War Dead. That heading was followed by many names, going back to the War of 1812. The last entry was Frame, Hartley E., U.S. Army, Pfc. Viet Nam.

Zyzmchuk closed the file. Leaving the computer on at the opening menu, he walked out of the Alumni Affairs Building and drove to the 1826 House restaurant, across the street from the motel. He sat by a window facing the road and ordered coffee. Then he waited.

It wasn't long before a small car turned into the motel lot and parked in front of number 19. The dark-haired woman got out, unlocked the door and went inside.

Zyzmchuk paid for his coffee and drove across the street. "I'd like a room," he said in the office. "Is number twenty available? That's where I'm parked."

"It is," said the clerk, "but there's no fireplace. Eight has a fireplace, though, and it's empty."

"Twenty will be fine."

"They're the same price."

"I like twenty."

"Okeydoke."

Once inside his room, Zyzmchuk pressed his ear against the wall. He heard the woman talking on the other side, but couldn't make out her words. There were no other voices. Zyzmchuk examined his phone, following the wire to an outlet in the back wall. He opened the window and looked out. A telephone cable was strung along the foundation, a few inches above the ground. At each room a small plastic circuit box was wired to it.

Zyzmchuk got his toolbox and climbed out the window. The motel backed onto a rocky meadow, occupied by half a dozen cows. They raised their heads, looked him over, stuck their noses back in the grass.

Zyzmchuk opened the plastic box outside number 19. He clipped his own wire to the leads and ran it into the circuit box outside number 20. Then he climbed back inside and closed the window.

Zyzmchuk picked up his phone. A man said, "If that's supposed to be a joke, it's not a very funny one." Click. Zyzmchuk heard breathing; it sounded very near. Then the line went dead. He hung up.

Zyzmchuk lay on the floor, next to the dividing wall. The 1826 House had thick broadloom, nice furniture and fireplaces in some of the rooms, but it didn't have soundproof walls. Zyzmchuk could hear the woman moving around. She got on the bed, got off the bed, ran water, turned on the television, turned it off, picked up the phone.

Zyzmchuk picked up his.

"Boucher's Dodge and Dodge Trucks. Buddy here," said a voice that oozed bonhomie.

"It's Jessie Shapiro, Mr. Boucher." The woman sounded nervous, as though she were about to ask for a loan.

"Who?"

"Jessie Rodney."

"Oh yes, Mrs. Rodney." His stores of bonhomie were drying up fast.

"I wondered—"

"Sorry. Nothing new."

"He hasn't been back yet?" The woman's voice dropped; Zyzmchuk could hardly hear her.

"Nope. And nothing on the BMW, neither."

"Please call me if anything—"

"What's that?"

The woman cleared her throat and spoke louder. "Call me

if anything happens. Collect. I'm at 413-656-7098. Room nineteen."

"Sure thing."

Click.

Zyzmchuk heard the woman walk slowly across the room, heard her lie on the bed; bedding rustled. Silence. Zyzmchuk's eyes began to close. He pictured a bird's-eye view of the 1826 House with its roof taken off: he and the dark-haired woman lying a few feet from each other, on opposite sides of a wall. Then, quite distinctly, he heard the woman moan. It was not a moan of pleasure, but of despair.

She got off the bed. She moved around. She picked up the phone. Zyzmchuk picked up his.

"Yes?" said a man; he had a high voice, poised on the edge of a tantrum. A piano played in the background: the Goldberg Variations. It couldn't have been a record, Zyzmchuk thought: the pianist's left hand was almost nonexistent.

"Professor McTaggart?" the woman said; her voice was low again and forced.

"What? Keep playing, keep playing. No, no, from the third bar." The man's voice rose higher and higher. "Yes, what is it?" he snapped.

Again the woman cleared her throat and began with an apology, not the way to handle a yelling demon like the man on the other end. "I'm sorry to interrupt, but it's important. I'm looking for information about someone who was a Morgan student in the sixties. You were his faculty advisor, and I thought you might be able to help."

"Oh for God's sake," the man interrupted. "Who?"

"Hartley Frame. He was in the class of 'sixty-nine."

There was a long pause. Then the man said, "You've got the wrong number."

"But—"

"You want my ex-wife," the man said, his tone filled with spite. "Good-bye."

"God damn it," the woman shouted, not a hysterical cry, but one of rage, like a tormented animal. Zyzmchuk heard her over the phone and through the wall. Then something crashed and made a ringing sound. The phone: could she have detected

200

the bug? Zyzmchuk lay absolutely still. He waited to hear sounds of the telephone being taken apart or the back window opening. But room 19 was silent.

After a few minutes, Zyzmchuk heard pages turning. Then the woman walked across the floor. The door opened and closed.

Zyzmchuk peeked through the curtains. The woman went into the office. Still watching, Zyzmchuk called Grace at home. No answer. He tried her work number. Grace was there.

"It's Saturday," Zyzmchuk told her. "A day of rest."

"But I wasn't tired, Mr. Z. I was bored. What's your excuse?"

He didn't have an exact answer to that. "As long as you're there," he said, "I'd like the U.S. Army record for Frame, Hartley E."

"Frame?" she said.

"Right."

"Gotcha."

The dark-haired woman—Jessie, Jessie Shapiro or perhaps Jessie Rodney—came out of the office and got in her car. Her face looked puffy, her eyes exhausted, and yet . . .

"Mr. Z.?" said Grace. "You still there?"

"Yes." The dark-haired woman got in her car. "I've got to go," Zyzmchuk said.

"Ciao."

The dark-haired woman backed her car and turned onto the road. Zyzmchuk followed. She drove to the southern edge of town and down a short dead end. Zyzmchuk parked on the corner. His phone buzzed.

"Mr. Z.?"

"That was quick."

"And futile. The Hartley Frame records are flagged. I can't get into them without assistant director authority or higher."

"Who flagged them?"

"I don't know. Do you want me to call Mr. Keith?"

The dark-haired woman was at the door of a little house at the end of the street, talking to someone Zyzmchuk couldn't see. Then she went inside; the door closed.

"Yes or no?" said Grace.

"Yes or no?"

"About calling Mr. Keith. He's got the authority."

"No, don't call Mr. Keith. But see if you can dig up anything on Jessie Shapiro. Or Jessie Rodney."

"In army records?"

"In any records, Grace. Any at all."

23

The dark-haired woman was a good driver, but she never checked her rearview mirror. Following her north on Route 7, Ivan Zyzmchuk wondered about that. There were all kinds of people in his business, but they had one thing in common: they checked their rearview mirrors. Frequently.

It was only four o'clock when the two cars crossed the state line, but the sky was already darkening. Zyzmchuk might not have looked so closely at the southbound Jaguar had it been any color other than cherry red. It stood out, even in the fading light. Zyzmchuk knew someone with a car just like that, so his eyes were on it as it flashed by. And he saw the someone he knew, hunched over the wheel. Keith.

Decision time. Zyzmchuk's hands and feet made it for him. They threw the Blazer into a controlled right-to-left skid and swung it around. A noisy business, but no one was around to be bothered by it except the cows in the fields. Moments later, Zyzmchuk was heading south. Welcome to Massachusetts, said the road sign. It was a personal message from the governor, whose signature was at the bottom.

The Jaguar had been going fast—seventy or eighty, Zyzmchuk thought. He didn't pick it up until the outskirts of Morgantown. The Jaguar rounded a corner, not totally in control, and quickly slowed down and pulled into a gas station, parking by the pumps.

Zyzmchuk drove in right behind the Jaguar and stopped with his bumper inches from it. He got out and approached on the driver's side. The window slid down. Beatles' music floated out. They were singing about fixing a hole. "Fill her up," Keith said.

"Premium, I suppose?"

Keith's head snapped up. "Zyz!" he said. He added, "Old buddy," in a lower octave. "What the hell are you doing here?" He switched off the music.

Zyzmchuk leaned on the roof and tested the suspension. The car bounced up and down.

"Please don't do that," Keith said. "I asked what you're doing here."

"My job. And you?"

"Oh, right, right," Keith said, as though remembering that Zyzmchuk had one. "Then it's not really a coincidence."

"What isn't?"

"This serendipitous event," Keith said.

"Serendipitous?"

"Fortunate. It comes from a story about the three pri—"

"I know where it comes from." Zyzmchuk bounced the car a few more times. Keith frowned, but said nothing. "I don't know why it applies to this event."

"Because. It's a chance to have a talk outside the office. Let our hair down a bit. I should have realized you'd be here. After all, she's here."

"Who?"

"Alice Frame." Keith glanced up at Zyzmchuk's face. "I have a feeling we're talking at cross-purposes, Zyz. I'm here to attend the unveiling of the memorial. The senator couldn't fit it in, and he asked me to stand in for him, as it were. Alice is here, too, of course. And that's why you're here. There. Does that all add up?"

"You need new shocks, Keith," Zyzmchuk said.

Keith laughed. "You've got a great sense of humor, Zyz. We're going to miss that. How about dinner? You can bring me up-to-date on the investigation."

"Dinner sounds good."

"Super. Know anywhere?"

Zyzmchuk recommended the 1826 House restaurant—the coffee had been good.

"No, no," Keith said. "We can do better than that."

"You know this town?"

"I spent my salad days here, Zyz."

"Doing what?"

"Becoming a gentleman. Learning to love art, poetry, Western civilization. Within limits. Picasso yes. Allen Ginsberg no. That's what Morgan's famous for. I'm an alumnus."

"I thought you went to Harvard."

Keith shook his head. "That came later. The B school. This was the scene of my undergraduate career."

Keith knew somewhere. Le Cochon d'Or. The interior evoked a French country inn. They sat in a dark corner, overhung with strings of garlic cloves. "It's on me," Keith said when the menus arrived. Zyzmchuk ordered mushroom soup and a steak. Keith ordered a lobster soufflé and ris de veau. His French wasn't bad, Zyzmchuk noticed, certainly better than the waiter's. "You like wine, Zyz?"

"Sure."

Keith scrutinized the list. "How about the Chiroubles?"

"Fine."

Candlelight glowed on Keith's glasses, and the creamy collar of his button-down shirt. There was a tiny red spot near the neckline, the kind that comes from a shaving cut. "So," he said, "How goes the Little Miss Muffet affair?"

The first course arrived. Keith poked at the soufflé with the point of his knife. The soufflé quivered, but didn't deflate. "Perfection," he said, cutting off a piece and popping it in his mouth.

He chewed it carefully, lips pressed together. Zyzmchuk had the impression he was counting the chews.

"Ah," Keith said, dabbing his mouth with a napkin. "Soup okay?"

"Fine."

"Good, good." Keith went to work on another bite. When the chewing and the dabbing were finished, he said, "You haven't answered my question."

Zyzmchuk put down his spoon. He'd been hungry, but watching Keith eat had dulled his appetite. "There's nothing to report."

"What kind of nothing?"

"The boring kind."

Keith stared at his reflection in the blade of his knife. "Isn't that always the way?" he said.

How would you know, thought Zyzmchuk, you've spent your life in an office; but he just nodded. The waiter refilled their glasses; they were both drinking quickly. Keith had some more soufflé and said, "What's she been doing?"

"Nothing of any interest to us."

"Nothing that might clarify the polygraph?"

"No."

"Dahlin is very anxious to avoid unpleasantness with the powers that be."

"Who isn't?"

Keith smiled. "He has career ambitions."

"Like what?"

"It would only be hearsay." He tipped the glass to his mouth once more. "Good, huh?"

"Yes."

Keith was staring in the knife blade again. He dipped the corner of his napkin in a water glass and patted the spot of blood on his collar. Putting down the knife, he said, "Chiroubles is my favorite of the Beaujolais crus."

Zyzmchuk nodded but didn't speak.

"What's yours?"

"The red kind," Zyzmchuk replied. "Unless they're pouring white."

"Ha ha. There's that sense of humor. But you're not fooling me, Zyz. I know what you are."

"What am I?"

"A sophisticated man. A man of the world. For example, I bet you could tell me the eight communes of Beaujolais that are allowed to put their names on the label."

"You lose. Can you?"

Keith leaned forward in his chair, like an eager student, and counted them off on his fingers. "Chiroubles, Juliénas, Saint-Amour, Morgon, Moulin-à-Vent, Brouilly, Côtes de Brouilly, Fleurie. Eight."

He'd omitted Chénas—there were nine—but Zyzmchuk didn't mention it. Instead, he asked, "Is that the kind of thing you learned here?"

Keith laughed. "What a reputation this school has! No, Zyz, I learned from my father—he had a little cellar." Keith smiled at the memory, swirled his wine around, drank and said, "What kind of people has she been seeing?"

"No one special."

"So you think there's nothing to it?"

"I always have."

Keith nodded. "You're probably right. I trust your judgment, Zyz." He stared deep into his wineglass. "That Rumanian caper. Incredible. I still don't understand how you got out."

"On a regular commercial flight," Zyzmchuk said.

"I meant how you were able to do that."

Zyzmchuk couldn't imagine that Keith really wanted to know. He emptied the bottle in their glasses and said, "When did you graduate?"

"From here?"

"Yeah."

"Nineteen sixty-nine."

"Not so long ago," Zyzmchuk said. He would have thought Keith older than that. Keith looked older and acted older. Or maybe it was just that Zyzmchuk preferred to believe he really wasn't so much older than his boss.

"It seems like a century," Keith said. He ordered another bottle of Chiroubles. "Those were crazy times, Zyz. Student strikes, demonstrations, drugs, Viet Nam."

"You were involved in all that?"

"Well, not actively. I was too busy. But I soaked up the atmosphere."

"What were you busy doing?"

"My studies, of course. And the drama club. We did an adaptation of *The Wind in the Willows* my senior year. Played to full houses for a week. All male, then—now everything's totally changed." Keith reached for his wine. His hand shook a little.

"You look tired," Zyzmchuk said.

"Jet lag."

"Where have you been?"

"You name it." Keith looked at his gold watch—a Rolex, Zyzmchuk noticed: perhaps it came with a feature to tell him where he'd been. "How much more time do you think you'll need?"

"For what?"

"Miss Muffet."

None was the answer, of course. But Zyzmchuk said, "A few more days."

"A few more days," Keith repeated. "I hope you're not being . . . overzealous. It was just a publicity stunt, after all, as Dahlin said."

"So was Nagasaki."

Keigh laughed. "I love your perspective, Zyz. I really do. Okay. A few more days. We'll expect a report on Wednesday then. The day before Thanksgiving."

"All right."

Keith asked for the bill. He paid with a gold card. He had a gold card, a gold watch, a golden past and a golden future.

They rose. Keith picked up his glass and was draining the last of his wine, when Zyzmchuk said, "Did you know Hartley Frame?"

Keith stopped drinking. A drop of wine trickled down his chin. "How do you know about Hartley Frame?" he asked.

"The memorial."

"Oh. Of course."

"And he was in the class of 'sixty-nine, too, wasn't he?"

"That's right."

"But he didn't graduate."

"You've been doing research."

"Not much. How well did you know him?"

"Fairly well, at one time. We were roommates freshman year. And sophomore. But I spent junior year abroad—a wonderful program. And after that I didn't see him as much."

"Did you meet the senator through him?"

Keith sat down. "Who have you been talking to?"

"Nobody. It fits, that's all."

"Yes, I met the senator through him. I interned in his office during the summers."

"Why did his son go to Viet Nam?"

"He flunked out. It meant the draft, in those days. You know that."

"But couldn't Frame have kept him out?"

"Maybe. But he didn't think it politic. He could see the headlines. Besides, they weren't really talking during that period."

"Why not?"

"The senator disapproved of Hartley's behavior."

"What was he doing?"

"The usual college shenanigans. But the senator's a very conservative man."

"How did Hartley die?"

"No one really knows. He was listed as MIA for a while. Then it was changed to KIA. I think the Red Cross had something to do with it."

"So you sort of stepped into the role?"

"What role?"

"Son."

Keith gave Zyzmchuk a long look. "That's not a very nice thing to say, Zyz old buddy."

"I take it back. It's a bit too pat, anyway."

There was a pause. Candlelight gleamed on Keith's glasses, hiding the expression in his eyes. "Pat?" he said.

"You know. Stereotypical."

"Oh. I see." Keith reached for his glass. It was empty.

"Here," Zyzmchuk said, pouring what remained in his own glass into Keith's.

"No thanks," Keith said. But he drank it just the same.

Keith had drunk half the first bottle and most of the second, but showed no sign of it. Zyzmchuk was impressed with him for the first time.

"I like the Beatles, too, Keith," Zyzmchuk said in the parking lot.

"The Beatles?"

"You had them on in your car."

"Oh," said Keith. "Just something to pass the time."

24

Night was falling as Jessie bumped along the dirt road to Spacious Skies. "Sure," DeMarco had told her. "Everything's a conspiracy. And Paul's dead, if you play the song backward." He thought that she was paranoid, a slave to discredited sixties notions of pervasive conspiracies. But were you still paranoid if it turned out everyone around you was lying? Start with her sister-in-law: Doreen Rodney, aka Blue. Her doubts about Blue had no fixed shape, but they were growing. They pushed open a gate in her mind, and all at once she made a connection.

Fuck, can't you answer your phone? Listen: you've got to split. I'm a—

Now Jessie knew what was familiar about Blue. It was her voice. She also understood Disco's reaction to the idea that Blue and Pat had been lovers. But that's all she understood.

The house was dark, and she didn't see the pickup. Jessie drove around to the other side. The pickup sat in the barnyard, but that wasn't what caught Jessie's attention as her high beams swept through the darkness. It was the barn. The door was open and the old Corvette was gone. Jessie parked beside the pickup, leaving her lights on and pointing into the barn, and went for a closer look. There was nothing to see but the tarpaulin, neatly folded on the floor. Eighty-seven miles in two decades. Now someone had finally decided to take the car for a spin.

Jessie turned off her headlights and walked around the house. She rapped on the door with the cracked crescent window. It swung open at her touch. Jessie hesitated, then stepped inside.

She listened. Silence. She called out, "Hello? Hello?" There was no reply but the house's, echoing her voice. That didn't mean the residents were out. Not at Spacious Skies. Jessie felt along the wall until she came to a switch. She flicked it. Nothing happened.

She moved along the hall and tried the next switch she came to. Again nothing happened, except her fingers got wet. She tried a few more switches and gave up. Slowly she made her way past rooms once overflowing with the barn painters and their music, now full of shadows, to the kitchen. She smelled burned sugar.

The kitchen lights were out too. Jessie felt through drawers until she found a box of wooden matches. She lit one and looked around the room.

Except for one chair, overturned on the floor, everything seemed exactly the same as the day before. There was even a cookie sheet on the table, bearing chocolate-chip cookies in neat rows. Jessie touched one of them. Still slightly warm. The power hadn't been out for long. She was thinking about that when she noticed something about her hand, caught for a moment in the circle of yellow match light. The tips of her fingers were red.

Her fingers began to tremble. She raised them to her nose and sniffed. The redness had a smell, but not of paint. More like copper dust. Jessie touched her fingertip to her tongue and tasted salty blood.

Jessie walked back along the hall, struck another match and held it to the light switch. Red fingerprints drew an arc above the switch, then trailed down the wall, as though someone had tried fingerpainting and quickly tired of it.

Jessie went into the hall and looked out the crescent window. There was nothing to see. She lit another match and started climbing the stairs. The tiny flame drove the shadows on ahead of her—up the stairs, down the long hall, into Disco's room. His wheelchair sat in the corner, but he wasn't in it. Neither was he in the bed. Or under it.

Jessie walked back along the hall. Her foot was on the top stair when a car door closed outside. Jessie blew out the match and backed into the shadows.

The front door opened. A man entered. In the darkness, Jessie could see only that he was tall and moved athletically.

The man sniffed the air. He had something in his hand. He held it out. A light flashed on. He aimed it down the hall. For a moment, his face was caught in the edge of its beam, and Jessie glimpsed high cheekbones and straight blond hair, platinum blond. It was a face Jessie had seen once before by flashlight.

Mr. Mickey.

He moved down the hall. Jessie took her shoes off and walked softly to Disco's room. She felt for the closet door, opened it and shut herself inside.

The closet was deep, its back wall beyond Jessie's reach. She crouched on piles of clothing. Rough fabric hung down around her head. She smelled sweat. She saw blackness. She heard silence.

Time passed, unquantifiable in a sensorially deprived environment. Then sound came to Jessie's world: footsteps, padding on the hardwood floor. Jessie shrank back in the closet, pulling clothing on top of her. The footsteps grew louder and louder. And then light poked through the crack at the bottom of the closet door.

Jessie wriggled further back. The doorknob turned. Jessie pulled something woollen over her face, reached into the depths of the closet for more clothing. The door swung open.

And in that moment, her hand, deep in the closet, touched human flesh.

Jessie froze. She felt nothing but what was under her hand— soft hairs, a knuckle, blood pumping in a vein. Light probed the darkness. Blood pumped in the vein. And from the other side came a little breeze, as though someone was fanning the air near her head. The breeze went away. The light vanished. The door closed.

The footsteps retreated, quieter, quieter, then nothing. The knuckles turned. A hand gripped hers. "Blue?" whispered a voice. It was Disco.

"Shh," Jessie hissed. Their palms dampened together. Jessie didn't risk any movement until she heard the faint sound of a car starting. Then she withdrew her hand—she had to jerk it out of Disco's grasp—and scrambled from the closet.

"Blue," said Disco, still whispering, "don't leave me."

Jessie kneeled outside the closet, her body shaking. She was soaked with sweat. "Oh, God," she said.

"You're not Blue," Disco said, no longer whispering, his voice now high and full of fear. "Who are you?"

"Jessie." Her voice, too, sounded high-pitched. She fought to control it, not very successfully. "I talked to you yesterday. Don't you remember?"

"I—I think so."

"It was only yesterday."

"I said I think so, didn't I?"

"What happened here? There's blood on the wall downstairs."

Disco's voice rose higher. "Whose blood?"

"I'm asking you."

"I don't know. I don't know anything. The power went out. Then they came into the house and started talking to Blue. Downstairs. They were mad."

"Who's they?"

"I don't know."

"Yes you do."

"Shit, shit, shit." Disco rocked back and forth, like an Orthodox Jew in prayer. "Yes, I know. It was Ratty. Ratty and another man. I hid in the closet. Then you came in. I thought you were Ratty. I thought I was going to die. Then you touched me. Like—a woman. And I thought it was Blue. Where is she?"

"I don't know."

Jessie heard Disco moving in the closet. He grunted. "I'm all twisted up in here."

"Do you want help?"

"That's my role in life."

Jessie didn't know the reply to that. She pulled Disco out of the closet, dragged him to the wheelchair and propped him up in it. She tried to be gentle, but his body was tense and inflexible and heavier than it looked. Disco groaned.

"What's wrong?" Jessie asked.

"It hurts, for fuck sake."

Jessie was silent. She heard an airplane, far above. She heard Disco's breathing; gradually it resumed a normal cadence. "Who is Ratty?"

"A scumbag."

Jessie described Mr. Mickey. "Is that him?" she asked.

"No."

"That's the man who just left."

"I don't know him. I just know Ratty. He's responsible for everything."

"What do you mean?"

"My eyes. My legs. My night flight to oblivion."

"Why is he responsible?"

"He gave me the acid."

"You didn't have to take it."

"What do you know? I've seen things you'll never see."

There was nothing to gain from fighting with Disco. "Maybe you have," Jessie said.

He grunted, and went on: "I've never had acid like that. It made me want to die and fly."

"When did this happen?"

"A long time ago. When we decided to go for the big enchilada."

"Who is we?"

"Just me, I guess. Blue was against it. She already had the little enchilada. That was fine for her, but what did it do for me? Piss all. So I went after the big one. That's when Ratty came up. I never liked Ratty. I didn't like the way he played."

"What did he play?"

"Me. We went up Mount Blackstone with two blue tabs and a jug of wine. We did up and sat on the edge of the lookout. The stars were right fucking there—you could reach out and touch them. I felt like God. But then Ratty turned it into a bummer."

"What's Ratty's real name?"

"Scumbag."

"How did he turn your trip into a bummer?"

215

"He said things that weren't true. It broke up my mind. Not blew it. Broke it up."

"What did he say?"

"Things about Blue. That Blue and Hartley Frame were getting it on behind my back."

"Did you have a relationship with Blue?"

Disco raised his voice, almost to a scream. "We were fucking childhood sweethearts." He took a deep breath and continued more calmly. "We almost got married when we were seventeen. Blue had an abortion instead. We were still very tight. So I knew it couldn't be true. But my mind broke up anyway, and I looked into Ratty's eyes and got freaked out. Those eyes weren't human. And I couldn't stop looking at them, snake eyes in a human face. Ratty had short hair that night. Real short. Instead of long, like normal. He hadn't been around for a year or two. Ratty saw I couldn't stop looking. And then he said, 'This is just a warning, fly-boy.' "

"What did he mean by that?"

"He meant forget the big enchilada."

"What was the big enchilada?"

"Bread. Enough to last a lifetime."

"I don't understand."

There was a long silence. Then Disco said, "I guess I didn't either."

"Why do you say that?"

"Because."

Jessie waited for him to go on. When he didn't, she said, "Then what happened?"

"That's the last thing I remember. Till I woke up in the hospital."

"Did you fall or were you pushed?"

No reply. Jessie lit a match. "Did you fall or were you pushed?"

Disco shrugged.

"Who is Ratty?"

"The drummer."

"In Pat's band?"

"Once or twice. But it wasn't Pat's band. It was that fucker Hartley Frame's. He always got whatever he wanted. Hendrix gave him the Stratocaster. Just like that." In the weak light of the match, Disco's eyeless sockets were two black holes. "Do you think he was balling Blue, what's your name again?"

"Jessie. Why not ask her?"

"I did."

"And what did she say?"

"Yes."

"Then it's probably true."

"No." Disco pounded the arm of his wheelchair. "She's lying."

"What does it matter now? What matters is where she is and what happened here tonight."

"Blue's all right. She's as tough as they come."

Then why had she sounded so scared on Pat's answering machine? "Blue called Pat last Saturday and left a message, telling him to get away. Why did she do that?"

"You're so full of shit, you know that?"

"What do you mean?"

"You figure it out."

"You help me. What did Pat have to get away from?"

"All your questions." Disco laughed a barking laugh.

"What do you mean?"

"Nothing. I don't never mean nothing."

"Was it Ratty?"

Disco snorted.

"Then who?"

"Leave me alone. I don't know anything. I'm blind as a bat."

"That doesn't make you stupid."

"I was stupid before I was blind. Why don't you go away? Blue doesn't want you around here."

"Why not?"

"She said so."

"All right. I'm leaving. But you must have some idea where she might be."

Disco didn't answer right away. Jessie waited. He needed Blue, and she was mobile. Finally he said quietly, "Try the cookie store."

"What cookie store?"

"Blue's cookie store in town." He told her the phone number.

Jessie went downstairs. As she passed the switch in the hall, she struck another match. The red fingerpainting was gone.

In the kitchen she picked up the phone to call the cookie

store. She'd almost finished dialing before she realized the line was dead.

She went outside. She rechecked the barn. The Corvette was still gone.

Jessie drove into Bennington and found the cookie store. It was open, but Blue wasn't there and no one had seen her. Her store had a special on chocolate-chip cookies and a well-painted sign showing two dancing gingerbread men. Above them it said: EGGMAN COOKIES. D. RODNEY, PROP.

25

Ivan Zyzmchuk was glad when the phone started ringing. He'd had enough of lying in his bed at the 1826 House, staring at the floral wallpaper. The mattress was too soft, the room too hot, the painted flowers too dainty. He picked up the receiver and said, "Hello."

"I'm just calling to say good-bye." It was Keith.

Zyzmchuk sat up. "You won't be at the unveiling?"

"No. I've been summoned by the master."

"Senator Frame?"

"You've got such a sunny disposition, Zyz. Always ready with a quip. I'm sure it hasn't kept people from taking you seriously." Keith paused to let his words sink in. Then he said, "Dahlin is the master, as I hope you know. Good-bye."

Zyzmchuk got out of bed. His reflection flashed by in the mirror—a broad, powerful figure with a long curved scar on the right shoulder and a shorter one on the left thigh, like brackets around a qualifying clause. He went to the wall and pressed his

219

ear against it. No sound came from the dark-haired woman's room. Her car was parked outside. Zyzmchuk put on his sweatsuit and went for his run.

The sky had cleared overnight. Now it was the kind of dome a minimalist would like, pale blue and empty: no clouds, no jet trails, no birds. Zyzmchuk felt very small running around beneath it.

On the way back, Zyzmchuk went by the music building. A few dozen people stood on the lawn, facing the veiled memorial. Alice Frame, her mink coat buttoned to the top, was making a speech. Zyzmchuk moved closer.

". . . and because Hartley loved music so much, his father and I have decided to establish a scholarship, to be called the Hartley Frame Memorial Fund, which the chairman of the music department will be free to award to the most promising music student in the senior class. To mark the inauguration of the scholarship, we are very proud to present Morgan College with this work of art." Alice Frame tugged at the tarpaulin. It stuck. Jameson T. Phinney, in a fur hat, stepped up to help her. The tarpaulin came loose, sliding off a huge steel figure that might have been a man bent over a guitar. At its base a plaque read: IN MEMORY OF HARTLEY FRAME, 1947–1971. The reflected sky washed the memorial in pale blue.

People began to clap in a well-bred way. Cracking sounds echoed discreetly across the quad. A tall black woman in a red jacket bowed and smiled. Alice Frame shook her hand. Phinney shook her hand. The crowd fragmented; a few people moved forward, waiting for a word with the sculptor, Phinney or Alice. One of them was the dark-haired woman. Jessie Shapiro. Or Rodney. She held out her arm, trying to attract Alice's attention. From Zyzmchuk's angle, it connected the two women like a hyphen.

He cut through the mass of slower-moving people, in time to hear the dark-haired woman say, "Mrs. Frame? May I talk to you for a moment?"

"Certainly," Alice replied. She looked puzzled, possibly by the intensity of the dark-haired woman's tone, clearly audible to Zyzmchuk, twenty feet away.

"It's a bit complicated," the dark-haired woman began. "I—"

At that moment, Phinney put his hand on Alice's shoulder,

turning her away. "Alice, I'd like you to meet an old and val-
ued . . ."

Zyzmchuk circled the statue, using it as a screen. He didn't
want the dark-haired woman to see his face, but he wanted to
see hers. Alice was shaking hands with a man in an impresario
coat. The dark-haired woman's eyes darted from one to the
other. She leaned forward slightly, as though into the teeth of
a prevailing wind. Then her hand slipped into the pocket of her
suede jacket. Zyzmchuk got ready to run between them. But
when she withdrew her hand, it held not a pistol, but a broken
barrette. Zyzmchuk let his weight shift back on his heels. The
dark-haired woman glanced down at the barrette; she didn't put
it back in her pocket, but kept it in her hand, tightly grasped.

The man in the impresario coat moved on to the sculptor.
The dark-haired woman stepped in front of Alice Frame, inside
the orbit of personal space. Alice blinked.

"It's about Pat Rodney," the dark-haired woman said.

Alice blinked again.

"He was a friend of your son." Her voice was low; Zyzmchuk
came closer, until he stood behind the man in the impresario
coat.

"Yes?" said Alice.

"I—I was hoping he might be here. But I haven't seen him."

"What did you say his name was?"

"Pat Rodney. He might be with a little girl. My daughter."

"I'm afraid the name isn't familiar."

"But they were good friends." The dark-haired woman's
voice grew edgy. Phinney, listening to the sculptor, cast a quick
look at her. "They played in a band together. They went to
Woodstock together."

"I'm sorry."

"But you must—"

"Alice," called Phinney, a little louder than necessary, "may
we borrow you for a moment?"

"Excuse me," Alice said to the dark-haired woman; she half-
turned and Phinney, reaching for her arm, drew her away. They
were as smooth as Rogers and Astaire; they might have made
quite a couple, Zyzmchuk thought, fit to be monarchs of some
other world where good manners counted for everything.

But back on earth, they meant less and less. The dark-haired woman spoiled the choreography. Hurrying after Phinney and Alice, she tried again. "Mrs. Frame, think back—Hartley must have spoken about some of his—"

"I'm sorry." Alice was turning pale.

The dark-haired woman planted herself in front of Phinney and Alice. Zyzmchuk had a clear view of her face, a beautiful face, but every feature sapped by anxiety. Leni had looked like that the last time he saw her, the night of the kiosk fiasco.

"What about the funeral? Didn't some of Hartley's friends come? I'm sure Pat—"

"Funeral!" Alice rounded on her. "What sort of funeral do you have for a dog tag and a telegram?"

The dark-haired woman faltered. "What do you mean?" she said.

Alice might have been about to reply, but Phinney spoke first. "This is not the time for whatever it is you want. Now if you will please excuse us." Holding Alice by the arm, he pushed past the dark-haired woman. For a moment, Zyzmchuk thought she would resist with her body—he could see she was strong—but she gave way. Alice and Phinney joined remnants of the crowd climbing the steps of the music building. The dark-haired woman walked slowly the other way. She went right past Zyzmchuk, but didn't see him. Her eyes were hot and cloudy.

Zyzmchuk watched Alice and Phinney enter the music building. Sounds of musicians tuning their instruments drifted through the open door. He turned and followed the dark-haired woman. She walked back to the 1826 House and went into her room. Zyzmchuk entered his. He pressed his ear to the wall. He heard the squeak of box springs, the soft knock of a headboard against the wall. Then nothing.

Zyzmchuk showered, dressed and returned to the music building. He followed the sounds of the Mozart horn trio to a performance hall on the second floor. But he didn't go inside: Alice Frame was talking on a pay phone outside the closed doors.

Zyzmchuk walked past her and stopped in front of a bulletin board. He took out a notepad and pen and began copying random notes from the bulletin board. "Ride needed to Boston—share gas." "Movie at Slocum House Sat. nite: Eraserhead, $1." Zyzmchuk was conscious of Alice Frame's eyes on him, heard her lower her voice. He kept writing on the notepad.

"It makes it so final," Alice said. There was a long pause. "Yes, we've been through it a hundred times. That doesn't make it easier. In fact, it was harder, if anything. A woman was asking questions about one of his friends. It brought everything back. That's—" Another pause. "I don't know. Pat somebody . . . I don't think she gave her name . . . Dark hair, not bad-looking, does it matter? The point is it was upsetting. Because we really didn't know his friends, did we?" Zyzmchuk heard tinny sounds of anger coming over the wire. Alice raised her voice, too. "I am blaming you." Again Zyzmchuk felt her gaze. She lowered her voice. "Partly." The tinny sounds diminished, dipped below Zyzmchuk's hearing threshold. It didn't matter—he couldn't keep up the bulletin board pretense any longer. He closed his note-book and walked away. He heard Alice say, "All right, Edmund. I'll expect you." The receiver clicked into its plastic cradle. By that time he was around the corner and on the stairs.

The Morgan College library stood on a hill overlooking the music building. It was an even grander structure, combining excesses drawn from Greek and Roman styles and guarded by two stone lions with angry faces. They roared, "Knowledge is power," in case anyone thought libraries were for wimps.

Zyzmchuk pushed open the massive oak door and went in. His shoes clicked across the marble floor. A stern man in a powdered wig looked down in disapproval from a gold-framed painting over the main desk. The woman behind the desk had oily fingerprints on her glasses and the same disapproving expression on her face. She directed Zyzmchuk to the periodical section. In half an hour he had found what he wanted.

WAR CASUALTY

Pfc. Hartley E. Frame, ex-'69, son of Senator Edmund S. Frame '43, and Alice Frame of Sweet Briar Va. and South Morgantown Mass., was removed from the Missing-in-Action list and declared dead by the U.S. Army on January 5, 1971. The action followed the visit of an International Red Cross team to a North Vietnamese prison camp in December.

Private Frame was sent to Viet Nam in January 1970. He was last seen during heavy fighting around Pleiku the night of February 3 of that year. He was listed as MIA in

March. A memorial service will be held in the chapel on Sunday.

—from the *Morgan College Record*, January 10, 1971

Zyzmchuk photocopied the article and pocketed it. He was about to leave the periodical room when a long shelf loaded with fat purple-bound books caught his eye: copies of the college yearbook, going back to time immemorial, or at least 1845. "For earlier volumes," said a notice, "consult the librarian." Zyzmchuk selected the 1969 volume and sat down to look at it.

The 1969 *Morganian* was like a stranger's home movies: pictures of people and places that meant nothing without the catalyst of the viewer's nostalgia. Zyzmchuk looked at faces of young, long-haired men on playing fields, in marching bands, at parties dancing with young, long-haired women, carrying a banner that said: "Hey hey L.B.J.—How many kids did you kill today?" He remembered his own yearbook, Chicago 1951, with a picture of himself, sole Z, on the last page. The yearbook had been left behind in some apartment or rented room. Nostalgia was death in sentimental disguise. No need to rush things.

Individual photographs of the graduating seniors appeared alphabetically at the back of the 1969 *Morganian*. Hartley Frame wasn't among the F's; he hadn't graduated. Zyzmchuk checked the R's for Rodney and the S's for Shapiro, finding neither. But Keith was there. He'd been thinner in 1969, with long hair worn Prince Valiant style. The hair surprised Zyzmchuk, but after a moment or two he noticed that Keith was wearing the kind of horn-rimmed glasses he still wore, noticed the sober expression of a budding *homme sérieux:* perhaps, with the long hair, an homme of the eighteenth century. Under the photograph, it said, "Drama Club 2, 3, 4; Band 1; Art Appreciation Club 3, 4; Rifle Club 1, 2, 3, 4." Zyzmchuk turned back to the first page, searching for other pictures of him.

He found four.

The Art Appreciation Club: Keith and four other young men in tweed jackets, standing around a table set with upended wine glasses and half a dozen bottles of wine.

The Band: a ragged corps on a rainy football field. Keith was in the middle, a bass drum with the word "Morgan" on it strapped to his shoulders. He didn't look happy.

The Rifle Club: a line of marksmen at a firing range Keith stood at the far end. His form looked perfect.

The Drama Club: "The Blizzard of Gauze." This, Zyzmchuk saw, was some sort of political spoof. The Wizard wore a Ho Chi Minh mask; the Wicked Witch of the West had on a Lyndon Johnson one. Dorothy, in a polka-dot dress, had been played by Keith. He'd worn so much makeup Zyzmchuk had to read the caption to make sure.

26

An evangelist was on TV. He had a florid, well-fed face, suffused with love of God and contempt for his fellow man. Jessie didn't switch him off. All the other channels had shut down for the night; she couldn't sleep, and she didn't want to be alone. Even the preacher's malign company was better than nothing. He whispered, he shouted, he cried, he paraded across the stage like an albino peacock in his white silk suit.

But at last the organ music rose, and people came forward from the audience to be saved. It made a good background for rolling credits, and the director rolled them. Then he cut to a bare studio where the preacher, in a more somber suit and a mood to match, explained his current financial requirements and asked that they be met by return mail. After that he turned to snow and left Jessie alone with her thoughts.

But the activity taking place in her mind couldn't really be called thinking; it was too disorganized. Fragments of thoughts popped out at her like bogeymen in a funhouse, vanishing before her mind could fit them into patterns. She was left, at two-thirty in the morning, lying fully clothed on her bed at the 1826 House, exhausted, sleepless, staring at her suitcase across the room. It was open: a sleeve of Kate's red sweater hung over the edge. Beneath it she could see the blue-striped leather of one of her Reeboks and a corner of *Jane Eyre*.

She thought for the first time that Kate was dead.

The idea struck her with the force of a blow, opening a hole in her subconscious that spilled out unbearable images: Kate's funeral, sorting her things, the empty space on the fridge where the "My Mom" poem had been.

"Enough," she said aloud and pushed herself off the bed. Having such thoughts was one thing; dwelling on them another—a masochistic self-indulgence. Like an El Greco martyrdom, there was something sick about it. And worse, it led nowhere.

Jessie sat at the desk and took out the motel stationery. So far, she had coped with Kate's disappearance like a bloodhound: searching for her trail, nose to the ground. That hadn't worked. Perhaps it was time to step back, to see from the perspective of the bloodhound's handler. That meant putting her thoughts in order. It meant developing an explanation for Kate's disappearance first, finding her trail second.

Explanation 1: the theory, half DeMarco's and half hers, that Pat was on a toot down memory lane with an old buddy. This was getting harder to believe. His old buddy Hartley Frame was dead, for starters. Explanation 2, or more properly 1A: Pat had come for the dedication of Hartley Frame's memorial. This was invalidated by his absence from the ceremony. Besides, neither theory accounted for Blue's frightened message on Pat's answering machine. Or Mr. Mickey. Or the bag lady who had watched Pat's house. Jessie could only imagine one context where all that would fit: drug-dealing. Had Pat been involved in some drug enterprise with his sister? Maybe for years? Was that what the ten-thousand-dollar payment to Eggman Cookies was about?

If all that were true, then Mr. Mickey and the bag lady might be Pat's competitors or suppliers with some grievance against him. Blue had discovered that they were about to move against him, but her warning had come too late. On Friday Pat had been in Los Angeles. On Monday he was at Buddy Boucher's. A second man stayed in the car. How had Buddy Boucher described him? He hadn't. The second man had stayed in the BMW—a little rocky, Buddy said. Could the second man have been Mr. Mickey? Why not? She hadn't seen him till the following Thursday—he'd had plenty of time to return to L.A. And then to cross the country again. Why? Had he found out she'd been to Spacious Skies? Had he been searching for her when he came up the stairs to Disco's room? Or for Disco? Or for someone else?

And if the second man had been Mr. Mickey, it meant that Pat had shaved his head. Why?

Jessie looked down at the motel stationery. She'd drawn a box. Inside the box she'd written three names: Mr. Mickey, Bag Lady, Ratty. Beneath the box dangled another, also containing three names: Pat, Blue, Disco. Beneath it dangled a single, boxless name: Kate. Around the whole, she drew a barn. Then she crumpled the paper, tossed it in the wastebasket and rose. The motel supplied a flashlight in every room. Jessie took it and went outside. The bloodhound-handler approach led back to Spacious Skies.

The night was cold, cold enough for snow, but the sky was clear. The moon, so big and orange in L.A., here seemed small; and as white as false teeth. Jessie got in her car and drove north.

There was no traffic. Jessie found herself pressing on the accelerator—fifty-five, sixty, sixty-five. Then she saw headlights approaching from the Vermont side and slowed down. The headlights seemed to be approaching quickly, but Jessie was not prepared for the speed of the oncoming vehicle. It flashed by so fast it rocked her little rented car in its wake and was far down the road behind her before her brain processed what she'd seen: a black van with a red streak on the side and a white head behind the windshield, too briefly glimpsed to record any of its features but the baldness on top.

A jolt went through Jessie, like an electrical stimulus meant to activate the muscles of laboratory animals. She stepped on the brakes, much too hard. The wheels locked in a skid that swept her across the road and into a field on the other side. The car spun around several times and came to a stop; the motor stalled.

Jessie's senses were suddenly acute. She could smell, almost taste, burned rubber in the air, could hear the popping sounds of metal changing temperatures and, far away, the fading noise of another engine. But, although her hand was not quite steady when she turned the key, she felt no fear. The urge to follow the black van was too powerful to allow any other feeling. Kate was in that van. Jessie was sure of it. She stamped the accelerator to the floor; the car roared out of the field, tearing two strips in the earth, and swung out onto the road to Morgantown.

Jessie hunched over the steering wheel, peering ahead for a glimpse of the black van's taillights. But she didn't see them. She sped south through Morgantown, past the 1826 House, dark except for her own room and the one beside it, past the campus, and into the shadowy hills beyond. A sign pointed the way to Pittsfield, Stockbridge, Connecticut, New York. The black van might have gone that way; or it might have turned off the road in Morgantown, might now be parked on some side street. Jessie stopped the car, more carefully this time, turned it and drove back to town. Morgantown wasn't a metropolis; she would search every strip of pavement if she had to.

It was easy in theory, in practice much harder. Morgantown's streets weren't clearly marked; some circled back on themselves, some ended in cul-de-sacs. After an hour, Jessie had seen only two signs of life—a dog trotting across a playing field and a student, her black face momentarily caught in the glare of Jessie's headlights, trudging along a sidewalk with an armful of books. Her mind pictured the van flying south, across the Connecticut line, heading for New York; the image was forcing her to face the fact that she had made the wrong decision, forcing her to look into an uncharted future.

Then she saw the van.

It was parked on a tree-lined crescent, in front of a student residence. There were no streetlights, but the light of the moon was strong enough to illuminate the red flames on the bodywork, the temporary Vermont license plate. Other cars were parked in front of the residence, but the space behind the van was empty. Jessie pulled into it and shut off the engine.

Nothing happened.

No light came on in the van. Its doors remained closed.

Taking her flashlight, Jessie got out of the car. She heard a dog barking, faintly, and a guitar, fainter still. Not a sound came from the van.

Jessie walked around it. She moved very quietly, without really knowing why. The windows, as Buddy Boucher had told her, were opaque, all except the windshield. Jessie put her face to it and looked in.

There was no one in the front; beyond lay darkness. Jessie switched on the flashlight and shone it through the windshield. The back of the van was closed off by a plastic curtain. The cheap material gleamed in the light of her beam. Litter lay scattered on the front seat, piled on the floor—McDonald's cartons, Coke cans, cassette tapes: *Fresh Cream, In-A-Gadda-Da-Vida, Strange Days.*

Jessie moved onto the sidewalk and knocked softly on the van's side door. No sound came from within. No one sat up in a moment of panic, no one stirred in her sleep. Jessie knocked again, harder, hard enough for the sound to echo off the brick wall of the residence and rebound over the broad lawn.

She leaned closer to the door, so her mouth almost touched the cold metal, and called, "Kate. Kate?" And heard her own voice as it really sounded, high and scared. She lowered it, gave it more force, and said, "Pat. Are you in there?" She heard nothing but the voice of someone pretending not to be scared.

What is wrong with you? Act. Move. Jessie reached out, took the handle and turned it. The door was locked. She walked around the van, trying all the doors—all locked.

Jessie stood uncertain on the sidewalk. She scanned the residence. Only the lights in the stairwells were on. She shone the flash into the van's front seat and saw what she had already seen.

Jessie returned to her car. She opened the glove compartment and took out Buddy Boucher's Polaroid: same van, same license plate. She took a deep breath, trying to make herself patient. Unless Pat had abandoned the van, he'd be back. All she had to do was wait. She had him.

Jessie waited. She forced her body to be still, but she couldn't control what was happening inside it. Her heart raced lightly, pounded, raced again. Waves of fatigue swept through her, waves of panic swept them back. Much stranger, her breasts began to feel heavy, as though they were filling with milk. She hadn't had that feeling in nine years. Reaching under her sweater,

Jessie felt her nipple. It was wet. But that was a biological impossibility. Her mind told her that.

But her body was telling her that Kate was very near. She got out of the car.

It was then Jessie noticed something she had seen from the beginning, but hadn't appreciated. Across the sidewalk from the van, on the edge of the grass, was a square hatch cover, painted gray. It was the right size to protect a steam vent, perhaps; or maybe it had something to do with the sprinkler system. The hatch cover had a hasp on one side so it could be locked down. But now the hasp was thrown back on its hinge. Going closer, Jessie found the lock in the grass. The bolt had been cut in two.

Jessie bent down and raised the cover. She switched on the flashlight. Its beam didn't shine on sprinklers or a steam vent, but into a deep round hole, lined with brick. A steel ladder, bolted to the wall, led down.

We used to drop acid and jam in the tunnels. The sound was incredible. We had a little room at the end. With a little mattress.

Jessie crouched over the hole, playing her light into it. The beam glinted on the steel ladder, found the floor below, a dirt floor, leading off into shadow. What had she heard when she first stepped out of her car behind the black van?

A dog barking.

And a guitar, very faint, as though the sound came from far away. Or from underground.

Leaving the hatch cover open, Jessie rose. She examined the van. The driver, with the empty space behind him, had parked close to the car in front, no more than a foot away. Jessie got into her car and inched it forward until the bumper pressed against the rear of the van. She engaged the emergency brake, got out, locked the car. Then she lowered herself into the hole and climbed a few rungs down the ladder.

Warm, moist air rose up from below. Jessie stepped down to the tunnel floor, felt its slick dampness under her feet. She took the flashlight out of her pocket and turned it on.

There was just enough room in the tunnel for Jessie to stand up without bumping the pipes overhead. She saw a naked bulb in the ceiling, another one farther on and a switch on the wall.

231

Jessie reached for it, then stopped. She had no way of knowing whether the switch controlled only the bulbs nearby or the lighting system of the entire tunnel. So, although craving strong light, she left the switch alone and moved forward with only the dim glow of the unsteady flashlight beam to guide her.

The tunnel was a narrow world of its own, with its own sights: cables, wires, pipes; its own smells: wet earth, urine, decay; its own sounds: dripping water, the quick scratching of running rodent paws, the occasional flushing through an overhead pipe or clicking in a transformer box. And there were Jessie's sounds too: her quiet footsteps, her breathing, shallow and rapid.

That was the totality of the tunnel world. Jessie had almost grown used to it when someone started talking.

A man. Or a boy. Jessie stopped. She switched off the flashlight. Blackness.

The talking came from above, clear but slightly distant, like a voice from the next room. The man, or boy, said, "I know it's the middle of the night. I'm sorry." Silence. Then he spoke again: "I said I was sorry. But Mom? I hate it here. I want to come home." Another pause. "But I don't want to call you at the office. I want to talk about it now. Can't you . . . shit." Plastic clicked on plastic. Heavy footsteps creaked above Jessie's head. She must be under the residence; she thought she'd gone farther than that. She turned on the flash and shone it in the direction she'd come from. All she saw was a cone of light, edged in shadows, ending in darkness. Perhaps she had gone farther; perhaps it was another residence above her. She fought off an urge to go back and moved on.

Jessie hadn't taken many more steps before the tunnel divided: two dark corridors, parting at a forty-five-degree angle. She halted, shining her light along one, then the other. They looked identical. Kneeling, she examined the dirt floor, searching for footprints. There were many: a few deep corrugated impressions that might have been left by work boots; some smoother, flatter prints; one made by a waffle sole. The problem was the prints appeared with similar frequency in the entrances of both halves of the tunnel. And none appeared small enough to be size four.

Jessie stood up. *Be smart. Go back. Wait by the van.* But

she didn't go back. She stayed where she was. She heard water dripping, heard her own breathing, rapid and shallow. And then, out of the right-hand tunnel, floated the sound, very faint, of a guitar. Was there a voice too, a singing voice, high and wobbly? Jessie held her breath, listening as hard as she could. She wasn't sure. Suddenly she felt very cold. She started to shiver and couldn't stop. She stepped into the right-hand tunnel and kept going.

If there had been a singing voice, it was now quiet, but the sound of the guitar seemed to grow louder. Then it faded again, until Jessie could no longer hear it at all. She stopped. Had the sound filtered down from another residence? Could she be under the music building? Or had it come from somewhere in the tunnels?

Jessie turned back. After a little while, she heard the guitar music again, not so much in the tunnel, she now realized, as drifting behind the wall. The left-hand wall. She shone her light along it as she walked: cables, wires, damp brick. And then she saw a padlocked door set in the wall, with a sign on it saying, DANGER! HIGH VOLTAGE!

The door was low, no higher than Jessie's waist. She squatted before it, checking the padlock. It was a heavy brass padlock with a thick bolt, securely fastened to another bolt in the door frame. Jessie put her ear to the door. She heard the guitar music, clearer now. Chords. She almost recognized the song—the title wavered on the edge of her consciousness, then sank away.

She tugged at the padlock on the chance that someone hadn't bothered to snap it into place. No chance. Then, for no particular purpose, she grasped the doorknob, rattled it around and pulled. The door opened. The padlock was fastened to the doorframe, all right, but the frame was fastened to nothing. It came open with the door. Looking closely, Jessie saw that the frame had been pried off and the nails flattened on the other side.

Jessie aimed her beam into the doorway. The yellow cone illuminated a tunnel quite different from the one she was in. The ceiling was much lower. Cobwebs hung from it in thick, overlapping mats. A hairy-legged spider scrambled from one to another like a high-wire artist in a spotlight. The guitar playing was even clearer now, although Jessie had the strange sensation that it came from somewhere below. She got on her hands and

233

knees and crawled into the tunnel. The guitar playing stopped.

Jessie stopped too. It was very quiet in the low tunnel, the air dusty and stale. Jessie felt something moving in her hair. She reached back and batted away some feathery thing with a hard core, barely stifling a cry of disgust. Then she crawled forward.

The earthen floor was dry and covered with animal feces; they cast little shadows—round, oblong, cylindrical—but down the center of the tunnel most of them were flattened. Jessie paused from time to time to brush away cobwebs; then she would listen again for the guitar, fruitlessly, and keep going.

She sensed rather than saw the opening in the tunnel. The impression came on a cool draught against her face, a change in the sound of her knees sliding in the dust. A minute or two later, the yellow beam spread across a small, round cavern. Jessie crawled into it and stood up; her hair brushed against the roughly finished ceiling.

She looked around. The cavern had two openings: the low one she had just come through, and a higher one leading the other way. The walls seemed to have been blasted out of the rock. They were covered in faded paintings, psychedelic paintings, she saw as she went closer, executed in cheap poster paints. Naked lovers wrapped in robes of their mingled hair; giant eyes with fish leaping out of the pupils; penises ejaculating mushrooms: cave art by cavemen under the influence of Aubrey Beardsley and fantasy comics. Over the entrance to the higher tunnel were words, painted in rainbow colors, now barely legible: "I Kill Therefore I Am."

And in a little alcove on the far side, Jessie saw a narrow bed: a mattress, the ticking stained and dirty, resting on a rusty frame.

La Bohème.

Jessie entered the alcove. She saw more words lettered over the bed, white paint in wobbly lines on the rock: "Woodstock Nation." She touched the W. It was sticky.

The mattress, though soiled, was free of dust. Jessie raised one corner. Something fell to the floor. She felt under the bed and picked it up: a U.S. passport. Her index finger had just slipped under the front cover, but she hadn't opened it, when the scream came.

234

It was a wild scream, a man's or a woman's, Jessie didn't know: maybe not even human. It lifted her right off the ground. She banged her head on the rough ceiling, lost her balance, fell crouching, her heart beating crazily, the shaking flashlight aimed at the opening of the high tunnel, from where the sound had come.

For a moment, there was silence. Then Jessie heard a child crying.

A girl-child.

Jessie ran. She ran with all her strength into the high tunnel, following the jerking beam of light. Cobwebs and animal feces, distance and time—all went unnoticed. Jessie ran. The girl cried, not far away now. Not far away but . . . but what? Somewhere below. That realization was just striking her when her lead foot came down on emptiness, and she fell spinning through air. Her light stabbed out flashing views of brickwork and a glinting steel ladder. Then she hit the floor. The flashlight spun away, crashed on bricks, went out.

Jessie lay in utter blackness, the wind knocked out of her chest. She felt no pain, but couldn't move.

Silence.

Then footsteps.

A candle shone. Partly blinded by its light, Jessie could make out nothing more than a gleam on a bald head.

"Pat?" she said.

"Smarty pants," said a man. It wasn't Pat. It was the singer with the high, wobbly voice.

He came closer. He looked down. A smile appeared in the darkness, a surprised smile, Jessie thought, surprised and pleased. She tried to get up. She was still trying when something swished through the air. Then she felt pain, rocketing through her head and exploding into nothingness.

27

Zorro didn't look quite so young anymore.

The observation pleased Bao Dai. But maybe it was just the dim light. He interrupted the blues riff he was playing on the guitar—it wasn't plugged in, so he alone knew how hot the music was—and picked up the candle. He held the candle close to Zorro's face. Zorro flinched away from the flame, but not before Bao Dai saw it was true: he looked older.

"Look," Zorro said, "I think we should try to work something out." He spoke in a whisper, because the little girl was sleeping.

Bao Dai plugged in the guitar and turned the volume up to 5. "Like what?" he said, picking up the blues riff where he'd left off, or maybe it was another one.

"Don't do that," Zorro said. "She's sleeping."

"I'm playing a lullaby." He moved into "Big Rock Candy

236

Mountain," sang a few lines until he forgot the words, ran off a little solo. He saw that Zorro was listening, saw he didn't think it was very good. Had he missed a note? Or two? Maybe his technique wasn't the best. It was the style that counted. Couldn't people see that?

Bao Dai stopped playing. "You think you're such a star."

"I don't."

"A bigshot professional guitar player."

"There are hundreds of guys like me."

"There's no one like me."

The girl writhed in her sleep. Maybe the nylon ropes were bothering her. Bao Dai had removed the copper wire for sleeping, but he couldn't risk the ropes.

"Couldn't we work this out?"

"You mean make a deal?"

"Something like that, yes."

"Like the last deal we made?"

Bao Dai held the candle close to Zorro's face. Zorro flinched

"I'll do everything I can to make it up to you," he said.

Bao Dai didn't speak. He just held the candle close to Zorro's face.

"Just tell me what you want."

"Everything," Bao Dai said.

"Everything?"

"Everything you took. Your house. Your Zorro house."

"I didn't take the house from you."

"No? Whose name is it in?"

Zorro had no answer.

"The house," Bao Dai repeated.

"All right."

"The guitar."

"What guitar?"

"This one. It's mine anyway, by right."

"But—" Zorro started to say Bao Dai's name.

"Don't you ever call me that. My name is Bao Dai."

"Okay, but you know the guitar is mine."

"Just because he gave it to you? It's mine, by right. You stole my style."

"That's not true either. Can't we handle this in a reason-

237

able way, before something . . . irrevocable happens?"

Before something irrevocable happens? The remark outraged Bao Dai. A raw red tide spilled through his mind, washing away all thought, all capacity for thought. He shoved the burning candle into Zorro's nose.

Zorro screamed.

The girl sat up. She screamed too.

Bao Dai pulled the candle out. Up until that moment he hadn't laid a finger on Zorro. He was sorry. "I'm sorry," he said. The raw red tide receded.

But it left him feeling good. He hadn't felt so good since he'd done what he did to Corporal Trinh. He felt the same sense of release, of freedom, of justice.

Bao Dai relit the candle. Zorro and the little girl were watching him. There was a change in their expressions. He was God in a three-cornered world.

They were still watching him a few moments later when the little world suddenly changed. From nearby came a heavy thud. The thud was followed by a tinkling sound, like a rolling hubcap.

Bao Dai was on his feet, the candle in one hand, the wire cutters in the other. "Not a sound." Bao Dai mouthed the words, rather than spoke them, then quickly moved away through the shadows.

A body lay on the floor. A woman's body. It moved. A face peered up into the candlelight.

"Pat?" said the woman.

Bao Dai recognized her.

Wifey.

Or ex-wifey. The one with the nice tits.

"Smarty pants," he said and brought the wire cutters down on her head, not too hard. Kind of gently, in fact.

Bao Dai opened the door near the stairs and dragged the woman inside. Then he went back and bound the little girl in copper wire. He hadn't removed Zorro's wire in the first place. Now he added more.

Bao Dai returned to the woman. Her chest rose and fell with her breathing. She was fine, just fine. Bao Dai bent over and raised her sweater. Her tits—nice tits—stiffened in the cold air. Bao Dai watched them stiffen. After a while, they

238

stopped stiffening and relaxed a little. Bao Dai wanted to see them stiffen some more. He reached out and touched one. It was smooth and soft and springy. Did he feel a little stirring in his groin? Or had he imagined it? He put the candle on the floor to free his other hand, then reached for her again.

Bright lights went on all around him.

Part Three

Part Three

28

Ivan Zyzmchuk's eyes
snapped open.

How long had he been asleep? He checked his watch. 2:18
A.M. No more than half an hour. He lay still on the too-soft
mattress, listening. It was quiet. He no longer heard the dark-
haired woman moving on the other side of the dividing wall, no
longer heard the voice of the TV preacher. The only sound was
the diminishing whine of a car, fading away to the north. Nothing
abnormal; he closed his eyes.

But he didn't sink back down into sleep. Although his body
was tired, his eyelids now wanted to stay open. After a while
he stopped fighting them and got out of bed. He looked out the
window. Light leaked through the curtains of the room next
door, pooling in the dark-haired woman's parking space.

It was empty.

Wearing his bathrobe, Zyzmchuk opened the door and went
outside. The whining car had passed out of hearing range. He

243

peered into the window of number 19. Through the finger-breadth gap in the curtain he could see a tapering expanse of beige carpet, the leather suitcase he had lifted off the carousel, now open, with a red sweater on top, and a corner of the still-made bed.

He was still looking at this long, narrow scene when he heard more car sounds, again from the north; but these grew louder instead of fading away, and so rapidly that he barely had time to step into the shadows before the car itself appeared, flashing by at enormous speed. But it was a van, not the kind of car he was looking for, and it was out of sight in seconds, leaving behind three or four notes from a car stereo, bent once by musicians, bent again by the Doppler effect, and a glimpse of painted flames.

Zyzmchuk returned to his room, splashed cold water on his face and dressed. As he was tying his shoes, he heard another car go by, also very fast, also headed south. It had disappeared by the time he went outside. He didn't give it much thought: the sound of the dark-haired woman driving off must have awakened him. He got into his own car and drove north.

On the other side of Zyzmchuk's windshield, an all-black world glided by. The sky was blackest, next the strip of road, finally the fields and trees on both sides, shading almost into gray. He hit ninety miles an hour as he crossed the state line, leaning over the wheel, searching for two red dots in the blackness. But they never appeared. Zyzmchuk drove into Bennington, turned around and went back to the 1826 House. The lights in room 19 were still on; the open suitcase with the red sweater still visible through the parting in the curtains. Zyzmchuk entered his own room, undressed and went back to bed. There was nothing else to do.

But he couldn't sleep.

It wasn't just a matter of eyelids determined to spring open; the little outing had stimulated his heart. It had pumped fresh blood through his arteries, waking him fully.

3:10.

Zyzmchuk lay impatiently in bed until four, listening for cars, and when none came, hoping his body would slow down. Then he gave up, put on his sweats and his J. C. Penney sneakers and went out. Roadwork.

Zyzmchuk set off toward the campus. He hadn't gone a mile before he realized the falsity of this nighttime surge of energy. In the back of his mind, he had known he would pay for his lack of sleep; he hadn't known the payment would be demanded so soon. Now, as he pounded past the music building, with its hulking shadow of the steel guitarist, he faltered. Faster, he willed himself, as he had many times in the past; he knew his body—sometimes it had to be driven, that's all, but once it reached the plateau, it remained there. Faster. Faster. Push. But this time, and it was the first time in his life, his legs, thick, strong, powerful, did not obey. He ran on, but pounding slowed to plodding, slowed still more. Zyzmchuk stopped and sat down, resting his back against the cold steel guitarist. He wasn't at all winded, didn't ache anywhere, yet knew he couldn't go on. He pressed his thigh with his fingers, as though examining a strange object: it seemed, as always, full of muscle. But when he got up and tried again to run, the same thing happened.

Zyzmchuk walked slowly across the campus, still feeling the cold steel at his back and absorbing the implication, immense yet mundane: you're going to be fifty-seven in a few weeks. This is what it means.

Zyzmchuk walked past the music building, down stone steps and around a square brick structure that had the look of a dormitory. He crossed the lawn and came to a street, quiet and still. A van was parked by the curb—a black van with a flash of red on the side, possibly the van that had sped by the 1826 House a few hours before. Zyzmchuk stared at the van for a minute or two before he realized that he knew the car parked right behind it.

Zyzmchuk looked around. He scanned the façade of the dormitory, noted lights shining in the stairwells but not the rooms; saw a closed hatch cover on the lawn, poked it lightly with his foot; then, walking away, stepped on something hard: a broken lock.

A moment later, Zyzmchuk had the hatch cover open and was peering down a dark hole. His powerful flashlight lay in the toolbox at the motel. He considered going back for it, but first checked the cars parked on the street. Few of the drivers had bothered to lock their doors. Zyzmchuk found a book of matches on the dashboard of the fifth car he tried.

He struck a match at the mouth of the hole. Flickering yellow reflections marched down the shiny rungs of a steel ladder. Zyzmchuk followed them.

At the bottom he lit another match and examined the floor. Many feet had left prints in the moist earth; one set, much smaller than the rest, was bare.

The match went out. Zyzmchuk didn't bother to light another. He patted the brick wall on either side of the ladder, finding, as he'd thought he would, a switch. He flicked it; a bulb flashed on over his head, and others, every thirty feet or so, casting yellowish pools that didn't quite meet but provided adequate illumination down a long tunnel.

Zyzmchuk went forward. He moved quickly, aware of wires and cables, dripping water and fetid smells, all expected, all instantly ignored. He was looking for something else, although he couldn't name it: he'd know it when he saw it.

The tunnel divided. Zyzmchuk knelt, studied the floor. Footprints pointed back and forth at the entrances to both halves, but the freshest prints lay to the right. There were four sets of these: the first made by a man in leather shoes, the kind businessmen wear; the second by another man, heavier than the first, who wore waffle-soled shoes and might have been limping; the third by a woman in some sort of sensible shoes, loafers perhaps; and the fourth, not really a set, but a single print left by a small bare heel. Zyzmchuk followed them, not because they meant anything to him, but because they were the freshest.

A few minutes later, he found that the tracks led to a low, padlocked door in the left-hand wall. Zyzmchuk tugged at the lock, testing the possibility of ripping the hasp out of the wood. The door, and the frame, swung open.

Zyzmchuk crawled through. He was in another tunnel, more dimly lit than the main one. He kept going. Cobwebs swept through his hair, stuck to his face; he didn't pause to wipe them away. He was hurrying now, although he couldn't have explained why.

Space opened around him. Zyzmchuk found himself in a round, rock-walled chamber with a higher ceiling, but not quite high enough for him to stand upright. Lying in the dust in front of him was a U.S. passport.

Zyzmchuk opened it. He saw a photograph of a man he didn't know and a name: Gerald Brenner. He leafed through the pages. There were many stamps in Gerald Brenner's passport, too many to examine now.

Zyzmchuk rose, stooping, and examined painted walls, a bed and the entrance to another tunnel, over which he read: "I Kill Therefore I Am."

A perversion of Descartes's aphorism; beyond that, it meant nothing to him. Probably it represented some undergraduate joke; still, he quickened his pace even more as he entered the tunnel. But he had to slow down almost immediately: the tunnel was unlit. Glass crunched under his shoes. He stopped and lit a match. A broken light bulb lay at his feet. And a few yards ahead, the tunnel floor disappeared abruptly in a void.

Zyzmchuk moved to the edge and spun the match into the blackness. Before it went out, he glimpsed another steel ladder, leading ten or twelve feet straight down, and the continuation of the tunnel at a lower level.

Zyzmchuk climbed down the ladder, lit another match. To one side of the ladder was a cracked wooden door, sagging on its hinges. He thought for the first time of his gun, locked in the safe in his apartment, as he pushed the door open.

It led to a small, dusty storage room. In the flickering match light, Zyzmchuk saw another smashed light bulb, broken furniture in crooked stacks, moldy cardboard boxes, littered fast-food wrappers and soft drink cans. One of the wrappers contained a half-eaten hamburger with onions and ketchup.

Zyzmchuk sniffed it—not at all spoiled—and moved farther into the room. A couch stood against the side wall, in reversed position, its high back facing the room. He held the match over it and found the dark-haired woman, supine on the other side, her sweater drawn up around her neck.

Zyzmchuk pulled the couch away from the wall, quickly but gently, and knelt by the woman's head. Blood, glistening deep red in the feeble match light, had soaked her hair, still seeped through it onto torn and dirty cushions. Zyzmchuk touched her throat. The skin was cool and dry; a slow, heavy pulse beat beneath it. Lowering his head to hers, he felt her breath on his face. Warm breath. It smelled of nothing. Perhaps blood.

Jessie Shapiro. Or Jessie Rodney. She breathed on his face two or three more times. He pulled the sweater down over her breasts.

He spoke her name. "Jessie? Jessie?"

There was no answer. Her eyes, he saw as the match went out, remained closed. Long lashes curled in the yellow-brown light, then vanished.

Zyzmchuk lit another match, his last, and examined her head. The wound was over her right ear, not deep but long and jagged. He had nothing clean to cover it with. His clothes were dirty from the tunnel, so were hers. All he could do was wipe his hands together hard in the hope of rubbing away the dirt and then lay one of them on the wound. He applied pressure.

The dark-haired woman's blood wet Zyzmchuk's palm, seeped through his fingers. He sat on the couch, rested her head on his lap and pressed harder. Time passed in black silence. Her blood stopped flowing.

"Jessie?"

No reply.

No, he thought, reaching for her throat. But she wasn't dead: he felt the even pulse, stronger than before, felt her breath on his face. He ran his hand over her body, searching for more wounds, or signs of internal damage. He found none.

Then Ivan Zyzmchuk lifted Jessie Shapiro in his arms and took her out of the storage room. He knew at once he'd have no trouble carrying her out of the tunnels, or much farther if he had to. His fatigue was forgotten. He didn't feel her weight at all.

29

The sound of crying played like background music in her sleep. It seemed, as before, to float up from somewhere below, but not, this time, from the bottomless depths of a flooded basement. This time, she knew even without investigating, the crying came twisting up through endless black tunnels.

That was one difference.

The other was that the crier was no longer Kate, but herself. And the words she cried were, "Daddy, Daddy."

When it became unbearable, Jessie opened her eyes.

Silence. The room was thick with silence. It had the consistency of honey. Honey filled her ears, her head, formed a thin film over her eyes.

The room was her motel room. She recognized the floral curtains, the beige carpet, the TV where the white-suited preacher had pranced. Someone had rearranged the furniture, that was all. Oh yes, and removed the fireplace.

That and her suitcase. It was gone, too.

Jessie sat up. Up, up snapped her head, like something at the end of a rubber band. The room tilted and started whirling. Jessie fell back on the pillows.

The whirling slowed and stopped. The room righted itself. Honey flowed from her mind, as though a plug had been pulled. Memories flooded in. Jessie put her hand to her head and felt gauze bandages.

She tried sitting up again. This time she did it without unhinging the room. She shifted her legs to the side of the bed, pushed back the blankets. Every movement required great effort. She'd put on weight. Three or four hundred pounds.

Jessie lowered her feet to the floor and paused to gather her strength. After a while she gave up and took her chances at standing without it. There. Up. Not so tough. The room tilted again, but quickly settled back into place—just showing her it still had the power.

Jessie took a step. She instantly lost the three or four hundred pounds and grew several feet. That made walking a challenge—like stilts, only not so much fun. She moved her other foot and swayed like a sapling in the breeze. First one way, then the other. But soon she started to get the hang of it. In only two or three minutes, she went all the way to the bathroom.

Jessie looked at herself in the mirror. She didn't like what she saw. It wasn't just the pale skin, the purple pockets under the eyes and the white bandage wrapped like a turban that bothered her. It was the expression in the eyes themselves, an expression of fear and worse, much worse, helplessness too. The kind of look a woman couldn't show to the world, the kind of look Barbara hated. Could a bang on the head do all that?

Jessie turned away.

Maybe a bath would make her feel better; maybe a bath would wash that expression from her eyes. She reached for the taps and noticed for the first time that she was wearing a terry cloth robe. A nice robe—soft, clean, comfortable, but not hers. It was cut for a much bigger person, perhaps for the same person whose shaving kit lay beside the sink.

Jessie looked in it: A Bic razor, a hairbrush, a toothbrush, toothpaste. A Spartan kit, not at all like Pat's, or Philip's, bulg-

ing with grooming supplies. That was mildly interesting obser
vation number one. Mildly interesting observation number two
was that her own toilet bag wasn't there.

Jessie sat on the edge of the tub. She considered her options.
Call the motel manager. Call Buddy Boucher. Draw a bath. She
was still considering them when a key turned in the lock and
the front door opened.

Jessie rose, still shaky, and took the Bic razor from the
shaving kit. She moved to the bathroom door.

A man was standing in the main room: a big man in corduroys and a fisherman's sweater, with iron-gray hair, cut very
short. She knew right away that the razor wouldn't be much of
a weapon against him.

He was watching her. If he noticed the razor, held up in
her right hand as though it possessed the threatening power of
a gun or a knife, he gave no sign.

He said, "Where's the nurse?"

He didn't speak loudly, but his voice carried effortlessly, as
though from thick, long vocal cords, connected to something
deep inside.

"Nurse?" Jessie said.

The man turned, opened the door, looked outside. A pouter
pigeon–chested woman was ambling across the parking lot; she
wore a white dress and carried a white styrofoam cup.

"Hiya," she said to the man as she came in. "Just nipped
out for coffee."

"Nip on," he said.

"What?"

"You can go now," he told her.

The nurse's face tilted up belligerently; from that angle, she
had a good view of the look in his eye and reconsidered whatever
retort she had in mind. "I was only gone five minutes," she said
instead.

The man nodded; at the same time he held the door for her.
The discussion was over. The nurse's mouth opened. It closed.
She went out.

The man turned to Jessie. They looked at each other. Jessie
thought of saying, "Who are you?" The question sounded stupid
in her mind. She left it unsaid.

251

But he answered it anyway. "My name's—" he said; there followed a word beginning with Z; two or three strange syllables she didn't catch.

"And what . . . what do you want?" Jessie asked.

"Just checking up," the man said.

"Are you a doctor?"

"No. He's at the infirmary."

"What's wrong with my head."

"Slight concussion. And a cut. He stitched it up." The man's gaze shifted to the turban. He frowned. "Not as neatly as some." A look must have appeared on her face; the man saw it and quickly added, "But he got the job done, and nothing will show, when your hair grows back."

"Great," Jessie said. Her hand moved involuntarily toward the back of her head.

"Careful," said the man, "with that razor."

Jessie lowered her hand, stuck the razor in the pocket of the terry cloth robe. "How many stitches did I get?"

"Not too many. Twenty-five or thirty, I think."

The room wobbled slightly, as if about to go into the tilting routine.

"Are you all right?" the man asked.

"Fine, thank you," Jessie said, a little icily, to counter any helplessness he might see in her eyes.

"You're welcome," said the man. "Why don't you sit down?"

"I like standing."

Jessie watched him watching her. He had gray eyes to match his iron-gray hair. Was there something familiar about him? "Are you with Mr. Mickey?" she said. The words were out before she'd given them any thought.

"Mr. Mickey?"

"Or it might be his first name. I don't really know."

If Z-man thought these remarks nonsensical, he didn't let it show. "Why would I be with him?" he asked.

"I don't know. It was just a thought." Maybe the two men were connected in her mind by their size and the strength they exuded; this man was not as tall as Mr. Mickey, but much broader.

"A thought springing from what, exactly?"

"I don't know. I don't know what I'm saying, exactly." The man's expression, until now neutral, shaded toward the unfriendly, without any physical change Jessie could identify. "Who are you?" she asked, this time aloud.

"I told you my name."

"I didn't catch it."

"My name doesn't matter." There was a pause. Then the man said, "I think I'll sit, even if you don't."

"Make yourself at home."

"Why not? It's my room."

He sat in the soft chair on the other side of the bed. His movements were easy and economical; they might have been called graceful in a smaller man.

"And this is your robe?"

"Yes."

"Where are my things?"

"Next door. In your room."

Jessie opened her mouth to say something, stopped herself.

"Go on," said the man.

"I—I'm a little confused, that's all."

He nodded. "A blow on the head will do that," he said and in the same relaxed tone, added, "Who gave it to you?"

"I—how did you know it was a blow?"

"A glancing one," the man said. "But with something heavy. You're lucky to be alive."

"Is that what the doctor said?"

The man shook his head. "He thinks you hurt yourself in a fall."

"Why?"

"Because that's what I told him. Of course, any good doctor would have known it was a lie. But, as I explained—"

"He wasn't a very good doctor."

The man smiled, very quickly. It was gone in a moment.

"Why did you lie to him?"

"Because it made no difference in terms of your treatment. X-rays. Stitches. Tetanus shot. Painkiller. And blows on the head lead to questions, the police, etcetera. I wasn't sure you wanted all those complications."

Jessie gazed across the room at the man, trying to see through to the meaning behind his words. She couldn't. The room wobbled again.

"Why don't you sit down?"

"I'm fine."

"The doctor thought you should spend the day in bed."

"But you said he was a lousy doctor. You can't play it both ways."

He gave her a long look. "Suit yourself."

But all at once the idea of sitting was irresistible, perhaps because she was elongating again, and the room was turning white. Jessie took a few steps forward, controlled, balanced steps, she thought, and sat on the edge of the bed, not too heavily. She waited for the man to say, "That's better." He didn't. He didn't say anything at all. His gray eyes had an inward look, as though they'd gone behind the clouds.

Jessie took a deep breath. Colors flowed back into the room. "Did you find me in the tunnel?" she asked.

He nodded. The clouds in his eyes drifted away.

"Are you a policeman?" Something about him reminded her of DeMarco—DeMarco was about the same height, although not quite as wide.

"No," he said.

Like DeMarco, but less aggressive, she decided. So she asked, "Are you with campus security?"

He smiled his quick smile. "Security in general."

"What does that mean?"

"It means I'd like you to tell me what you were doing down in the tunnels."

"And if I don't?"

"Then I'll have to fill in the blanks myself. That'll waste time, and worse than that, I might not be able to do it."

"What were *you* doing in the tunnels?"

"Looking for you. What do you do for a living by the way?"

"Why do you want to know that?"

"No reason."

Jessie told him.

"I'd never have thought of that," he said. He shook his head, smiling to himself. Then he asked, "Who hit you on the head? Pat Rodney?"

"How do you know Pat?"

"I don't."

He didn't know Pat. He didn't know Mr. Mickey. "How do

you know about him, then? I don't understand your interest in all of this."

"All of what?"

Jessie said nothing.

The man rose, walked to the window, parted the curtains. Light rain dripped from a low gray sky. "When I was a kid I had a book," the man said, still looking out the window. "It was the story of two coal miners. Bazak and Vaclav. They don't know each other. They're from different villages and work in different mines. Then one day they both swing their picks, and the wall between them falls down." He drew the curtains, turned to Jessie. "It was a picture book. I still remember the look on their faces."

"Is that supposed to be a parable?"

"Just a memory." He reached into the pocket of his corduroys. "Here's your mail. It came while you were asleep."

He leaned across the bed and handed Jessie an envelope. It had Appleman and Carr printed in the top left-hand corner and was addressed to her at the 1826 House. It was also torn along one side.

"It's been opened," Jessie said.

The man gazed at her unblinking and didn't speak.

"You had no right to read my mail."

He sat down in the chair. "You might as well read it too," he said. "Otherwise we can't discuss it."

Angry thoughts shot through her brain, but none of them translated themselves into effective language. Jessie opened the envelope. Inside was a letter from Dick Carr, enclosing a money order for five hundred dollars. "In going through Barbara's papers," he wrote in the last paragraph, "I found a file labeled with your name. It contained a memo written by Barbara on the day of her death, raising the possibility of applying for a court order to examine your ex-husband's bank records, in hope of tracing him through recent transactions. I took the liberty of so applying, and aided by Lieutenant DeMarco's warrant of the twentieth, was successful. Enclosed please find a copy of all Mr. Rodney's savings and checking transactions for the past two years, as well as the contents of his safety deposit box. I hope this will be of some help."

Jessie hadn't known that Pat kept a safety deposit box. Now she examined what Dick Carr had found in it.

On top was a clipping, slightly yellowed, from *The New York Times*, January 6, 1971:

HARTLEY FRAME

The Pentagon announced today that Hartley E. Frame, son of Sen. Edmund S. Frame (D. Va.) and Alice Frame, has been removed from the Missing-in-Action list and declared dead. The action resulted from an inspection tour of North Vietnamese prison camps by a Red Cross delegation.

Pfc. Frame was born on October 4, 1947, in Sweet Briar Va. He attended the Hill School in Pottstown Pa. and Morgan College, Morgantown Mass. He is survived by his parents.

The second enclosure from the safety deposit box was a sheaf of counterfoils, stapled together. Each recorded a ten-thousand-dollar payment to Eggman Cookies; each was dated March 18. They were annual payments from 1971 to last year.

Jessie looked up, into iron-gray eyes. "I need to know what side you're on," she said.

"What sides are there?"

"I don't know." Jessie realized the truth of her words as she spoke them and suddenly knew the helpless look was in her eyes. "I don't even fucking know that," she said. And then she was crying, uncontrollably, in front of a stranger, the way she had cried "Daddy, Daddy" in her dream. The room began to tilt and spin. Jessie rolled over, buried her face in the sheets.

She was half-aware of the man moving across the room. Then she felt him bending over her, sensed his hand moving toward her.

But he didn't touch her.

He moved away. Water ran in the bathroom. He returned. "Here."

He held out a glass of water and two vials. Jessie wiped her face on the sheet and sat up. "What are those?"

"Amoxicillin," he read from the label. "One every four hours. And painkillers. As needed."

256

Jessie took the antibiotic, drained the glass. She was very thirsty.

"What about the painkillers?"

"I'm okay," Jessie said, returning them unopened. Her head was hurting, but she needed to think clearly. The man was watching her very closely, almost as though he could gauge her pain just by looking. "It says 'as needed,' right?" she asked.

"Right." He took the empty glass, holding it in both his broad hands like a thing of value.

"You might as well talk to me," he said. "I already know you're looking for Pat Rodney. I know he's your ex-husband. I know he's got your daughter. I know he's with another man. I know you're interested in Hartley Frame. I know you tried to trace him at the Alumni Affairs Office and that you questioned Alice Frame about him, not too successfully."

"How do you know all that about me?"

He looked surprised. "I didn't think you were trying to hide your movements."

Jessie stared at him for a moment. Then, despite the tears on her face, despite the pounding in her head, she laughed. Not loudly, not long, but a real laugh. He smiled again. "You must think I'm pretty stupid," Jessie said.

"I don't."

"Try your name on me once more."

"Just call me Ivan."

"That's a funny name for an FBI agent."

"What makes you think I'm an FBI agent?" There was a new tone in his voice; if she had had to guess, Jessie would have said he sounded insulted.

"Doesn't the FBI guard senators and that sort of thing?"

"I don't guard senators."

"Then why are you interested in me?"

"Fill in the blanks. Then I'll know."

Jessie made a decision. She made it on the basis of little things, because she didn't know enough about the big things to form an opinion. Little things. The glass of water. Reaching out to touch her and then not. The quick smile. The thoughtful look that had drifted across the gray eyes. It wasn't logical. It was impulsive, intuitive, feminine—all those things that hadn't made America great.

257

"All right, Ivan," Jessie said, "where do I start?"

"Where you like," he said.

Jessie started on a Sunday afternoon in Santa Monica, with the sun a strange white ball low in the sky and a long wait for a blue BMW that never came. She told Ivan about the message on Pat's phone, about Blue, and Spacious Skies. She told him about Pat's blackboard, Mr. Mickey, the house in Malibu. She left out nothing—not Gato's record store, not Philip, not DeMarco. Not Barbara. He brought her suitcase from next door so she could show him the broken barrette and the Reeboks with the blue stripes. Zyzmchuk had to get a key from the office; Jessie couldn't find hers.

She also showed him the picture of Kate at the beach, standing like a stork. He put on glasses to look at it. "Just for close-up work," he muttered, so low and quick she hardly heard him. Then he studied the picture for a long time—much longer, she thought, than necessary for just the memorization of Kate's image. He handed it back without a word and took off his glasses.

At the end, Jessie was exhausted. Her head ached; she didn't have the strength to get off the bed. But she felt a strange relief. She had emptied her mind into his.

Ivan sat for a while, the thoughtful look in his eyes. Then he said, "Was Mickey, or Mr. Mickey, the man in the tunnels?"

"I don't think so. The man in the tunnels wasn't big enough. And Mr. Mickey's not bald. But who else would have been trying to kill me?"

"Whoever it was didn't try to kill you."

"Why do you say that?"

Zyzmchuk thought of her bare torso, the sweater pulled up over her breasts. He probably should have had the doctor examine her for signs of sexual penetration, probably still should. But he just said, "Because you're not dead."

She was watching him. She had eyes he didn't want to lie to. "Is that the whole reason?" she asked.

"What else would there be?" It was an evasion, not a lie, but it brought the helpless look briefly to her eyes, and he wasn't happy with himself for that.

"I don't know," she said.

Zyzmchuk rose briskly, rubbing his hands, trying to kindle optimism in the air. "Tell me about the words on the blackboard."

"They said 'Make hay while the sun shines.' In phonetic Arabic."

"But what were the exact words?"

What were they? Jessie remembered Philip, thinking they were French: You something the you. "Toi giet la toi."

"Spell it."

She did.

"What makes you think that's Arabic?"

"Mr. Mickey told me."

"It's not Arabic."

"What is it?"

"Let's find out." Ivan picked up the phone, dialed. "Hello, Grace," he said. "I need a translation. . . . The phrase is 'toi giet la toi.' " He gave the spelling and hung up.

Ivan sat in the easy chair. Jessie sat on the bed. A minute went by, then another. The phone rang. He picked it up. "Zyzmchuk," he said; this time Jessie caught the name. He listened for a few moments and put down the phone.

He looked at Jessie. " 'Toi giet la toi'—there are accents, apparently—is Vietnamese," he said. "It means, 'I kill, therefore I am.' "

Jessie thought of the words in the tunnel and the song she'd heard at Erica McTaggart's: "Descartes Kills." "I—I'm not sure I understand."

Ivan rose from the chair and came toward her. He held out his hand. "Bazak," he said, "meet Vaclav."

Jessie reached out. They shook hands.

30

Ivan Zyzmchuk, sitting at the desk in room 20 at the 1826 House, opened Gerald Brenner's passport. Jessie looked over his shoulder as he turned the pages.

Gerald Burton Brenner. A bald man with a round head and a big, loose smile. Born Oakland, California, 1951. He'd done a lot of traveling—Hong Kong, China, Japan, Australia, New Zealand, all in the past year. The most recent stamp was Thai: he'd entered Bangkok October 29, left on November 1.

"Seen him before?" Zyzmchuk asked.

Jessie examined the photograph. "No."

"Could he have been the man in the tunnel?"

"It was dark so I can't be sure, but I think the man in the tunnel had a different shape of head—longer and narrower."

He turned to her. "How many bald men can there be?"

"What do you mean?"

"One bald man at the car dealer, identified as your ex-husband. A second bald man in the tunnels and, let's assume, driving the van. You heard his voice. It wasn't your ex-husband's."

"No."

Zyzmchuk's index finger traced the outlines of Gerald Brenner's smile. "So is this baldy number three? Or is that stretching things a little?"

"Do you mean you don't believe me?" For a moment Jessie had a sickening feeling they'd swung suddenly onto the same detour she and DeMarco had taken.

But Zyzmchuk said, "Not at all," and turned back to the passport. On the last page he found Gerald Brenner's address in San Jose, California; his next of kin, Ginny Brenner, wife; and a phone number.

"What d'you say?" he said.

"What do *you* say?" Jessie replied.

She saw the quick smile. "Strike," he said, picking up the phone. "Strike, strike and strike again. Marshall Zhukov, or one of that crowd." He dialed the number in Gerald Brenner's passport, then held the receiver so Jessie could listen too.

The call was answered halfway through the first ring. "Hello?" a woman said, sounding small and faraway.

"Gerald Brenner, please."

There was silence on the other end. Then the woman said, "Who is this?"

"I'm a friend of Jerry's from Auckland. I'm in the States for a few days and thought I might look him up."

After another silence, the woman said, "What's your name?"

"Vaclav."

"I don't remember him mentioning you."

Zyzmchuk turned the pages of the passport until he came to the New Zealand stamp. Jessie noticed how unhurriedly his fingers moved.

"We only met in July," Zyzmchuk said. "But we seemed to hit it off. Are you Ginny?"

"Yes." Static buzzed in the line. Jessie could barely hear the woman say, "Did he mention me?" The connection seemed to be breaking and so, thought Jessie, did Ginny Brenner's voice.

"He did," Zyzmchuk said.

The woman began to cry. "Oh, Mr. Vaclav, something horrible has happened. Jerry's dead."

"No. What happened?"

"He was killed. Murdered. In Bangkok. He's been missing since the end of October, but they only found his body two weeks ago." She sobbed small, faraway sobs. "He—it was floating in one of the canals."

"But—why?"

"They say it must have been robbery. Jerry made a big sale over there on the thirty-first, and apparently there was some celebrating. No one saw him after that." Ginny Brenner's voice broke again.

"I'm very sorry," Zyzmchuk said. "Is it absolutely certain?"

"What do you mean?"

"That it was Jerry."

"Oh, yes. The—he was identified by the company's Bangkok subagent."

"This is terrible news."

"I know," said Ginny Brenner. "I know."

Zyzmchuk said good-bye and hung up.

Jessie backed a step or two away. "You were very good at that," she said.

Ivan Zyzmchuk was still for a moment. Then his head turned toward the photograph of Kate at the beach, which lay on the desk. He looked at it, then at Jessie. He wasn't angry, not even annoyed. "Are we going to discuss means and ends?" he asked.

"No," Jessie said, then added, "Not about this."

Zyzmchuk laughed, a full sound that, like his voice, seemed to rise from somewhere deep in his body. "My kind of ethics," he said. His eyes found hers for a moment, glanced away. "Do you feel up to a drive?" he asked.

"Where? Spacious Skies?"

"Bull's-eye," he said. "You don't need me at all."

Yes, I do, Jessie thought. But she didn't say it.

She got off the bed. White fog crept round the edges of her vision; the room started to play its tricks again.

"Sure you're all right?"

The question reached her through wads of cotton batting. She sat back down on the bed. "Just give me a minute," she said.

Jessie took a few deep breaths. She felt the gray eyes on her profile. Okay. Now. Slow and easy.

She stood up. Her vision stayed clear. The room stayed still.

"Let's go," Jessie said.

"Take one of these first." He was holding out the pain-killers.

Jessie shook her head. "I have to be smart."

"Take it for me."

"For you?"

"Yeah. It'll bring you down to my level. And I'll feel better."

Jessie took the pill.

They went to the parking lot. The cold found her weak spot right away, tracing the outline of her wound like an icicle tip. "Is this the kind of car the FBI hands out?" she asked, as he opened the door for her.

"Too fancy for the FBI," Zyzmchuk replied. "It's on loan from the White House."

They drove north, Zyzmchuk at the wheel, Jessie beside him in the passenger seat. Late afternoon: the sky hard blue, the earth gold, with the occasional blaze of a still-red tree.

"Do you have any children, Ivan?"

"No."

Jessie glanced at his face. He was watching the road. The question in her mind, a foolish question but one that had risen there abruptly, all on its own, was, Are you married? But what she said was, "You seem to have accepted my story."

"So far."

"But why?"

"That's a funny question. Why not?"

"Lieutenant DeMarco didn't."

"That's one reason right there."

"Surely you don't know him?"

"No. I meant you didn't have to tell me he didn't believe you. So you've told me the truth, or you're operating on a very high level of cleverness. Either way, I'm curious."

263

"Is that it, then: curiosity?"

"What other reasons could there be?"

"That's what I've been thinking about."

Outside a cow raised its head over a fence rail and looked right through them as they went by. Next came a little boy in a plaid lumber jacket, surrounded by bushels of apples. MACS AND CORTLANDS—79 CENTS A BOUCHEL. His eyes looked right through them too.

"And?" Zyzmchuk said.

"And I wondered whether you worked for Senator Frame."

"Why?"

"You said you saw me talking to his wife. And you've got a D.C. license plate. So I thought you might be here on account of him."

"I already told you I wasn't."

"You told me you weren't guarding him. You might be working for him in some other capacity. Or for her."

Zyzmchuk smiled. This one lingered on his face. "That adds up, all right, but not to the right answer. The senator and I have never met. I don't know his wife, either."

"But you knew who she was, what she looks like."

Zyzmchuk turned to her, an amused gleam still in his eyes. "How long is the interrogation going to last?"

"It's not—"

"Look," Zyzmchuk said, "I'm a government investigator. You've figured that out already. Why not leave it there?"

Jessie went silent. More cows passed by and an orchard, bare and deserted. "But what are you investigating?" she said when she couldn't hold it back any longer.

Zyzmchuk turned to her as he had before, but now the humorous glimmer had vanished from his eyes. "I'll know when I find it."

"It doesn't have anything to do with drugs, does it? You're not a drug agent?"

"I couldn't afford their haircuts."

Jessie wanted to say, Why can't you tell me? But it sounded like a nagging question, and she didn't want to nag. Why not? She wanted the information, didn't she? Yes, but she'd finally found someone who might be able to help her, and she didn't want to antagonize him. And there was a second reason, too, or the beginnings of one, farther back in her mind, which she didn't want to examine too closely, or too soon. Jessie remained silent the rest of the way, except for giving directions.

They followed Route 8 to the third turning on the left. Zyzmchuk slowed down by the mailbox with the handpainted blue flowers curling around the faded peace sign and stopped the car. He checked the mailbox. There was nothing inside, Jessie saw, but why hadn't she thought to do that, on one of her previous visits? There might have been mail in it, business mail. She might have made the Eggman Cookies connection a lot sooner. On the other hand, having made it, she was no further ahead.

Zyzmchuk's car rattled as it climbed the rutted dirt road to the top of the hill. The sun was setting—a red-gold ball low over the western rise. Its image burned in the windows of the white farmhouse on the far side of the meadow. And burned too, Jessie noticed, here and there on the shingle roof and through some of the white-trimmed dormers.

She was still noticing all that when the car surged forward, so abruptly her head was knocked hard against the headrest; it began to throb immediately. She touched her bandages as the car hurtled down the hill and across the meadow and felt dampness. But she had no time to worry about it.

Red-gold tongues lapped around the corners of the white house, licked up the walls, danced wildly in the downstairs windows, more sedately on the floor above.

Spacious Skies was on fire.

Something boomed at the back of the house. A black ball of smoke rose in the air, glittering with gold sparks. Zyzmchuk skidded around the house, stopped the car in a swirl of dust.

A man was squatting in the barnyard. A big man with pale blond hair, almost white. He was pouring gasoline from a red can into king-sized Coke bottles. He looked up in surprise.

"That's Mr. Mickey," Jessie said. Sudden fear rose in her like a storm tide, pitching her voice into a higher register.

Zyzmchuk got out of the car. Mr. Mickey stood up, and Jessie saw how big he really was: half a foot taller than Zyzmchuk and almost as broad. He held a bottle full of gasoline loosely in his hand.

Zyzmchuk took a step toward him. From the side, Jessie could see both how calm his face was and how rigid his back. Zyzmchuk asked Mr. Mickey a short question. Jessie knew it was a question from the tone, but that's all she knew. He'd spoken another language.

A language Mr. Mickey understood: his pale eyes widened; then, for an instant, his gaze shifted to the barn. Jessie saw pinstriped legs scissoring back into the shadows beyond the open door.

Perhaps Mr. Mickey had expected Zyzmchuk would glance that way too. Zyzmchuk didn't. Mr. Mickey threw the Coke bottle at him anyway. Zyzmchuk dipped his head to one side as the bottle flew past his temple, avoiding it with a minimum of fuss, like a boxer slipping a punch.

Then he moved in on Mr. Mickey, his hands curled into half-fists, held at waist level. Mr. Mickey didn't back away, didn't advance. He stood still and remained that way until Zyzmchuk was almost close enough to reach out and grab him. The next moment Mr. Mickey was in midair, his right foot a blur spanning the space between the two men. Zyzmchuk dodged. He was very quick. Mr. Mickey's foot shot past his chin, catching him on the left shoulder. The blow landed with the kind of thump a carpet beater makes and spun Zyzmchuk around.

Jessie saw Zyzmchuk's face go white, but he didn't fall. Instead he spun in a complete circle and came out of the spin like a projectile from a sling. Mr. Mickey wasn't quite ready. His other foot was on its way, but not so high this time, not so hard. Zyzmchuk curled over it. There was another thump, muffled, and then the two men were on the ground.

Dust rose.

Mr. Mickey cried out.

Zyzmchuk rolled on top of him.

Then a man in a pinstripe suit was standing over them. Jessie hadn't even seen him come. He had the gasoline can in his hands. He raised it high and brought it down on Zyzmchuk's head. Zyzmchuk toppled over and lay still on the ground.

That's when Jessie heard the siren sound, coming from the direction of Bennington. The man in the suit heard it too and looked up. Jessie had a good view of him—he was well-groomed, neatly barbered, wore horn-rimmed glasses. She'd seen him before, in front of Pat's house in Venice. He was the real estate man who had asked if the house was for sale, who reminded her of a commentator on TV. She couldn't tell whether he recognized her. Red-gold reflections shone on the lenses of his glasses, masking his eyes.

Mr. Mickey got up, slowly. He heard the sirens too. They grew louder. He said something to the real estate man. The real estate man picked up the gas can again and stepped toward the spot where Zyzmchuk lay.

No thoughts, no commands passed through Jessie's consciousness when she saw that. One moment she was watching, the next she was behind the wheel of Zyzmchuk's old car, turning the key.

The Blazer shot across the barnyard, straight at the real estate man. Red-gold gleamed at Jessie as he saw her coming. He jumped sideways. The fender clipped the gas can from his hand. He fell. Jessie braked, turned at the far side of the yard and started back. The sirens were very loud. Mr. Mickey was dragging the real estate man to his feet. He glanced at Zyzmchuk, lying on the ground, glanced at the approaching car, then threw the real estate man over his shoulder and loped into the woods behind the barn.

Zyzmchuk sat up. Jessie stopped the car and got out. She was going toward him when a loud crack came from the house, as though a giant bone had snapped in two. Enormous flames rose through the roof, unfurling like red-gold sails high into the evening sky. An invisible, scorching wave swept over the yard.

The fire roared.

Glass shattered.

And someone screamed. Someone in the house.

Jessie looked up. A face appeared in the window above the kitchen. An eyeless face.

"Disco," Jessie shouted, running under the window. The fire breathed its hot breath on her skin.

Disco bent his head down in her direction. The movement was unrushed, mechanical, as though he were in a trance. Then he screamed again, right at her, a shriek that cut through the noise of the fire and the sirens and made Jessie's heart leap in her chest.

267

"Disco," she shouted again. "You've got to jump. I'm right here. I'll catch you."

Disco laughed a wild laugh. "That's what Ratty said—'Jump.' Do you think I'm dumb enough to fall for the same trick twice?"

"I'm not Ratty, and that was a long time ago. Jump."

"Who are you trying to kid? Ratty's here. You're working for him."

A hulking flame sprang up behind him like a red-gold assassin.

"Disco, I'll catch you. You're going to die. Jump."

"Go fuck yourself."

"Jump," Jessie screamed over the fire, holding out her hands. "Jump." She scarcely noticed the firemen running across the yard, unrolling their net, pushing past her.

"Jump," Jessie screamed.

"Make me."

"Come on, buddy," said a fireman, "jump. Right in the net. Nothin' to it."

"He's blind," Jessie said.

"No, I'm not. The joke's on you. I can see for miles and miles." Disco laughed his wild laugh. "I'm stoned out of my mind, you motherfuckers. This is all a dream."

He had time to begin one more laugh. Then a red-gold curtain wrapped itself around him, choking off the sound. Disco's long hair went up like sparklers. And then he was gone.

Another giant bone cracked. The tremor unleashed another scorching wave. It blew the wall out, blew Jessie across the yard. She rolled over in the dirt—the earth felt cold despite the fire—and picked herself up. Then someone was leading her into the shelter of the barn.

The fire roared and roared again.

"Where are the hoses?" Jessie shouted. "Where are the hoses?"

"Too late for that, miss," said a fireman, watching with his arms folded across his chest.

Disco's window was gone. Jessie couldn't even find the place in the flames where it had been. The house had lost all structure and identity. It was just a heap of combustibles.

Jessie stepped out of the barn, her eyes searching for

Zyzmchuk. He came walking out of the woods. There, between the trees and fire, he looked for the first time small. Jessie went to him.

"Too late," was all he said.

Behind him, from some clearing in the woods, an unmarked, unlit helicopter rose and veered into the purple sky.

31

On the way to the station house, Jessie said, "I got a good look at the one who hit you on the head. It was the real estate man."

Zyzmchuk said, "Describe him."

"Medium-sized. Pinstripe suit. Glasses. A little over-weight." She shrugged. "Ordinary-looking. He reminds me of one of those commentators on TV."

"Which one?"

"I can't remember."

"Not Andy Rooney?"

"No."

"Thank God," said Zyzmchuk. "I'd hate like hell to have gotten the shit kicked out of me by Andy Rooney."

The fire chief and the police chief were brothers. The police chief was the firstborn. He'd hogged most of the dominant genes. The fire chief was younger and softer at the edges.

"We wouldn'ta known about the 'Vette at all," the police chief was saying, "if it hadn'ta been for a—what did she call herself again?"

"A ornithologist," the fire chief said, stressing every syllable.

"Bird watcher, to you and me," the police chief said. "Now, I ask you, what's a bird watcher doing in the middle of the woods at two in the A.M?"

"Studying owls," Zyzmchuk said.

The police chief gave Zyzmchuk a long look. The fire chief gave him a longer one. These weren't the first long looks Zyzmchuk had attracted since he and Jessie had entered the police station. The first one had come when Zyzmchuk showed them a card in his wallet. The police chief had taken it into another room, talked for a few minutes on the phone and returned saying, "Okeydoke. I'm s'posed to help you in any way."

"Help him in any way?" the fire chief had said. "Is he FBI or something?"

"Something," the police chief had barked at him, venting annoyance where he could, in an old, familiar place. The fire chief had shrunk in his chair.

The next long look had come from Jessie herself, when the police chief said, "Maybe you could give me some idea what this is all about."

And Zyzmchuk had simply replied, "It's a missing child case. Her child."

The police chief had glanced at Jessie and then said, "Do you mean the kid was on the chopper?"

"I don't think so."

"You don't think so. Do you want us to trace it anyway?"

"You can try," Zyzmchuk had said, "but it was a Sikorsky S-76, with no markings and a seven-hundred-mile range. It won't be easy."

"How does he know that?" the fire chief had asked. "It was dark."

The police chief had answered his brother with a glare. But Jessie thought it was a good question. That's when she had given Zyzmchuk her long look.

Now the police chief said, "Owls. That's right. Owls. Any-

271

way, this . . . bird watcher is camped out in the woods, not far from the state line—"

"Where the old lumber track runs," the fire chief interrupted.

"I'm coming to that." The police chief gave the fire chief a withering look. The fire chief stared at his boots.

"Where the old lumber track runs," the police chief continued. "Of course, no one uses it now. There's a sign up prohibiting any motorized traffic."

"That's to stop the dirt-bikers," the fire chief said.

"Shit, he doesn't want to hear about the dirt-bikers," snapped the police chief. "Pardon my French," he added to Jessie.

"Sorry," the fire chief said.

The police chief sighed. "So our bird watcher, camped out at two in the A.M., sees headlights shining through the trees and hears a car. It goes by, maybe a hundred yards from her. A little later she hears a person or persons, she's not sure which, walking back the other way." He paused. "Okay?"

Zyzmchuk nodded.

"Now, this bird watcher happens to be one of those—how would you say it?"

"Greenpeace types?" offered the fire chief.

"Close enough. So in the morning she calls the station to report a violation of the motorized vehicle prohibition. That was yesterday, but I couldn't spare a man to go over there until today. I just thought it was kids drinking, if you follow me. Didn't expect to actually find anything."

"Of course not," Zyzmchuk said. "Can we have a look?"

"Sure. In the morning."

"I meant now."

"Now? We can't do anything now. It's dark. In the morning, we'll go in with the jeep and give it a shot."

"That's fine," Zyzmchuk said. "I don't want to do any hauling tonight. Just look around."

The police chief gazed unhappily at his watch. "Well, if it's—"

"Thanks," Zyzmchuk said. "We could pick up your diver on the way."

The fire chief's jaw dropped and his brother's eyebrows rose, as though in demonstration of some Newtonian law.

"Davey?" said the police chief. "Davey's not going to want to go in the drink at this time of night. And besides, who's gonna pay his overtime?"

"I'll pay," Zyzmchuk said.

The chiefs exchanged a look. Some sort of communication was passing between them, Jessie saw, but very slowly.

"Plus a bonus," Zyzmchuk added.

That speeded things up. The chiefs nodded. "Okeydoke," said the elder.

Frost coated the windshield of the police chief's car. His brother scraped it off. "Going to be a cold winter," he said to no one in particular.

They drove through the quiet town, the police chief and Zyzmchuk in front, Jessie and the fire chief in back. There were no other cars on the road. The fire chief said, "Joanne picked out the turkey this aft."

His brother grunted. Jessie wondered what had happened to the turkey at Spacious Skies.

After a while, the fire chief said, "They say rain for Thursday." Later, gazing out the window, he added, "But I think snow."

The police chief snorted.

Davey lived in a tiny shingle house on the edge of town. He was waiting in the driveway, beside a rusty pickup. "I'll follow you," he said. Davey's eyes were wide in the night; he had a few wispy hairs on his chin and looked about seventeen.

"Well, now, Davey," the police chief said through his rolled down window, "you know the way up to Little Pond, don't you?"

Davey blinked. "Sure. I was there this afternoon."

"Then maybe you could take our friends by yourself. They just want a look-see."

Davey's eyes went from one to another. He'd gotten lost somewhere on the ellipse of the police chief's thought.

Zyzmchuk showed him the next move by saying, "Fine with me."

"Okay," said Davey.

The police chief turned to Zyzmchuk. "I'll be saying good night then."

"Good night."

Zyzmchuk and Jessie got out of the car. The fire chief jumped out of the back and hurried into the front. The car was rolling before he could close the door.

Davey looked up at Zyzmchuk. "All set?"

They climbed onto the torn front seat of the pickup, Davey behind the wheel, Jessie in the middle, Zyzmchuk on the outside. As Davey started the motor, the door of the house opened and a woman in a housecoat ran out.

"Here," she said, thrusting a Thermos through Davey's window. She didn't look at Davey's passengers. "I'll leave egg salad in the fridge. You can make sandwiches."

"Okay, Mom."

She ran back into the house.

Davey backed out of the driveway and drove east on Route 9, into the mountains. He leaned over the wheel, eyes fixed on the road. So were Zyzmchuk's. Jessie tried closing hers, but that only made her head hurt more. She wondered how Zyzmchuk's head felt: he hadn't said anything about it. In the dim light of the cab, she looked for damage on the back of his head. There was no dried blood—he'd been struck with the side of the gasoline can, not an edge—but she thought she saw a bump pushing through the iron-gray hair.

Zyzmchuk felt her gaze and turned. Their eyes met. "That was only round two," he said. "We'll get our licks in."

Jessie laughed, not so much at what he said as at the revelation that another mind was running parallel to her own. Davey glanced at them, looked quickly away. Jessie suddenly felt very safe, almost as though she could stay in the cab of the rusty pickup forever, with the alert boy at the wheel and the parallel mind at her side. Almost, except for Kate. Kate, who like Davey had a Mom: a Mom like a turtle shell. The cab of the pickup was her shell, and she was Kate's.

"I've been meaning to ask you something," Jessie said.

"Ask."

"What was it you said to Mr. Mickey?"

Zyzmchuk smiled. "Kaka idyot Polkovnik Grushin?"

"Meaning?"

"How is Colonel Grushin?"

"In?"

"Russian."

Jessie was aware of Davey's quick glance. She lowered her voice. "And he understood?"

"What do you think?" Zyzmchuk said, not lowering his.

"Yes," Jessie replied in a normal tone. "He has an accent. I thought he was Scandinavian. I even asked him."

"That must have amused him."

"It annoyed him. He said he was from Hermosa Beach."

"Is that on the Black Sea?"

"No," Jessie said, "near Redondo." And then she saw his smile. "So he's Russian, then?"

Zyzmchuk nodded.

"A Russian . . . agent?" The phrase, so common in the papers, on TV, in the movies, sounded unreal.

But Davey's darting look was real, and so was Zyzmchuk's voice. "Looks like it," he said.

"But how did you know?"

Zyzmchuk replied with a sound that might have been the beginning of a laugh, a bitter one, or maybe just a grunt.

Davey turned onto a dirt road that climbed a hill into thick woods. An old stone wall ran along the right side. The road was rough. Every bump hurt Jessie's head.

"Slow down a little," Zyzmchuk said.

Davey slowed down.

"But what connection can there be between Kate and . . . Russia?"

An opening appeared in the wall. Davey slowed still more and turned into it. His headlights swept across a sign nailed to a tree: POSITIVELY NO MOTORIZED VEHICLES.

"Maybe none," Zyzmchuk said.

Leaves lay thick on the narrow track. Trees rose on all sides. Jessie was acutely conscious that they were living things, and this was their domain.

"Did Pat ever go to Russia?"

"No. Not as long as I knew him. He didn't like traveling."

"Did he have a passport?"

"No. Not that I ever saw. Who is Colonel Grushin?"

"It's a long story."

"I'm listening."

275

Jessie watched Zyzmchuk's face. He seemed to be gazing into the trees. For a while she thought he was formulating his reply. Then she realized he wasn't going to say anything.

Davey followed the track for another mile, maybe two. Then the track forked. The main branch led to the left. Davey took the other one, more a space between the trees than a track. He crept along for about ten minutes, then stopped at the bottom of a short rise.

He pointed. "It's just up there."

They got out and walked up the rise. It ended in a flat shelf of rock. The night opened in a circle all around. The moon, now less than full, shone on a still sheet of water twenty feet below, black water with a broken silver line shimmering across to the other side.

"Little Pond," Davey said. He took a flashlight from his pocket and walked, crouching, to the end of the rock. "Here," he said. "See?"

A thin layer of earth and gravel covered the rock. Davey's light shone on the impression of a lone tire tread, a few inches from the edge.

"I see," Zyzmchuk said. He looked down. "Got your gear?"

"My gear?" Davey said. "You want me to go in now? I was just in this afternoon, and I told the chief what I saw."

"Not you," Zyzmchuk told him. "I want to see for myself."

"In that case . . ." Davey went silent. He was looking at the broken silver line; Jessie saw its pattern repeated in his eyes. "Are you certified?"

"What?"

"Have you had much experience with scuba?"

"Some," Zyzmchuk said.

"It's deep. I hit fifty feet on my gauge, and I wasn't on the bottom."

"I'll be all right. I'll pay for any damaged equipment."

"It's not that," Davey said. He sounded hurt.

"Good," Zyzmchuk said. "Let's get started."

They returned to the pickup. Davey laid out the equipment: mask, snorkel, fins, regulator, tank, wet suit, weights, light.

"You'll never get in that wet suit," Jessie said.

"She's right," Davey said. "I think I can find you a bigger one by tomorrow."

Zyzmchuk shook his head. "We'll have to manage without."

"Are you kidding? It's November. You wouldn't last three minutes in there."

"Have you got any Vaseline? For lubricating the zippers and stuff?"

"Yes," Davey admitted.

"That'll do."

Davey found the Vaseline. Then, carrying the dive bag, he led them along a path around the base of the rock to a small, stony beach.

Zyzmchuk stripped off his clothes. Jessie thought of going back to the pickup or averting her eyes, like some Victorian damsel. That seemed silly, so she just looked.

Zyzmchuk's body was white and hard in the moonlight, like stone, except for the scars. He rubbed Vaseline all over it: polished stone. If he was conscious of her watching, he gave no sign.

"Here," Jessie said. She stepped forward, took the jar and rubbed Vaseline on the part of his back he couldn't reach. His skin felt warm, much warmer than hers.

He lifted the tank over his head, wincing slightly—Jessie noticed only because she was watching for it—and strapped it on. He put on the fins; spat into the mask, rinsed it in the pond; donned the weight belt; turned on the light.

Then he walked into the water. "Jesus Christ," he said. He laughed.

"Why not wait until morning?" Jessie asked.

But he had put the regulator in his mouth and slipped below the surface before the last word was out. The moment he was gone Jessie remembered her dream: diving down to the deep place where Kate was crying. A horrible thought germinated in her mind.

Silver bubbles broke nearby on the black water. A trail of them led steadily toward the base of the rock, shrinking smaller and smaller and finally vanishing.

"Did he used to be a football player or something?" Davey asked.

"I don't think so," Jessie said.

She and Davey stood on the stony beach. Jessie, in her wool sweater and suede jacket, still felt cold. She wanted to hug

277

herself warmer, but didn't because of Zyzmchuk down in the pond.

"Five minutes," Davey said. Then there was silence until he said, "Ten."

"Have you got another tank?" Jessie asked.

"Not here. There'd be nothing—"

Yellow light glowed up through the water near the base of the rock. "Here he comes," Davey said.

Jessie saw silver bubbles. They grew bigger. Zyzmchuk stood up in the water, a few yards from the beach. The polished stone had turned from white to blue. He raised his mask and spat out the regulator.

"I'd like to open that trunk," he said. His words were slurred, as though his lips and tongue had thickened. "What have you got?"

"Like a torch?" Davey said. "I left it at home. The chief said this was just for—"

"A crowbar will do."

"I don't have that either. I've got a screwdriver."

"We'll try it."

Davey ran to the pickup.

"Ivan?" Jessie said.

"Yeah?"

She'd been about to say, Why not come out now? Or, Leave it till tomorrow. Something in his eyes told her not to. So instead she said, "How's the water?"

He laughed. He was still laughing when Davey returned with the screwdriver. Davey tossed it to him, and he dipped out of sight.

"Is he okay?" Davey said.

"Seems like it."

They watched the silver bubbles. The bubbles had lost some of their luster; the moon was slipping down the sky. An unbroken line of cloud was closing behind it like a sliding door.

"Five minutes," Davey said. "I hope he's watching his air. A big guy like that can go through a lot of air."

Time passed. It seemed like a long time to Jessie.

Davey said, "Six minutes. Shit. Does he know how to make a free ascent?"

"What's that?"

"Jesus." Davey started to pace, up and down on the stony beach, checking his watch every few seconds. "Why couldn't he wait till morning? Nothing's going to change. It's only a few hours, for God's sake."

Jessie thought about that. Was it that Ivan Zyzmchuk was a driven man, like some Type A executive who had to have things done his way and when he wanted? Or did it have to do with something else, such as losing the fight in the barnyard and letting Mr. Mickey and the real estate man get away? Was he punishing himself down there? Or just getting his licks in?

Jessie didn't have time to think it through. Underwater, yellow glowed again, and silver bubbles grew bigger. "Here he comes," Davey said.

"Have you got a blanket?"

"In the truck."

"Get it."

Davey ran off.

Zyzmchuk rose in the water, just a few yards away. He was shaking. He didn't come forward. Jessie realized that he was shaking so hard he couldn't manage the last few steps to the beach. Jessie went in and got him.

Davey wrapped the blanket around the hard blue body. Together he and Jessie pounded on it. "Here," Davey said, holding out a cup of steaming coffee from the Thermos. Zyzmchuk couldn't hold it. Jessie tipped it up to his lips. His teeth were chattering; Jessie could hear them. She held the back of his head to steady it. He no longer felt warm, but icy cold.

Some of the coffee went in. Then more. "Okay," Zyzmchuk said. "I'm all right." His speech was so slurred Jessie could hardly understand him.

He said something else. She put her ear close to his mouth. "Couldn't open the trunk," he said.

"They'll do that tomorrow."

"But I found something else."

"What?"

He looked away, across the pond.

"Tell me."

Zyzmchuk licked his lips. "Another car."

"Another car?" Davey said. "I didn't see another car."

"It was under the Corvette. They must have been pushed off the same spot."

"What kind of car?" Jessie said. "Tell me."

Zyzmchuk opened his shaking hand. On his palm lay a metal disk with the letters BMW printed on it.

32

It took longer than the police chief had expected. The Corvette didn't come up until three o'clock, the BMW until after four. Both cars gushed water as they swung over Little Pond, up onto the big rock: white water from the Corvette, muddy water from the BMW.

The two cars, sitting side by side, had some things in common—low mileage: the BMW had seven thousand miles on the odometer, the Corvette one hundred and three, sixteen more than when Jessie had seen it under the tarpaulin; color: they were the same shade of blue; ownership: soggy papers taken from the glove compartments showed that both cars were in Pat Rodney's name.

But there were differences. The BMW had a current sticker on the license plate. The Corvette's vanity plate—PAT 69— read 1969 and hadn't been updated. And the trunk of the BMW was empty. That wasn't true of the Corvette. A body, jammed into fetal position, lay in the Corvette's trunk—a woman's body with a big gold hoop dangling from one mushroom-colored ear.

It was Blue Rodney.

She was fully dressed—jeans, Birkenstock sandals, an embroidered Mexican shirt—but the shirt buttons had popped open, so it was easy to see the round, bloodless hole between her breasts. That made Jessie remember the red fingerpainting around the light switch at Spacious Skies and the taste of blood—Blue's blood—in her mouth.

An ambulance arrived. The attendants laid Blue on a stretcher and carried her inside. As they set her down, her head flopped to one side. Brown water ran from her slack mouth and down the white bodywork of the ambulance.

"Oh God," Jessie said. The words made almost no sound. She was so rigid with tension she could barely speak.

Then Davey, in a bright orange wet suit, surfaced from his last dive. He swam to shore. It seemed to take a long time. Jessie's eyes were glued to him, straining to pick out some body movement that would reveal the news he carried. At last he stood up in shallow water, pulled off his mask, let go his regulator, wiped the snot from his nose and stepped onto the stony beach. Jessie was waiting for him.

"That's it," he said and shivered like a dog.

No more bodies.

Jessie's worst fears weren't realized, but they'd grown more palpable, less abstract, fed by hours of watching the work at Little Pond. Now they didn't go away, but merely receded a little, like an army biding its time.

Two tow trucks came. They towed away the Corvette and the BMW. The ambulance left. Then the police chief, the fire chief, Davey. Cold drizzle drifted down from the sky.

Jessie turned from the pond to find Zyzmchuk watching her. "I could use a drink," he said. "How about you?"

She nodded.

They stopped at a little inn off Route 9 and sat before a fire. It hissed and crackled in the grate, but it didn't warm Jessie. She felt cold, almost as cold as mushroom-colored skin.

"What'll it be?" Zyzmchuk asked.

"Anything."

"Two brandies," Zyzmchuk said to the innkeeper. He didn't look like the kind of innkeeper who came from a family of innkeepers; he looked like the kind of innkeeper who'd abandoned a high-paying city job in pursuit of some country squire dream.

"Will that be genuine Cognac from France or Spanish brandy?"

"Genuine Cognac for the lady," Zyzmchuk said. "Rotgut for me."

"I assure you," the innkeeper began, reluctantly adding, "sir. Our Spanish brandy is rather—"

"Make that rotgut all around," Jessie interjected. The words came out unbidden.

Zyzmchuk laughed. The innkeeper closed his mouth and went away.

Spanish brandy came. Zyzmchuk raised his glass. "To picadors," he said.

The Spanish brandy burned Jessie's throat and radiated heat through her body, as though it had distilled the power of the Spanish sun.

"Sometimes Spanish brandy's just the thing," Zyzmchuk said. "Especially the kind with ten or twelve stars on the bottle."

They sat on a couch, not at opposite ends, not touching. Blue-tipped flames nipped at each other in the grate. A Vermont yellow pages lay on a side table. Zyzmchuk picked it up, leafed through.

"That's funny," he said. "They're not listed."

"Who's not listed?"

"Big-Top Motors in Bennington."

"Who are they?"

"The dealership that sold the Corvette, according to the chrome writing on the trunk."

"Why do you want to talk to them?" Jessie was aware of the note of irritation in her voice, but was too tired, too worried to overcome it.

Zyzmchuk ignored it. "Someone—the man you call Mr. Mickey—went to a—"

"I don't call him Mr. Mickey. He calls himself Mr. Mickey."

"I meant it's unlikely to be his name. There aren't a lot of Mickeys in Russia."

Jessie and Zyzmchuk looked at each other. Anger sparked between them, like electricity between two terminals. Zyzmchuk switched it off by raising his hand, palm out, and saying, "Peace, Bazak?"

Jessie laughed, not hard, not long, but a laugh. "Peace, Vaclav."

They ordered more brandy. "I knew you'd like it," the innkeeper said. He poked the fire, emptied an ashtray, straightened his ascot and went away.

"The man who calls himself Mr. Mickey," Zyzmchuk resumed, "went to some trouble not just to hide the body, but to hide the Corvette as well."

"Why?"

"That's what we have to find out."

"And what about the BMW?"

"Good question: we can't hang that one on Mr. Mickey yet. Maybe never."

"What are you saying? Surely the same person—"

Zyzmchuk shook his head. "Four people have died. Blue Rodney and Disco and possibly—probably—your friend were all killed by Mr. Mickey and Andy Rooney. But what about Jerry Brenner?"

"I don't know."

"Me either. That's why we've got to take one car at a time." Zyzmchuk stared into his drink. "I liked those cars down there, in a neat little pile and all. Of course, one was on the bottom a few days before the other." He rose and went to the pay phone in the hall.

But the operator had no listing for Big-Top Motors, not in Bennington, or anywhere else in Vermont.

"Maybe Buddy Boucher knows," Jessie said.

Zyzmchuk smiled. "Now you're cutting coal," he said.

Jessie called Buddy Boucher at home.

"Hi there," he said. "Nothing to report. I'll let you know as soon as anything happens. Trust me."

"It's not that, Mr. Boucher. I thought you might be able to help me locate another car dealer who used to be in Bennington."

"Looking to buy a car?"

"No. Just find the dealer."

"Because I'll beat any price in the tristate area."

"I'm sure you will, but I'm just looking for the dealer."

"What's his name?"

"I don't know. The dealership was called Big-Top Motors."

There was a pause. Then Buddy Boucher said, "Why are you looking for this dealer?"

"It's very complicated, Mr. Boucher. But I think he sold my ex-husband a car in nineteen sixty-nine, and he might be some help in finding him now."

"Are you talking about your ex-husband Mr. Rodney?"

"That's the only ex-husband I have."

"Then the answer's no. Big-Top Motors never sold him a car."

"How do you know?"

"Because I never forget a customer, Mrs. Rodney. That's one of the golden rules in this business."

"I don't understand."

"I was Big-Top Motors, Mrs. Rodney, until nineteen seventy-two. That's when I sold up and went over to Dodge. Big-Top went belly-up two years later."

"But I've just seen a Corvette with your chrome plate on it, registered to Pat."

"What year Corvette?"

"Nineteen sixty-nine."

"What color?"

"Blue. The same blue as the BMW."

"Azure blue," Buddy Boucher said. "A convertible?"

"Yes."

"I think I remember a car like that, Mrs. Rodney. I've got a good memory for cars. That one probably went for about five-one or five-two. A lot of money in those days. But it wasn't bought by anyone named Rodney."

"Who bought it, then?"

"I don't recall offhand, but if it's important I can find out. I've got all the Big-Top files in the basement."

"It's important."

Buddy Boucher went away. Jessie hung on. In Buddy Boucher's house, a child yelled, "I'm the Terminator."

A second child yelled in a higher voice, "No, I am. I'm the Terminator."

Flesh smacked flesh. Yelling turned to crying. "Stop it," a woman said. She'd taken over the yelling. "You can both be the Terminator."

285

The crying stopped. "That's stupid, Mom."

Buddy Boucher returned. "You still there?"

"Yes."

"I've got the file. Azure blue Corvette Stingray, white walls, 327 V-8, radio, leather seats, serial number 43567978?"

"That sounds like it. I don't know the number." She felt a tap on her shoulder. Zyzmchuk was there, holding up a piece of paper with a number written on it: 43567978. "Yes," Jessie said. "That's the one."

"I sold that car on the twenty-ninth of August nineteen sixty-nine, for five thousand one hundred and twenty-five dollars. Cash deal. I've got a photocopy of the check right here."

"Who wrote it?"

"Like I told you, not Mr. Rodney. The signature here says 'Hartley Frame.' "

"Hartley Frame?"

"Right."

"Just a minute." Jessie covered the mouthpiece and said, "He's got a photocopy of the check."

"Get it."

"Mr. Boucher? Could you send me that photocopy? It might be a big help."

"I like to have complete records, Mrs. Rodney, in case the IRS ever comes calling."

"How about a photocopy of the photocopy?"

"I guess that will be all right."

As she gave him the address of the 1826 House, Jessie felt another tap, gentle, unrushed. She looked again at Zyzmchuk. He mouthed the word "bank."

"What bank was the check drawn on, Mr. Boucher?"

"Morgantown National. In Massachusetts."

"Thanks," Jessie said. "Goodbye."

Buddy Boucher was saying, "But I don't see how it matters if it wasn't your—" when she clicked the receiver into the cradle.

Jessie looked at Zyzmchuk, saw he'd heard Buddy Boucher's remark. "I'm not sure I do either," she said.

"Po-iti po-dyengi," Zyzmchuk replied.

"What does that mean?"

" 'Follow the money'—Trotsky, or one of that crowd," replied Zyzmchuk. "All ye know on earth, and all ye need to know."

"Little Pond?" Erica McTaggart said. "I haven't been there in ages."

Erica McTaggart was sitting on the worn velvet couch in her tiny living room, wrapped in a blanket. It was a draughty house, and there was no fire in the grate, only a mound of ashes.

Jessie, leaning against one end of the couch, said, "Did Pat ever go there?"

Erica's eyes darted to her, to the easel, now empty of men doing what they had to do, of any canvas at all, to Zyzmchuk standing with his back to the fireplace. "I think so," Erica said. "A group of us used to go there for picnics sometimes. In the spring. 'Sixty-eight or -nine. He would have been part of it."

"Who else?" Zyzmchuk said.

"Who else?"

"Would have been there."

"Different people. Sergeant Pepper."

"Sergeant Pepper?"

"The name of the band," Jessie explained.

"Right," said Erica. "And maybe a few girls from Bennington."

"Hartley Frame?"

"Of course. It was his band."

Zyzmchuk and Erica looked at each other for a moment. She turned away, hugging herself.

"How about a fire?" Zyzmchuk said.

"There's wood outside, but I think it's wet."

Zyzmchuk went out the back door.

Jessie said, "Who was in the band, besides Hartley and Pat?"

"It kept changing. I sang sometimes. There was a piano player for a while, but he flunked out. Different drummers. Hartley's roommate was one of them." Erica glanced toward the back door. Her voice grew confidential. "Is that your boyfriend?"

"No."

Erica nodded. "He's a little old for you anyway."

The back door opened. Zyzmchuk came in with an armful of logs.

"What was the name of Hartley's roommate?" Jessie asked.

"Dennis Keith," Erica said immediately.

"You've got a good memory," Jessie said.

"Not really," Erica answered. "He was a local boy."

"Like Pat?"

"Not at all. Not at all. Dennis was one of the few who makes it to the college. His mother used to clean for me."

Zyzmchuk knelt and started sweeping out the grate. "Is she still around?" he asked.

"No. She died a few years ago."

"What about his father?"

"Didn't have one. He died in Korea, I believe."

Zyzmchuk snapped a piece of kindling in two. "Have you got any pictures of him?"

"The father?"

"The son."

"No. I had pictures. I had a whole sixties' album filled with shots from those days—Hart, the band, the big demonstration at the police station, the strike, everything—but it wound up at Ross's after the divorce, and he threw it out before I even realized I didn't have it. Can you imagine anything so petty? I was going to use it in a collage."

Zyzmchuk arranged the kindling in a little platform, rolled a sheet of newsprint under it and piled one split log on top. He struck a match. The paper caught fire, then the kindling. The log smoked. He blew on it. A tiny flame flickered on the edge of its bark and slowly spread.

"I've got a picture of her, though," Erica said. "Of Mrs. Keith."

Erica led Jessie and Zyzmchuk into her bedroom. A big charcoal drawing of two lovers hung over the unmade bed. It looked like a product of drawing class, not as well-executed as some Jessie had seen but a lot more graphic than most. Erica's signature was prominent in the lower right-hand corner.

The photograph was one of many taped to Erica's dressing table mirror. It couldn't really be called a picture of Mrs. Keith. Erica stood in the foreground, a younger Erica in a very small bikini. She was laughing into the camera; her body hadn't been

288

so wiry then. Jessie had some idea of why she'd offered to show them the photograph. She wondered whether she'd have made the same offer in Zyzmchuk's absence.

An old woman stood deep in the background, wearing a shapeless polka dot dress. Her gray hair was tied in a bun; deep shadows surrounded her eyes.

"That's Mrs. Keith," Erica said.

"She cleaned for you?" Zyzmchuk said.

"Me and others. They were poor."

"But her son went to Morgan."

"On full scholarship. He was a hard worker. Much more like the students now. And he knew how to get ahead. Hartley didn't even know that the concept of getting ahead existed. Maybe that's where his charm came from."

"Are you implying that Keith used Hartley to get his job with the senator?" Zyzmchuk asked.

Erica turned to him. Jessie saw her profile in the mirror, eyes narrowed, neck slightly bent, a prefiguring of old age. "You seem to know something about him."

"Not much," Zyzmchuk said. "What's the answer?"

"Are you a policeman?"

"No. Just a friend of Jessie's. Helping find her daughter."

The image in the mirror relaxed a little. "I wouldn't say Dennis used Hartley, exactly. It was just normal clubmanship, really, the way men go about those things. The job didn't work out anyway."

"It didn't?" Zyzmchuk said. "I thought Keith interned every summer in the senator's office."

Erica shook her head. "Just one summer, and only part of that. It didn't work out."

"Why not?"

"I don't know. I don't think Hart ever told me. It wasn't a big deal."

The three of them stood before the dressing table mirror in Erica's bedroom. They looked in silence at the laughing, near-naked woman and the little old one behind her.

"Does the phrase 'I kill, therefore I am' mean anything to you, Mrs. McTaggart?" Zyzmchuk asked.

"Sure." She looked at Jessie. "It's from that song I played you—'Descartes Kills.' "

"What does it mean?"

"Mean? What it says. You want a gloss on it?"

"Yes."

"Well, it's satire, I suppose. My ex-husband is a big fan of Descartes. The last man who knew everything and all that crap. He was also a big fan of the war in Viet Nam. That's what inspired it."

"You wrote the song, then?" Jessie said.

"Just the words. Hart wrote the music. Do you want to hear it again?"

Jessie looked at Zyzmchuk. "No thanks," he said. "But I'd like to know why it's written on the wall in the tunnels."

"What were you doing down there?"

A tone entered Zyzmchuk's voice that Jessie hadn't heard before, cold and hard. "I told you. We're looking for Jessie's daughter."

Erica's face changed. It grew more confident in a way. And the expression in her eyes said Zyzmchuk wasn't her type after all.

"We wrote it on the wall. That's how it got there. I can't explain why. It's like trying to explain humor. You get it or you don't." She looked at her watch. That didn't require an explanation.

They walked out of the bedroom, through the living room to the front door. The fire had gone out.

"I told you the wood was too wet," Erica said.

Jessie and Zyzmchuk went outside. The door closed. A lock clicked. A bolt slid. Another lock clicked. And another bolt.

There was a silence. Then Zyzmchuk said, "She forgot to turn the key."

Jessie stared at him for a moment before she realized he was joking. There was a new expression on his face: all at once it was easy to picture him as a mischievous little boy. Jessie started to laugh. She laughed and laughed. She hadn't laughed like that since the night she'd sat with Barbara in the kitchen. This time it didn't end in tears.

A curtain twitched in the window of Erica McTaggart's drab little house. Zyzmchuk glanced at it, then said, "How does Spanish brandy sound?"

"Perfect."

"But first to work."

Two young men in lumber jackets and chinos were coming down the steps of the Morgan library. "I've got an exam at nine tomorrow," one said. "What's Kierkegaard all about?"

"You're fucked," the other replied.

"That's how I read him, too," Zyzmchuk told Jessie as they entered the building.

The study halls and carrels were crowded, but except for one young woman leafing through *Money* magazine, Jessie and Zyzmchuk had the periodical room to themselves. Zyzmchuk threaded a reel of microfilm from a box labeled "NYT May–Aug. 1969" onto a viewer, wound it quickly through to August, then slowed down.

"There it is," he said, stopping at Friday, August 15: the first day of the Woodstock festival.

The *Times* had devoted a story a day to the festival. Jessie and Zyzmchuk read them all. The editors had taken several approaches, treating it first as an amusing human interest story, like the hula hoop craze or Amazonian mud rituals; then as a natural disaster, (but only two people had died, not nearly enough for even a local fire, except in Manhattan, to make the paper, to say nothing of the front page); finally as a financial disaster (but a disaster that didn't appear to bother the promoters—that was the only clue that something new had happened).

Zyzmchuk drew a calendar on a sheet of paper. "Woodstock," he wrote across boxes fifteen to seventeen. In box twenty-nine, the last Friday in the month, two weeks after the beginning of the festival, he wrote, "Corvette."

"What are you getting at?" Jessie said.

"I don't know yet," Zyzmchuk replied. "On August fifteenth, Pat Rodney, Hartley Frame, and some others went to Woodstock. Two weeks later, Hartley bought a car that was put in Pat's name."

"Does that mean Hartley bought Pat a car?"

"That's the simplest explanation."

Jessie remembered her first conversation with Disco. He'd told her the festival had been the end of the commune at Spacious

291

Skies. *Everyone went away.* Had it marked the end of the commune or caused it? Had something gone wrong at the festival? *What have you heard about Woodstock?* All she knew was that the band had jammed in the woods with Jimi Hendrix and that Hendrix had given Hartley his guitar: the guitar that had hung on the wall in the music room in Pat's house in Venice and had disappeared, she suddenly realized, along with Pat and Kate. Jessie remembered too the tape of Joni Mitchell singing "Woodstock" in Pat's cassette machine.

"Hartley may have given Pat something else around that time," she said.

"What?"

She told him about Jimi Hendrix's guitar, adding, "but Pat always said he bought it at an auction. Why would he lie?"

Zyzmchuk didn't say anything.

"And why would he take the guitar with him when he went west to California, but leave the Corvette in the barn?"

Zyzmchuk had no answer for that either.

They left the library. Jessie had lost her desire for Spanish brandy. They drove back to the motel. Jessie went into room 19, with fireplace, Zyzmchuk into room 20, without.

In front of the bathroom mirror, Jessie unwound her turban of bandages. She couldn't see the part of her head where the hair had been shaved, but she could feel it and feel the line of stitches, like bridges over a dried-up river.

She heard a knock on the door; holding the bandages, she went to it and called, "Yes?"

"It's me," said Zyzmchuk.

Jessie raised the bandages with the idea of quickly rewrapping them, then decided not to bother. She opened the door.

"Let's see," Zyzmchuk said, moving behind her. She felt his breath on the bare patch of skin. "Not bad," he said. "You're a quick healer."

He sat on the chair, Jessie on the edge of the bed.

"Hungry?" he said.

"No."

"Thirsty?"

She shook her head.

"I had a phone message," he said. "I have to go back in the morning."

"Home?"

"Home?" he said. "No. The office. I have to give a report. And there are one or two things I might be able to do while I'm there."

"Like what?"

"Examine Hartley Frame's army records, for one."

"To find out what?"

"I'm not sure."

She started to say something, stopped herself.

"Go ahead."

"You said four people had died. You didn't mention the fifth."

"The fifth?"

"Hartley Frame."

Zyzmchuk smiled. "No. I didn't."

"You think he might not have died in Viet Nam, don't you?" Jessie said. "And that he's come back now, using Gerald Brenner's passport."

"Maybe. It's no use speculating until I see the records."

"Why? We already know there was no body." *What sort of funeral do you have for a dog tag and a telegram?*

"All right, then," Zyzmchuk said. "Where's he been all this time?"

"A prisoner over there. Now he's escaped. And shaved his head to look more like Gerald Brenner."

"There's no evidence of any Americans held against their will in Vietnam."

"But it's possible."

"Maybe. Or maybe, just assuming he didn't die, he remained voluntarily."

"And?"

"And was sent back."

"Why?"

Zyzmchuk shrugged. "That's why it's too early to speculate. We'd have to know more about Jerry Brenner for starters. And his passport. Did his killer take it? Or was it found on the street? Or by the police? Was it sold on the black market? Who bought it?"

"I see," Jessie said. She felt weak and tired. She pulled herself further onto the bed and lay down. She closed her eyes.

Disco's fringe of long hair went up like sparklers inside her eyelids. Then it was Kate's hair, dark and frizzy, catching fire.

"I'll try to be back tomorrow night," Zyzmchuk said. "Someone's coming in the morning to be with you till then."

"Who?"

"A friend of mine."

"Is it necessary?"

"No point taking chances," Zyzmchuk said.

Time passed. It was quiet in room 19, and cold. Jessie pulled the covers over her. Later she heard Zyzmchuk walking on the carpet. The lights went out. She heard his body sink into the chair.

"Are you going to stay here all night?" she asked.

"Just to be on the safe side."

A car buzzed through the night like a giant insect. Then quiet returned, a muffling quiet, Jessie thought, as though she were buried under pillows of snow. She heard nothing except her own breathing and felt nothing but cold and the ache in her head. She needed sleep, but every time she closed her eyes she set her daughter on fire.

Jessie scanned the darkness. In it loomed darker shapes— the TV, the open door to the bathroom, the closed curtains, the closed front door, Zyzmchuk in the easy chair, like a hillock.

"Ivan," she said, one day ago a strange name, exotic and unreal.

"Yes?" A deep sound, but soft.

"Come here."

Silence. No sound but her own breathing. And then footsteps on the carpet. Slow, hesitant footsteps. He brushed against the bed, started to sit down on it.

"No," said Jessie, lifting the covers. "Inside."

Silence. Then he was beside her, and she heard his breathing and felt his warmth. She reached for him.

"Maybe I've forgotten how," he said.

But he hadn't.

It was perfect.

And after, he still held her tight. His eyes, inches from her own, were open wide.

33

Jessie opened her eyes. He was watching her.

"Where were you August fifteenth, nineteen sixty-nine?" he said.

"Is this an interrogation?"

"Yes."

"What am I charged with?"

"Having a past I know nothing about."

"Is that a crime?"

"Unforgivable."

"I've got nothing to hide," Jessie said. "August fifteenth, nineteen sixty-nine. The summer before my freshman year. I was probably at the beach. Where were you?"

The gray eyes looked far away. Then Ivan Zyzmchuk smiled. "Hunting ibex."

"Ibex?"

He nodded. "With the Shah." He raised his head an inch or two off the pillow. "What's that look on your face?" he said.

"Horror. That's my look for horror."

He seemed about to laugh, but he didn't. Then he said, "Let's not talk."

He put his arms around her and drew her body against his.

"You'll make me an addict," Jessie said.

He said nothing.

Soon she was sleeping a dreamless sleep. When she awoke, her headache was gone, and so was he. But she wasn't alone. Another man sat in the easy chair.

Jessie sat up, holding the covers over her breasts.

"Don't be alarmed," the man said. He had a reedy voice, but his accent reminded her of the Gabor sisters. "I'm a friend of Ivan."

Although his chin jutted forward in a state of permanent aggression, the man didn't look like a bodyguard. The rest of him, small and shrunken, made Jessie think of an old banty rooster.

"My name is Bela."

"I'm Jessie."

"Yes," he said. "I know."

"When did Ivan leave?"

Bela studied his watch. "Not so long ago," he said. "He'll be back tonight. Meanwhile we stay here. In the room."

"I'd like to get up."

Bela's chin jutted forward a little more. "Up, okay. But not out."

He sat in the chair, chin jutting out. Jessie remained in the bed, the covers held over her breasts. Then he realized the problem. A faint pink blush rose to the surface of his waxy cheeks. "I'll be right outside," he muttered, getting up and going out the door.

Jessie showered and dressed. "All clear," she called.

Bela came in. He stopped, looked her up and down. "You're how old?"

Jessie told him.

"Ivan's fifty-six," he said sharply. "He'll be fifty-seven in two months."

296

"I know."

"Peh. You know."

He sat down in the chair, took a book from his pocket and started reading. The title was in a language Jessie didn't recognize. Bela's eyes flickered back and forth, back and forth; then he licked his forefinger with the tip of his tongue, a very white tongue, and turned the page. His eyes flickered back and forth. Jessie wondered if he was a bit mad.

"Do you work with Ivan?"

He looked up, forefinger marking his place on the middle of a page. "So what am I doing now?"

"I meant at his office."

"I'm too old to work in this land of opportunity," he said. He raised his forefinger, jabbed it at her. "And so is Ivan. They're getting rid of him."

"Who?"

" 'Who?' she says. You don't know anything about him. He doesn't have two nickels to rub together. He's going to have to find a job. At his age." Bela's eyes returned to the book. They flickered back and forth, back and forth; the white tongue licked the fingertip; the page turned.

"What are you reading?" Jessie asked after a while.

"The life of Verdi," he replied, in the kind of tone that suggested she couldn't possibly be interested.

"What language is it in?"

"My language," Bela said. "Hungarian."

He snapped the book shut, returned it to his pocket. His hand emerged with something else: a silver-framed photograph. He rose and placed it on the mantel. Then he went to the window, parted the curtains and looked out.

Jessie crossed the room to the mantel. The photograph was in black and white. It showed a woman seated at a small, round table. She was dark and smiling, very pretty and very young.

"Who is this?" Jessie asked, still regarding the picture.

She heard Bela turn. "Leni," he said. "My daughter." He came closer, like a flower drawn by the sun, until he too stood before the photograph.

"She looks very nice," Jessie said.

She wished she'd chosen a better word, especially when

297

Bela repeated, "Nice." There was a silence. Now he was looking at her, his chin pointed at her eyes. "Nice. Sure. Nice. I suppose he told you about her."

"No." And then it hit her. "Are they married?"

"Married?" Bela said with fury.

Jessie stepped back. She tried to guess what had enraged him. "Divorced?"

For an instant he seemed to inflate and grow much younger. She thought he was going to hit her. But he didn't, not physically. "She's dead. They killed her a month after that picture was taken. So they never got married." His voice rose. "And they never would have got no divorce. Never."

Jessie took another step back. "I'm not sure I understand," she said. "Did this happen recently?"

"Recently? Is nineteen fifty-six recently?"

Her voice rose too. "I was four years old," she said, as though he'd accused her of complicity in the death.

This seemed to shock him. He deflated. "Yes," he said, quiet now. "You're young." His gaze was drawn once more to the photograph. "She was young too. Younger than you, maybe. I don't know young people's ages anymore. How old are you?"

Jessie told him again.

He nodded. "She was younger. Twenty-two, when that was taken." His finger reached out, but not for jabbing. He gently laid it on the image of Leni's shoulder. "She was pregnant. Five months pregnant. The whole world was in front of her." Bela's voice had fallen into a maudlin tone, but his eyes were completely dry.

"What happened?"

"There was a newspaper vendor. Grushin got to his wife."

"Colonel Grushin?"

"That's right. What about him?"

"Ivan mentioned him. But I'm not sure who he is, exactly."

"The Russian," Bela said. A long silence followed, so long Jessie thought the explanation complete. Then Bela said, "He wasn't so high and mighty then. Just another Russian thug. He's the one who . . ." Bela abandoned the sentence; his eyes returned to the photograph. "Did he tell you about Leni?"

"No."

"No?" All at once his face seemed very old and drawn. He

put a hand on the mantel, as if steadying himself in rough weather.

Jessie opened her wallet. "I've got a picture too," she said. She took out the photograph of Kate at the beach. "This is my daughter." Bela didn't look at it. "The one who's missing," she added. "The one Ivan's helping me find."

Bela turned slowly to the photograph of Kate. He studied it for a few moments without speaking, then said, "What's her name?"

"Kate."

"How old?"

"Ten."

"Ten," he said and exhaled heavily. It might have been a sigh. "She's missing?"

"Yes."

"Does Grushin have her?"

"Oh no," Jessie said. "It's nothing like that." But a chill ran down her spine and spread through her body. She wanted to step into that photograph, grab onto Kate and not let go.

"Nothing like that," Bela said, waiting at the end of her thought. "Then why is Ivan involved?"

"I don't know. I don't even know what he does, exactly."

Bela's dry eyes regarded her without expression. Then he took Kate's photograph from her hand and stuck it in the corner of the silver frame. Jessie noticed that Leni had frizzy hair too, not much different from Kate's, or hers.

"I hate the fucking Russians," Bela said.

He sat down in the easy chair and took out his book. "You like Verdi?" It was more a statement than a question.

"I don't know much about him."

"I meant his music."

Jessie's mind echoed faintly with the sounds of childhood Sunday mornings, when her father took control of the record player, but she couldn't sort them out. Bela was waiting for an answer. "I saw the film of *La Traviata*," she said. "I liked it very much."

"The film of *La Traviata?*" Bela's mouth pursed, as though he'd just tasted something bad. "Who was in it?"

"Placido Domingo and Teresa Stratas."

"Peh," Bela said. "Who sang the father?"

"I don't remember."

299

"Peh." Bela opened the Verdi book, found his place and started reading. His eyes went back and forth; his wetted finger turned the pages.

Later, Jessie said, "Are you hungry?"

Bela didn't look up. "No."

"I am." It was true. She hadn't really felt hunger since the day Kate disappeared; all at once she was famished. She didn't want to look into the reasons too deeply. Sex lay at the bottom of it, and sex meant that life goes on, no matter what. That was the thought she would not accept.

Bela closed the book. "Okay. What do you want?"

"Let's just go across the street."

"No. I'll go. You stay here. You don't let anyone in. Understand?"

"Yes."

"No one in. No one out."

"I've got it."

"So. You got it. What do you want?"

Jessie almost said, "Nothing." But she *was* hungry. "Scrambled eggs. Toast. Orange juice. Coffee. Bacon."

"Bacon?"

"And maybe some kind of fish, if they've got it. Salmon or trout."

"Scrambled eggs," Bela said, rising. "Toast. Orange juice. Coffee. Bacon. Fish." He looked up at her; he was an inch or two shorter. "That's the way Leni ate too. Like a man. But she didn't get fat." He gave her a quick inspection. "You're not fat either." It was a reluctant concession.

Jessie took a twenty-dollar bill from her wallet. "Here."

Bela pushed it away. "I don't want your money," he said, going to the door. "Lock it and use the chain." He went out.

Jessie locked the door and slid the chain in place. Right away she wished she hadn't asked for so much food. What was Kate eating for breakfast? What had she eaten for the past twelve days? Jessie's appetite curdled inside her. She stood motionless in the middle of the room, paralyzed by her thoughts.

There was a knock at the door. Jessie went to answer it. She had one hand on the knob, the other on the chain, when she realized Bela couldn't possibly be back yet, unless he'd forgotten something. Like the key. She glanced quickly around the room, but didn't see it.

"Bela?" she called.

Silence. Then a voice, a cultured male voice, spoke. "Ms. Shapiro?"

Jessie was silent. She didn't recognize the voice. It certainly wasn't Mr. Mickey's or the real estate man's or the bag lady's strange high-low voice.

"Ms. Shapiro?" came the voice again. "I was told I could find you here."

Why be silent? Whoever it was had heard her movements through the door. "By whom?" Jessie said.

"By my wife. Alice Frame."

Jessie opened the door, but didn't unhook the chain. Outside stood a man in a down jacket and heavy tweed pants. "Senator Frame?" Jessie said.

He smiled. "You can call me Ed."

Despite his casual turnout, he didn't seem like the kind of man she wanted to call Ed. He had well-barbered silver hair, manicured fingernails and a face that would have looked good on Mount Rushmore, or at least a postage stamp; now she recalled it from TV news reports and photographs beside newspaper stories she never read. She didn't call him anything. She just said, "I didn't tell your wife where I was staying."

He smiled again. "Not exactly. But this is where everyone stays." Jesse had never understood the phrase "practiced smile." Now she did. "May I come in?" he said.

Jessie looked past him, to the restaurant across the road. Through the windows she saw featureless people sitting at tables, moving around; she couldn't tell which one was Bela.

"Or would you rather come out?" Senator Frame said. "I only want a few minutes of your time."

U.S. senators were polite. They didn't hit people over the head with gasoline cans or kidnap them on unmarked yachts. Jessie unhooked the chain and opened the door. "Come in," she said.

"Thank you," he replied and having taught her "practiced smile" now demonstrated "courtly bow." He glanced around the room. "Very nice," he said. "I stayed here once—I mean in this very room."

"When your son was at Morgan?"

The smile came again; Jessie wondered if it were something like a nervous tic, or perhaps the only facial expression a senator needed, like a pitcher with a good knuckleball. "No," he said. "We had the cabin by then. This was for my tenth reunion. Nineteen fifty-three, it must have been. The next big one will be the fiftieth. I can hardly believe it." The senator paused for a moment, as though contemplating the passage of time, and then said, "But I didn't come to bore you with reminiscence. My wife tells me you're married to an old acquaintance of my son."

"I was. But . . ."

Senator Frame raised his eyebrows—prominent overhangs like snowy cliffs—and said, "Go on. I won't bite."

"Your wife said she'd never heard of Pat."

He spread his hands in an almost priestly gesture that spoke of compromise and forbearance. "Alice hasn't been herself lately. The business of the memorial has roused some old demons, I'm afraid."

"So she did know Pat?"

"I wouldn't say 'know.' Alice and I met him once or twice— if it's Pat Rodney we're speaking of."

"We are."

Senator Frame reached into his pocket. "I'd like to make sure." He handed her a passport-sized photograph. Jessie felt his eyes on her as she examined it.

"That's Pat," she said. A teenage Pat, his good looks incipient, his fair hair a few shades lighter then, not quite Sergeant Pepper length.

Senator Frame took back the picture, put it away. "Where do you and Pat live?"

"We're divorced. Both in the Los Angeles area."

"Malibu?" he asked.

"No. I'm in Santa Monica, he's in Venice."

"Ah," he said. "The colorful names you've got out there." He parted the curtains, looked out the window. The room seemed to make people do that, Jessie thought.

Senator Frame turned to her. "My wife says you're in some sort of trouble."

"Pat and I have a daughter." Kate's picture was still in

Bela's silver frame. Jessie took it out and showed it to him. He barely glanced at it.

"Yes?" he said.

"They both disappeared."

"When?"

"Almost two weeks ago."

"Wednesday the nineteenth?"

"Not quite two weeks. It was the Sunday."

"And this was in Los Angeles?"

"Yes."

"Then what brings you here?"

Jessie didn't answer right away. The senator made another gesture that reminded her of priests and blessings. "We'd like to help, Ms. Shapiro. Alice and I. Unless you've got some other assistance?"

"Why do you want to help me?"

The smile came again. "I admire your bluntness, Ms. Shapiro—I see it more and more in young women these days. Perfectly understandable." The smile faded, very slowly, like an actor prolonging his exit. "We'd like to help for the simple reason that your husband—your ex-husband—was a friend of our dear boy." He opened his mouth to continue, then stopped and turned up his hands in a hopeless gesture. Dampness rose in the senator's eyes, not enough to overflow, more like two thin films of dew. He blinked and it was gone. "If you'll allow us," he added.

"All right," Jessie told him. "I'm here because Pat and Kate were seen in Vermont soon after they disappeared." She told him about Buddy Boucher. "And there was another man with them."

"Another man?"

Jessie found herself crossing the room, parting the curtains, looking out. She saw dead leaves blowing across the parking lot. "Senator Frame?" she said.

"Yes?" His voice was quiet and gentle.

"Were you given solid proof that your son died in Viet Nam?"

There was a long pause. Jessie turned. His face was very pale, much like the color of Mount Rushmore itself. "What do you mean?" he asked.

Jessie took a deep breath. "Is there any way he might have survived? Might still be alive?"

The water level rose again in his eyes. "I hope you have a good reason for putting me through this, young lady."

Jessie fought off the urge to say, "I'm sorry." She wasn't sorry enough to stop herself from going on. "I don't have proof," she said. "But it's the only explanation for what's happened, unless you know for sure that he's dead." She told him about the words on the blackboard and Gerald Brenner's passport.

Senator Frame's eyes dried as she spoke, but his complexion stayed chalky. "I don't know for sure," he said when she had finished. "There was no . . . body, if that's the sort of thing you mean. But it was all confirmed by the Pentagon. Besides, all those stories of MIA's in jungle prison camps over there are just bunk. I've seen the intelligence reports." He sat down in the easy chair, rather heavily. He stared at his shoes, thick-soled walking shoes made of rich, supple leather. "But it's possible. I guess. It's possible." He looked up at Jessie. "Have you told the police about this?"

"Not about your son. That all came later. The police thought it was routine divorce warfare, or Pat on a toot."

Senator Frame nodded.

"You and your wife disapproved of Pat, didn't you?"

"I had no opinion."

"Your wife, then."

" 'Disapprove' would be going too far. In any case, it's ir-relevant now. Is anyone helping you, Ms. Shapiro?"

"Not exactly."

"You have help then?"

"One or two friends." She thought of Barbara and added, "The names wouldn't mean anything to you."

"Here or back home?"

"Both."

"You wouldn't have any friends in Washington?"

Jessie hesitated.

"A man named Keith, for instance?"

"No."

He was watching her very closely, like a human lie detector, she thought. Then he bared his teeth again. "You have a friend in Washington now, Ms. Shapiro."

"Thank you, Senator Frame."

"Ed. Really. All my friends call me Ed."

"Ed."

"And may I call you Jessie?"

"Yes."

"A lovely name. Biblical." He rose and held out his hand. "And how appropriate. The Bible is full of miracles and this would be a miracle. To see my son again, I mean. A miracle. Here's hoping."

She shook his hand. His skin was cold, almost as cold as Ivan's after the dive in Little Pond. "What are you going to do now? Call in the FBI?"

He frowned. "Not yet, I think. First we'll have a long talk with the army. We'll go from there." He took a card from his pocket and wrote a number on it. "We're at the cabin on Mount Blackstone till the Monday after Thanksgiving." He drew a map on the back. "Call if you need me." He went to the door, then stopped and turned. "But don't say anything to Alice." Another misty weather system moved across his eyes. "I don't want her heart broken again."

He paused to let his words sink in. He was still pausing when the door opened and hit him in the back. He whirled. It was Bela, carrying a loaded tray. The next moment the tray was on the floor and a gun in Bela's hand. It happened so quickly Jessie wasn't sure where the gun had come from. He pointed it at the senator's chest. The senator backed away, into the easy chair. Jessie thought he was going to dive behind it.

"Who the hell is this?" Bela snapped at her, his eyes on the senator.

"Put that away," Jessie said. "The man is a U.S. senator."

"I don't care if he's President Roosevelt. My orders were no one in, no one out."

Jessie saw the senator's eyes flicker in her direction. "He's trying to help, Bela."

"Be quiet," he said to her. And "Out" to Senator Frame.

The senator moved past him, looking at Jessie. There was no smile now. "You haven't been quite truthful with me, Jessie."

"Out," Bela said.

"She's right," Senator Frame said to him. "I do happen to be a senator, and this kind of treatment—"

"Out," Bela said, no louder than before, but more sharply pronounced. The reedy voice, the Hungarian accent, the gun— all now combined to make Jessie see Bela in a new light. He could be dangerous.

The senator saw that too. He went through the doorway, half-turning so he could keep his eyes on Jessie. "I didn't think you had this sort of friend. Where do you suppose his orders—"

Bela slammed the door on the rest of his question. He locked it and drew the bolt. Then he parted the curtains and looked out. Senator Frame was climbing into a big jeep, the kind that seemed more suburban than military in origin. He drove away.

Bela turned to Jessie. The gun was still in his hand, loosely held now, but pointing in her direction. "Leni used to do things like this too," he said. "Stupid things. That's how come she got killed."

"That man was a United States senator, not a killer," Jessie said. Her voice rose in anger, and she made no attempt to rein it in.

"So?" Bela said. "The guy who shot Leni was a Hero of the Soviet Union. It makes no difference."

"God damn it," Jessie shouted. "I don't give a shit about Leni. I want my daughter back. That's all."

Bela glared at her. His face slowly reddened, as though he had caught fire deep inside. For a second or two, Jessie thought he might shoot her.

But he lowered his eyes and put the gun away. Then he knelt and picked her breakfast off the floor.

34

"Your wife has nice tits," Bao Dai said.

They were on the mattresses: Bao Dai squatting, Zorro curled like a fetus, the little girl asleep.

"What are you talking about?"

"Tits. Nice ones. I had a little feel. Your wife's."

"I don't have a wife. I'm divorced. I told you. Anyway, she's in California."

Bao Dai smiled and shook his head. "I had a little feel. How could you walk away from tits like those?" He stopped smiling. "But you were always good at finding tail, weren't you?"

No answer.

"I asked you a question."

"I don't know."

"Don't be modest. You had a nose for it. Right? Poontang—you know what I'm talking about."

No answer.

"Was your wife a good fuck?" Bao Dai tried to remember his last erection, not a puny little stirring, but a hard-on. He couldn't. All he could remember was Corporal Trinh's yellow cock and what Corporal Trinh did to him in the Year of the Pig, or maybe before that, in the year of some other animal. "I asked you a question."

"What?"

"Was your fucking wife a good fuck?"

"Why are you asking these questions?"

"Don't raise your voice at me."

"Why are you asking these questions?" (Quieter.)

"I told you—I felt her tits. You don't believe me?"

No answer.

Bao Dai got up and splish-splashed across the room. He took the key out of his pocket and held it up. 1826 House, read the plastic tag. And a number: 19. "She's here, all right. She thought I was you."

That struck Bao Dai as very funny. He laughed. The girl stirred.

"Where is she?" Zorro asked in a whisper.

That was a good question. Bao Dai looked at the room key, rubbed it and put it away. "Does she like to drop acid?"

"No. Why?"

"I've got some. Feel like dropping acid?"

"No one drops acid anymore."

Bao Dai felt like hitting him in the face. But that was too easy. Instead he stepped back and said, "I missed everything, didn't I?"

"I feel badly," Zorro said. "I told you—if you let us go, I'll do what I can to make it up to you."

"Let's start now."

"What do you mean?"

"By starting over."

"Starting over?"

"Yeah. We'll go on a trip. Two trips. A real one and the other kind."

"Where?"

"Bethel."

"But why?"

"That's square one. Where else do you start over?"

308

No reply. What could you say to logic like that? Bao Dai went upstairs to say good-bye. Ma was in the kitchen. "That smells like good pie, Ma. What is it? Apple? Rhubarb? Banana Republic? Just joking, Ma."

"Rhubarb," said Ma. "Your favorite." Worried eyes. "Is everything all right?"

No—the cellar was leakier than ever, but Ma didn't like to think about worrisome things, so Bao Dai just said, "Sure."

"I meant . . ." Ma began softly, but Bao Dai didn't hear. His attention had suddenly been drawn to the old crucifix, on the wall where it had always been. Maybe the paint was a little more faded, but he could still see the five red trickles. The crucifix got all mixed up with Pa's lash, and Corporal Trinh, and the Year of the Pig. His mouth felt dry, his throat constricted.

He swallowed. "Go to the hardware, Ma."

"The hardware?"

"I need nails."

"What for?"

"Just fixing a hole, Ma. Six-inchers'll do."

"Will that stop the flooding?"

"It better."

Ma returned with nails and a bouquet of flowers. Then she went out again, taking the flowers with her. Bao Dai brought Zorro upstairs to the phone. He took out the room key. The phone number was on the back.

"Let's have a little party."

"What do you mean?"

"Call her. Make the arrangements."

"I won't."

"What's wrong with a party? I have the right to get to know her a little, don't you think?"

"I won't do it."

Bao Dai took out the whalebone knife and held the point lightly against Zorro's ribs. Not too lightly. He felt a trembling in his fingers, wrapped around the handle. Zorro felt it too, and his eyes filled with fear. "You will. See, if you don't . . ." Bao Dai pointed the knife at the floor, toward the basement below, and gave it a little twist. "First her, then you. But I don't want to do that."

"You don't?"

"Of course not. If things go well at the party, I might even let you go away somewhere."

"All of us?"

"Sure."

"I mean me, the girl and Jessie?"

"Jessie?"

"My ex-wife."

"That's her name?"

"Yes."

"I like it."

"But is that what you mean? The three of us?"

"You want it in writing?"

"No." Zorro's eyes were still afraid. He wasn't nearly as brave as Corporal Trinh. "Do you mean it, that's all."

"Sure," Bao Dai said again and handed him the phone.

But there was no answer in room 19.

"Let's hit the road," said Bao Dai. "We'll try later."

35

" 'Krund,' " said Bela.

He was sitting in the easy chair, a folded copy of the local paper in his lap. He'd been staring silently at the Jumble for some time. Jessie had been staring silently at her breakfast. Scrambled eggs, bacon, toast, smoked trout—all mixed together now and cold. Jessie didn't want to eat. She sipped from the dented orange juice carton and tried to think of something to say to Bela. She'd just about given up when he raised his eyes from the paper and said, " 'Krund.' "

And she replied, " 'Drunk.' "

" 'Drunk,' " Bela repeated. He filled in the blanks. "It fits."

Peace was restored. Bela's anger had passed like a sudden squall.

"What about 'frashter'?" he asked.

" 'Frashter'?" "Frashter" was tougher. "May I see?"

Bela handed her the paper. She gazed for a while at "frash-ter." Then she moved on to the other words: "juraif" and "nymiost." She couldn't get them either. The cartoon clue showed a frightened bagpiper with ghosts materializing from his pipes. The caption read: "What the pied piper paid." "Frashter." "Juraif." "Nymiost." The pied piper. Jessie played with the letters. She got nowhere.

"This is impossible," she said.

Bela didn't answer.

Jessie looked up from the puzzle. Bela was asleep, his head sunk on his chest. His hair was very white and so fine she could see his pink scalp through it.

Jessie turned the page. She read an article about turkey prices. She read *Doonesbury*. She checked the personals column; it was empty. Her eyes wandered down the last page. They stopped at a very small headline near the bottom.

SERVICES FOR LOCAL WOMAN

Funeral survices for Doreen Rodney, late of Bennington, Vt., will be held this morning at eleven A.M. at the Church of St. Mary in North Adams, Mass. Burial will take place in the North Adams cemetery.

"Bela?" Jessie said quietly.

He didn't stir.

She stood up. Blue Rodney was Pat's sister. He'd been giving her ten thousand dollars a year since 1971. Wasn't it possible that he would go to her funeral?

Jessie gazed down at Bela's baby-fine hair, his pink scalp. *No one in. No one out.* He wasn't likely to agree to an expedition to North Adams, not without a lot of discussion, and it was already 10:30. She put on her jacket, left a note on top of the Verdi book—"Back at one, gone for a walk"; a little breezy, perhaps, but she didn't like being a prisoner—and slipped out the door.

North Adams was separated from Morgantown by a short drive and two hundred years of barely making it. Jessie parked in front of the Church of St. Mary at five to eleven. It was a small, faded white building with an army-navy store on one side and a vacant lot on the other. The advertised sermon for Sunday was "Thanksgiving in a Thankless World." Jessie went inside. No one was there but an old red-nosed man sweeping up.

"The Father moved it to ten," he explained. "So's he wouldn't miss the game."

The old man directed her to the cemetery. It lay at the end of a road that went by a gas station and a junkyard. The grass needed mowing and the paths needed raking. Jessie walked along one of them, past gravestones so weathered that the names of the dead had vanished along with the rest of them.

She met the priest coming the other way. He was an old man, older than the caretaker at the church but not quite as red-nosed. He wore a white surplice and muddy shoes and in no way resembled the rabbi with the paisley tie. But he checked his watch with the rabbi's same hurried gesture as he went by, and Jessie thought of Barbara and a spiffier graveyard in a spiffier part of the country.

As though some heavenly bylaw were in force, all colors were shades of gray: the sky, the earth, the tombstones, the lone woman at the end of the path. Pat wasn't there. Neither were the aging, long-haired mourners she had half-expected There was only the gray woman at the end of the path. Now Jessie saw that she was holding a bouquet of yellow gladioli. The flowers glowed like a sun in an empty corner of space.

Jessie approached the woman. She stood beside a partially filled hole in the ground, looking down at the newly turned earth. A gravestone lay in a wheelbarrow nearby. "D. Rodney" was etched in the marble.

The woman heard Jessie coming and looked up. "They're on a break," she said.

The woman wore a thin cloth coat and a kerchief printed with palm trees; wisps of gray hair curled out from its edges. She had the hoarse voice and wrinkled skin of a lifelong smoker. But Jessie didn't notice much of that at first; what she noticed were the woman's brilliant blue eyes.

"I'm late," Jessie said.

"That's all right," the woman replied. "Nobody came. It's all been so sudden. I guess the news didn't have time to get around. Because Doreen had friends. Lots of them," she added, in case Jessie thought of arguing. "Are—were you a friend of hers?"

"I knew her," Jessie said. "What about you?"

The woman's eyes had prepared her for the answer, but it

still shocked her when it came. "I am Mrs. Rodney. Doreen's mother."

Jessie was silent, but not because she had nothing to say; her mind worked frantically to put her thoughts in order. The woman was Pat's mother; her own ex-mother-in-law; Kate's grandmother. Yet Pat had always said that his parents died in a car crash before he went west. Either he'd been lying or, perhaps, he and Blue weren't full brother and sister. Pat's eyes were blue, but not the startling China blue of this woman and her daughter. Jessie tried to remember any hint from Blue that she and Pat were less than full siblings and couldn't.

What was the right approach? Jessie had no idea. She plunged ahead: "Do you have a son named Pat?"

Mrs. Rodney squinted at her. "Why do you want to know that?"

"Is it true?"

Mrs. Rodney's fingers tightened around the stems of the flowers. "You never did tell me who you were."

"My name is Jessie Rodney."

"Rodney?"

"I was married to Pat for five years. We have a daughter."

Mrs. Rodney sucked her lips into her mouth and bit down on them hard. She didn't speak.

"I can see that this comes as news to you," Jessie said. "Your existence is news to me. Pat told me you'd died in a car crash."

"I wish I had." Mrs. Rodney's eyes filled with tears. They rolled down her cheeks. She took no notice of them and didn't make a sound.

"What do you mean?" Jessie said. "Why did Pat lie about you?"

"Oh, go away. I don't want to talk." She looked down into the grave. "Haven't you got any decency?"

"I know this is a bad time for you." Jessie reached out to touch her arm. Mrs. Rodney backed away. "But it's a bad time for me too. Pat disappeared, and he took our daughter with him. Your granddaughter."

"I don't have any granddaughter."

"Yes, you do," Jessie said, feeling in her pocket. She took out Kate's photograph and showed it to Mrs. Rodney. The woman

314

turned away. Then Jessie did something that appalled her even as she was doing it: she grabbed the back of Mrs. Rodney's head—so thin and bony—and forced her to face the picture.

"That's Kate," Jessie said. "She's your granddaughter and she's still alive." Her voice was shaking. She let go of Mrs. Rodney. "But you've seen her, haven't you?"

"I don't know what you're talking about. I've never laid eyes on that child. Maybe everything you say is true. But I haven't seen her. And I haven't seen Pat in years and years. Not since he went away to that horrid concert."

"What concert?"

"The Woodstock one."

Mrs. Rodney looked again into the grave. Her hands twisted the gladioli stems.

"I don't believe you," Jessie said.

Mrs. Rodney made a low sound. It might have been a groan. Then she opened her purse and fumbled inside. She found a pack of cigarettes, stuck one in her mouth, found a lighter, lit the cigarette. With the flowers, it was a lot for her unsteady hands to manage. She lost her grip on the glads; they fell into the grave. Mrs. Rodney stared down at them. She made the low sound again and then drew deeply on the cigarette.

"You've seen them," Jessie said. "Haven't you?"

Mrs. Rodney shook her head quickly from side to side. Sparks flew off the end of her cigarette.

"Where are they?"

"I don't know what you're talking about," Mrs. Rodney said, her lips clenched around the cigarette. "I'm not even sure who you are. You accost me like this at my own daughter's funeral in the middle of my grief, with all your rough questions, but I don't know who you are. He never men—"

Mrs. Rodney cut herself off, but too late.

"That's it," Jessie said. "I'm coming to your house."

"You have no right."

"We're talking about my daughter." Jessie's voice rose, cold and hard. "I have every right."

"I could call the police."

"You could. They're looking for him too."

"They are?"

Jessie nodded.

Mrs. Rodney sucked her cigarette down to the filter and tossed it aside. A gust of wind caught it and blew it into the grave, down with the flowers. "Oh God help me," Mrs. Rodney said. "I can't take any more." She got down on her hands and knees, reaching for the cigarette butt. Her arms were too short. She bent further; her skirt rode up, exposing her scrawny legs.

"Here," Jessie said, kneeling beside her. She picked up the cigarette butt and the flowers. The butt she ground under her heel, the flowers she lay in the wheelbarrow, beside the gravestone.

"Where's your car?" she said.

"I don't have one. I came on foot."

"I'll drive you."

They walked down the path to the parking lot. A dog barked angrily behind the junkyard fence.

"What if I don't tell you where I live?" Mrs. Rodney said.

"Then I'll find it some other way."

They got in Jessie's car. Its front end had been battered by the black van that night outside the residence and the windshield was cracked, but Mrs. Rodney didn't seem to notice. She sat silently in the unmoving car, looking at nothing, for half a minute, maybe more. Then she said, "Turn right at the end of the road."

Mrs. Rodney lived close by, on a rutted street lined with decaying tract houses. Her house had decayed the most. It had blocked gutters, peeling paint, dirty windows and a tiny brown lawn. All that Jessie saw in passing. What she noticed right away was the absence of the black van and Mrs. Rodney watching her out of the corner of her eye.

Mrs. Rodney unlocked the front door and stepped in ahead of Jessie. Her eyes darted around the gloomy interior. Then she turned, almost pirouetting like a far-gone house-proud frau, and said in a very bright voice, "See? Nobody home."

Jessie pushed past her. She went from one dark room to another, snapping on lights. She saw grimy wallpaper, sagging furniture, everything chipped, broken, ruined. She saw no sign of Pat or Kate.

Jessie returned to the front hall. Mrs. Rodney hadn't moved.

"See?" she said again.

"Is there a basement?"

316

"No," Mrs. Rodney replied. But her eyes slid toward a closed door across the hall. She was a poor liar.

Jessie went to the door and swung it open.

"I wouldn't go down there," Mrs. Rodney said. "It's always flooded."

"Flooded?" Jessie felt for the switch, turned it on. A weak yellow light shone somewhere below. She moved toward it, down a wobbly staircase.

The basement reeked. Water gleamed dully under a bare bulb. But it wasn't depthless and didn't swallow Jessie up when she stepped off the last stair. It didn't even top the edges of the soles of her shoes.

Three mattresses rose out of the water like islands. These looked almost as seedy as the one in the tunnel, but they weren't completely bare. Blankets, threadbare and rumpled, covered at least some of the ticking; there were other things as well: soft-drink cans, fast-food wrappers, scattered bits of tinfoil, a blackened pin, several bent lengths of sturdy copper wire. And under one of the blankets lay a Coca-Cola T-shirt, size extra-small.

Jessie picked it up and pressed it to her face. The Coca-Cola T-shirt had no smell, but she kept it there for a few moments anyway.

Then she explored the rest of the basement. She found a stone staircase leading up to bulkhead doors. She pushed them open and looked out into a small backyard. It was muddy, muddy enough to show clear tire tracks, leading away from the bulkhead and around the side of the house.

Jessie closed the doors and went upstairs. Mrs. Rodney was still in the front hall. Jessie held up the Coca-Cola T-shirt.

"They went," Mrs. Rodney said.

"Who went?"

"You know."

"Pat?" Mrs. Rodney nodded. "Kate?" She nodded again. "And who's the other?"

"You know."

"Hartley Frame?"

Mrs. Rodney nodded a third time.

"Where did they go?"

No answer.

"When?"

"This morning, I think. I didn't actually see them. They used the hatch. They weren't here long. Just since Monday. I knew nothing before then. I swear by all that's holy."

Monday. The day after she had gone into the tunnels. Hartley Frame had had to move on, taking Pat and Kate with him. They were on the run.

"Why did you let them stay here? Didn't you realize something was wrong?"

Tears were glistening again on Mrs. Rodney's cheeks. "It's all my husband's fault."

"Your husband? Is he alive too?"

"In Purgatory."

"He's dead?"

"Yes. But not soon enough." Her voice cracked.

"What do you mean?"

"I mean he's the cause of everything, if you know anything about psychology. He was a vicious brute. He used to beat Pat and beat him and beat him and beat him." Mrs. Rodney came closer. The tears were flowing now, down her face, dripping off her chin. She gripped Jessie's arms; her hands were small and bony, but surprisingly strong. "Beat him and beat him. I want you to understand that and try to forgive. Pat doesn't mean to be violent."

Jessie jerked herself free. "What are you talking about? Pat's not violent."

Mrs. Rodney started to speak, stopped herself, then said, "It wasn't all my husband's fault, even though he was a brute. It was Dennis Keith's fault too."

"Why?" asked Jessie, thinking of the photograph of another old woman, in Erica McTaggart's bedroom.

"I don't mean to blame him. Not like I blame Patrick senior. They were friends, after all, when Pat was little. His mother and I worked at the plant together. But Dennis was different; he had plans."

"What the hell are you talking about?" Jessie said. The woman's elliptical comments were leading her away from where she wanted to go.

Mrs. Rodney's voice rose with hers. "He introduced my boy to Hartley Frame and his free and easy ways. It put a lot of ideas in his head that were too much for him."

"Such as?"

"Such as getting away with things. Such as their music and their . . . their immorality."

"Are they selling drugs, Mrs. Rodney?"

She looked down at the worn carpet under her feet. "I don't know. I don't know anything. I'm a stupid old worthless bag."

"Are they on the run from whoever killed Blue?"

Now, at last, sound came to accompany Mrs. Rodney's tears. She howled. And howling, she slumped against the wall and sank to the floor. Jessie reached out and laid her hand on the woman's shoulder. Mrs. Rodney didn't acknowledge her touch, but made no move to knock her hand away.

Jessie crouched in front of her. Mrs. Rodney's eyes were no longer brilliant blue, but opaque with thick tears; her wrinkled face was smeared with fluids. "Where did they go, Mrs. Rodney?"

No reply.

"You have to tell me. Do you want your son to die too?"

Mrs. Rodney howled again, a high horrible sound that pierced the air like sirens. "Not the little girl," she cried. "Just not the little girl."

"She has a name. Kate. She's your granddaughter."

"Oh, if that was only true. I'd give—I'd give . . ." She couldn't think of anything. It was very quiet in the ruined house. When Mrs. Rodney spoke again, her voice was so low Jessie could hardly hear. "Don't you see? He's still my son. Nothing can change that."

The crying stopped. Jessie helped Mrs. Rodney to her feet. She wiped Mrs. Rodney's face with the sleeve of her jacket.

"You're kind," Mrs. Rodney said.

Jessie shook her head. "Where did they go?"

The bleary eyes gazed up at her. "Square one," Mrs. Rodney said softly. "Back to square one."

"I don't understand."

"That's what Pat said. Back to square one."

"What did he mean?"

"I don't know. I'd tell you if I did. I swear to God I would."

319

36

The visible world was still composed of shades of gray, but as Jessie drove back to the motel, the darker ones predominated. When she parked in front of room 19 and got out of the car, cold wind gusted in her face. She looked up. The sky was wild.

Jessie felt in her pockets for the key, before remembering that she no longer had one. She knocked on the door and waited for Bela's angry face to appear in the doorway. But no one answered her knock. She tried number 20. No answer.

Jessie went into the office. No one was there. Keys lay in wooden slots behind the desk. Jessie took the one from box 19.

She let herself into her room. Everything was the way she'd left it, except that her note was gone and Bela wasn't sleeping in the easy chair. The Verdi book lay there in his place.

She called room 20 and let the number ring. No answer.

"Shit." Was Bela somewhere out in the cold, searching for her?

She put down the phone. It rang immediately.

"Yes?"

Whoever was on the other end didn't speak. "Yes?" Jessie said again.

"Jessie?" said a voice.

A man's voice. She barely recognized it. But she did. "Pat?"

"Yes. Is that you, Jessie?"

"It's me. Oh God. Where the—" Many thoughts warred for Jessie's attention. "Is Kate all right?" was the one she spoke.

"Yes, she's all right."

"Let me talk to her."

There was a pause. Jessie thought she heard muffled talk. Then Pat said, "She's not here right now."

"Where is she?"

Another pause. "Outside."

"What do you mean outside? Go get her."

"Just a—" Muffled talk.

"Where the hell are you?" Jessie said, only half-conscious of how loudly she was saying it. "What the hell are you doing?"

Another voice came on the line. Another man. "Hi there, Jessie," he said.

Jessie wasn't aware of how hard she was squeezing the phone or how hard her heart was beating; her whole being was concentrated on the faint electronic hum at the other end of the line. "Is that Hartley Frame?" she said.

The man laughed. She didn't like that laugh at all. "Got me there," he said.

"I want to talk to my daughter."

"She can't come to the phone right now. Is there any message?"

"Why not? Have you done something to her?"

"Me? Of course not. You're welcome to come and get her."

"Where?"

"Where? You want me to tell you where?"

The sound of that was worse than his laugh. "You said I could come and get her."

"Sure I did. And I meant it. I'm just having a little fun. But the thing is—who's coming with you?"

"No one."

"That's good. Because it wouldn't be right. It's too . . . soon, you know what I mean?"

There was a long silence. He was waiting for an answer. "You're not ready yet?" Jessie said.

"Yeah. That's it. So just come alone, for now. After everything that's happened I wouldn't want to feel . . . like threatened, if you understand."

Jessie understood. At least she recalled the gist of all the articles she'd read and movies she'd seen about the emotional problems of returning war veterans; and realized this was much worse. "I'll be alone," she said. "But where?"

"Three guesses."

"But I have no idea."

"Try."

"The cabin on Mount Blackstone."

He laughed. "That's one."

"Please. Just tell me."

"Try."

"Spacious Skies?"

"That's two."

"Look, I don't know the answer. Why don't you just—"

"Come on, Jessie. Be a good sport."

She thought. "In the tunnels?"

"Nice try. That's three. Give up?"

Jessie was about to say yes when it hit her. "Woodstock," she said. "At the site of the festival."

There was a pause. Then he said, "Well now, you are something, aren't you? Got it in four. It really shouldn't count, but I'll bend the rules a little."

"And you'll give me back my daughter?"

"I promise. If you come alone."

"How do I know she's all right?"

"Because I told you."

"Let me speak to her."

"Why? Don't you believe me?"

Oh, God, Jessie thought. The articles and movies hadn't explained how to handle this. Then she remembered Alice Frame. "It's not that," she said. "It's just that I'm her mother, and I miss her. Like your mother misses you."

"What do you know about my mother?" The phone vibrated against her ear.

"She thinks you're dead. You'd make her very happy if you came back and saw her. It would remake her life."

Pause. "How do you know?"

"I talked to her."

"When?"

"Sunday."

"Is that today?"

"No."

"You didn't see her today?"

"No."

A long pause. "We've got a lot to talk about," he said.

"Yes," Jessie answered, thinking of him and his mother.

"I mean you and me."

"You and me?"

"Check."

There was another silence. Jessie listened for sounds on the line. There were none. They were very near. Kate was very near. She felt it.

"How do I know that Kate's all right?"

"You don't trust me?"

"It's not that. It's just that I'm a mother. Like your mother."

"Like my mother?"

"Yes."

He laughed the laugh she didn't like. "That's a good one," he said. More muffled talk. Then he said, "Okay, mother, here she is."

Bumping sounds.

Breathing sounds.

"Kate? Kate? Is that you?"

"Mom?"

The sound of that word cut down to the core of Jessie's being. "Oh, Kate, darling, are you all right?"

Kate's voice trembled, but she didn't cry. "Mom, don't—"

The line went dead. Jessie stood by the phone, waiting for it to ring again. It didn't.

37

Grace's office had changed. The big desk was still there, the comfortably padded swivel chair, the VDT, the keyboard, the printers, the file cabinets, the government-issued framed photographs of the Grand Canyon. But the can of Almond Roca was gone. And so was Grace.

A young man sat in her chair. A very young man, with short dark hair and a closely shaved baby face. He wore something that made the room smell like a pine forest.

"Where's Grace?" Zyzmchuk said.

"Grace, sir?"

"Who are you?"

"Fairweather, sir. I'm the new GR-3."

"Since when?"

"Yesterday, sir. I'm very pleased about the promotion and anxious to get down to some hard work."

"At what?"

"At what, sir?"

Zyzmchuk went into his own office. No one was sitting in his chair. He sat in it. He called Grace's home number. No answer.

Zyzmchuk pressed a button. Fairweather came into the room.

"You must be Mr. Zyzmchuk, sir. According to the office floor plan." His right hand twitched, as though anticipating possible handshaking. None ensued.

"Is Dahlin in yet?"

"Mr. Dahlin, sir? He's in Brussels. Mr. Keith said to tell you that the meeting has been pushed back to one."

"Is he in?"

"Who, sir?"

"Keith."

"Mr. Keith, sir? He'll be in at twelve forty-five."

Fairweather had a crisp delivery; it made all his words sound urgent. Zyzmchuk was tired of him already.

"Do you know where Records is, Fairweather?"

"From the floor plan, sir."

"Go to the Russian section. I want pictures of all Russian consular employees, including commercial, in the Los Angeles area."

"Yes, sir." Fairweather turned, almost militarily, and quick-marched to the door.

"Make that all of California, Fairweather."

"All of California, sir."

Zyzmchuk picked up his phone. He called the Morgantown National Bank. "The manager, please," he said.

"That would be Mr. Spring. May I tell him who is calling?"

"Ivan Zyzmchuk. From Washington."

"One moment."

Buzz.

"Hello, Mr. ah . . ."

"Zyzmchuk."

"Yes. This is Ronald Spring. What can I do for you?"

"I'm calling from Veterans Affairs, Mr. Spring. It's about some property that may be owned by a deceased soldier. We're

325

trying to verify the ownership, to help settle the estate. It may have been paid for with a check drawn on your bank."

"When was this?"

"August nineteen sixty-nine. The twenty-ninth."

"That's a long time ago. I wasn't here."

"But do your records go back that far?"

"Not on the computer."

"But somewhere?"

"Yes. Somewhere."

"Then I'd appreciate it if you'd have a look."

"Now?"

"That would be perfect. We're trying to close some of our old files, what with the new budget."

"That may be. But there are certain channels you have to go through for this kind of thing."

"Even for a dead man's bank account?"

"I'd have to look into that. The problem is—"

"Oh, by the way, Mr. Spring," Zyzmchuk interrupted, "I forgot to mention that we like to send framed citations to co-operating officials in the private sector. Signed by the secretary of defense."

"Framed citations?"

"Suitable for hanging."

"I see. It's Ronald B. Spring, by the way. I don't suppose the citations are ever signed by the president."

"Only in unusual circumstances. I could put in a favorable word."

"I see," said Mr. Spring again. "What name will the account be under?"

"Frame. Hartley E."

"A check on August twenty-ninth, nineteen sixty-nine."

"Right."

"I'll give it a try. Mr. ah . . ."

"Thanks." Zyzmchuk gave him the number and hung up. He buzzed Fairweather.

"Just coming, sir."

Fairweather entered with a stack of folders. "Here are the pictures, sir. All Soviet consular employees, including commercial, in California. I asked for 'Russian' as you directed, sir, but the woman said everything was filed under 'Soviet.' "

326

"My mistake," Zyzmchuk said. He would never stop making it.

Fairweather laid the folders on his desk. "Anything else, sir?"

"Yes. Answer any calls on my line 'Veterans Affairs, Estate Accounting Department.' "

Fairweather's eyes widened. This was the kind of excitement he'd been anticipating. "Forever, sir?"

"Just until I tell you to stop."

"Of course, sir." He quick-marched away.

Zyzmchuk began opening the folders. He examined passport-sized photographs of Russian faces, mostly male, some female. The faces wore the solemn expressions of business people going about their affairs. One or two had allowed themselves a faint smile, to show they were regular guys at heart. Or perhaps they just couldn't contain their amusement when they saw the official job descriptions.

Mr. Mickey was one of the smilers. His platinum hair and pale eyes made the photographic resolution seem poor, but Zyzmchuk never had trouble remembering the faces of people who tried to kill him. Mr. Mickey was listed as a technical advisor in the trade section of the San Francisco consulate. And underneath the picture was Mr. Mickey's name: Mikhail Tsarenko. His age: thirty-eight. And a notation: GRU member. Rank— Major (as of Sept. 1984).

Zyzmchuk was still looking at Mikhail Tsarenko's picture when his line buzzed. "It's a Mr. Spring," Fairweather whispered. "I told him it was Veterans Affairs. He didn't seem surprised."

"Put him on."

"Hello," said Mr. Spring. "Mr. ah . . . ?"

"Yes," Zyzmchuk said. "That was quick."

"Just because it's not in the computer doesn't mean we can't find it," Mr. Spring said, a little huffily.

"Right," said Zyzmchuk. "And did you?"

"Five thousand one hundred and twenty-five dollars, made out to Big-Top Motors in Bennington, Vermont, August twenty-ninth, nineteen sixty-nine?"

"That's it."

There was a slight pause. Then Mr. Spring said, "Is it the

same Hartley Frame they put up a monument for the other day? The senator's kid?"

"Yes. It must have been one of the last checks he wrote."

A longer pause. Zyzmchuk heard rustling paper. "Second last," Mr. Spring said. "I can't imagine his parents being concerned about tracing five grand from twenty years ago."

"That's got nothing to do with me," Zyzmchuk said. "When was the last one?"

"The last what?"

"Check."

"Do you need to know that, too?"

"We value complete records, just like you," Zyzmchuk said. "Was that Ronald *B.* Spring, by the way?"

Mr. Spring made a breathy sound. It might have been a sigh. "Yes," he said. "B for Barry."

"Do you want the citation to read Ronald B. or Ronald Barry?"

Silence. "Ronald B., I guess. That's the way they know me up here."

"Tell me about the last check, Ronald B."

Paper rustled. "The last check. Okay. It was made out to Mojo Guitars Limited, Reno, Nevada. Four hundred and sixty-four dollars, thirty-three cents."

"When was that?"

"January fourteenth, nineteen seventy. It left seventeen dollars and eighty cents in the account. The account was ruled inactive in nineteen seventy-one and the money transferred into general funds."

"Do you have the two checks in front of you, Mr. Spring?"

"I do."

"Look at the signatures."

"I'm looking."

"And?"

"And what?"

"Is there anything unusual?"

"Unusual?"

"Think back to your teller days."

"I was never a teller."

"But if you had been," Zyzmchuk said, "would you notice anything unusual about the signatures?"

328

Pause. "No. They look fine to me. 'Hartley Frame.' That's all."

"Are they identical, Mr. Spring?"

"Oh, that. Yes. Identical. At least as far as I can tell. But I'm not a handwriting expert."

"Okay," Zyzmchuk said. "Thanks."

"Mr. ah . . . ?"

"Yes."

"When might I expect the citation?"

"We'll try to get it out by Christmas," Zyzmchuk said. "But you know the government."

Mr. Spring giggled. They said good-bye.

Fairweather came in. "Mr. Keith called, sir. The meeting's postponed till two-thirty."

"Why?"

"He didn't say, sir."

"Where's he calling from?"

"I don't know, sir. He said he can't be reached."

"Stop calling me 'sir.' "

"Yes . . ." He stretched out the "s" so that it sounded like the beginning of the forbidden word. "What should I call you then?"

"Anything but 'sir.' "

"Yess."

Zyzmchuk glanced out his window. In the past few hours, a solid line of clouds had slid across the sky like the roof of a convertible. "Call me when he arrives."

"Yess."

"And Fairweather."

"Yess?"

"Do you know how to work the computer?"

"That's what a GR-3 does, s—."

"Then get me the army records for this man." He wrote "Hartley E. Frame" on a slip of paper and handed it to Fairweather.

"I'll get right on it," said Fairweather.

Zyzmchuk walked down the hall to Dahlin's office. No one was there but Gorbachev, pissing against the hedge. He crossed the hall and looked in Keith's office. Keith didn't have photographs on his walls. He had maps. There was nothing strategic about them. They were maps of the wine-making regions of Europe. He also had a nice Picasso calendar and the plushest furniture, deepest rugs and biggest plants in the building. None of it was government issue—he'd paid for everything himself.

A copy of *The New York Times* lay on his desk. It was opened to a Frank Prial article on Bordeaux futures. "How are things in your daddy's wine cellar?" Zyzmchuk asked aloud, just in case anyone was listening. Then he sat down at the desk and called Keith's home number. It rang twenty times before he hung up.

2:30. No Keith. Zyzmchuk went downstairs for coffee. "There's going to be a big storm," a cleaning woman by the machine was saying.

"Rain or snow?" said the janitor.

"Rain here. Snow up north."

Zyzmchuk poured himself a cup of coffee and went to the front door. The clouds had grown darker and looked swollen, as though they were holding their breath. He returned to his office and called the 1826 House, room 19. There was no answer.

At three Fairweather entered. "Mr. Zyzmchuk?"

"Yes?"

"Is it okay if I call you 'Mr. Zyzmchuk'?"

"Yes. What is it?"

"Oh. Mr. Keith called. He's been delayed. The meeting's not till five."

"Is he still on the line?"

"No, Mr. Zyzmchuk."

"Where is he?"

"He said he can't be reached."

"But the call came from somewhere."

Fairweather backed up a step or two. Zyzmchuk realized he'd raised his voice. "I think he was in his car, s—Mr. Zyzmchuk. I heard some honking."

"Get him on the line."

Fairweather rang the phone in Keith's car. No one answered. "Maybe he stopped for gas or something," Fairweather said.

"Try again in ten minutes."

Fairweather tried again in ten minutes. And ten minutes after that. But he couldn't reach Keith.

"Did he sound nearby?" Zyzmchuk asked.

"Nearby?"

"Or far away."

Fairweather thought. "I really couldn't say, Mr. Zyzmchuk. I was concentrating on getting the message right, you know?"

Fairweather returned to his office. Zyzmchuk tried room 19 at the 1826 House again. Still no answer. He tried room 20. No answer. Outside his window the clouds kept darkening and growing more massive. Lights shone in all the buildings on the skyline.

Five o'clock. No Keith. Fairweather came in. "Tomorrow's Thanksgiving, Mr. Zyzmchuk."

"That's right."

"I wonder if I might . . . go home now. Call it a day, kind of. I wanted to get cracking on the stuffing."

"Did you find Hartley Frame's army record?"

"Oh, that," Fairweather said. "I forgot to mention. There was no army record for Hartley Frame."

"You must have made a mistake," Zyzmchuk said. Grace hadn't told him there was no record; she had said it was classified.

"No, Mr. Zyzmchuk. I can show you if you like."

Zyzmchuk followed Fairweather into Grace's office. Fairweather sat before the screen and started tapping the keys. His hairless fingers had a quick light touch, like a pianist's. "Okay," he said, after a minute or two. "We're in army records." He typed, "Frame, Hartley E."

The rest of the screen remained blank for several seconds. Then a message appeared: "Error 57—Invalid File Name."

"Meaning?" said Zyzmchuk.

"Meaning, I think, sir, Mr. Zyzmchuk, that Frame, Hartley E., was never in the army. Would you like me to try the other services?"

"No."

There was a long silence. Zyzmchuk felt Fairweather's eyes on him. For a moment he believed Fairweather might be thinking along with him. "What is it, Fairweather?"

"Will that be all, then?" Fairweather asked, proving he wasn't.

"Yes."

"I can go?"

"Yes."

"Thank you, Mr. Zyzmchuk. It'll be a pleasure working with someone of your experience. Happy Thanksgiving."

The first raindrops landed softly on the window and ran down the glass in hesitant streams.

38

Grace lived in a one-room apartment just east of the Georgetown campus. Ivan Zyzmchuk pressed her buzzer in the lobby. Grace's voice didn't come over the intercom; the lock didn't click. Two men in business suits came down the stairs and opened the door. "I've got to get my hands on some Redskins tickets," one said in French.

"I'm desolated," the other replied, also in French. "Je ne peux pas vous aider."

Zyzmchuk went through the doorway and up two flights. At the end of a corridor, he knocked on Grace's door. No one answered, but he heard tinny excitement on the other side of the door, the kind of excitement that comes out of a box with rabbit ears.

He knocked again. "Grace," he called. "It's me. Ivan." Mr. Z., he'd almost said.

Grace opened the door. She wore a quilted pink housecoat

and fluffy pink slippers. The color matched her eyes. He thought she'd lost weight. It didn't suit her.

"Oh, Mr. Z.," she said. "They fired me."

Her lip trembled. He thought she was going to cry, but she didn't. "May I come in?" he said.

"It's a pigsty. It's a dump anyway, but now it's a pigsty too."

"I don't care."

Grace stepped aside. Zyzmchuk went in. Framed prints hung on the walls, Degas prints, all of them with subjects from the ballet. The slender girls in tutus looked down on Grace's room: the unmade single bed; the litter of newspapers and magazines; the unwashed coffee mugs on every surface; the game show contestants on the box in the corner, jumping up and down at the sight of a toaster.

"I told you," Grace said. "It's a pigsty."

Zyzmchuk cleared a space on the couch and sat down. "What happened, Grace?"

She was gazing at the TV. "They fired me," she said quietly. "What am I going to do?" Drums rolled. Trumpets blared. A beautiful woman in a tight dress pulled back a scarlet curtain. Waiting on the other side were a microwave oven and a VCR. Applause.

Zyzmchuk got up and switched off the set. "Who fired you?"

"Mr. McKenna. He does all the firing."

"Did he give a reason?"

"Poor job performance."

"That's ludicrous. Your record's outstanding."

Grace shrugged. There was no fight in her; she needed an office to function, the way a honeybee needs a hive.

"McKenna doesn't know anything about your work. Who gave him his orders?"

"I don't know. It could have been anybody."

"It couldn't have been anybody, Grace. Who could have done it?"

"You mean technically?"

"Yes."

"I'd have to think."

"Think."

Grace's eyes cleared a little; he'd plugged her into office

routine, no matter how temporary, how hopeless. Zyzmchuk picked up her phone. He called the 1826 House, first one room, then the other. The phone rang and rang. Grace was waiting for his attention. He hung up.

"There are only three people with the authority, Mr. Z. Besides Mr. McKenna." She counted them off on her fingers. "Mr. Dahlin, Mr. Keith."

"That's two. Who's the third?"

"You, Mr. Z."

He smiled, but was conscious of how quickly it came and went. Time was short and he was far away. "It wasn't me," he said.

Grace's lip trembled. "Oh, I know that."

"So who was it?"

She thought. Her eyes grew blurry again. "I just don't know. Neither of them ever expressed any dissatisfaction with my work. And Mr. Keith hasn't even been in the office much lately."

"Did anyone know you'd been helping me?"

"Helping you?"

"Looking for Hartley Frame's army file."

She shook her head. "Not unless someone accessed my logs."

"You logged the Hartley Frame search?"

Grace nodded. "And the woman. I log everything, Mr. Z. I always go by the book. Or went by the book, I should say." She glanced around her room, as though taking in where that had got her.

"What woman?" Zyzmchuk said.

"The one you asked me to look up." Grace was watching him closely. "Jessie something. She had two last names. There was nothing on her. I tried the Bur—"

"You logged her too?"

Zyzmchuk realized he had raised his voice; he was also on his feet, although he didn't recall standing up.

Grace backed away, one hand holding her housecoat tightly closed at the throat. "Did I do something wrong?"

Zyzmchuk struggled to make his voice reassuring. "No, Grace. Who could have accessed your logs?"

"Anyone with my code."

"Who has your code?"

335

"It's no big secret. D-base has it, Mr. McKenna, even computer maintenance."

Zyzmchuk turned and paced across the little room. He pulled back the curtains. A wind had risen from the north. It was blowing the rain at a slight angle across the sky.

"Mr. Z.? Have you done something wrong? Is that why I got fired?"

He closed the curtains and looked at Grace. She was afraid. He had no reassurance to give her. "What happened when you tried to get Hartley Frame's record?"

"I told you. It was classified. We needed A.D. or higher to get into it. I asked you and you—"

"I tried to get into it today, Grace."

"By yourself?"

"No. There's a new . . . GR-3."

"Already," she said softly.

"Yes," Zyzmchuk said. Grace's lip was trembling again. He waited for it to stop. Then he said, "He couldn't find any file for Hartley Frame."

"He must have made a mistake."

"Not that I saw. He got an Error 57 message."

Grace said nothing. He could see she had chosen silence over repeating that her replacement had made a mistake.

"What came up when you tried?" Zyzmchuk asked.

Grace looked surprised. "I told you, Mr. Z. It was classified."

"But what came on the screen? Exactly."

"Word for word?"

"Yes."

Grace screwed up her eyes like a child. "First came the classification code. It was an NP-6; that's the A.D. level. Then the entry, Frame, Hartley E. Then his unit, and that was all."

"His unit?"

"Yes. It was the 173rd Airborne Brigade."

"Will they have their own records?"

"Separate from army records, you mean?"

"Yes."

Grace thought. Her eyes had an inward look, as though she were gazing back on twenty-five years of directing paper traffic in Washington. "They do," she said.

"Let's go," Zyzmchuk said.

"Like this?" Grace spread her arms.

"Why not? Just throw on a coat."

Grace threw on a coat. They hurried out to her car. Her pink slippers flapped on the sidewalk, a foot of quilted housecoat hung down past the bottom of her coat, but there was a spring in her stride.

"Do you want to drive?" she said, digging the keys out of her purse.

"You drive," Zyzmchuk said.

Grace drove. She drove fast and well. She parked in Zyzmchuk's space, but could have parked anywhere; it was after six and the lot was empty. They rode the elevator, walked quickly down the hall to her old office. Grace sat at the terminal. Her fingers tapped the keys, then froze in midstroke.

"I can't sign in," she said. "The machine won't accept my code."

"Use mine. I've got it written down in my desk." He turned to go.

"Don't bother," Grace said. "I know it. I know all the codes."

"Dahlin's?"

"Yes."

"Use it."

Grace smiled. "You're funny, Mr. Z."

Her plump fingers dove down to the keyboard. Letters and numbers appeared and disappeared on the screen. They meant nothing to Zyzmchuk. He watched Grace's fingers instead, how they hesitated, hovered, tapped—sometimes a single key, sometimes a flurry. Then the screen went black except for the cursor, pulsing in the top left-hand corner.

"We're in," Grace said.

"And there's nothing?"

"No. I haven't entered him yet."

"Go ahead."

Grace's fingers flicked across the keys. "Frame, Hartley E." lit the screen. A few moments passed; nothing moved but the pulsing cursor. Then words began running across the screen, line after line.

"Bingo," Grace said. Her fingers were still. Zyzmchuk leaned over her shoulder; his eyes strained to take it all in at once.

FRAME, Hartley Edmund
HT.: 5'11"
WT.: 170
EYES: Blue
HAIR: Blond
BUILD: Medium
DISTINGUISHING MARKS: None
IQ: 132
EDUCATION: College, three years
DRAFT STATUS: 1A, as of Jan. 1, 1969
PHYSICAL: Sept. 1, 1969. Fort Dix. Passed for active ser-
vice.
INDUCTION: Oct. 3, 1969. Fort Dix.
BASIC TRAINING: Oct. 3, 1969–Dec. 1, 1969. Fort Dix. As-
signed 173rd Airborne Dec. 3, 1969. Rank: Private
MOVE ORDER: Dec. 22, 1969.
EMBARKATION: Jan. 10, 1970. U.S.S. Oriskany. San Diego.
DISEMBARKATION: Jan. 28, 1970. Cam Ranh Bay.
PROMOTION: Feb. 6, 1970. Pfc.
MIA: March 10, 1970. Pleiku area. See note 1.
DECEASED: Between March 1970 and December 1970. Exact
date unknown. See note 2. Declared dead Jan. 5, 1971.
See note 3.
DECORATIONS: Combat service ribbon. Purple heart. Bronze
star. All posthumous.
NOTE 1: (From report of S. Sgt. Millard Flemming, March
11, 1970.) Pfc. Frame was point on a six-man sweep
north of Pleiku March 9–March 10, 1970. Our bivouac
was surrounded by 30 to 40 N.V. regulars at about
22:30 March 10. A firefight of about ten minutes followed. Enemy withdrew. Our casualties were two
wounded, one seriously, and Pfc. Frame who was not
seen after the fighting.
NOTE 2: (From report of M. Gilles Ricord of International
Red Cross, Dec. 3, 1970.) I send under separate cover
dog tags (number 237–32495, name Hartley E. Frame)
and fingerprints furnished by the Government of North
Viet Nam. Bodily remains apparently lost in a fire which
destroyed buildings in D-1 camp.
NOTE 3: Prints match those taken at Fort Dix, Sept. 1, 1969,

from Hartley E. Frame—J. M. Morris, MD, Central
Identification Laboratory, Hawaii.

"Is that all?" Zyzmchuk said.

Grace tapped a key. The words scrolled out of sight. "Yup,"
she said. "Does it help?"

Zyzmchuk stared at the empty screen. "It raises some question," he said.

"Like?"

Like how could Hartley Frame have written a check to Mojo
Guitars Limited in Reno, Nevada, on January 14, 1969, if he'd
sailed for Viet Nam on January 10?

"You don't know or you just don't want to tell me?" Grace
asked.

But Zyzmchuk was silent, lost in a maze of thought that
changed shape with every mental move he made. Outside darkness had fallen, dark as the blank screen. Rain beat on the
windows.

At last he spoke, but it wasn't to answer her question. "I've
got to get to the airport, Grace."

"I'll take you," she said.

39

Rain cut down from the sky in slanting lines, like strokes painted with the edge of a palette knife. Jessie drove out of the Berkshires, into New York and across the Hudson. The rain and wind were busy knocking the last leaves off the trees. That made the trees whip their bare branches around like flagellants in a fury of mortification.

Jessie held the wheel tight in both hands and drove as fast as she dared; but the little rental car didn't handle as well as it had before the battering outside the campus residence, and when she turned on the headlights, Jessie found that only one was working. After almost an hour she tried the radio. It wasn't working well either. The only clear station had an oldies format and an announcer with the voice of a B-movie seductress.

"All your favorite ear candy from the fifties, sixties and early seventies," breathed the woman.

"Ball and Chain" by Janis Joplin. "She Said She Said" by

the Beatles. "Rip This Joint" by the Stones. Then the Levi's commercial came on. Jessie snapped it off before the ringing guitar part. She just drove. Her mind became a box, enclosing one word. The word was "please."

Jessie entered Woodstock a few minutes after four. It would have been a beautiful town in any other weather. But now the lawns were muddy brown and the tidy, freshly painted shops on the main street looked like a movie set after the lighting men have gone home.

Jessie parked outside a store with a pumpkin in the window and went inside. A bell tinkled as the door closed behind her. It was a cheese shop. A woman in a black cashmere sweater and designer jeans had a white display card in her hands. She was writing the wrong accent over the e in chèvre. "May I help you?" she said. "We've got some lovely Camembert just in."

"Not today," Jessie replied. "I'm looking for the site of the festival."

"Festival?"

"The Woodstock festival."

"Oh, that. I wouldn't know. We just opened last month. We're from Manhattan, but we couldn't take it anymore. Try one of the locals." From the way the woman said "locals," Jessie suspected her migration might not be permanent.

She drove to a gas station and filled the tank. "I'm looking for the site of the Woodstock festival," she told the attendant.

He stuck his head in the window. Perhaps he was a local. He needed a shave, deodorant, a dentist, eyedrops. "On a day like this?" he said. "You people." He laughed. Jessie didn't. "I'll tell you what I tell them all. The famous Woodstock festival didn't take place within spitting distance of Woodstock." His voice grew a little sibilant, as if he was tempted to do some spitting himself. "We wouldn't have none of it. Not then. Not now." He laughed again. Rain ran down the bill of his Red Sox cap and dripped on Jessie's shoulder.

"Where was the site?" Jessie said.

"Why down in Bethel," he said. "I can never understand how come none of you pilgrims ever knows that, if you're so gung ho about that whole business."

Jessie leaned away, out of the drip. "Where is Bethel?"

341

"Well, first you got to loop around the reservoir," the attendant began, and he launched on a discourse full of town and route names that didn't stick in Jessie's mind.

"But how far is it from here?"she interrupted, expecting an answer like five or six miles.

"Fifty miles," he said, with the smug sureness of a joker delivering a tried-and-true punchline. "Take you an hour to get there in this weather. At least."

Jessie drove southwest, into cloud-covered hills. The rain was falling harder, and the air growing cold. Jessie turned on the heat. The roads were narrow and winding, passing through many small towns. There wasn't much traffic, but it was after five by the time Jessie drove into Bethel, and almost dark.

Bethel showed no signs of being a magnet for burned-out New Yorkers. It looked like a simple country town. Jessie went into a simple country store.

"Just closing," said an old man in a smock.

"I'm looking for the site of the Woodstock festival."

He sighed. "Straight on through to Hurd Road. Take a right and keep going till you come to four corners. That's it." He dropped a handful of steel bolts into a paper bag. They exploded softly on landing.

Jessie drove out of Bethel. Rain drummed on the roof and flowed down the cracked windshield into the track of the wipers. On the far side of the clouds the sun must have been going down: for a few minutes everything turned a faint shade of purple. She found Hurd Road and turned right.

Rolling empty farmland stretched into the wooded distance. Nothing moved across it—not a tractor, not an animal, not a man. There was no sign of the black van, Kate, Pat or Hartley Frame. Jessie approached a crossroads and slowed down. She saw a small, gray shape in the brown emptiness, not far from the roadside, and pulled over.

Jessie got out of the car, stepped over a shallow ditch and walked into the field. Cold rain fell on her; mud sucked at her shoes. The gray shape, she now saw, was a stone marker. Under a bas-relief of a guitar neck bearing a dove, a plaque read: "This is the original site of the Woodstock Music and Arts Fair."

Jessie looked around. She was alone. She gazed at the inscription, her mind a blank. Rain, finding its way into her collar and trickling down her back, broke her trance.

Had Hartley Frame lied to her? Why? If he was going to lie, why telephone her in the first place? Jessie didn't have the answer. All she could think of was trying Mrs. Rodney again.

Move, she told herself. But she didn't want to move, didn't want to get in the car, didn't want to see the decaying house in North Adams again. She stood in the rain, looking at the stone marker in the empty field, once filled with half a million strong. The Joni Mitchell song started playing in her mind. It had also played, she recalled, in Pat's cassette machine, when she'd pressed the button in his music room.

What had happened that Friday night in Venice? It must have been Friday night—they'd driven across the country by Monday.

Hartley Frame had knocked on the door, perhaps only minutes after she'd dropped Kate off. How had he found out where Pat lived? From Blue Rodney. She tried to warn her brother, but the warning had come too late.

Who had opened the door? Pat? Kate? Had Pat even recognized Hartley at first? They had let him in. Or he'd forced his way in. And then? All she knew were two facts: They'd played the Joni Mitchell song. They'd driven away in the blue BMW. Perhaps they'd stopped at Pat's bank: Buddy Boucher had been paid in cash.

Had it turned ugly somewhere along the way? Or had it been ugly from the start?

Jessie remembered something else. Jimi Hendrix's guitar. The Stratocaster that hung on the music room wall. The one Pat had said he bought at an auction, but Disco said had been given to Hartley by Jimi Hendrix at the festival. It had been missing too. So, fact three: they'd taken the guitar with them. Adding it all up, she was no further ahead. That left only Mrs. Rodney.

Jessie looked up from the marker. The rain fell harder now, blowing into her face from across the field. Only the weakest tinge of purple remained in the clouds; the sky was growing dark. Jessie was just about to turn toward the car when she noticed something moving at the edge of the woods. It was no more than a blur, a dark blur. She closed her eyes, opened them. The dark blur was still there, but it had stopped moving.

Jessie took a few slow steps across the field. The light was fading quickly now, but the blur began to assume a rectangular shape. And, at the very limit of her vision, she saw a tiny flash of red. Jessie started running across the field as fast as she could.

The blurry rectangle hardened its outline and became the black van. The tiny flash of red blossomed into the painted flames along its side. Soon Jessie could even distinguish silvery dents on the corner of the back door and a bend in the rear bumper.

She ran. There was no sound but the rain, the sucking mud and her own breathing. *Be smart,* said a voice inside her. But what was the smart thing to do? She didn't know. She ran right up to the van.

The van was parked under a big bare tree at the edge of the woods. No sound came from inside. Jessie was so close she could reach out and touch the van. She reached out and touched it. Cold and wet. She wiped water off the windshield and looked through. No one was in the front seat. The plastic curtain was drawn behind it.

Jessie walked around the van. She tried the two front doors, the side door, the back door. All locked. She put her forehead against the opaque windows, but could see nothing inside. She tried the side door again, harder this time, jerking the handle up and down. The door remained locked.

But something stirred inside. And someone—no, not someone, but Kate—said, "Who's there?"

"Katie! Katie! It's me!"

"Mom?"

"Oh, yes, yes, yes. Are you all right, darling?" Emotion surged through Jessie; she felt as though her whole body would dissolve in it. She struggled to control her voice. "Can you open the door?"

"I'm tied up. Hurry, Mom."

"It's okay. I'll get you out." Jessie bent down and picked up a rock. She smashed the window on the passenger side door. Her hand was through the hole and on the lock when a man shot out from under the van and bounced to his feet. He wore a filthy summer suit and a big smile. His teeth were brown and rotten.

"Welcome to Woodstock, Jessie," the man said, spreading

his arms. His head had been shaved, but new hair was growing back in a dark stubble. Rain ran through it and dripped down his hollow face.

"Hartley," Jessie began; but the word faltered on her lips when she noticed the color of his eyes. "I want my daughter back."

The smile faded. "That's not my name," he said. "My name is Bao Dai."

Oh God, Jessie thought. She had no idea what to say, how to deal with him, how to get Kate out of that van.

"Bao Dai," he repeated. "It's an emperor's name. Emperor of the V.C. Emperor of the mud."

"I know. You wrote 'Toi giet la toi' on Pat's blackboard." It was the first thought that came to Jessie's mind.

His eyes narrowed. "That's not how you pronounce it." He came a step closer. She stepped back. "You're afraid of me, Jessie."

"That's obvious."

He showed his rotten teeth again. "You don't need to be. I like you. Come." He held out his hand.

Jessie didn't move. "Come where?" she said.

"Just for a little talk."

"Let's talk here. My daughter's in the van. I want to be with her. I want to see her."

"She's fine. She's kind of my daughter too, you know. By right." He thrust out his bony jaw, as though waiting for an argument. Jessie said nothing. "Come," he repeated, holding out his hand again.

Jessie didn't move. He reached into his belt and took out a knife. Jessie recognized it—Pat's carving knife with the scrimshaw handle.

"You made me show you this," he said, almost sounding insulted. "I didn't want to. But you couldn't just come nicely." He lunged forward and grabbed her hand. He was very quick and very strong. His hand felt hard and rough. Jessie tried to pull away. He tightened his grip and drew her toward the trees.

"You said I could have my daughter. You said you weren't going to hurt anybody."

"And I meant every word. But I wasn't stoned then. I'm a bit stoned now."

"Mom?" called Kate from the van.

He jerked Jessie into the woods before she could answer and pulled her, half-running, half-stumbling, about twenty or thirty yards through the trees. Then suddenly he stopped. Another man stood against a tree. He was bound to it with nylon rope. He was drenched, dirty and shivering, long fair hair matted to his skull. It was Pat.

He saw her. Tears came to his eyes. "Oh, Jessie, I'm afraid," he said. "He's got some acid. He made me take some. I'm afraid."

The hard hand relaxed its grip. The other one showed her the knife. Jessie slipped free and, making no abrupt motions, went to Pat and put her hands gently on his shoulders. After all he'd done—placing Kate at risk, helping set this trap for her, other things she only half-understood—Jessie still couldn't say the bitter, angry words she'd meant to say when she saw him again. He was already down; and he was still Pat.

"Everything's going to be all right," she said and tried to mean it. But one look into Pat's eyes, and she knew there would be no help from him. She was on her own.

"Sure it is," Bao Dai said behind her. "I took some too. Blue ones and red ones. We're buddies. We share everything." Jessie turned. He took a vial from his jacket pocket. "And I've got some for you too."

"I don't want any," Jessie said.

"Don't be shy. Turn on. Tune in. I forget the other part." He opened the vial and took out a tablet. "Blue cheer," he said.

"No."

"Yes. It's good acid. I see all kinds of colors." He looked around. The only colors Jessie saw were gray and brown and the bright blue of his eyes. "We'll make up for lost time." He came toward her, the tablet between his fingers.

Jessie spun away, dodged around a tree and ran. She gave everything she had to that run. *Get to the van. Unlock the door. Grab Kate. Run.* That was all she had to do.

Jessie was only a few steps from the edge of the woods, ten yards from the van, when he caught her. He was very fast. He brought her down. Her head hit the muddy ground, not very hard. But it was the second blow in three days.

It couldn't have been more than a few minutes before Jessie

opened her eyes. The sky hadn't grown much darker; the rain wasn't falling much harder. She was lying on her back in the woods. Her head hurt worse than the first time. She tried to get up. She couldn't.

Her wrists and ankles were bound with copper wire that had been fastened to tent pegs driven into the ground. Jessie pulled and tugged and strained with all her might; but she couldn't move.

Then she heard voices, not far away. A man, the man who called himself Bao Dai, said, "It was right around here someplace, wasn't it? Lie down."

Another man, Pat, said, "I don't want to. Why don't we—"

There was a thump. Then Bao Dai said, "When I say lie down, you lie down. There. Like that. That was rule number two."

"Please don't. Please don't. I'm begging you."

"I begged plenty of times. I begged Corporal Trinh plenty of times."

"But you can't blame me for that. Who could have known what would—?"

"Who else can I blame?" Bao Dai interrupted, his voice rising. "Christ, I'm stoned out of my fucking mind. But you know what?"

"What?"

"It's just what I was afraid of. A bad trip. You know? Real bad."

"Maybe . . . I can help," Pat said. Jessie could feel him thinking; she wished she could be doing the thinking for him.

"You? You? You're the one, baby, the one who fucked me good. Better than Corporal Trinh. You know that? I should cut off your yellow cock."

"Oh God."

"Sure. Oh God. You'll find that's a big help. But don't you worry. Would I do a thing like that?"

"No."

"Keep your fingers crossed." Bao Dai laughed. Then he said, "Just don't make offers to help, that's all. If I'm having a bad trip it's your fault. Right?"

"Right."

"Goddamned right." Pause. Then Bao Dai's voice rose again. "It was right here, right fucking here, where you stole the guitar Hendrix gave to me—"

"He gave it to me. You know that."

Jessie, listening, was thinking, *Pat, you fool*, even before Bao Dai yelled, "Shut up." There was a cry of pain. Then Bao Dai said, "It was right here. You said, 'Do you want to try something far-out?' That's what you said: 'something far-out.' Isn't that the most . . . the most . . ." Bao Dai gave up his search for the phrase. "And I was just a dumb fucking townie, and I said, 'What?' And you said, 'I'll make it worth your while.' "

"And I still will, if you let me."

"Oh yeah?" Bao Dai laughed the laugh Jessie didn't like, but this time it went on and on. "With another car? Another sporty car for sporty me?"

"If you want. But much more than that. I promise you'll never have to work again."

"I've never worked yet." Bao Dai was laughing again, high, higher, out of hearing.

"And you'll never have to. I'll give you everything you want."

"I don't want money."

"Then what do you want?"

"All those years."

"But I can't give you that." Pat started to cry.

"Sure you can. I'll take the girl, for starters."

"You know that's impossible. But you can visit sometimes, and—"

"You son of a bitch." Jessie heard Bao Dai's voice rise to the limit of control and then beyond. "Visits. You're giving me permission to visit my own life. Can't you see that? Can't you? Can't you? Well, let me tell you something. Do you know what's in my kitchen?"

"Your kitchen?"

"This."

"Oh no. Oh God, no."

"Oh God, yes."

Then there was a hammering sound. And Pat screamed a horrible scream. And another. Bao Dai shouted over his screams. "It's not even enough. You stole my life, Hartley Frame, and

348

you have to pay." His voice sank suddenly, almost to a whisper. "That's rule number one."

"Please Pat, don't do this to me."

"It's done."

"Please, please." Jessie heard the cries of her ex-husband. They faded to moans and soon to silence.

Then she heard footsteps, soft footsteps coming closer. The man who called himself Bao Dai stood over her. His eyes were mad. "It's time to pay the price." He stripped off his filthy tan suit and the button-down shirt. He wore nothing underneath. He had a thin, hard body; his arms and legs were thin and hard too, criss-crossed with scars: arms and legs that glistened in the rain like something other than flesh and blood. He didn't seem to notice the rain at all.

Bao Dai squatted beside her, unbuttoned her jacket and raised her sweater.

"I've done nothing to you," Jessie said.

He rubbed her breasts with both hands. They were hard hands and rough.

"You've got no reason to hate me," Jessie said. But he wasn't looking at her, wasn't listening. He was looking down between his own legs at his penis. It was soft and limp.

"Do you know how long it's been since I had a hard-on?"

He pinched her nipples, then gave them a twist.

Don't show pain. Somehow Jessie knew that. It was all she knew at that moment.

He twisted her nipples harder. His penis began to swell. Jessie wanted to bite her lip to keep from crying out, but she couldn't risk that either. She just didn't cry out.

One rough hand kept twisting her nipple. The other hand raked down her stomach slowly and began fiddling with the snaps of her jeans. They frustrated him. He got the knife and started cutting the material. The point pricked her skin. Blood seeped out of it. He smiled at the sight, and his penis swelled a little more.

Jessie saw her future. It was short and brutal. There was only one possible way out. It all depended on how well she understood him; it also meant going against every grain of her being. But she didn't calculate the cost of doing that: there wasn't much reason to think she would live to pay it.

"Look at me," Jessie said, trying to imitate the B-movie seductress voice from the radio. "Look at my face."

He looked, reluctantly. Jessie stared right into his deadly eyes as though they were the eyes of a lover, a demon lover who had her completely under his spell, and she softly said, "You don't have to do that, honey. Just untie me and I'll cooperate."

Both his hands stopped moving. There was a silence. It seemed to Jessie to last forever. Then he said, "Shit." He looked down between his legs. His penis was shrinking. "Why'd you have to go and do that?" He brought one of his hands to it, but it was no use. "You've ruined everything," he said. He was angry now, but that was all. He grabbed her breast and squeezed it like a rubber ball. This time Jessie had to bite her lip, bite it until she tasted blood, but she didn't make a sound. She understood him. His penis stayed limp. "You've ruined it."

He rose, reached for his clothes in the mud. By the time he was half-dressed, Jessie could tell his mind was already on something else. He didn't even see her. And then he was gone. Footsteps went away. An engine started. Its sound, too, faded away.

Jessie lay in the mud. She wanted to cry and never stop. But there was no time for that. *Don't think of what a coward you are. Think of Kate.* She began to struggle with her bonds. The rain helped her, softening the earth around the tent pegs. After a while she worked one arm free. A few moments later she was on her feet.

She followed the moaning sounds. She didn't have to go far. After only twenty or thirty yards, she came to a shallow pit surrounded by newly turned earth. A few spadefuls had been tossed back into the pit, not nearly enough to cover the man lying inside. Clods of dirt lay on his face and soiled his long, fair hair. His eyes were closed. He moaned: the father of her child, the only man she'd really loved.

He was lying on something. At first the image didn't focus in Jessie's mind. Then she took it in. He'd been crucified on Jimi Hendrix's guitar.

She saw the big nails, driven through his upper arms—one into the body of the guitar, the other into the neck. His right arm had bled very little, but the left one, nailed to the fingerboard, had bled a lot, soaking his shirt and the mud below, and was still bleeding.

Jessie ran forward, dropped to her knees, laid her hand on his forehead. He opened his eyes. They saw her, recognized her. "Jessie." His voice was quiet as a whisper, but he wasn't whispering. "I should have told you a long time ago."

She hadn't really known until that moment. Now she did.

"Oh . . ." Jessie didn't say his name. She had no name for him now. She brushed the dirt off his face and out of his long, fair hair.

He closed his eyes. "Jessie," he said. She could hardly hear him. "I wish we could have made it. It was all my fault."

"That's not true."

His eyes opened. They filled with alarm. "You've got to go," he said. "Hurry. He said he's taking her to Grandpa's."

"Grandpa's?"

"The cabin. He's going to do something. He thinks my father—" His face twisted in pain, as though someone had jerked on invisible wires.

"First I'm getting you to the hospital."

"No. Leave me."

Jessie tore strips off her shirt, wrapped them tightly around his arms, above the nails.

"Leave me."

"You're going to be all right. You've lost a little blood, that's all." She knelt behind his head, took his shoulders, tried to sit him up. He moaned. She pushed. The neck of the guitar jammed under a stone. He cried out. She couldn't free him. The head of the nail rose a fraction of an inch from the surface of his arm. He screamed. Jessie grasped the head of the nail and pulled it out.

He sat up, half free of the guitar. He stopped screaming. His lips turned up in a weak smile. Then Jessie saw the blood. The nail had ripped a huge hole in his arm. Blood was spurting out of it, soaking the tourniquet, soaking her.

"Oh God," she said, frantically pressing her bare hand on the wound. Blood poured out through her fingers. "Oh God." His eyes closed. He sank back into the bottom of the pit. Jessie kept her hand on the wound, praying for the blood to stop.

351

Finally it did. But his breathing stopped too. Jessie put her mouth to his, blew her breath into him. His chest rose. Her breath came out. His chest fell. Her breath went in. Her breath went out. It was no good, but she stayed there by the pit for a long time, trying to breathe life into him.

At last she gave up. It was night now—starless, moonless darkness, full of icy rain. Jessie got him out of the pit, half-dragged, half-carried him out of the woods. It was a long way to the car. There was no time. But she couldn't leave him there.

She dragged him across the field. It took forever. The guitar came loose. She left it in the mud. Rain turned to snow, colder than the rain and almost as hard. The wind blew it wildly over Yasgur's farm.

40

The plane swung to the right. It swung to the left. It bounced up a few hundred feet. Then down. All seat belts were buckled. They'd been buckled the whole flight. No food, no drink, no last minute money-making with calculators and lap-top computers. Outside the oval windows lay a black night full of white swirls. The plane circled an invisible airport, wobbled down, hit the runway, hit it again, and again, and once more. Then it rolled to a stop in front of the terminal, and everyone got out, sick smiles on their faces. They closed the airport five minutes later.

The Blazer waited in the parking building where he'd left it. Ivan Zyzmchuk circled down the ramp and stopped at the tollbooth. "It's chaos out there," said the attendant happily, taking Zyzmchuk's money. "Thanksgiving's the busiest time there is. Couldn't be wilder."

Zyzmchuk drove out into the night. A gale was blowing from the north, driving snow through a roaring sky. Cars were

353

stuck on every hill, wheels spinning; they skidded sideways through intersections, sat abandoned by the side of the road. Zyzmchuk stopped. He didn't have snow tires, but in the back were chains he'd owned for twenty years. He put them on, shifted into four-wheel drive and wove through maddened traffic to the turnpike.

A barrel with a flashing light on top blocked the entrance ramp. A state trooper stood beside it, bundled in a heavy coat. Zyzmchuk drove up to him, rolled down the window. "Closed, pal," shouted the trooper. "Go home."

"How much is shut down?"

"The whole goddamn pike. Here to the end of the state."

"I've got to get on it."

"Think again. It's closed. Get it? They're not sanding. They're not even plowing—that's how bad it is."

"I'll take the chance."

The trooper laid a hand on the butt of his gun. "Are you going to make trouble, pal?"

"No. I've got special authorization. I'm going to reach into my pocket and show you."

The trooper drew his gun. Zyzmchuk took out his ID. The trooper put his gun away, took the ID and shone his torch on it. He frowned. "I've never seen one of these before."

"Now you have."

The trooper turned it over and gazed at the blank side. "I'll have to call someone in."

"There's no time for that."

"Why not? How far do you think you'd get anyways? There's drifts out there tall as a man."

"I haven't got time for speculation," Zyzmchuk said.

"What?"

Zyzmchuk threw the Blazer in gear and floored it. The bumper swept the lighted barrel off the road. In the rearview mirror, Zyzmchuk caught a glimpse of the trooper fumbling with the ID, the torch, the gun; then he was out of sight.

Zyzmchuk ran up through the gears and stamped on the pedal. *Drive like a bugger, you old fool. Drive like a bugger.*

He drove. There were no other cars, not moving ones. All he saw was white, white with a yellow hole in the center. *Just stay in the yellow hole, that's all you've got to do.* He didn't call

354

himself an old fool again. It was true, but what was the point?

Zyzmchuk stayed in the yellow hole for four hours. The old chains bit into the snow, the rusty bumper crashed through the drifts. Zyzmchuk saw white and yellow, and red, when the warning light flashed that the engine was overheating.

Don't you fucking overheat on me. He had a crazy vision of himself ripping the Blazer apart if it let him down. The vision passed. He drove on, pedal to the floor.

Snowdrifts were piled four feet high in the parking lot of the 1826 House. Zyzmchuk left the Blazer on the highway, lights flashing, and fought his way through the drifts. Snow rose halfway up the doors of rooms 19 and 20. There were no tracks.

Zyzmchuk knocked on room 20. No answer. He tried 19. The same. He had no key. He looked at the windows of the office. No lights shone inside. He put his shoulder to the door of number 20 and broke it down.

Number 20 was empty.

He broke into number 19. Number 19 wasn't empty. It was a shambles.

Bela lay in the middle of it. There were scratches on his face and bruises on his forehead. Zyzmchuk knelt and felt for a pulse. There was none and his skin felt cold. His right hand was curled in a fist. Gently, Zyzmchuk opened it. Bela held a handful of platinum hair, torn out by the roots.

Zyzmchuk got up. He saw Bela's Verdi book lying open on the floor beside the overturned easy chair. At first he thought it was the only object that hadn't been disturbed. Then he picked it up and found the other one underneath: Bela's gun.

Zyzmchuk examined it: fully loaded, unfired. He pictured Bela reading, getting sleepy, putting the gun on the floor, laying the book on top, closing his eyes. Sometime later Major Tsarenko came in; the old man woke up slowly, fuddled, couldn't find the gun right away.

Then Zyzmchuk had a thought that made him charge into the bathroom, flick on the light and look around wildly. But the bathroom was empty. No more bodies.

Not here.

Zyzmchuk stuck Bela's gun in his pocket and left room 19 with murder in his heart.

41

Jessie drove down out of the hills, back across the Hudson, up into the Berkshires. Snow fell around her, thicker and thicker, wrapping her in a silent, floating, white cocoon. She was alone in it with her ex-husband's body in the backseat.

The wind blew harder as Jessie climbed into the mountains. It found every chink in her car, tossed plumes of snow through the headlight beams, sent drifts licking across the road. There was no question of driving fast; it was all she could do to keep the car on the road. She saw no sign of the black van ahead of her, saw no other cars at all until she reached Morgantown.

She drove to the 1826 House, but didn't enter the parking lot. Snow was drifting across it, three feet high in some places; and piling up in front of the doors. No lights shone in rooms 19 or 20 or in the office. And the Blazer wasn't there.

Jessie turned around, retraced her path for a few hundred yards, then took the Mount Blackstone road. It was narrow,

356

steep and winding. The air grew colder, the wind blew stronger. Her lights ended in a fuzzy glow of yellow and white a few feet in front of the car. Her tires whined as they fought for traction. Jessie made the mistake of stepping on the gas. The tail swung out, clipped a snowbank; then the car slid helplessly to the other side of the road, finally stopping in a small clearing, buried to the hubcaps.

Jessie got out. She waded out of the clearing and onto the road, hunched forward against the wind. Jessie was aware of it tearing through her thin clothing, but she didn't feel the cold. Her attention was focused on two blinking red lights, farther up the road.

When she drew closer, she saw they didn't come from the van, but from a small car halted before a massive drift blocking the road. The engine was running; Jessie could hear it, although she couldn't see the exhaust—the wind whipped it away as fast as it came out of the tail pipe. She approached the driver's door. Music found its way out of the car into the night, but Jessie couldn't see who was listening: a thin layer of snow covered the window. She brushed it aside and looked in.

Two figures embraced in the front seat. Eyes opened, saw her. A woman screamed. Jessie stepped back. The door opened. A tall man got out. Jessie recognized him from the ceremony at the memorial, but she could tell he didn't recognize her.

"What is it you want?" he said.

Before Jessie could answer, a woman spoke from inside the car. "It's her again," she said. It was Alice Frame.

"Her?" he said. The wind rose. His voice rose to match it.

"Yes. The one who got me so upset."

"Oh," said the man. He looked at Jessie, eyes narrowing with irritation.

She pushed past him and leaned into the car. Alice Frame sat in the passenger seat, huddled in a thick fur. She looked up at Jessie, fear and anger in her eyes. "I've got bad news," Jessie said. "About your son."

"How could there be bad news about my son?"

"There is," Jessie said. She felt the tall man trying to pull her away and shook him off. "You'd better come," she said to Alice Frame.

"Oh, God," Alice said. "It never ends." She got out of the car.

357

"Don't do anything she says," the tall man told her.

"Just hold my hand, Jamie," Alice said to him. He did, but he put his leather glove on first.

Jessie led them down the road to the little clearing. The wind should have been at her back now, Jessie thought, but it was in her face again. She thought about that instead of about what she was doing to Alice Frame. She had to be sure.

Jessie opened the rear door of her car. The overhead light went on. She stepped back. Alice looked in.

Three waves swept across her face. They would change it forever. The first was recognition. The second was horror. The third had no name that Jessie knew.

"What's going on?" the tall man said.

Alice went to her knees in the snow.

"Who is that?" the tall man said, peering in the car. "Is he drunk or something?"

Alice began to wail. "He came back, he came back." She looked up, blinking, at Jessie. "He was alive the whole time."

Jessie shook her head. She was shaking it at the first statement, but maybe it applied to the second as well. She turned to the tall man.

"Did you see a black van go by?"

"How could anything go by? The road's blocked."

"How long were you parked there?"

"Why do you want to know?"

Alice screamed, "Answer her!"

He made his voice a little more polite, but he didn't answer the question. "Why do you want to know?" he repeated.

"Because the man who killed him is driving that van." She looked at Alice. "And he's got my daughter tied up inside. Your granddaughter."

Alice gazed at her in the weak glow cast by the car's interior light. Tears were freezing on her face. Jessie could see that she didn't fully understand, but that she knew a world of many possibilities was opening up before her. They were all bad.

Jessie bent down and helped Alice to her feet. There was no strength at all in Alice's body. "We're going to need your help," Jessie said to the tall man.

"For what?"

"He may have gone up to the cabin before you came."

"Who may have? I don't understand a word you're saying. All I know is you come harassing Alice with your questions, then you bring a . . . a dead person here and start handing out commands." He paused and looked at his watch. "I think the best thing I could do would be to get the police."

"There's no time," Jessie said.

He ignored her. "Come, Alice."

Alice wiped her face on her mink sleeve. "You come with me."

"Now, Alice, you know that's not such a good idea, not with Edmund there. It could lead to all sorts of . . ." He lowered his voice. "And Maggie thinks I'm out of town."

Alice flinched, but the pain came and went very quickly. There was nothing more that could be done to her, not tonight. She turned and started up the hill. Jessie went with her. He watched them go.

The higher they climbed the harder the wind blew. It made noises in the treetops, not as high-pitched as howling, but lower, more like moaning. Alice didn't say a word until they came to a narrow lane on their right. Then she said, "Where was he?"

"Do you mean—"

"All those years."

"California. He has—had—a house in Venice."

"Venice?"

"California."

They turned into the lane. The trees grew close together, muffling the wind. Jessie could hear Alice's quick breathing.

"What happened?" Alice said, her voice low and thick.

"They made a deal at Woodstock. A rotten deal."

Lights shone through the trees. Jessie felt Alice's hand suddenly squeeze her arm, very hard. "Did my husband know? Did he know the whole time?"

Jessie had no answer to that question, although it gave her an inkling into what Ivan Zyzmchuk was doing. But she didn't have time to think it through: that moment they rounded a corner and saw the black van stranded in the snow.

Jessie ran to it. The side door was unlocked. She threw it open with the foreknowledge that no one was there. She didn't

359

need to see the bare plywood platform, burger wrappers, soda cans; or the wire cutters and the few short pieces of copper wire. One glance and then she was running through the snow. Alice called out behind her, but Jessie didn't hear, didn't stop. She was half-aware of a shadow, or maybe two, moving through the trees, but that didn't stop her either. She came to the cabin door.

The door was not fully closed. She smelled wood smoke, heard a voice, a man's voice. She caught only one word: "Daddy." But she knew that voice. It belonged to Pat Rodney, the man who called himself Bao Dai. And perhaps he was right to; perhaps that's what he had discovered, on his trip across the sea, on his mental trip in the woods: there was no more Pat Rodney.

Softly, Jessie pushed the door open a few more inches and stepped inside. She stood in a big entrance hall; the floor was gleaming pine; skis and poles hung on the walls. Three carpeted stairs led up to an open doorway. Jessie climbed them and looked through.

She saw a big room with windows on three sides, a thick red Persian rug, a dying fire burning in a massive stone fireplace, and three people: Senator Frame, Bao Dai, and Kate. Senator Frame stood with his back to the fireplace. He had a shotgun in his hands. Bao Dai had Kate: one arm around her chest, the carving knife at her throat. The girl had wet her pants. It made Jessie want to kill.

None of them saw her, standing in the doorway. Bao Dai's eyes were on the shotgun; the senator was watching Bao Dai. Bao Dai said, "Put it down. You wouldn't want anything to happen to your boy, would you Daddy?"

The senator's jaw muscles bulged. "I'm not your daddy."

"Then why did they send you my dog tags?" Bao Dai's pupils had grown so big that the bright blue irises were reduced to outlines, almost invisible. He wiggled the knife, waiting for an answer. None came. Kate opened her mouth as though she would scream, but no sound came. "And what about your cute little granddaughter?" Bao Dai said. "I know you wouldn't want anything to happen to her."

Jessie took a quiet step into the room, then another, trying to move along the wall behind Bao Dai.

"I have no granddaughter," the senator said. "I don't know what you think you're doing, but I'm an expert with a twelve-gauge, and I'm not afraid to use it." He raised the gun into the firing position and sighted along the barrel.

"No," Jessie said.

Bao Dai and the senator jerked their heads around to look at her. Kate's head moved too, not much, but just enough to break the skin against the blade and send a few drops of blood down her neck. Again her mouth opened, but no sound came. In the next moment Bao Dai had backed against the nearest wall of windows, where he could keep his eye on Jessie and the senator at the same time. He had a big smile on his face. Then Alice walked into the room and the smile broadened.

She moved toward her husband, slow but steady, like a figure in a trance. "You knew everything," she said. "Everything."

"I don't know what you're talking about, Alice. You're in my line of sight. We've got a madman in the house."

"Oh, that we do," Alice said. "That we do."

Bao Dai laughed, a high laugh that cracked and went silent. "Put it down, Daddy. We can still be pals."

The senator stepped to the side, sighted again along the barrel. Bao Dai wiggled the knife. Then Jessie saw the sinews quiver under the skin of his hard forearm.

"No." She dove at him.

She was still in midair when a cracking sound came from outside. The window shattered on Bao Dai's back. He fell on the red rug. Kate went down with him. Jessie landed on the floor, rolled, and grabbed her. "Kate. Kate. Are you all right?"

Kate didn't answer, but her eyes were open, she was breathing and there was no blood, except for Bao Dai's.

Cold wind rushed into the room, whirling snowflakes around their heads. A man in snowshoes and a ski suit climbed through the window, a pistol held loosely in his hand. It was Mr. Mickey. He stooped to unstrap the snowshoes. Then he walked across the room, took the shotgun from the senator and laid it carefully on a couch beside him.

"Who are you?" the senator said.

"A friend." Mr. Mickey rolled Bao Dai's body over with the

toe of his boot. His eyes were still open and in death had resumed the striking blueness they shared with his mother's and sister's; the grin was still on his face. Mr. Mickey made a little clucking sound, as though the man on the floor had done something naughty. Then he looked up and said, "It's a little draughty. Why don't we all get closer to the fire?" He didn't raise the gun; he didn't put it away, either.

"You still haven't told me who you are," the senator said.

Alice's eyes went to her husband, then to Mr. Mickey. They were numb, confused, afraid: the eyes of a dreamer falling through one nightmare to another.

Mr. Mickey said nothing.

The senator said, "I want my gun back."

"I'm sure you do," Mr. Mickey said. "But this is what your people would call a damage control situation, I think. An excellent expression—it so well encapsulates the quality of your civilization." Mr. Mickey paused. He glanced around the room. "Perhaps," he resumed, "if it were just you . . . But your wife knows too much. And this woman"—he flicked the pistol at Jessie—"knows much too much."

"I don't understand you," the senator said. The Mount Rushmore face was suddenly shining with sweat. "May I remind you that I am a senator of the United States?"

"None of this would be happening if you weren't," Mr. Mickey said. "Or if it didn't mean so much to you."

"You're not making much sense."

"No?" said Mr. Mickey. "Do you know what your code name is in Moscow?" Mr. Mickey glanced around the room again to make sure he had everyone's attention. Then he said, " 'Faucet.' " He permitted himself a smile at the humor of this.

Maybe the senator thought Mr. Mickey couldn't smile and be alert at the same time. Maybe he knew what was coming. Maybe he disliked the code name. He made a move toward the couch—a clumsy move, not very quick. Mr. Mickey had plenty of time to bring the barrel of his gun down on the back of the senator's head. But in that moment, Jessie lifted Kate and ran from the room.

Run.

Down the three stairs. Into the big hall. But through the

362

front doorway, still partly open, she saw a man standing outside in the storm. Rather, not a man, but snowshoes, legs, shadows. Jessie turned and bolted through a kitchen, past a trussed turkey on the counter and up a staircase. She heard the crack of a gunshot. And Alice's muffled voice saying, "No." And then another crack.

Jessie reached the second floor, ran down a long hall, into a room. She felt Kate's small hands clinging to her. "Oh Mom. You took so long."

"I know, sweetheart. But everything's going to be all right."

Heavy feet bounded up the stairs. Jessie glanced wildly around. There was no other door, no way out. She went to the window, put Kate down, manipulated the locking mechanism. It was a double window; she couldn't figure out how it worked. The footsteps came quickly down the hall. Jessie picked up a wooden chair and hurled it through the glass. The storm howled into the room. Jessie took Kate in her arms. Mr. Mickey came through the doorway, the pistol in his hand. He pointed it at her head and said, "Too late."

Perhaps because of the storm, he didn't hear Alice Frame coming up behind him. Blood trickled from her mouth. She stumbled against his arm and tried to grab the gun. Mr. Mickey jerked it away, but Alice held on to his arm. For a moment her eyes met Jessie's.

"Jump," she said.

The gun went off. Alice slumped to the floor. Mr. Mickey pulled the gun free and turned toward Jessie. She jumped out into the night.

It wasn't a long fall, not nearly as long as the fall in Malibu. But there was no water waiting below, and she had Kate in her arms. They began a slow spin in the air. Jessie stuck out one hand to break the fall; with the other she held on to Kate as hard as she could. Then she was lying on her back, breathless in the snow.

"Kate. Kate."

"I'm okay, Mom," said a voice against her breasts. "Are you?"

"Yes." Jessie sat up. She put a hand in the snow to push herself to her feet and felt pain in her forearm. She tried again.

It was worse. She got her legs beneath her, heaved herself up. Then, with Kate in her good arm she took a step away from the house. She sank to her waist in the snow, fell forward on her bad arm. She bit her lip to keep from crying out. A cracking sound came from above, almost inaudible in the wind. She worked one leg free, plunged forward on her bad arm, sank; worked a leg free, plunged forward, sank; worked a leg free.

She was at the back of the house. Mount Blackstone rose before her, an immense shadow in the driving snow. She reached the trees.

"Hold onto my neck, darling."

Jessie felt freezing hands on her neck. That freed her good arm. She used it to pull them through the trees, a foot at a time, plunging, sinking, plunging, sinking. But Kate's hands kept slipping away; her lips chattered from the cold. She wasn't wearing a coat. Jessie tried to remove her suede jacket and wrap it around her, but couldn't get it off her bad arm. It dragged uselessly behind them.

Plunge. Sink. Plunge. Sink. Jessie climbed the mountain, Kate in one arm, the other arm dangling behind.

"I'm getting cold, Mom."

"I know, darling. It's going to be all right."

Plunge. Sink. Plunge. Sink. The next time Kate said she was cold, her voice was so thick Jessie could barely distinguish the words. And she herself didn't have the strength to answer. She just kept going. Her clothes hardened with frozen sweat.

Kate's teeth stopped chattering. Her body went limp and she didn't speak. There were no sounds but the angry ones of the wind and the desperate ones of plunging and sinking. Once she thought she heard the whine of an engine. The sound died. She plunged and sank, plunged and sank.

After a while, Jessie grew aware of a new sound, a soft clicking sound from behind, as though someone were knocking pencils together. She turned, saw nothing but the lights of the cabin, far below. She plunged on.

But the clicking continued. It grew louder. Jessie turned again. Now she saw something. First it was a shadow behind a screen of slanting snow. Then it was a figure. And then a man. He didn't plunge and sink, plunge and sink, but strode along the top of the snow. The clicking came from the frames of his snow-shoes.

Jessie turned and kept going. Plunge. Sink. *Click click.* Plunge. Sink. *Click click.* Closer and closer. Then she heard him breathing, the deep, even breathing of a distance runner.

She plunged. Sank. Plunged. Sank. Then a hand pressed against her back. It bent her down, pushed her in the snow, face down, Kate beneath her. Kate squirmed frantically. Jessie squirmed too, with all the strength she had left. She rolled over, onto her side, and looked up into Mr. Mickey's eyes. They were without expression. He was a man with a job to do—Bao Dai's opposite: for him, murder carried no moral baggage, nothing damning, nothing redemptive.

Mr. Mickey had his gun, but he wasn't bothering to use it. Perhaps he hated waste. He just took her neck in his huge hand and began forcing her head down into the snow.

Jessie tried to move. She tried to bite. She tried to scream. She could do nothing.

Then a white bear rose up behind Mr. Mickey. It raised its white paws high in the air and brought them crashing down on Mr. Mickey's head. Mr. Mickey slumped forward, on top of her.

Sirens sounded down below. They could have been the screams of very small things, like butterflies. Then Mr. Mickey was no longer on top of her, and the bear was bending down, peering into her eyes. The bear's own eyes were very worried and a little wet.

Click. Click. More clicks. The bear looked up. Mr. Mickey was on all fours, his head hanging down. He raised it very slowly, just in time to see a much smaller man come clicking out from behind a tree. He had a ski mask on his face and a gun in his hand.

Mr. Mickey's lips twisted up in a little smile.

The sirens screamed their little screams.

The gun cracked.

Mr. Mickey dropped dead in the snow.

"Got him, Zyz," said the man in the ski mask.

"Keith?" said the bear.

"To the rescue," said the man in the ski mask.

The sirens sounded.

The bear picked her up. He picked Kate up. He carried them down the mountain.

"I can walk," Jessie said.

"You don't have to prove it," the bear replied. He didn't let her go.

They were almost at the bottom when Jessie put her lips to the bear's ear and told him a secret. It was just two words: "George Will."

42

"Imagine," Keith said, "a desk man like me saving the ass of an old hand like you, Zyz!"

Thanksgiving morning. The wind had died, the snow had stopped falling. The sky was bright blue; snow covered everything, thick and white. The whole world was blue and white, dazzling blue and glaring white. Just being in it—there outside the cabin on Mount Blackstone, watching the ambulance attendants carry out the bodies of the senator, his wife, Major Tsarenko and Pat Rodney—made Zyzmchuk's eyes hurt.

"You've got a good imagination, Keith," he said.

Keith laughed. His cheeks glowed in the cold air like polished apples.

"Better than mine," Zyzmchuk said. "Sometimes I have trouble imagining things."

"It's your Central European background, Zyz, if you don't mind my saying so."

Zyzmchuk smiled. Keith smiled. "That must be it," Zyzmchuk

said. "Some sort of sociogenetic block. There are certain things I just can't imagine."

"Like what, Zyz?"

"Like your father's wine cellar."

Keith's smile froze on his face. "My father's wine cellar, Zyz? What about it?"

Three state troopers came out of the cabin, the rolled-up red rug on their shoulders. "What sort of collection did he have?" Zyzmchuk asked.

Keith's smile relaxed. "A modest one, really, I guess. Mostly Burgundies, if I remember. It's been a long time."

"Did your mother like wine too?"

"My mother?"

Zyzmchuk nodded. "Did she enjoy going down there and rooting out a nice bottle?"

"Sometimes, I suppose."

"Like after she'd come home from scrubbing Erica Mc-Taggart's floors?"

Keith looked up into Zyzmchuk's face. The glare made him squint, reducing his eyes to slits. "What are you saying exactly, Zyz?"

Zyzmchuk gazed past him, at the white mountain. "Got your watch on?" he asked. "The gold Rolex?"

Keith frowned. "Yes."

"What time is it?"

Keith pulled back the sleeve of his coat. "Eight-twenty."

"That's a nice watch," said Zyzmchuk, looking at it. "Did your mother ever see it?"

Keith tugged down his sleeve. "She passed away years ago."

"I know. I saw a picture of her the other day. I think she would have been impressed by a watch like that."

Keith squinted up at him. "Why do you think that, Zyz?"

"Because she was poor."

"I wouldn't say that. More like middle-class."

"Middle-class people don't scrub floors for a living. You were poor, Keith. No father, and a mother who cleaned up for the McTaggarts. Now you've got a gold watch, a red Jaguar, a house in Malibu. You've come a long way."

Keith's brow wrinkled. "There's no house in Malibu, Zyz."

"Sure there is. A nice little investment. Just not in your

name, that's all. Do you know Fairweather? He's flying down to Panama this afternoon to get all the details. He's very excited about it." A police helicopter came around the mountain and dipped over the cabin. "You made it big, all right," Zyzmchuk said, "but it must have been hard being a poor scholarship student, and a local boy too, at Morgan. What with all those rich kids. Like Hartley Frame."

Keith squinted up at him for what seemed like a long time. Then moisture squeezed out from between his eyelids. And his voice cracked a little when he said, "It was hard, Ivan. Sounds silly, now, maybe, but it was hard. I wanted so much to . . . belong. I suppose I embellished things a little. Some things. From time to time."

"Perfectly understandable. In fact, there's only one thing I don't understand."

"What's that?"

"Why Frame fired you, that summer you interned in Washington."

The moisture stopped leaking through Keith's eyelids. "I don't get you, Zyz. I worked there every summer, for one thing, and he never fired me. I left on my own, but that was just two years ago, when I came over to your outfit."

Zyzmchuk shook his head. "You worked there one summer, Keith. And you were fired. What happened? It couldn't have been too serious, or he wouldn't have taken you back, would he? Was it your long hair?"

Keith said nothing for a few moments. A plow came slowly up the lane, folding blankets of snow before it. Keith sighed. "I had a brief, very brief, affair with Alice. At her instigation." Keith's eyes flickered toward him, then looked away. "It amounted to nothing, but Frame found out."

"That's going to be hard to verify," Zyzmchuk said. "In the circumstances."

Keith shrugged.

"Still, he fired you."

"Yes."

"But later he hired you back."

"Yes."

"So he forgot and forgave."

"I suppose you could say that."

369

"When did he take you back?"

"A year or so after I graduated."

"Around the time the Red Cross visited Hartley Frame's prison camp and declared him dead?"

Keith glanced around. Zyzmchuk didn't. He already knew what there was to see: the mountain on one side, state troopers on the other. "I don't remember the exact date," Keith said.

"No? How about Woodstock? Do you remember that?"

"Woodstock?"

"The festival. That's when Hartley and Pat made their little deal in the woods."

"I don't know what you're talking about, Zyz."

"You were there. It was just the kind of rich man-poor man stuff you understand so well. Pat went to the army physical as Hartley, in return for the blue Corvette. The one you dumped in Little Pond." Right on top of the BMW Pat Rodney dumped there; it wasn't surprising, Zyzmchuk thought—local boys always knew the best spots for dumping things, and they were both local boys. Their mothers had worked together at the plant. The sons had started together at the bottom; one had used the other to rise to the top.

"Maybe they both thought Pat would flunk the physical," Zyzmchuk continued. "Maybe just Pat did. Maybe he didn't care much one way or the other. Maybe he thought going to Viet Nam was worth the car. Maybe there would be more payments when he came back. Maybe he was just a dumb kid. He passed the physical. His fingerprints went into the records as Hartley's. He went, as Hartley, to Viet Nam. He got captured. Meanwhile Hartley went, as Pat, to California.

"Then the Red Cross visited the prison camp, and enough evidence was produced to declare Hartley dead. That made the switch a fait accompli. Of course, it was smart to keep Pat Rodney alive. There might have been a propaganda use for him further down the line, if the senator ever ran for President, say. Meanwhile, everyone who knew about the switch tried to profit: Doreen Rodney blackmailed Hartley; Disco made a clumsy attempt to get to the senator. He came up here, didn't he?"

"You must be very tired, Zyz. You're not making sense."

"No? Don't you remember intercepting Disco and taking him on a little trip?"

Keith looked around again. The mountain and the troopers hadn't moved.

"But they were small-timers compared to you," Zyzmchuk went on. "You're the one who made it all happen. I've been checking the army records. They're badly organized—it took some time to find them." Keith bit his lip. "The funny thing is that Hartley's whole unit could have been wiped out easily, but all they did—North Vietnamese regulars, by the way—was take one prisoner. Isn't that odd?"

"Odd?" Keith's voice was low.

"Yes. Almost as if it were a setup. Almost as if they knew who their prisoner really was from the beginning."

"This is a lot of wild talk, Zyz. I can't follow you at all."

"Sure you can. When Pat Rodney went to Viet Nam, some-one—someone with a good imagination—walked into the Russian embassy and told them about the Woodstock deal. Oh—I meant to ask you something. You mentioned you spent your junior year abroad."

"That's right."

"Where?"

"It was an art study program. Arranged by the Art Appreciation Club."

"But where?"

"Various museums. The Uffizi, the Tate, the Louvre."

"Did you squeeze the Hermitage in there too?"

Keith nodded.

"That must have been a nice year," Zyzmchuk said. "Meeting all kinds of people, and things. We'll have to talk about it someday. Or someone will. Anyway, an imaginative fellow walks into the Russian embassy and tells them about the Woodstock deal. Sells them the information, I'm sure, although it will be hard to prove. The Russians appreciate imagination. They decide this imaginative fellow might be useful. They send him back to the senator. He tells the senator about the switch, explains how the senator's career would be over unless he cooperates. Perhaps the senator never even knew the Russians were involved. Maybe he didn't want to know. Was that it, Keith?"

Keith opened his mouth to speak, then closed it without uttering a word.

"What I like," Zyzmchuk said, "is that you were running

371

him. I thought it was the other way around for a while. That confused me. You were much better than I thought. Not just a desk man, Keith. A real pro. It'll take years to figure out all the stuff the Russians got, if we—if they—ever do."

A police car followed the plow up the hill, parked in front of the cabin. Grace got out and came toward them, carrying a shopping bag.

"But Major Tsarenko was running you. It must have been a bad day when he told you Pat Rodney was on the loose."

Keith's brow wrinkled. "Are you talking about the Russian, Zyz? The one I saved you from last night?"

"That proved what a pro you were," Zyzmchuk said. "But the timing was a little off. Not your fault, but the major wasn't a factor by the time you fired. I was the one you wanted of course, but you realized it was too late, once you heard the sirens. So you shot your master, keeping him out of the hands of the interrogation boys."

"This is quite a theory, Zyz. But utterly unprovable."

"We have a witness."

"A witness?"

"She saw you outside the house in Venice. You just missed catching Pat Rodney there, didn't you? The real Pat Rodney, I mean. That was unlucky." Zyzmchuk smiled. "It meant having to deal with Jessie Shapiro."

Keith didn't reply.

"She saw you again at the barn in Vermont. Said you looked like one of those commentators on TV. Couldn't remember which one at first. I don't think she watches much TV. But it finally came to her: George Will."

"Is this a joke, Zyz? I've been in the same room with him on several occasions, and I assure you I don't look at all like him."

"I've always thought you do, Keith. So will the jury."

Grace came up to them. She didn't look at Keith. "I went to his house as you said, Mr. Z. I found this." She opened the shopping bag. Inside were a gray wig, a polka dot dress and a pair of wraparound sunglasses.

" 'The Role of Disguise,' " Zyzmchuk said, " 'in the Modern Intelligence Matrix.' "

"You had no right to enter my house," Keith said. Grace

didn't answer. He turned to Zyzmchuk. "Dahlin will bounce you the moment I tell him."

"Dahlin was bounced himself an hour ago," Zyzmchuk said. "You should have run last night, Keith. You might have caught the Aeroflot out of Montreal."

Keith was silent for a moment. Then he said, "Not with the roads the way they were."

"Probably not."

They looked at each other. Keith turned away.

"I'll do what I can for you, Keith, if you tell me where to find the Picasso."

"The Picasso?"

"The Rose Period one. Alice Frame reported it stolen about ten years ago, and I'm sure she thought it was. You and the senator knew differently, of course. I'd kind of like it to go to her granddaughter."

Keith didn't reply.

Zyzmchuk took Grace's arm, started to turn, then stopped. "What role did you play in *The Wind in the Willows?*"

There was another silence. It went on and on. Then a very small smile crossed Keith's face. "Ratty. The review was very favorable, if I recall, even if it was just the college paper."

Zyzmchuk led Grace away. The mountain stayed where it was, but the troopers began moving toward Keith.

"A Lieutenant DeMarco called from Los Angeles," Grace said. "He left his number."

"Throw it away."

Zyzmchuk said good-bye to Grace and got into the Blazer. He drove down the mountain, came to Route 7. It hadn't been plowed. He stopped. South meant Washington, north meant back into town. Zyzmchuk stayed where he was for a few minutes, unmoving in a world of dazzling blue and glaring white. He thought, I'm too old; I know nothing about being a father; it wasn't real, but only because of the danger she was in.

He thought those thoughts, but he turned north anyway. It couldn't hurt to say good-bye.

He drove to the 1826 House, parked in the lot. Rooms 19 and 20 were sealed. A policeman stood at the door of number 1. He stepped aside to let Zyzmchuk go by.

Ivan Zyzmchuk opened the door. It was warm inside. A fire

burned in the grate. Jessie Shapiro lay sleeping in the bed, her broken arm in a cast, her other arm around her sleeping daughter. Piles of quilts covered them. Their dark, frizzy hair mingled on the pillow.

He closed the door. He thought, I'm too old; I know nothing about being a father; it was only because of the danger. But he wanted to lie down, if just for a moment. How could that hurt? He wouldn't fall asleep—he wasn't much of a sleeper anymore—but just lie down for a while, not disturbing anyone, then get up when the first plow went by and follow it out of town.

He lay on the bed.

Not long after, the first plow did go by the 1826 House. But by that time, inside room 1, Ivan Zyzmchuk was sleeping a deep sleep, his arm resting across Jessie and her little girl.